MYSTIQUE

The dark shape emerged from the summerhouse and demanded, "Shut your eyes, mam'selle."

Charlotte did as she was told, trembling in sudden, thrilling expectation. The next thing she knew, she felt him tie a cloth tightly around her head, blindfolding her. His hands fell on her shoulders and drew her against his body where his long curls brushed her cheek. Beneath a soft shirt, his heart beat faster.

One hand moved suggestively down her body, pressing her hips closer to his own. She caught her breath, and started trembling again when he removed the rose and slid his hand inside her neckline . . .

She made no move to stop him, although his touch seemed almost more than she could bear. Her head fell back, her senses hungry for him as the Frenchman growled her name . . .

SPINE TINGLING ROMANCE
FROM STELLA CAMERON!

PURE DELIGHTS   (0-8217-4798-3, $5.99)

SHEER PLEASURES   (0-8217-5093-3, $5.99)

TRUE BLISS   (0-8217-5369-X, $5.99)

MYSTIQUE

Marion Clarke

Zebra Books
Kensington Publishing Corp.

http://www.zebrabooks.com

ZEBRA BOOKS are published by

Kensington Publishing Corp.
850 Third Avenue
New York, NY 10022

First Printing: September, 1997
10 9 8 7 6 5 4 3 2 1

Printed in the United States of America

Chapter 1

With a sinking feeling, Charlotte realized that their troubles were not over. As the Virginia stagecoach rumbled out of sight, not a soul came forward to meet them. She and Amy strained their eyes in every direction, but the depot was shut tight and only rain and darkness engulfed the empty road.

Another problem to be faced, Charlotte thought wearily. The journey to Stone Gardens from New York had been one disaster after another. First came the breakdown of the new train line; next their trunks had gotten lost, shunted somewhere onto the wrong depot; and then, the stagecoach horse threw a shoe, causing another long delay.

Everything had culminated in the coach leaving them beside a deserted platform where the signpost stating "Beauville Five Miles," had fallen in the mire, and therefore pointed nowhere.

Amy huddled closer to her sister's side. "Why is no one here to meet us?"

Charlotte drew in a breath. "Well, we are about six hours

late, you know. They probably waited for quite a while and then gave up, thinking we had been delayed enroute and must have gone to some inn for the night."

"Oh, I wish we had. It's so cold and dark here . . . a-and rain is dripping down my neck." Amy tugged at the limp, wet ribbons once tied so bravely underneath her chin. "Our bonnets will never be the same."

Charlotte silently agreed. After only a few moments under the leaky station roof, their capes and carefully refurbished hats had become completely soaked. Without their trunks, they couldn't even change into dry clothes when they reached their destination. All they had with them of any value was the reticule Charlotte carried on her arm, containing the meager remains of her father's legacy. Her fingers tightened on the cord. Suppose a vandal came along the road and snarled, "Your money or your life?" Oh, no, that was nonsense. No robbers would be abroad in such awful weather.

She shook her head and sighed. "Amy, staying at an inn would have meant an outlay of cash, which we can't spare. After paying all the doctor bills, we had just enough to get us here and have a small reserve for emergencies. We must be careful with our funds. We really don't know how things will work out at Stone Gardens."

"You're right, Charlotte. I won't moan any more. You always know what's best."

Oh, do I? Charlotte wondered. Had it been wise to leave New York for an unknown plantation in Virginia and an aunt who had been so upset when her sister married a "Yankee"? But with the bookstore under new ownership, Charlotte's duties were taken over by the son and she had been unable to find any other work in these troubled times.

Aunt Clara had been the last hope, and at her dying father's urging, Charlotte had written, asking if she could find employment for herself and Amy in return for room and board. A stiff reply in the affirmative had sent Charlotte and Amy on their way as soon as their father had been laid to rest.

But now Charlotte couldn't help feeling disturbed that no one had waited to meet them, at least a servant with a conveyance of some sort. No, it did not bode well for a warm welcome at Stone Gardens Plantation.

Years of caring for an invalid father and a sister eight years younger had convinced Charlotte that action was the best approach to trouble. She squared her shoulders and said briskly with an optimism she was far from feeling. "Let's start walking, my girl. A little more rain won't hurt us. We are wet already. We can take the post road that the stagecoach traveled, and I'm sure we will find shelter somewhere."

Amy glanced doubtfully up and down the dark, abandoned road. "Which direction shall we go?"

"Well, I'm not sure, but at least we will be warmer walking, and someone should come along to help us." Charlotte summoned up a smile, feeling as she had so often since both parents died, that she was the mother and Amy her child. At seventeen, Amy's flower-like beauty had lost its look of immaturity and was ripening into womanhood. It was hard to acknowledge that someday Amy would no longer need her. Why, the child even had an admirer in New York. Tim Deane, son of the new bookstore owner, had asked if he could write to Amy and even hinted at paying her a visit.

Charlotte felt certain that Amy was indifferent to the lanky, sandy-haired young man, so she answered that she could hardly issue an invitation since she and Amy were going there to work. There was no use wondering at this juncture what chores would be expected of them. The main thing now was to arrive all in one piece.

For a while, Charlotte plodded silently, squishing in the

sucking, red mire of the Virginia countryside. The rain plastered cold wet strands of brown hair against her face and soon mud-splattered skirts and sodden boots made progress a bone-wrenching effort. Chilled muscles began to ache and her stomach growled with hunger.

She knew Amy must feel equally uncomfortable and finally she stopped and groaned, "I think we have gone far enough in this direction. We better turn around and—"

"Listen!" Amy interrupted shrilly, grabbing Charlotte's arm. "Do you hear that? Someone's coming." She dashed into the middle of the road and waved both arms. "Stop, stop! Help us, oh, please help us!"

With a cry of alarm, Charlotte jerked Amy back to safety just as a carriage came careening around the bend.

"Oh, we're going to be rescued," Amy shouted.

The driver pulled back on the reins while his startled beasts reared and neighed, pawing wildly at the air. "Who are you?" he demanded. "What are you doing out in this storm?"

Fired by desperation, Charlotte's voice drowned out Amy's excited jabbering. "Please sir, can you help us? We are looking for Stone Gardens, the home of my aunt, Clara Bainbridge Wilson. No one came to meet us at the depot so we tried to go on foot, but now—"

"Now we are almost exhausted," Amy burst out.

"Could you direct us to some shelter?" Charlotte asked.

The man hesitated and Charlotte strained her eyes to see him better, but the descending rain and darkness conspired to make his image just a blur.

It may have been Amy's young, importuning face or just the desperate appearance they both presented, but at any rate, the driver swung down from the carriage and pulled open the door with a sweeping gesture.

His voice now sounded husky with an almost gutteral

accent, *"Est bien, mademoiselles,* I shall drive you to Stone Gardens myself. Please get in."

"Oh, thank you, sir," Amy exclaimed fervently, throwing him a grateful glance. Without a second urging, she scuttled deep inside the coach.

About to follow suit, Charlotte suddenly had a clearer view of their rescuer and a swift alarm darted through her. Why, the man was *masked.* He wore a short, dark cape draped across one shoulder with a heavy cord, full knee breeches, and a wide-brimmed high-crowned hat, all in the style of the old French cavaliers. An enormous head of black curls cascaded to his shoulders.

Something was not right. Charlotte backed away and called, "Amy, perhaps we better walk, after all. Get out of the carriage."

Amy poked her head out briefly. "Charlotte, what are you saying? It's too wet and cold to walk. Haven't we been waiting for someone to come along and rescue us? What ails you?" Indignantly, she withdrew into the interior of the carriage.

This was a fine time for Amy to flout her authority. "Amy, come on," Charlotte called again.

The man gave an exclamation of impatience. Placing his hands upon his hips, he said, "I have said that I will take you to your destination, *mam'selle.* Now, will you please get in out of the rain?"

Charlotte swallowed and demanded defiantly, although her voice quavered, "Are you a highwayman? I warn you, sir, we are practically penniless. A-and anything else you might have in mind—" She gave a convulsive gulp. "We both would fight like tigers."

"Mon Dieu!" He uttered a short bark of laughter and wiped a hand across his dripping chin. "Do you actually think I would use a night like this to force your submission in a cold, damp carriage? How exceedingly uncomfortable!

And as for money, if you had any, I am certain you would not be on foot, crawling along this miserable road.''

His teeth flashed briefly below the mask. ''Come now, do I not make good sense?''

''B-but, why are you—''

''Masked? I have been on a journey requiring discretion. I fear you will just have to trust me. Or continue walking in the rain and the little one, she is delicate, no? As I see it, you have little choice.''

Charlotte pushed back wet strands of hair and gave a longing glance into the interior of the coach where Amy sat curled up like a little kitten. ''Please get in, Charlotte,'' she implored.

Feeling defeated at last, Charlotte turned back to the driver. ''Very well, I'll come.'' Thinking how ungracious that sounded when perhaps he would be driving out of his way, she added, ''I can offer you a little payment for your trouble.'' She felt inside her purse, but he waved away the coins she offered.

''Non, non. Although your beauty tempts me to seek your sweet red lips for payment, right now this will suffice, eh?'' He reached out and drew Charlotte's hand up to his lips which felt soft and wet against her suddenly racing pulse.

Astonishment immobilized her—and some other strange emotion, but when his lips warmed, moving seductively back and forth, she jerked away with a gasp and dove into the coach. She heard him give a chuckle as he slammed the door.

Dropping on the seat, she placed a hand against her chest. Did he actually refer to her ''beauty''? And then the way he'd kissed her! Never had a man's touch affected her so. Granted, her experience with kisses had been limited to fleeting encounters with a very small number of admirers. A few dinners, concerts, strolls in City Park, all leading eventually to her boredom and the dismissal of their suit.

This time . . . this man . . . who or what was he? It was all so strange. The storm, the deserted road, and then the masked man emerging to give aid like some hero in a novel.

Charlotte raised her voice above the sound of pounding hoofs and rain drumming on the carriage roof. "Amy, did you observe the strangeness of our rescuer? His wig and mask and the odd costume he wore?"

"Of course, I did." Amy giggled, busily engaged with wiping her face and hands on a sodden, cambric handkerchief which she now stuffed carelessly inside her reticule. "How could I miss it? I supposed that he was coming from some masquerade party."

That wasn't the reason that the man had given. He had said, "a journey requiring discretion," which might mean that he had come from a rendezvous with a married lady. That still did not stop him from kissing Charlotte's wrist and making remarks about her lips.

Her cheeks grew warm, and impatiently, she pushed aside her hat, feeling her brown hair sag like a damp ball inside its crocheted snood. She must not dwell on his odd behavior—at least they were on their way. "I guess we should be very thankful that he stopped for us. If we don't develop pleurisy or something worse from this night, we'll both be lucky."

"I know. What heaven it will be at Aunt Clara's, warm and dry." Amy sighed blissfully. "I hope she'll give us something to eat. I am starving—absolutely *starving.*"

An uneasy thought crossed Charlotte's mind. Suppose he took them somewhere else, a distant and secret place? Had they been fools to get into a stranger's carriage? But they had been so miserable . . . The alternative of struggling through the storm was just as daunting. She sat rigidly while Amy chattered away, not requiring any answers, and the coach careened swiftly along the storm-swept road.

At last they came to a rocking halt and a brisk rap sounded on the roof. Charlotte let down the window and craned her head upward. "What is it? Are we at Stone Gardens?"

"As you can see, *mam'selle.*" The man gestured with his whip toward a house whose tall chimneys could just be glimpsed beyond a line of trees. "Stone Gardens lies at the end of that curving drive. I cannot take you closer, *je regrete.*"

"Oh, that's quite all right." Relief flooded Charlotte at having arrived safely. As she and Amy emerged from the carriage, both thanked him fervently. Ashamed of her suspicions, Charlotte added, "We are exceedingly grateful, sir."

He saluted with his whip, then flicked the horses and thundered out of sight, leaving Charlotte staring after him. He was certainly a man of mystery whose kiss had sent her pulses hammering. If that had been exciting, what would it be like to feel his kiss against her lips? She grew a little dizzy at the thought and turned quickly to follow Amy.

"Wasn't that an adventure?" Amy cried as they hurried up the driveway. "I wonder if we'll ever see him again?"

"I'm just glad to be here, at last. We've had quite enough adventure for one night," Charlotte answered.

"Look, Amy. Isn't it beautiful? Just the way Mama described her childhood home: white pillars, a wide front porch, the flowering bushes and all the trees. Oh, and there's the colored fanlight above the door. Someone must still be up." Dashing onto the porch with Amy right behind her, Charlotte grasped the handle of the bellpull and gave it a resounding jerk. It pealed several times before the door cracked ajar and a grey-haired Negro peered out, surveying them cautiously.

Then he flung the door wide open and quavered shrilly, "Lordamercy, I think they's here, Miss Clara."

A woman's voice called from the upper hall, "Cicero, who is at the door?"

Charlotte moved past the wavering figure of the old retainer with a smile and greeting before she called up the stairs. "Charlotte and Amy Davenport are here. Is that you, Aunt Clara?"

The butler held aloft a smoking candle, his mouth agape as he surveyed their mud-splattered capes and rain-soaked hair. "Miss Clara," he croaked. "These are the lost lambs I was waitin' on, for sure. Praise the Lord!"

"We feel more like drowned rats." Amy giggled as she dropped her cloak on the marble hallway and stepped out of her shoes. Running forward, her golden hair escaped its snood and tumbled about the shoulders of her dark blue wrinkled dress. "Oh, Aunt Clara, I'm so glad to be here. Just think, we were delayed six hours. We've had such an adventure."

Their mother's older sister, tall and stately, advanced in a quilted, cream-colored wrapper and lace nightcap, from which dangled a dark black braid. "So—Amy and Charlotte, we meet at last." She embraced them rather gingerly, her long face filled with astonishment.

"Whatever happened to you? Cicero waited for hours. We finally decided that you had gone to stay at the town inn overnight. Heavens, how wet you are. Come into the parlor by the fire."

While herding the girls forward, Clara issued commands: "Cicero, stir up the fire in here and get blankets to wrap them. Then rouse Aunt Becky to bring some hot soup and toast."

Charlotte and Amy huddled gratefully near the hearth while Cicero lit the lamps and fire began to crackle in the green-veined marble grate.

Charlotte glanced wearily around at the large, high-ceilinged room with its long plush drapes and green and black furniture resting on a flowered rug. Vaguely, she thought it all looked luxurious and quite imposing. Aunt Clara seemed to fit right in, regardless of her robe and braid.

Amy carried the burden of the conversation, making it sound like they had had the greatest lark. But when she described their rescuer, his clothes and accent, Aunt Clara gave a little scream.

"The Frenchman! That notorious villain! Saints above, it's a miracle you girls escaped unscathed.''

Amy giggled. "I just knew he might be somebody exciting. Oh, here is our soup. How delicious it looks. Thank you." She scrambled into a chair and accepted the tray across her lap.

Charlotte also received onion soup, some hot toast oozing with butter, a wedge of cheese, and a glass of foaming milk. She couldn't speak for several minutes while devouring the food, but when she revived, she asked her aunt, "Why do you call the Frenchman a villain? What has he done?" She felt a slight regret. He had been kind to them, albeit a little too romantic, but a kiss upon the wrist was scarcely villainy.

Aunt Clara sniffed, tossing back her braid and leaned forward from the green plush sofa. "I will tell you. He's a member of the Underground Railroad. He steals slaves from their rightful owners and spirits them away up North."

"That hardly sounds like villainy," Charlotte said indignantly, then held her tongue as she watched her aunt's face, grow scarlet.

"You sound just like your father." Aunt Clara said. "That Yankee talked the same way when he came here. You better watch your tongue, my girl. Sympathy for people like the Frenchman will get you in a lot of trouble."

"Oh, Aunt Clara," Amy burst out, "We are both so fatigued, I doubt if Charlotte can utter a word of sense.

As for myself, I feel quite faint—" Rising, she swayed and put a hand up to her head, but not before Charlotte saw her give a warning wink.

Clara came instantly to Amy's side. "Of course, my dear, you must go right to bed. You're delicate, just like my little sister was. Oh, how I worried when she went up North. She couldn't bear that climate and it slowly killed her." She jerked a bellcord for a servant and led Amy from the room.

Immediately, Charlotte regretted her tactless outburst as she followed them. In the hall, they both thanked their aunt, but Clara's eyes looked cold until Amy kissed her impulsively on the cheek. For the life of her, Charlotte couldn't follow suit. Besides, she had a feeling that Aunt Clara would not enjoy a kiss from the niece who in any way reminded her of the deeply resented "Yankee."

Chapter 2

Charlotte didn't rouse all night, and it was only a warm shaft of sunlight falling across her face that made her lift her eyelids.

Blinking, she stared from the blue, fringed canopy above her fourposter bed to the tall windows where an autumn sun filtered through heavy, flowered drapes. She finally focused on the figure of a girl sitting in a chair, surveying her intently.

"Who—who are you?" Charlotte stuttered, raising up to rest upon her elbows. "Oh—you must be Vanessa, Aunt Clara's daughter."

The girl leaned over so Charlotte could see her face and her head of glossy black ringlets. "Well, I was anxious to meet you, Cousin Charlotte, since you are supposed to be my companion."

So this was to be her employment? A confidante to this young beauty who looked anything but pleased? Her long-lashed violet eyes had a curious expression—cold, wary, and somehow hostile.

She evidently doesn't want me for a companion, Charlotte thought with a sinking feeling. What a disadvantage to meet this gorgeous cousin while flat in bed wearing someone else's long-sleeved muslin nightgown.

Vanessa looked like a fashion plate in an azure morning gown of polished chintz with a tiered skirt edged in broderie anglaise. At the opening of her round, lace collar, she had pinned a handpainted floral brooch depicting forget-me-nots. With no chance to indulge in current fashions, Charlotte still had a hidden love of pretty clothes, and she admired the picture Vanessa made, even though her welcome was anything but warm.

"There is a little problem." Vanessa cleared her throat. "I have met Amy. We had a long talk, and I found her most congenial. Frankly, Charlotte, I don't think you and I would suit. Mama told me about your outburst last night and how much you seemed like the Yankee my Aunt Rose married. Amy is so sweet and docile and—ahem—I prefer to have her for my companion. She's young, too, just the right age for me since I'm eighteen."

And I am almost decrepit? Charlotte's mouth twisted. Yet she knew at twenty-five, she was supposed to be "on the shelf".

She had to admit, though, it was logical that Vanessa would be drawn to the girlish, happy-natured Amy. Of course they would be better suited, but Charlotte stared back uneasily, at a loss for words. If Amy was the choice for Vanessa's companion, what work was destined for herself?

Vanessa grew impatient at Charlotte's unresponsiveness, and her little foot in its black satinet slipper tapped the flowered rug. "I guess we will just have to find another occupation for you, Charlotte. What can you do?"

Did Vanessa expect to hear: "cook, sew, clean?" Charlotte raised her chin. "I worked in my father's bookstore before he sold it. I wrote letters, kept records, ordered new books, waited on the customers . . ."

Vanessa shook her head. "That doesn't sound like anything that we could use. What else?"

Charlotte pushed up higher in the bed. "Vanessa, I don't blame you for wanting Amy, but I have just recovered from a very trying journey and I am waking up to find myself in a place where I'm not needed. Can't this discussion about my future employment be postponed until I have dressed and eaten breakfast?"

Vanessa had the grace to look embarrassed. "Certainly. Forgive me. I just felt afraid that you might not like the switch to Amy and would act unpleasant. I can't stand arguments."

She rose and smiled. Now that she had gained her way, Vanessa's manner became more friendly. "I heard that you met the notorious Frenchman last night. When Amy described him, I knew at once who it was. Thank heaven, I've never met the villain. I should simply swoon with fear."

"Who is he really underneath that wig and mask?"

Vanessa shrugged. "No one knows his real identity. He has only been seen in that ridiculous disguise. Some say he isn't really French at all. Probably a Northerner. He steals slaves from their masters, you know, and aids them to escape."

"So that is his sole claim to villainy?"

"Isn't that enough? It is even rumored that he is a member of the infamous Underground Railroad. It isn't really a railroad," Vanessa informed her condescendingly, "just a chain of hiding places for runaways."

"I've heard of it." Charlotte didn't add her own views knowing now how unpopular they would be down here.

"There is a price on the Frenchman's head," Vanessa continued avidly. "I just can't imagine what possessed him to bring you girls almost to our doorstep in his carriage."

"Human compassion, I suppose," Charlotte murmured.

Coyly, Vanessa twisted her blue hair ribbon. "Some silly girls say he looked attractive when they glimpsed him dashing by. What did you think?"

"It was impossible to tell, since he was wearing that disguise. I thought he seemed eccentric, but at that point, Amy and I were so cold and wet, we probably would have taken refuge with him even if we *had* known his reputation. Where is Amy, by the way?

"Goodness, she's been up this age and went to pick some flowers. We've both had breakfast, but you can still get something downstairs. I will send Tibby up with water for your washing. She can be the maid for you and Amy. Tibby's new to housework and very young and green, but she was absolutely useless as a field hand. Just be firm and tell her exactly what to do."

With that, Vanessa sailed out of the door in a swirl of azure ruffles, and Charlotte sank back against the pillows. A maid? She was about to have a firsthand experience with a slave, like it or not.

She had already met one slavery dissident and her curiosity about the Frenchman was intense. If he really was a member of the Underground Railroad, he would be in constant danger of arrest. She had heard that both Northerners and Southerners belonged to this secret fraternity, it included anyone who believed that the evil of slavery should be abolished. Its members were called "conductors" and they sent runaways to "stations," which might be a barn, a secret room, a Quaker's cellar or attic, a Yankee cargo ship, or just a haystack where a person could be hidden on his way up North by a sympathetic farmer.

Southern turmoil existed on every hand, and Charlotte knew she must guard her tongue regarding her own views. Right now, there was the problem of work to find and she slid out of bed, determined to get dressed and talk to Amy.

However, at that moment, someone scratched upon the door. When Charlotte called, "Come in," a young, brown-skinned girl staggered into the room, carrying a large can of steaming water. She was barely able to tip it into the china washbasin, and in the process, some of the water splashed onto the carpet.

"Oh, 'scuse me, miss." Eyes dilated with fear, the girl bent down and scrubbed frantically with her long, white apron.

"No harm is done," Charlotte said briskly, sliding out of bed. "Are you Tibby, my new maid?"

"Yes'm, Tibby's my name and I'm to care for you." She stood before Charlotte with downcast eyes, long lashes curving against youthful cheeks, looking not a day over fourteen.

Since she never had a personal maid before, Charlotte felt a little awkward. "Well, Tibby, you may call me 'Miss Charlotte,' a-and I need some towels, please."

Tibby promptly scurried to the door and from a basket in the hall, produced geranium soap and linens. "If you tell me what to do, Miss Charlotte, I do it right quick. Just—just say." She continued in a desperate whisper, "I'm new to the big house, but I surely do want to 'blige."

Charlotte glanced around the room. "The clothes that I wore last night, where are they?"

"I cleaned and ironed everything while you was asleep, Miss Charlotte." Tibby darted to the wardrobe doors and flung them open.

Chemise, drawers, hose, and petticoats hung beside Charlotte's traveling gown, now looking fresh and clean. Even her low boots were scrubbed and polished.

"Oh, you did a fine job," Charlotte beamed. "Well, you may go now. I'll let you know when I need you. And, Tibby, don't be afraid of me. I would never harm you."

Charlotte smiled encouragingly, but Tibby only flicked

a tremulous glance in her general direction, then flew from the room on soundless feet.

Charlotte sighed. What a sweet, pretty girl, but so timid and fearful. What kind of treatment was she used to receiving? A thrashing if she spilled some water? This was something Charlotte had not considered. She had imagined her aunt and cousin would be easy-going and kind-hearted, treating their slaves with compassion.

After all, her mother had come from here and had been so sweet and gentle. She had loved the people who cared for her at Stone Gardens and often told young Charlotte about the singing in the evening after work, the laughing children, the ones who had been her playmates as a child. It had seemed that everyone had loved her mother and she had never seen the ugly side of slavery.

If only Rose had lived, things might have been so different. Papa might have clung more eagerly to life, instead of sliding into a weak acceptance of his declining health and leaving his two girls to face an uncertain future with no money.

And now that future must be faced. Determinedly, Charlotte slipped out of her nightgown, dipped her washcloth in the warm water and sponged thoroughly before donning the clean undergarments that smelled of fresh starch and lavender.

As she brushed her hair, she walked curiously around the room. Viewed superficially, the pale pink rug, flowered damask drapes, and rose-patterned wallpaper all gave the impression of wealth and taste. But then, as she looked more closely, she noticed surprising signs of deterioration: darns in the satin bedspread, chips in the marble washbasin, streaks of rust along the wall. The armoire, dresser, and bedstead of golden oak gleamed with a patina that age could not destroy, but they had all been cleverly arranged to cover worn spots in the rug.

Shaking back her long, dark hair, Charlotte went to look out of the window. Would the garden show the same, sad signs of neglect? Ah, no, at least not from this distance. She caught her breath with pleasure. In the lawn below, a white cupid rose from a marble pool containing waterlilies. In all directions stretched crowded beds of richly blooming plants: red and lavender dahlias, yellow chrysanthemums, snowy asters, as well as many flowers she did not recognize. Beyond the garden, evergreens towered with other trees whose leaves had changed to autumn hues of crimson, gold, and copper. Many had fallen in great mounds and drifts of dazzling color.

Lost in admiration of the scene, Charlotte suddenly saw Amy start across the lawn, carrying a bunch of roses. She was talking with great animation to a large, dark-haired man, but then each took a different direction while Amy continued toward the house.

Charlotte wondered how many family members lived at Stone Gardens? She knew Aunt Clara was a widow with one child, but there might be other people. She had heard from her mother that the South was noted for its hospitality.

Charlotte had barely finished dressing when Amy burst into the room wearing an unfamiliar lavender dress instead of her blue traveling outfit.

"Where did you get that?" Charlotte exclaimed.

Amy twirled around. "Vanessa gave me this dress and it fits me perfectly. You can hardly see the worn spots at all. Isn't it beautiful?"

"Indeed, it's most becoming." Although Charlotte admired the pretty poplin with its belling, braid-trimmed skirt and short-sleeved bolero, she didn't like she and her sister being patronized by Vanessa. Pride, however, was a luxury they could ill afford.

"It's all right to wear it, isn't it? The color, I mean,"

Amy asked anxiously. "Papa told us not to go into mourning, but I don't want to look disrespectful to his memory."

Charlotte smiled, touching a long, golden ringlet which brushed Amy's round, pink cheek. "No, pet, I'm sure Papa wouldn't mind."

For such a long time, Papa hadn't minded anything as his lung infection worsened. The bookstore soon was neglected and finally had been sold at a loss. Papa, though, had insisted that Amy and Charlotte should go to their mother's home in Virginia. *Where we are reduced to accepting charity,* Charlotte thought bitterly.

Misinterpreting Charlotte's expression, Amy's blue eyes clouded. "Perhaps Vanessa has some clothes for you also."

Charlotte raised her chin. "No, thanks, I am sure we will get our trunks back soon. But I am glad she gave you something, dear. I know how much you love pretty things, and there have been few enough in your young life. You should be having beaus, going to teas and parties, having lots of new clothes—"

"Oh, I don't need all that, truly. I am just so happy that we are both here together in this fine home and that Vanessa seems to like me. Only . . ." Her cheeks flushed and she bent her head, fingering the black braid frogs decorating her bolero. "There's just one bad thing . . ."

Charlotte gave a rueful laugh. "I know. Vanessa rushed in to tell me that she wanted you to be her companion instead of me. I wasn't even out of bed yet, but she couldn't wait."

"Oh, that was bad of her."

"Now, never mind," Charlotte answered quickly. "This will be a fine thing for you. You will be cared for and petted like the adorable little kitten that you are. I am much better able to survive out in the rough world."

Amy interrupted with a cry and ran to fling her arms around her sister. "Oh, Charlotte, you are not thinking of leaving here, are you? Trying to find work elsewhere? Oh, please, I don't want you to go. If you must, promise that we will go together.''

"Now, don't fret, little one." Deftly Charlotte wound her hair up into its crocheted snood. "Let's see how things go for a while. After all, we have only just arrived. Perhaps Aunt Clara has some other plans for me. Anyway, I wouldn't know where to go and I'm certainly not going to rush away this instant. Now, come along and show me where I can find some breakfast.''

As they descended the stairs, Charlotte asked, "By the way, who was that man I saw you with out in the garden?''

"Oh, that's Devlin Cartright. He rents the guest house from Aunt Clara and guess what? He's a writer. Perhaps Papa sold some of his books?''

"I never heard of him.''

Amy shot her a sidelong glance. "He's rather handsome in a craggy sort of way and probably not too old, though his hair does have a touch of silver. He said he lives alone,'' she added slyly.

Charlotte smiled. "Perhaps he's interested in Vanessa. She certainly is a beauty.''

"No more so than you.''

"Amy, Amy,'' Charlotte gave a burst of laughter. "You see me with the eyes of love. I am no beauty.''

"Why, you have gorgeous chestnut hair, a sweet, intelligent face. You carry yourself just like a queen. Any man would admire your figure.''

"Amy, love, I'm not here to find a man.''

"What about the Frenchman?'' Amy tittered. "I saw him kiss your hand and you just stood there, letting it go on and on.''

"You little monkey! You never said a word.''

"Well, neither did you. And I see you're blushing. Perhaps you'll meet the Frenchman again. Wasn't it lucky that he came along? Without his aid, we might have languished beside the roadside for hours, instead of revelling in all this grandeur."

"Believe me, I am grateful to be here." Charlotte's eyes dwelt on the wide, oak staircase carpeted in shades of green, the high, white ceiling carved with plaster fruit and flowers and the ornate paintings in their gilded frames. The curving staircase ended in the marble hallway where doors stood open leading to other rooms.

Remembering the strange shabbiness of her bedroom, however, Charlotte was not surprised to see chipped cornices, cracks and stains along the woodwork and frayed edges on the stair treads. She said nothing of this to her sister and tried to stiffle the uneasy feeling that financial difficulties might have beset Stone Gardens . . . and now her aunt had the added burden of herself and Amy. The necessity of finding work loomed larger. She must find a way to contribute to their keep.

Amy led Charlotte through the hallway to a small room at the rear where a linen-covered table was set with silver and china. A wide, lace-curtained window overlooked a garden of multi-colored roses, most of their rain-drenched petals littering the ground.

"I was able to find some flowers for the table," Amy said, pointing to a silver bowl. "Vanessa said that would be one of my duties."

Duties? Was Vanessa going to pile a lot of chores on Amy in return for her castoff clothes?

"This is the morning room," Amy continued, "where breakfast is served. Aunt Clara has a tray up in her room. I have already eaten, but the sideboard still has food keeping hot over little candles. Isn't that a good idea?"

She stopped abruptly as two men entered from the garden door. "Oh, Mr. Cartright, we meet again," she said.

"This is my sister, Charlotte, whom I've mentioned. I think you two will have a lot in common."

Seen up close, Devlin Cartright was indeed a good-looking man—tall, well-built, with thick dark hair and eyes. But when Charlotte smiled and said his name, he merely nodded. A brief glance in her direction had not revealed any attempt at friendliness. Though he had a large, full-lipped mouth, a crease down each cheek gave him a remote, controlled expression.

The words on Charlotte's tongue which meant to ask about his writing, went unuttered. A little hurt, she turned her eyes to the other man who still stood in the garden door.

Hat in hand, he was clothed all in black with work pants tucked into high boots. His stance held no hint of servility and Charlotte thought she had never seen such a tough, hard-bitten face.

His eyes were not on her, however, and when she observed the direction of his concentrated gaze, a flash of consternation swept her.

Chapter 3

The man's bold black eyes riveted on Amy as though he had never seen anything so desirable. Hungrily, he assessed every inch of her from the crown of golden curls to the dainty slippers peeping from the lilac skirts.

Charlotte caught back an indignant gasp. How dared the rude fellow look at Amy in that manner? Who was he, anyway?

Mr. Cartright now supplied that information. "Charlotte and Amy Davenport, meet Martin Cord, the overseer."

Cord dragged his gaze from Amy and drew a deep breath. He touched a finger negligently to his forehead in token of the introduction, then raked a hand through his thatch of rough black hair. "I must speak to Miss Clara. One of our slaves is missing."

"My aunt is not up yet." Suddenly, Charlotte's interest quickened. "Did you say a slave has gone? How did that happen?"

"How? If we knew that, we might put a stop to it," Cord

spat out. "He is the second slave to escape this month, and it's the work of that damned Frenchman, I'll be bound."

Charlotte pressed a hand against her mouth. The Frenchman! And they had been with him just last night. Had he been returning from a run on the Underground Railroad when he rescued them?

"Why are the slaves running away?" Charlotte made bold to ask. "Are they being mistreated?" If they were, probably this hard-faced overseer was to blame.

Anger leaped to the man's swarthy features. "No, by God. All slaves here get the same treatment. No problems, if they do their duty."

"And what happens if they don't?" Amy interposed anxiously, moving up beside her sister.

The overseer met her blue-eyed beauty with an immediate softening of his harsh expression. "That should be no concern of a fine little lady like yourself."

"That's right," Charlotte snapped. "Come away, Amy." She took hold of the door to close it. "I shall see your message is delivered to my aunt, Mr. Cord."

The overseer stubbornly refused to budge. "Miss Amy, if you would like to see the slave quarters, you can judge things for yourself. I would be most honored to show you around the plantation."

Charlotte thinned her lips. The gall of the man! How dare he make such an offer to her sister on such brief acquaintanceship.

Before Charlotte could voice a rebuke, to her astonishment, Amy smiled at him. "Why, thank you, Mr. Cord. I would like that."

"Send a servant for me when you want to go." His black eyes swept Amy again from head to toe, as if he wanted to memorize the vision he beheld. He cast a brief glance at Charlotte. "As for Miss Clara, I want to speak to her in person. I'll be back." With that, he swung away and the door closed smartly after him.

"Amy," Charlotte hissed, "you are not to have a thing to do with that odious person. I saw the way he looked at you."

"Like a cat looking at a dish of cream," Mr. Cartright grunted, turning to pick up a plate from the sideboard.

"It was insulting," Charlotte flamed.

Amy drew back the lace curtain from the garden window, her eyes on the vanishing black-clothed figure. "He didn't mean to be insulting. I think he likes me."

"Amy! Now listen to me—you don't understand—"

"Oh, Charlotte, dear, don't get upset." Amy whirled around, her laughter bubbling. "Didn't you say I should have beaus?"

Charlotte clenched her teeth. "Not someone like that. A tough, hard-bitten man so much older than yourself."

"He's not that old, I think. Probably not yet thirty and rather handsome, too, I thought." Amy slid her sister an impish glance. "Don't worry, I promise to behave. Now, I'm going to see if Aunt Clara is up yet, so I can wish her a good-morning. Meanwhile, eat some breakfast, dear. Perhaps Mr. Cartright will keep you entertained."

Entertainment was not what Charlotte wanted . . . and it was highly unlikely that the withdrawn author would supply it. Morosely, she surveyed the chafing dishes on the buffet. Would Cord present another problem besides her own difficult and ambiguous situation? How could she leave Stone Gardens now to look for work elsewhere? More and more it became apparent that her place was here where she could watch over her young sister.

She didn't really feel like eating, but took a bowl of milky grits, which her mother had described as being a staple of southern breakfasts. She poured syrup and butter in the center, then filled a cup with coffee and sat down at the table.

Across from her, Mr. Cartright concentrated on a large breakfast of ham, eggs, beaten biscuits, and coffee. He didn't seem disposed to talk until his plate was empty. Then he leaned back and dabbed a napkin to his lips.

After a minute, Charlotte glanced at him again, wondering why he didn't leave, and found him staring at her with his unrevealing, heavy-lidded eyes. What went on behind that controlled, hard-planed face?

His silence proved unnerving. If he wouldn't speak, she would. "What kind of books do you write?"

"Swashbuckling adventure."

"Indeed?" For a minute, Charlotte was at a loss for words. She would have thought adventure was the farthest thing to interest this laconic individual. "Er—lots of derring-do and swooning maidens?"

"My maidens seldom swoon and they don't stay maidens very long."

Embarrassment flooded Charlotte's face. She said awkwardly, "How—how interesting. I don't think my father ever stocked any books by a Devlin Cartright. We had a little shop—"

"Your sister told me. Have you ever heard of Rodney Rogue?"

"That's you?" She gaped, recalling the books quite well, sagas of very hot-blooded Scottish clans. She had read one, and in spite of being stunned by the detailed, passionate love scenes, she had been glued to the swift-paced pages until the end.

"I have turned to the South for my next book," he continued, "and have encountered a dilemma. My clerical assistant became ill and had to leave. For the past month, my work has been piling up."

Charlotte stared at him as an incredible hope flared.

Was it possible he might need her help in some clerical capacity?

"I wish to hire someone to copy my manuscripts in a good clear hand before I send them to my publisher. Your sister said you did clerking in your father's bookstore and now you are seeking work." His narrowed eyes glinted at her briefly. "Interested?"

Charlotte swallowed. "Why—why, yes—" Trying to subdue the surge of hope that flooded her, nevertheless she felt as though a lifeline had been tossed to her in a stormy sea.

"Come to the guest house in an hour and I'll show you exactly what I need, then we'll discuss this further." He poured himself another cup of the rich, chicory-flavored coffee and drank it while staring out the window.

Charlotte observed him silently. This strange man might be difficult to work for. She knew nothing about him except that he was a successful writer. Would he be a demanding, fault-finding employer, asking her to perform many extra duties? Did he have a sharp, unreasonable temper? She firmed her lips. No matter. She had struggled with difficult types in her father's shop: buyers, salesmen and creditors. Some were amorous while others tried to cheat her since she was a woman. She had learned to hold her own with all of them.

No matter how taxing, the most important thing was to remain at Stone Gardens so that she could keep an eye on Amy, especially after observing her reaction to Martin Cord. True, the man had a certain rough handsomeness, rather like a hungry wolf, but Amy was too young and innocent to recognize a dangerous lecher.

Charlotte rose to her feet. "Very well, Mr. Cartright, I will see you later—"

She broke off as voices sounded at the hallway door.

Amy and Vanessa entered dressed for an outing in shawls and bonnets.

"Ladies." The writer stood up, giving the girls a brief nod.

"Hello! Vanessa is going to take me for a drive to see the countryside," Amy chirped, then shot Charlotte an apologetic glance. "The pony cart just seats two."

Charlotte smiled. "I'm sure you will have a lovely ride now that the sun is shining and all is fresh after the rain."

Ignoring Charlotte, Vanessa twittered to Mr. Cartright's side with an arched expression. "I missed you at breakfast this morning, Devlin. Were you writing all night again? I vow you are just going to work yourself to death. You really do need someone to take care of you."

She clasped his arm with a provocative pout, and Charlotte saw him answer with a smile. She could scarcely blame him. There was no denying that Vanessa made an entrancing picture and was well aware of it. Her rose-trimmed straw hat lent color to a flawless cheek and the black velvet bow beneath her chin emphasized the whiteness of her throat.

"I may have solved one problem," the writer said. "I am considering hiring Miss Charlotte to work for me."

With a joyous exclamation, Amy ran to Charlotte's side and flung an arm around her waist. "Oh, what could be better? Then you can stay right here at Stone Gardens doing the same kind of clerical work you did for Papa."

Vanessa frowned. "That's not the proper sort of thing for a lady. Men have always worked as clerks." Her face held a sudden angry light as she stared across the table.

Could she possibly be jealous, Charlotte wondered, because I would be working close to Mr. Cartright?

Not leaving anything to chance, Amy turned to Devlin and told him earnestly, "My sister is awfully clever. She did everything in our father's bookstore—buying, selling, keeping records . . . She can do any kind of office work, I'm sure. And is as good as any man." This last remark she aimed at Vanessa with a little grin.

The beauty shrugged. "Well, I must admit Charlotte does give the impression of being a hard worker in that serviceable grey gown and tightly wound hair."

"I hope your observations are correct," Mr. Cartright said silkily and took a step toward the door.

Vanessa stopped him with a hand upon his arm. "Devlin, now that I think about it, this may be a good thing for us. Perhaps you can come riding with me more often. How about this afternoon?" She walked her fingers up his sleeve, all sweet coquetishness again.

"I will let you know, Miss Vanessa, but now I have some work to do. Please excuse me, ladies." With a short nod, he strode off through the garden door.

There went a man who knew his own mind, Charlotte mused, and probably never could be made to do a thing against his wishes, even if it meant thwarting Vanessa's equally strong will.

"Come, Amy," Vanessa said a little petulantly. "Let's not stand about all day indoors."

"Enjoy your ride, girls," Charlotte said. "I think I shall go and speak to Aunt Clara about some things—"

To her surprise, Amy ran back to her side. "No, Charlotte, wait, please don't say anything to her. I promise to be most circumspect. You won't have a thing to worry about."

Charlotte stared blankly. "I just want to tell her about our lost trunks. What is the matter with you?"

Amy dropped her eyes. "N-nothing. I told her about our trunks, and she is going to send someone to the depot so they can pass the word along the railroad lines."

As the girls left, Charlotte heard Vanessa say to Amy, "What did you mean about being circumspect?"

"Just—just that I want to please everyone."

"Oh, well, you can do that, never fear."

Staring after them, it occurred to Charlotte that Amy might have thought she was going to tell their aunt about Martin Cord's interest in her. Judging by her sister's reaction, this matter was becoming more serious by the minute.

Drawing a deep breath, Charlotte felt she must get a little fresh air before her interview with Mr. Cartright and she went upstairs to fetch a hat and shawl. She must try to appear calm, intelligent, and quickly grasp Mr. Cartright's instructions. He didn't seem the sort to "suffer fools gladly."

When she came back down the stairs, she saw Cicero admitting a visitor, a tall, older woman in a black riding habit the skirt caught up in her hand by a silver chain. Handing her crop and plumed hat to the butler, she suddenly saw Charlotte and called out in a high-pitched tone, "Hey, girl, don't run off. I've come to meet you. Where's your sister?"

"She's out riding with Vanessa. How do you do? I am Charlotte Davenport."

"Miss Charlotte, this here is our neighbor, Mrs. Beaulah Hartley." Cicero made a creaking bow. "May I bring you ladies some refreshment in the parlor?"

"Later, Cicero, and don't call Clara yet." Shrewd, dark eyes went over Charlotte. "Were you going out?"

"Yes, I thought a brief stroll in the garden might be pleasant."

"Mind if I join you? I recall your lovely mother very well, you know."

"Oh, do you?" Charlotte cried eagerly. Together, they went out the front door.

A splendid glossy mare stood tethered on the grass verge, drinking from a water trough of carved grey stone. Mrs. Hartley gave the animal a warm pat as they passed it on their way around the house. "Do you ride, Charlotte? You don't mind first names, I hope. I answer to Miss Beaulah. I say manners should be sensible and not a lot of folderol, meaning nothing."

"I agree. Please call me Charlotte. And, no, I don't ride. Oh, Miss Beaulah, tell me what you remember of my mother. She died when I was eight, so I only saw her through a child's eyes. I thought she was so dear, always sweet and considerate of a little person like myself."

"You saw her truly. Her parents doted on her and were very bitter when she ran off with 'that Yankee,' their words, not mine. She told me how she met him in his bookshop on a trip up North. After that, they corresponded and finally James Davenport came South and carried Rose away. I saw him once—a handsome, strong-minded devil who couldn't take his eyes from Rose. Well, Clara was devastated at losing her beloved little sister and became as bitter as her parents. I'm surprised she has welcomed you."

"Perhaps she felt guilty about inheriting everything," Charlotte said, "and is trying to make amends. However, when I wrote to her, I said we expected to earn our keep and she agreed. Amy is to be a companion for Vanessa, and Mr. Cartright is considering me as secretary. If he does, I can contribute to our board and room."

The lady nodded. "The plantation is not doing well since the senior Mr. Bainbridge and Clara's husband Frank died. Well, Vanessa is a spoiled beauty, but her demands should not be hard if she likes your sister. I've met Devlin Cartright only a few times, although he's been in residence a month. I found him quite reserved, but I also think he's sensuous and shrewd. I read one of those daring books he writes. Shocking, but I couldn't put it down." She chuckled. "I'd be on my guard, if I were you."

"Why?" Charlotte asked, startled.

"You'll find out. That's all I've got to say just now. What do you think about Stone Gardens?"

"I haven't seen much of it. How did it get that odd name?"

"Your mother didn't tell you? Well, she might have thought it was too grim for your little ears. I think she closed her mind to any trouble with the slaves. Come, I'll show you why it's called Stone Gardens. I warrant you've never seen anything like it."

As they walked through the extensive plots of live flowers, alternating with ornamental bushes, benches, arbors and swaying trees, Charlotte wondered if her mother and father had wandered here, however briefly. Perhaps they had paused to kiss while he placed a betrothal ring upon her little hand. Grief seemed imminent and Charlotte had to thrust the image from her mind. Perhaps they were together now and happy.

"The garden is so beautiful," she told Miss Beaulah, "but terribly neglected." She shook her head at the briars and roses twining up tree trunks, petals littering the ground. Weeds and dried grass poked up wherever they could find a foothold in the herringbone brick path.

"The flower beds here used to be quite famous," Beaulah Hartley said, "but they don't get proper care anymore. Perhaps you and Amy could help out there."

"I'd be glad to do some wedding and pruning. We only had a tiny plot up North, but I used to help my mother with my own little tools."

"It's a ladylike pursuit, as Vanessa says, but her only contribution is to cut some posies for her own adornment. We have a rather nice rose garden that my husband cares for. I raise horses. He raises flowers. You'll have to visit us soon."

"Do you live nearby?"

"About five miles away. I am the closest neighbor. My

niece and nephew will be coming any day and then we'll have a party, perhaps a picnic by the river. I haven't seen them since they grew up, but my sister says they are beautiful and lively. My sister and her husband are going to Europe for a visit, so I asked the children to stay with me."

She broke off abruptly as they rounded a corner where a high ivy-covered wall faced them with a closed arched door. Mrs. Hartley waved her hand dramatically. "Here it is. The Stone Garden, built entirely by one man, a clever slave who was an outstanding artist. His only previous training had been the carving of gravestones." She lifted up a latch and with a groan, the door swung open.

As they entered the strange place, a chill swept over Charlotte and she shivered, even though the sun was bright. Words failed her and she could only stare. The whole area contained a multitude of grey stone objects, some shaped like flowers: roses, tulips, lilies, huge squat blossoms that rested on beds of gravel edged with scalloped cement bricks. Small trees suggested conifers and palms with stiff, flat upright "leaves". In a round pool, grey stone fish "swam" on a waterless bottom.

Walking slowly with a silent Mrs. Hartley at her side, Charlotte marveled at a well and bucket, a sundial, a summerhouse twined with carved flowers and vines, as well as benches, urns and statues. All of it was lifeless stone, cold and hard as death itself. Although it certainly was awesome, Charlotte felt repelled.

"What do you think of it?" Beaulah Hartley's voice sounded hushed, subdued, as though the eerie place had cast a cloud over her former liveliness.

Charlotte inhaled deeply. "It is . . . amazing, incredible and must have taken years and years to make. But it's a dead world, no scent, sound or color. Nothing has any life. I still would like to know a little more about the man who made it."

"Well, here comes someone who can tell you." Mrs. Hartley waved her hand as Devlin Cartright strolled toward them, his feet crunching on the gravel, hands thrust in the pockets of his brown corduroy jacket.

"Good-morning, Miss Beaulah. Are you showing Charlotte Davenport the 'Graveyard of Dreams'?"

What a perfect name for the place, Charlotte thought. It would take a writer to think of that.

"Charlotte is stunned but interested. I shall leave you to tell her the history, Devlin, as I know you've studied it. I must go in and visit Clara. She probably wonders where I am. Nice to meet you, Charlotte." She hurried down the walk, waving back as Charlotte thanked her for the tour.

"Am I late? Were you looking for me?" Charlotte asked a little nervously when she and Devlin were alone.

"You're not late, but I am anxious to discuss the work that I need done. However, perhaps you should hear the story of the Stone Garden first. It's the main reason I came here."

Chapter 4

Instead of going directly to his studio, Devlin motioned Charlotte toward a stone bench and took a place beside her. For a long moment, he stared across at the carvings without speaking.

Surreptitiously, Charlotte studied him, recalling Mrs. Hartley's description: "reserved, sensuous and shrewd." His profile looked almost as strongly carved as the nearby objects, as she noted a keen precision in his features: wide brow with dark eyebrows above thick white lids seeming to mask inner thoughts. A slash down each flat cheek held a full-lipped mouth in check. Strands of silver glinted on his brow in the dark waves of hair worn long behind his ears.

How old was he? Did he have a wife? Children? Where was his home? Charlotte hadn't expected to be so interested in his private life and had to quickly reel in her thoughts as he began to speak.

"I read this account in a book about Virginia landmarks before I came here and it inspired my current novel.

"About two hundred years ago, one of the Bainbridge ancestors wanted a garden built for his new plantation. He had a strong young slave named Erasmus, whom he considered selling because he had been trained to make gravestones and would bring a good price on the auction block. But the slave begged his master not to separate him from his family and said that he would make such a garden as had never been seen before—all carved out of stone. Intrigued, the owner agreed not to sell him nor any of his family until the garden was completed.

"The canny slave saw to it that the garden took many years, but one day the owner broke his word and sold off Erasmus's two sons. In retaliation, the slave began to destroy the carvings. He didn't get far before the patrol discovered him and then he was shot right here among the unique objects he had made." When he finished, a silence fell for several moments.

"It's a sad and bitter story," Charlotte mused. "Rather like Scheherazade and the tales she told each night to the king to put off her execution."

"I doubt if the slave ever heard of the Arabian Nights, but he certainly built an unusual place. There is even supposed to be an old secret tunnel in here which leads to the house, in case of Indian attacks."

"No wonder my mother never mentioned this place," Charlotte said with a shudder. Evil deeds still haunt it.

Devlin gave her a narrowed glance. "Your father was a Northerner, wasn't he? How do you feel about being in a slave state?"

Charlotte knew she must speak carefully. "It's too soon for me to judge."

He said no more but rose and led her from the strange garden. Charlotte noticed for the first time that the stones were chipped and weather-worn. Probably no one ever came here except the wind or rain. The slave had created a dead world. Had he been trying to illustrate his own sad plight?

"The Stone Garden is depressing, in spite of its uniqueness." Charlotte drew her shawl closer around her arms, trying to subdue the eerie feeling of doom and ancient sadness that the place engendered. Perhaps a miasma lay upon the whole South with its thousands of enslaved souls. Would it cause a holocaust someday, as her father had believed?

When she drew a ragged breath, Devlin caught her arm in firm, hard fingers. "I see the place affected you strongly. You must be very sensitive to atmosphere. Are you all right?"

"Oh . . . yes . . ." He released her and she swallowed hard. For some reason, his touch had sent a tingling sensation clear up her arm, but it had helped to clear her brain.

They were now in the real gardens, with the sunshine and humid warmth. Bees buzzed in the over-ripe grapes spilling from a long arbor. Birds chirped among the golden leaves drifting constantly to the worn brick paths. The fragrance of roses scented the air along with rampant honeysuckle vines on every wall.

"It's lovely here, but so neglected." Charlotte sighed.

"Hard times. Your aunt is selling off workers that she can't afford to keep."

"Is that why they are trying to escape? They must be terribly unhappy to risk severe punishment if they are caught. Why do they continue trying?"

"Wouldn't you?"

An odd remark, and Charlotte didn't answer, wondering if it was an indication of the writer's own feelings about slavery? As a resident on the plantation, however, he would have to be discreet.

When they left the flower beds, a small white building appeared beyond a row of elms. Only one story high, it

had a railed porch, green-shuttered windows of uncur-
tained glass and even a small chimney.

"How cute—it looks like a play house," Charlote
exclaimed.

"It's big enough. One bedroom and a sitting room with
a fireplace to give heat, if needed." He extracted a key
from a ledge above the door. "While you're working here,
the door can be left unlocked. Otherwise, use the key if
we both are out. I don't want curious children of the
workers wandering inside."

"Of course not." It sounded as though her hiring was
an accomplished fact and, happily, she glanced around
the room with its fireplace and closed door, probably leading to a bedchamber. The main area was taken up with
two big tables, wall shelves, several chairs, a small plush
loveseat and two oil lamps.

There seemed to be a great deal of disorder: boxes of
notes; books strewn about; some teetering in piles upon
the floor; and scattered everywhere were the tools of his
trade—pens, pencils, notepads, paper and ink bottles. She
saw drawings tacked upon the wooden walls and moved
closer to observe them. Perhaps these were to remind the
writer of his subject's physical attributes. There were many
types: strong-faced men, weak, small men, some old, some
young, villanious expressions, heroic faces, a few with Afri-
can features. And then the women. Not so many of them,
mainly several studies of one voluptuous, black-haired
beauty. Her poses, executed with attention to detail, were
brazen, sad, frightened, thoughtful or seductive.

"These are very good. Did you study art?" Charlotte
asked.

He grunted a short laugh. "No. They are characters in
my new book, *From Dreams to Flames.*"

"That's the title? And you're incorporating the Stone
Garden?"

"There is a synopsis of my plot on the wall over there. You can read it later. It might help you to understand what I am doing. Now, Charlotte, if you will sit down here, I'll explain what I want done."

Charlotte? Without the southern "Miss"? So, informality was to be the rule. Much better. She had been afraid from his cool manner when they met that it might presage a distant, unfriendly relationship. However, she would call him Mr. Cartright until he suggested a first name basis, which of course might be never. It was all very well for him to call her Charlotte, but he was her employer.

He drew two chairs up to the big table, supplying her with foolscap, ink, and a steel-nibbed pen. "Let me see what kind of hand you have. Copy this paragraph."

She must not let his intense closeness make her shake. She drew a sheet before her, and dipping in the inkwell, began slowly and carefully to copy the first few lines of a manuscript he showed her. *Aurelia, marry me tonight. My ship sails on the James at dawn, and I must be on it, even though my soul cries out for more of your sweet surrender.*

His writing was a careless scribble, evidently written at high speed, but it was legible—at least thus far. "I could do better if you weren't watching me," Charlotte muttered.

"You're doing well. You write a strong, clear hand. Leave enough space between each line for the editor to write his comments and also an inch margin all around. Be sure to number pages consecutively. Begin each new chapter halfway down the page and at the top write "Dreams" for manuscript identification. Understand?"

Charlotte nodded, but not leaving anything to chance, she took a scrap of paper and scribbled down his instructions.

"You can work at your own pace, but I would like at least three chapters done each day." He shoved back his chair and gathered up a notebook and pencils. He named a generous sum for wages. "I'm going out for several hours. When you leave for lunch, remember to lock the door and replace the key."

"Then—?"

"Yes, you're hired. I think we shall work well together. You don't babble."

Charlotte flushed with pleasure and called after him. "I think this will be a very interesting occupation." By that time, he was out the door and she drew a breath of pure excitement. Heavens, she was going to be in at the birth of another Rodney Rogue novel. Before it reached an eager public, she would know its pages contents from cover to cover.

She decided to read the synopsis and rose to seek the pages tacked upon the wall. She discovered that the hero, Jarvis Hamlin, was outwardly a pirate of the high seas, but secretly a man who aided slaves in the South to escape harsh masters. The beautiful mulatto heroine, Aurelia was only seventeen, yet had caught the master's eyes, as well as those of Jarvis. Aurelia had a Negro half-brother who was carving the Stone Garden and his hatred ran high for any whites, including Aurelia, for the mixture of blood had creamed her lovely skin. There soon would be a duel to the death between her lovers and an uprising of the slaves to be subdued. In the end, Jarvis and Aurelia would sail away, knowing they never could marry in the South, but will find sanctuary on some West Indies island.

Charlotte, filled with enthusiasm, returned to her copy work and continued for several hours, unaware of the passing time. Finally, her back ached, her hand felt cramped, and she realized that her skimpy breakfast would not keep her going any longer. It must be time for lunch.

Just as she pushed back her chair and corked the ink bottle, she heard an odd sound from the porch. A whimper, then a groan. She jerked around and saw a dark face

peering in the window. A shaking hand shaded the creature's desperate, reddened eyes below a blood-soaked rag.
A tattered shirt clung to its skeletal form.

Fear swept over her, and she was suddenly conscious of
the stillness and isolation of the guesthouse. For a long
moment, she didn't move. Neither did the figure at the
window.

Charlotte sucked in her breath. What was the matter
with her? There was a human being outside, evidently
severely injured.

"Who are you?" she called out, running to the door.
"What is the matter? Are you hurt?"

The apparition stumbled from the porch and backed
away with an inarticulate cry. He ran around the side of
the house and when Charlotte gained the path, the figure
had disappeared. Only a quivering bush at the far edge of
the trees marked his passage.

"Come back!" Charlotte shouted. "Let me help you."

No one answered. No one appeared. He had vanished
as completely as though there existed a real train in an
"Underground Railroad" and he had climbed aboard.
Charlotte searched for him among the trees, calling constantly, but all to no avail. Finally, she gave up and returned
to the studio.

To her surprise, Aunt Clara emerged from the garden
path, sedate and frowning in grey padusoy and black beading. "Where on earth have you been? We're waiting lunch
on you. Amy said you were working for Mr. Cartright, but
now—"

"Yes, I am." Charlotte pushed distractedly at her tousled
hair. "Oh, Aunt Clara, someone just came here to the
window, a terrible-looking black man with a bloody rag
around his head. He may be badly injured. When I came
out to help him, he ran away. Who could it have been?"

Her aunt stared blankly. "I have no idea. I would have heard if someone was running around our compound."

"Might it be the slave who escaped from here last night?"

"Oh, no, Elijah was sighted way down the river by the pattyrollers. Fiddle, I'm talking just like the Nigras." She gave a little snicker. "I mean the patrol, the slave catchers. They reported to me that they saw him board a Yankee freighter."

She started walking back toward the house and Charlotte quickly locked the door and hurried to catch up with her. "Then what happened?"

"Well, they tried to make the captain return to shore, but he refused and sailed away after cursing the patrol. Yankees are such a crude class of people. Charlotte, I sincerely trust that the Southern part of your nature dominates the Northern part."

Charlotte clamped her jaw. It was only the realization that she and Amy were dependent on her aunt's charity that kept her from a heated defense of "Yankees". Any one of her acquaintances would have shown more compassion for an injured person than her aunt just had done.

"What can be done about that poor man I just saw?" Charlotte continued doggedly. "Whoever he is, I know that he needs help."

"Yes, yes, but you must realize that colored people don't feel pain like a white person does. It has something to do with their inferior brains, I believe."

Charlotte nearly choked out a denial at this display of ignorance and bigotry, but said nothing.

"I will have someone look around," her aunt continued, "However, we are quite shorthanded."

"I've noticed. I shall contribute part of my wages for our board and room. I also thought I could do some gardening in my spare time."

"That would certainly be a help," her aunt conceeded.

"I hope that Amy and I won't be too much of a burden on you."

"Well, we had to take you in, since you had no other place to go. After all, you are close kin. What would people think if we hadn't offered you our home? Beaulah found out that you had written to us. I think Vanessa told her."

"It is very kind of you," Charlotte said a little stiffly. Groveling with gratitude for reluctant charity did not come easily.

"Yes. Well, I won't deny that my husband's death worked a hardship on Stone Gardens. We are forced to retrench in every direction since the bank, alas, refused to grant a loan to a mere woman. Anyway, it will save money to have Amy for Vanessa. My delicate child needs someone to fetch things and read to her when she has a headache, someone of her own class to be a companion."

Especially someone who doesn't ask for wages, Charlotte thought.

As they entered the house, her aunt waved a dismissing hand. "Now, hurry up and change for the midday meal, Niece. We are all waiting in the dining room."

"I'm sorry, but I have no other clothes until my trunk arrives." Charlotte smoothed down her grey skirt which had acquired some leaves and wrinkles during the morning's recent activities.

"Dear me, how tiresome for you." Her aunt patted the back of carefully-groomed black ringlets. "Well, come down as soon as you have washed."

Upstairs, Charlotte quickly cleaned her hands and face, brushed her hair back into a snood, then followed the sound of voices in the lower hallway until she came to a dark-paneled room. Here a long table was set with four places and a great deal of silver, crystal, and damask. Red dominated the color scheme with a flowered Turkish carpet, rose-colored chandelier of little glass bells, and gold-fringed crimson draperies looped back from tall windows.

Charlotte was startled when she discovered Amy standing by Martin Cord, who now wore a clean, white shirt, black string tie, and water-slicked hair. His hooded eyes stared down intently at the young pink-and-white face raised to his.

Charlotte must have made some sound, because the overseer glanced up and a caustic grimace twisted his mouth as he met her frown.

"Don't look so alarmed, Miss Davenport. I don't make a habit of dining with the gentry. Your aunt and I had some business to discuss and since we hadn't finished, she invited me to stay."

Aunt Clara inclined her head. "You are welcome at our table, Martin." She looked over her shoulder at the servants. "Miss Vanessa has gone out, so you may start serving now, Cicero."

With a rather rough courtesy, Cord held out Aunt Clara's high-backed, plush-covered chair, but Charlotte slid quickly into her own before he came to her. He then moved to Amy's chair and Charlotte saw the rascal brush her sister's shoulder with his fingers. Horrified, Charlotte looked away and gulped some water from her crystal goblet. What was she going to do about the man? It would require stern measures, and she might have to tell her aunt that he was too familiar with her sister. However, she hoped speaking again to Amy would be enough. It was too soon for them to begin complaining about anything at Stone Gardens.

Serving started, then, with dishes carried by a maid under the keen direction of Cicero. The table was soon covered with a large variety of items. Dismayed, Charlotte realized that the real dinner was served at midday instead of the light lunch that she always had up North.

This meal progressed from a thick, turtle soup to a boiled salmon with lobster sauce, sliced duckling, pickled beef, and side dishes that included cornpone, beaten biscuits, hominy, and vegetables swimming in rich cream sauces. In spite of financial difficulties, there seemed to be no retrenching on food.

When Aunt Clara and Martin Cord began a low-voiced discussion, Amy turned to Charlotte. "Did Mr. Cartright hire you? Do you like him? Will you enjoy the work?"

"Yes, to all your questions." Charlotte smiled. "But even if I didn't, it would make no difference to me. I must hold onto the job. It is important that we stay here. By the way, have you seen the Stone Garden?"

"Oh, no," Amy exclaimed. "Have you?"

"Yes, a visitor, Mrs. Hartley, showed it to me, then Mr. Cartright appeared and told me the whole history. Let's go together early tomorrow—"

Martin Cord's head snapped up and he threw Charlotte a defiant glare. "Your sister has promised to let me show her around the plantation in the morning."

"Aunt Clara said it would be all right," Amy quavered.

Their aunt nodded. "Both of you girls must see the plantation, and Mr. Cord is the one to explain it all. Take Charlotte, also. I just might come myself."

A look of frustration swept the overseer's swarthy face, and he set down his glass of Madeira with a little thud. "Do you want to go?" he questioned Charlotte in a tone that was anything but welcoming.

Charlotte glared at him. Thought he would have Amy all to himself, did he? "Certainly, I want to go. Tomorrow morning will be fine."

Amy's face flushed, but she didn't speak. She only picked at the iced Baltimore cake set before her, looking up with relief when a small boy appeared to pull the ceiling fans gently back and forth on a long rope which made the room much more comfortable.

Feeling that she had overcome one difficulty, Charlotte relaxed and enjoyed her dessert, but when the overseer pushed back his chair to leave, she suddenly remembered something.

"Just a minute, Mr. Cord, I want to tell you that a man came to the guest house while I was working there today. A terrible-looking creature, hurt, frightened, face all bloody. He ran away when I called to him and I don't know where he went, but I am certain he needs help."

"Oh, the poor man," Amy breathed. "I wonder what happened to him?"

"Really, Charlotte, I was going to tell Mr. Cord. I just forgot," Aunt Clara interposed testily.

"Colored?" the overseer barked. Charlotte nodded.

Cord drew a cheroot from a case in his pocket and rolled it slowly between his fingers, his eyes staring out the window. "There are no injured people in my compound and all are accounted for today, but I will keep my eyes open. He probably is a runaway from some other place."

He turned and the black eyes raked the table. "Did you know that the Fugitive Slave Law acquired new teeth the other day? Now anyone who aids an escaped slave had best watch out. They can be fined $1000 and get a jail sentence of from one to three years."

Aunt Clara thrust out her jaw. "It's about time some iron was put into that law. It's disgraceful and downright criminal the way Northerners have been stealing our property through the Underground Railroad."

Charlotte made a choking sound and her aunt's eyes swiveled to her face. "Oh yes, you made your views clear last night. But why should they not be called our property? They have been paid for, we give them housing, clothes, food . . . If they are sick, lazy or troublesome, we still take care of them. Then they repay us by running away. I say this law is long overdue.''

"I read about it," Charlotte burst out, unable to stop herself. "And, Aunt Clara, some aspects of the law are clearly wrong. There is no trial for escaped slaves to see if the person claiming them truly has a right to do so. There's also no inquiry to determine if they have been savaged. Bribes are offered to judges if they will send runaways back into slavery, and there are huge rewards for anyone returning slaves. Some unscrupulous people will surely profit—"

"Slave owners must be protected by any means necessary. Without our slaves, the South would perish." Aunt Clara rose, ending the discussion. "Well, girls, it's time now for our beauty naps. Good-day to you, Martin." Like a stately grey ship, she sailed out of the room.

Amy passed by the overseer with a little smile and Cord drew a deep breath, his eyes running over her with a hungry gleam. "I must go." He touched his forehead and strode out of the room, the black cheroot already between his bold, highly-colored lips, the lucifer match held ready in his hand.

"Come, Amy, we have to talk," Charlotte said firmly and took her sister by the arm. "After that, we'll visit the Stone Garden."

"All right," Amy said, but the meekness of her mien didn't fool Charlotte for a minute.

Chapter 5

"Wasn't there a lot to eat just now?" Amy whispered as they hurried from the house.

"Too much." Charlotte groaned and rubbed her stomach. "I shouldn't have eaten all that cake. At this rate, I'll start getting fat."

"Never. You have the height to carry your splendid figure."

Charlotte quirked an eyebrow at her sister as they slowly walked toward the garden. "Flattery will not get you out of a scolding, my girl. You know I do not like the interest you are showing in that overseer. You evidently don't realize what he is."

Amy shook back her curls. "I know what he is."

"And what is that, pray tell?" Charlotte demanded tartly.

"A lonesome man who has never had any softness or warmth in his entire life."

"Ha! I wager that the side street trollops are quite well-known to that hot-eyed character."

"Charlotte, that isn't love. He has never been married. He had no family and was raised in an orphanage."

"How did you learn all of this personal history?"

"We spoke a little before lunch." Color stole into Amy's cheeks and she looked away.

Charlotte stopped beneath the avenue of golden beeches and placed her hand on Amy's shoulder. "Listen to me. Don't you get any moony ideas about that man. He's a stranger, different from anyone you've ever known and that gives him a kind of glamour in your eyes. But I am older than you and I know what such men are like."

Amy tipped her head on one side, looking skeptical. "How, Charlotte, from books?"

"Books can teach you a lot. Amy, I fear that I must be blunt and crude, but you should be made aware of the facts. Martin Cord looks at you with naked lust."

Amy gave a burst of laughter. "Heavens, do you think he is about to rape me here on my aunt's plantation? Or risk losing a good job? Really, Charlotte! Besides, do you believe I would tamely submit to—to any indecencies from any man?"

Slowly, Charlotte released Amy and they started walking again. "No, but there are other things a man can do if he has evil intentions. Smouldering looks, casual constant touching, flattering remarks . . . Little by little, an unscrupulous rake can arouse a woman until she hardly knows what is happening. And that can lead to disaster—especially if she is a virgin."

Amy threw her a teasing glance. "Dear me, you have been reading some interesting books."

Charlotte didn't answer, but to her mind came scenes from Rodney Rogue's book that she had read recently in New York: The swift attraction between the protagonists which they had tried to fight, then the slow letting down of barriers, the awareness and longing, the unexpected nude encounter evolving into a desperate kiss. Then, the breaking off, the attempt to halt their headlong destiny, finally ending in passionate acceptance.

Charlotte's face grew warm and she pushed the memory from her mind, turning back to the problem at hand. "Amy, you are barely out of the classroom. You seem intrigued by Martin Cord and it worries me."

"Please don't be, dear. There is no need for concern."

"Well, I don't trust him one iota," Charlotte muttered. "At least promise me that you will be careful and come to me if he annoys you."

"Of course. And, Charlotte, I do know this much about men. Even the brashest and most forward of them need encouragement. Martin Cord is a proud man. He would never force himself on me."

That might not be true, Charlotte thought, but she said no more upon the subject. It was going to be hard to let Amy grow up at her own pace.

Relieved to have the matter closed, Amy gave a bright glance all around. "How beautiful the grounds are. Did you ever think to live among so many flowers? Vanessa also showed me the river. A tributary goes right past this grove of trees. There is a steep bank, then a pier and a boat. Maybe we could go rowing some day. What do you think?"

"I've only rowed around in City Park lake," Charlotte said a little dubiously. "We'll see. I guess that farther down, the James is wide enough for cargo ships. Aunt Clara said that the escaped slave, Elijah, was seen boarding a sympathetic Yankee's ship."

"Poor soul! I know your own views about slavery and I feel the same. But here we will have to watch our words."

"I am well aware of that." Charlotte sighed. "And speaking of slaves, behind that ivy-covered wall lies the Stone

Garden built by a most unusual man and the reason for the plantation's peculiar name.''

"What did Mama tell you?''

"I never asked about it—just supposing it meant some kind of a rockerie with plants. "Charlotte shoved on the door. "Just look at this. A slave carved every single thing in here about 200 years ago.''

Eyes wide, lips parted, Amy moved forward slowly, staring around in obvious amazement. As they walked along the graveled paths, Charlotte told the history of the carvings, just as Devlin had related it to her.

"How tragic,'' Amy whispered at the end. The place seemed to have a tendency to reduce ordinary speech to breathy murmurs, but Amy soon shook off her sadness and displayed the keenest interest.

"Look at this! And this—how did he *do* it?'' she cried darting from a bush of big stone fruit to a finely detailed jaybird, head peering sideways at the ground.

She was especially fascinated by the idea of a secret passageway. "Perhaps it was made for escape from the Indian attacks of those early days. When was this place built?''

"About 1650. Indians might have been a problem then. I remember reading that, in 1656, there was a terrible war with the Seneca Indians and the settlements in Virginia were under attack. People must have lived in constant fear in those early Colonial days.'' She narrowed her eyes and gazed around. "I would think that the most obvious place for a secret passage would be in the summerhouse. It has a small closed structure at the rear.''

"Let's look.'' Amy bounded up the steps, lifting her lavender skirts while Charlotte followed more slowly.

Except for one wall which housed a sort of closed, stone shed, the octagonal building had lattices half-way up with plain openings beneath the curving roof. Square blocks comprised the floor upon which rested several benches, a round table, and four ornamental urns.

Amy began thumping on the floor with her heels, and fired by her example, Charlotte got down on her knees to prod and press. Nothing gave or moved and she could find no way to open the shed which might be solid stone. What she did find, however, was a long black hair behind a flowerpot. She held it out. "Amy, look at this."

Amy examined it curiously. "Could it be Vanessa's?"

Thoughtfully, Charlotte drew it through her fingers. "It's not real. It's the kind of hair used for theatricals."

"A wig—of course," Amy breathed, round-eyed. "And we saw a whopper of a wig recently, didn't we?"

"What is it doing here?" Charlotte wondered. "A place where no one comes?"

"Could it have caught on your dress in the Frenchman's carriage and then have fallen out just now?"

"My dress has been washed and ironed since then."

Amy dropped her voice and glanced over her shoulder. "Know what? I think the Frenchman was right here in the garden. Perhaps looking for your window and another chance to kiss your hand." She gave a smothered giggle.

Charlotte rose and dusted off her skirts. "Don't be silly. Men are always kissing ladies's hands, and it doesn't mean a thing." However, for a moment, she relived that hard male pressure on her wrist, the damp lips moving slowly back and forth as though he enjoyed the responsive flutter of her pulse.

Impatiently, she thrust the memory from her mind and looked around at the cold stone objects, unable to suppress a nervous shiver. "This place makes me so uneasy. It seems to still hold the misery and hopeless bitterness of its creator despite all the years. Let's go, Amy. I must get back to work."

"Would it be all right if I took a peek inside the guest house?"

"Well, only if Mr. Cartright isn't there. I believe he's very careful with his work. He wants the door kept locked, and I can't blame him. His books fetch high advances, I'm sure."

"I'd like to read his novels. Vanessa said she would loan me one."

"I don't know if that's a good idea. Some love scenes are very frank."

Amy chuckled. "Don't you think I'm old enough to choose what I read?"

"Well, of course." Inwardly, Charlotte gave a helpless groan as they crunched along the gravel path. She wasn't Amy's mother, even if she often felt like one. There was nothing she could do. To make the books important would only add to their appeal. Forbidden fruit was always the most tempting.

They had nearly reached the guesthouse when, suddenly, both Devlin and Vanessa appeared on the little porch. They halted, staring, but it was Vanessa who spoke first in a shrill, unpleasant tone. "Really, Charlotte, where have you been? I thought you were going to be such a dedicated worker. At this rate—"

"At this rate," the writer cut in smoothly, "Charlotte has plenty of time to finish the last chapter. She has already copied two and three is the daily requirement." He gave a little nod to Charlotte. "And very nicely done. We are going for a ride. Do either of you care to accompany us?"

A quick flush of pique swept across Vanessa's beauty. "I'm sure they both are much too busy, even if they have riding outfits, which I doubt. Amy, I would like you to look over my wardrobe and see what gowns need refurbishing, tears, loose buttons, and so forth. Are you handy with a needle?"

Amy's face fell and Charlotte felt a rush of resentment that the little treat had been so summarily swept away. Amy had learned to ride in City Park with school friends, but Charlotte's work had left her no time for such relaxation.

It was obvious that Vanessa would brook no interference in her relentless pursuit of Devlin Cartright. She had changed into a black broadcloth riding habit and long-sleeved white blouse, the high collar pinned at the neck with a silver horseshoe. A beaver hat perched upon her curls with a provocative ostrich plume curling against her cheek, its shade the same entrancing color as her eyes. Whether or not money was scarce at the plantation, Vanessa's clothes seemed far from shabby or out of date.

"Of course, Vanessa," Amy said to her, "I'll see to your gowns at once. Thank you, Mr. Cartright, perhaps some other time."

He bowed as Amy, with one swift speaking glance at Charlotte, turned and fled across the garden.

Without another word, Charlotte entered the guest house, but not before she heard Vanessa say stridently, "Devi, dear, I must remind you that the girls are here to work, not play."

"Everybody needs a little relaxation," the writer protested mildly.

Fortunately, Vanessa's answer was obscured and Charlotte's mouth twisted with distaste. She didn't like Vanessa. Thank goodness, Amy had been chosen as the companion and so far they seemed to get along, mainly due to her sister's sunny disposition.

A little warmer feeling came to mitigate her annoyance when she considered Devlin's kind-hearted invitation. He wasn't nearly as austere and unfriendly as she had thought at first—just reserved. He was someone who kept his innermost feelings guarded.

She found herself wondering how that hard-planed face

would look suffused with laughter? Quickened with desire? Did he make love like his heroes? Taking long periods of skilled coaxing until his partner flamed into a crying need beneath the onslaught? Then came the dramatic ecstacy of fulfillment, which was not described in as much detail as Charlotte would have liked . . . even though she felt shamed by her curiosity.

Ever since she first read Rodney Rogue, vague feelings had begun to stir in her and now here she was copying the latest saga, with all its hot southern passion laid bare to her eyes. Would it cause a yearning to experience those mysterious thrills herself?

Was this what Beaulah Hartley had meant when she told Charlotte to beware of Devlin Cartright?

Chapter 6

Right on time next morning, Martin Cord appeared as Clara, Charlotte and Amy were finishing their breakfast. He removed his wide-brimmed, black hat and surveyed them with a rather grim expression. "Well, is everybody ready for the grand tour?" His defiant eyes quickly slid past Amy.

"Indeed we are." Aunt Clara trilled. "Just as soon as we put on our bonnets. Must preserve our complexions, you know, so we won't be mistaken for nigras." This last blithe statement was uttered in spite of the fact that Cicero and one of the maids still hovered in the corner.

"You don't want to cover up your pretty hair, do you?" The overseer spoke directly to Amy, allowing his eyes to roam over the bright, dancing ringlets.

Amy blushed quickly and shook her head.

Charlotte glared at him. Cord was being altogether too familiar. Reluctantly, she left him alone with Amy and hurried upstairs to her room. She had only her traveling pokebonnet of pleated grey faille, but she tied it on, wishing that she had the wider assortment contained in her trunk, although the meager contents probably would draw a sneer from Vanessa.

Oh, a fig for Vanessa's sneers! She had more important worries on her mind. Returning quickly to the breakfast room, Charlotte found her fears confirmed. The animal had his hand at Amy's waist while they gazed out of the window, murmuring together.

Charlotte folded her arms and began in a thunderous tone, "Mr. Cord, just what do you think you're doing?"

"Ready, ready, everybody's ready," Aunt Clara caroled, sweeping into the room. One hand held her big, daisy-trimmed leghorn hat, the other hand she thrust through Charlotte's arm, urging her forward. "Lead the way now, Martin. First to the Stone Garden, I think."

"We have already seen that," Charlotte said tightly, frowning at the overseer who had the cheek to grin a little as he moved away from Amy's side.

When they filed outside, Aunt Clara asked, "Where do you suggest we go, then, Martin, since they've seen the carvings?"

"Slave quarters, ma'am." He matched his step to Amy's, but didn't attempt to take her arm.

Aunt Clara soon began pointing out the places of interest. "Over there, girls, is our brick kitchen building through that tunnel of vines. That is where Aunt Becky prepares our delicious meals—although they never are quite as hot as I would like."

"Why isn't the kitchen in the house?" Amy wondered.

"Because there is always a danger of fire. And then, food odors are so unpleasant in the house. Now that is the milk shed with a spring running through it. It's built of stone, as you can see, and when it's cold enough, we can keep ice there in straw for several months, taking it from the river. Next is the herb garden. Hmm, it's rather gone to weed and seed, hasn't it? Pshaw, there just aren't enough servants here anymore to take proper care of things." She kicked petulantly at a drift of fallen leaves.

Drawing her cashmere shawl closer around her shoulders, she gave a heavy sigh. "Oh, you girls should have seen this place about twenty years ago. I vow we lived like royalty then. Your Uncle Frank had over five hundred slaves growing cotton, indigo and sugar cane. We had a whole stableful of blooded horses, three carriages, two boats . . . And how we entertained! Balls, picnics, hunts, musicals . . ." Her voice trailed off and her lips turned down. "Now those days are gone forever."

Martin Cord glanced back over his shoulder. "Your husband worked the land plumb out, Miss Clara, and never put a thing back in the soil—Just like most of the other southern planters."

Aunt Clara snorted. "And I suppose you could do it better? Have you ever owned a farm, pray tell?"

"No, ma'am, but I have a few ideas—"

"I've heard your ideas, and they all take money, which I don't have. Stone Gardens is crumbling about my ears."

Martin shrugged. "Well, anyway, the slave quarters are still in pretty good condition."

They all stopped at the fenced-in compound. The overseer took out a black cheroot and fired it with a lucifer, gesturing with the burning tip at the double row of whitewashed cabins. "Each family has a two-room place, a henhouse, a pigsty, and a garden patch. Some keep them in good shape, some don't. Those that don't have to make do with the weekly rations: three pounds of pork, a peck of cornmeal and a quart of molasses. They are allowed to trap racoon, rabbits, and fish in the river. They get two suits of summer clothes and one of winter wear. Not too bad a life, eh?" He peered at Amy and then the rest of them as though he was seeking some kind of vindication.

Charlotte pressed her lips together as she looked around. "The clothes are of tow linen and must scratch horribly. The babies are all mother-naked." She pointed to the little ones laughing and tumbling in the dust. "The houses have chinks between the boards and probably are freezing cold in winter. How many blankets are issued?"

"One to each adult."

Amy made a soft sound of dismay.

"Come now, we have seen enough here." Aunt Clara sounded cross. "I tell, you, Charlotte, these people are well taken care of. When they are sick, we call in a doctor and I visit them myself. No one under ten does any field work. The six and seven-year-olds only do gardening and light chores. It is true that they don't receive any schooling, like the Abolitionists are yammering for, but why in heaven's name should they need it?"

"What are their working hours?" Charlotte asked inexorably.

"Sun up to sun down." Martin Cord drew coolly on his cheroot. "Seen enough? Let's go to the fields next."

Aunt Clara, looking huffy, took Amy's arm and marched ahead.

Charlotte remained beside the overseer. Her eyes bored into his. "What about the flogging, Mr. Cord. Do you do it yourself? Do you enjoy it?"

His face darkened and he threw her a venomous glance. "No, to both questions."

"But you order it done, don't you? How many lashes? Forty? Fifty? A hundred? Until you break the blisters and the ground runs red?" Charlotte spoke for his ears only. These matters were too cruel for Amy's tender heart. "Do you beat women, Mr. Cord? Children?"

"My God," he spat, "you Northerners make me sick. All you yammer about is coddle the poor Negro. Do you think the lazy devils would lift a hand or foot without a touch of the whip to goad them? Why should they work harder than they have to? It isn't their land. They can't be fired. They can loll around, pretend to all kinds of 'miseries,' snarl up the machinery. Damn it, the only thing that makes them move is fear. Fear of the lash."

Charlotte's lip curled. "And you, Mr. Cord, have just given an excellent reason why slave labor is so poor and so wasteful: they have no incentive. And as for whipping them to make them work, the slaves will just run away, as many as possibly can." She finished triumphantly.

"Or revolt." Surprisingly, this time he agreed with her. "Like Nat Turner. Over fifty whites were killed in that rebellion. He was a preacher and well treated by his master, but he went crazy, I guess. Thought God was telling him to kill. I was just a boy in '31, but I can remember the terror that spread throughout Virginia and the whole South, for that matter. And it could happen again at any time, especially with a place going downhill like Stone Gardens. Slaves get frightened."

He puffed silently on his cheroot, then he said harshly, "Your aunt should sell and get out while she can."

"Leave this beautiful place, her ancestors's home? Good heavens, where would she go?"

"She should move up North. The South is a rotting society—a world that is as phony as the garden made of stone."

He left her, then, to catch up with the others, and when Charlotte reached them, he began to explain the workings of the tobacco field whose long, towering rows now stretched before their eyes.

"Virginia grows mainly chewing tobacco," Cord said. "Seeds are planted every spring. When the plants get six or eight feet high, they are harvested as you can see."

Between the rows of broad, green leaves, the workers swarmed, men, women, and children filling bags as quickly as fingers could strip and stuff, their eyes darting to the row bosses, mainly white men who urged them on while they suggestively stroked the thongs of black, snake whips and snapped them through the air.

A strong odor of tobacco from a long row of log cabins that Martin Cord said were the drying sheds and held slow-burning fires of hardwood, which were watched day and night for three weeks.

Amy fingered one of the big, bright leaves. "The stems are so tough. I should think it would hurt their hands to strip them so fast."

Aunt Clara and Martin both looked amused.

As her aunt moved out of earshot, Cord removed Amy's small fingers from the plant, spreading her hand across his own toughened palm. "That's the least of their worries. What they dislike most is hand-picking the worms and beetles that attack the plants. They seem to hate that."

Amy shuddered. "I would, too. I don't blame them."

Lingering nearby, Charlotte heard the overseer say softly, "You should never have to put such pretty hands to work. If you were my wife, you would 'sit on a pillow and sew a fine seam and dine upon strawberries, sugar, and cream,' just like in the nursery rhyme."

Amy gave a gurgle of laughter. "Good heavens, I don't mind working. I can cook and sew and clean. Charlotte and I have never been rich girls."

"If you were married to me—"

No longer able to contain herself, Charlotte whirled around and said quietly and firmly, jerking Amy's hand away, "Well, that is something that would never happen. And why wouldn't your wife have to soil her hands, pray tell? Are you such a man of means?" Her lips twisted in a sneer as she placed her arms akimbo.

He seemed to struggle with a wave of anger. His face

darkened and he spoke tautly. "I've saved up a bit. My wife could have a servant—"

"Oh, this is a ridiculous conversation. Stop talking about your prospective wife, heaven help her! We've heard enough."

Amy's blue eyes danced. "Oh, I don't know. I find it rather interesting."

Charlotte blazed at her. "Amy, you encourage this man's familiarity. He is disrespectful to you. I saw him in the breakfast room this morning."

Martin's face flooded with color. "Amy, I am not trying to be 'familiar' or disrespectful."

Charlotte clenched her teeth. "Her name to you is 'Miss Davenport,' sir. My sister is under my protection and protect her I will. Need I remind you that she is only seventeen?"

"I know that."

Amy had stopped laughing and looked worried. She threw a quick glance toward Aunt Clara, but she still was out of earshot, conversing with one of the row bosses. Amy put her hand on Charlotte's arm. "Please, dear, you are getting upset over nothing. Mr. Cord and I have just the barest acquaintance."

"Amy, run on ahead with Aunt Clara," Charlotte said impatiently, her eyes on Martin Cord. "I will join you in a minute."

Amy's face pinked. "Don't treat me like a child, Charlotte."

"Do as your sister says, Amy," Cord barked.

"Martin!"

"Oh, so it's 'Martin' and 'Amy' now, is it? Just bare acquaintances, I thought you said."

Amy threw them each a look of hurt anger, took her lavender skirts in both hands, and ran down the aisle of towering tobacco.

Cord and Charlotte disregarded her. Like two combatants, they faced each other squarely.

"I don't like your manner, Mr. Cord," Charlotte grated. "And I am warning you, from now on I want you to leave my sister strictly alone."

He placed his cheroot defiantly between his lips. "And if I don't?"

"I will take a horsewhip to you!"

His mouth curled. "I thought you were so against the use of whips. I guess it depends on who is wielding them, eh?"

Charlotte choked as the irrefutable logic left her speechless. For a few moments, they glared at each other in silence.

Then, suddenly, the battle was interrupted by a shriek.

"Amy! What is it?" Charlotte jerked around toward her sister, now standing in arrested flight at the far end of the row.

Another voice tore across the fields. Scream after scream. A voice filled with the ultimate in human agony.

All the field hands stilled. Even the row bosses froze, whips trailing on the ground, eyes studiously blank.

A trail of smoke hissed into the sky, and as Charlotte and Martin started running toward Amy, the unfamiliar, nauseating smell of burning flesh filled the air.

Amy was crying hysterically in Aunt Clara's arms. "They said—oh, God! The runaway was caught. They brought him back and b-branded him—like an animal—with an 'R.'"

The slaves who had divulged this information, melted quickly out of sight as Martin chased after them, roaring furiously, "Get back to work, you gossiping devils!"

For a moment, Charlotte felt unable to speak or move. But when she put out her hand to Amy and called her hoarsely, Aunt Clara shook her head. "I know what to do for her."

She led the sobbing girl away and Charlotte covered her face with shaking hands. The horror of the burning filled her mind as clearly as though she had seen it with her own eyes and she shivered, feeling sick and faint.

A strong pair of hands descended upon her shoulders and she looked up almost blindly into the face of Devlin Cartright.

"Come with me, my dear," he said and led her unresisting to his studio.

Chapter 7

"Sit down," Devlin ordered, directing Charlotte to the brown plush loveseat in the guest house. When she had removed her bonnet with a shaking hand, he handed her a glass of amber liquid. "Drink this slowly," He then poured some sherry for himself and sat down beside her.

He was silent for awhile, letting Charlotte's shattered nerves recover. The wine tasted sweet and warming and at last, she drew a tremulous sigh and leaned her head back on a pillow Devlin had arranged behind her. "I hope Amy is all right. That was an awful shock."

"Clara will take care of her. Your aunt seems very fond of Amy, perhaps being reminded of your mother."

Charlotte nodded. "Yes, I think you're right. It is easy to be drawn to Amy. Even Martin Cord—" She broke off and said bitterly, "Perhaps now Amy will realize what that overseer stands for. Why does Aunt Clara permit such atrocities on her plantation? Doesn't she care? I can't understand it!"

Devlin put their empty glasses on a table, then turned

sideways on the sofa so that he was facing her. "Charlotte, I don't know if I can explain—or if anyone can—but I will try. For a long time, ever since this country was founded, plantations have used slaves from Africa and this relationship has given slaveholders reason to look upon them as having emotions and intelligence far below the white man's."

"I know." Charlotte expelled an angry breath. "Aunt Clara said once that they didn't even feel pain as keenly."

"Exactly. I wager that idea helped to salve many a conscience. Of course, some of the owners treated their slaves with kindness and let the children learn to read and write and play with their own youngsters. But others didn't. All the planters surrounded themselves with a pampered existence of great wealth that created a rather isolated society, especially since the great estates were so far apart. They became content to go on living just as their forebears had done and ignored the problems of the Negro community. As long as crops were good and money plentiful, the owners could stay in their secluded, little world and that was all that mattered."

Charlotte moved restively. "But putting a hot iron upon a human being's skin . . . the pain, the disfigurement, the shame . . . How can anyone countenance that? How can they excuse it?"

"It's ignored. Did your aunt or Cord witness it? No. It was just an age-old punishment always meted out to runaways, branding them with an 'R' to make the slave easier to catch should he be desperate enough to try again."

Devlin stared grimly out the window, crossing his arms upon his chest. "I have seen worse things than that in my travels."

"Worse?" Charlotte echoed faintly, staring at his rock-hard profile.

"There are many cruel, inhuman tortures given for run-

ning away," he said. "Or for insubordination. As well as
any other offense that threatens the owner's world."

"And the slave has no recourse to the law?"

"No. A Negro can't testify against a white person."

Charlotte drew a ragged breath. "Oh, Devlin, what can
be done?" She colored as she realized her slip. "I mean,
Mr. Cartright."

"Devlin is the name my friends use so please call me
that. You see, I have used your first name without permission." His brown eyes softened as he looked at her. "Charlotte." He seemed to savor the name upon his tongue.
"You are such a sensitive, deeply-caring young woman.
What else are you so passionate about? Did you have a
sweetheart in New York? What was your life like?"

Charlotte dropped her eyes. "I—I have never been in
love." She knew he was trying to distract her from the
morning's ugliness and she gathered up her reserves in
order to speak calmly.

"We had a small house on the outskirts of the city with
a bookstore in the front. My father hated slavery, but he fell
in love with a Southern girl raised here at Stone Gardens. I
never heard them fight or argue, though her opinions
must have been quite different. She used to tell me about
happy days here. She thought that the slaves were contented, loving people, deeply religious and devoted to their
owners.

"Mama died when Amy was a baby and Papa never
seemed to laugh again. I helped him in the shop after
school, but more and more, he became indifferent, even
to his health. The only thing that roused him was to plead
with me to write to Aunt Clara and request asylum here."

Devlin's interest was so flattering, Charlotte spoke at
length, only wondering much later if she had bored him.

At the time, he showed no such indication. Finally, he
said, "You learned early to care for other people, didn't

you? Don't you ever think about yourself? What does Charlotte want from life?"

She gave a little laugh. "What anybody wants, I guess. A home of my own, people whom I can love and will love me in return. I have no talents to cultivate. I don't draw, sing or write."

That last item suddenly recalled Charlotte to her neglected duties and she started up. "Oh, my work—your writing—I have lots to do—"

"Not today, my dear." To Charlotte's consternation, he also rose and clasped both her hands in his big, warm ones. "Take your sister for a walk down by the river. Find ease in nature's beauty. If you wish to work this afternoon, I'll be gone."

He let her go and Charlotte gave a stuttering response as she hurried off without an argument. It wasn't only the morning's shocking incident that jumbled all her thoughts. Devlin, with his warmth and understanding, had touched a sympathetic core. The clasp of his hands had unleased a strange emotion. A very pleasant emotion, if the truth be faced.

She thought with a sense of wonder about their recent conversation and realized that, although he now knew the story of her life, he had not revealed one word about himself.

She found Amy alone in her own room, sipping tea and gazing out the window. Her face looked calm but grave, a little bit older than before. About to remind Amy of Martin's perfidy, Charlotte changed her mind.

She put her arm on Amy's shoulder, brushing back the golden curls. "Are you all right, baby? Would you like to take a walk down by the river? Devlin has told me to take the morning off."

Amy rose with a long sigh. "That would be nice. I can't help thinking about that poor slave. Wasn't that a terrible thing, just because he ran away? I don't understand Aunt Clara, do you?"

Charlotte tried to explain a little as they walked down the hall. She repeated Devlin's words, then added, "Of course, there is cruelty everywhere, Amy. In the sweat-shops of the North, in the child labor of Pennsylvania mines, in the fire traps of Manhattan, where garment and flower makers earn a pitiful fifty cents a week. But slavery is worse than any of these. I wonder if we did right to come to the South. We really don't fit into this kind of life."

Amy averted her face, but not before Charlotte had seen the dismay leap into her eyes. "Oh, Charlotte, you can't judge the South so quickly. There is beauty here, the flowers and trees, the rolling, blue-green hills. And I can hear the slaves singing and laughing when they come in from the fields. Surely a lot of them must be happy and content."

Charlotte felt too drained to argue the case against despotic rule, but for the first time she realized that Amy was exactly like their mother, seeing only a golden hue in life.

"Speaking of the 'happy' slaves," Charlotte tried to keep the irony from her voice as they started to leave the house. "I wonder if any of the older servants remember our mother?"

"I asked Aunt Clara about that," Amy said, "and there are very few left, Cicero and perhaps the cook. Of course they know who we are. Maybe they were told not to mention Mama's name after she ran off to marry Papa. Charlotte, do you realize we've never been shown portraits of our ancestors? Or taken on a tour of the house? Do you think we should broach the subject to Aunt Clara—"

"No, Amy. We have been taken in as workers, not accepted yet as relatives. We'll have to bide our time. Now, let's take a walk by the river."

As they strolled across the garden, there was no scent of burning flesh upon the humid air, only the rich ripe fruit, the full-blown roses, the flowering vines. The path led through the grove of trees and finally slanted downward to the James River.

The water flowed gently between moss-covered shoulders meandering slowly toward the distant sea. They turned their steps to the road beside the river, a stretch of hardpacked red clay lined with trees. A warm breeze stirred the spruce and hemlock and the only sounds were the lapping of the water and the twitter of cardinals and bluebirds making a flash of lovely color among the leaves.

"Indian summer weather," Charlotte murmured, suddenly recalling the story Devlin had told about a hiding place built in the old plantation. On just such a quiet, peaceful day, the isolated planters might have been startled by the peering face of a painted warrior. She gave a little jump when Amy clutched her arm.

"Look, Charlotte, here comes a rowboat. See how it glides, hardly making a ripple . . . and the water has such a lovely golden sparkle from the sunshine."

"A pretty sight," Charlotte agreed, smiling.

A dark-skinned servant sat in the stern, holding the oars while two young people lolled on cushions beneath a green and white striped awning. They both turned identical red heads toward the shore and waved at Charlotte and Amy as though they were old friends.

The young man jumped up and sketched a bow. "How do you do?" he called. "We are Keith and Katy Duncan here to visit our Aunt Beaulah. Aren't you the Davenport girls from up North? We will come to call on you right soon."

He nearly lost his balance at a sudden surging in the water, but his sister grabbed his arm and he tumbled back into the seat. They both began to laugh and wave as they were rowed away, their pilot adding a wide smile.

"My, how news travels." Amy twinkled. "Neighbors coming to visit us already."

Charlotte surveyed the departing couple with an approving eye. "They might be nice, young friends for you."

"Better than Martin Cord, you mean?"

"Exactly."

Charlotte cleared her throat as a sudden idea hit her. "What do you think of that Tim Deane whose father bought Papa's shop?"

Amy smiled. "He's nice. I promised him a letter."

"He told me he wished to visit Stone Gardens, but I don't feel secure enough to ask permission yet. Don't you agree? Perhaps a little later . . ."

"I might see what Vanessa says. She seems to like men and probably would welcome a new face."

"She should be interested in Keith Duncan then."

"He is cute," Amy murmured, "but rather young. Not a mature man like Devlin Cartright—or—or Martin Cord. I wonder what she thinks of *him?*"

"Probably considers him a servant—and that's all," Charlotte declared crisply.

"Aunt Clara seems to like Mr. Cord."

"He's her overseer, and I'm sure they are agreed regarding slaves. You must see Martin Cord in his true light now, don't you? He is a hard and callous man who is taken by your youth and beauty."

Amy gave a short laugh. "Charlotte, I am not a beauty. And you don't understand Martin Cord at all."

And you do, innocent little baby that you are? A pain shot through Charlotte. The hard-bitten overseer apparently still held a strong place in Amy's thoughts. If the beast harmed Amy in any way, emotionally or otherwise, he would answer for it.

* * *

When the sun moved past its zenith, Amy and Charlotte returned to the house for the midday meal, which was served between one and two o'clock.

It seemed a long time since breakfast. So much had happened: in the fields, in Devlin's studio and then the appearance of the twins. Charlotte actually felt hungry and tired. She left Amy in the lower hall and hurried to her room to freshen up.

After washing her face and hands, she brushed out her hair and wound it back up in a snood, the usual style she favored. In a weary burst of nervousness, she dropped the hairbrush and it clattered noisily on the china washstand.

It was then she heard it. A strange crackling. A rattling from the bed. Spinning around, she saw the spread move upward in a mystifying mound.

She jerked back the covers and gave a cry.

A small snake lay coiled upon a sheet of paper. As she watched in frozen horror, it glided from the bed, dropped upon the carpet and headed for the door.

Charlotte screamed and pulled frantically on the bell to summon Tibby. But it was Cicero who came to her door, took in the situation, and dropped his coat upon the viper.

"He's not dangerous, Miss Charlotte," Cicero told her soothingly. "Jus' a little garden snake." He bundled up coat and snake and flung them out her open window. "Now I has to fetch my coat." He smiled and bobbed his head, disappearing from the room before Charlotte could frame a question.

Still trembling, she sank down on the bed, feeling shaken, her thoughts awhirl. How did that viper get into her room from the garden, especially beneath the covers?

She looked down at the place where it had lain and saw

a sheet of paper. Printed on it in large block letters were
the words:

GO HOME, YOU DON'T BELONG HERE.

Trembling, she read it over and over, then thinned her
lips and sucked in an angry breath. Martin Cord, of course.
He knew for a certainty, after this morning's confrontation,
that Charlotte was his enemy.

She started up, the paper clutched in her rigid hand.
She would show it to everyone—No, wait. Suppose by some
chance, Vanessa had left the message, due to her jealousy
of Charlotte working closely with the writer. It might even
have been Aunt Clara, angered by Charlotte's critical manner on the morning's tour.

But somehow neither of the women seemed as likely to
have smuggled in a snake. It had to be Martin Cord. How
to handle the matter, however, posed a problem. For the
time being, she decided to make no accusations.

Downstairs in the dining room, Cicero had already
apprised Clara, Amy and Vanessa of the matter, and it was
passed off as an accidental entry by the snake. Amy was the
only face that showed concern, and for her sake, Charlotte
shrugged it all away.

She didn't mention the note to anyone. She would bide
her time and watch. There was bound to be another warning, maybe something more dangerous next time.

As for now, she would be on guard.

Chapter 8

Charlotte spent the afternoon working diligently on Devlin's manuscript, managing to clear her mind of everything except the task at hand. She couldn't afford to make any mistakes. His books were too important to his many readers hungry for the brand of exciting, daring men and beautiful, romantic women that he wrote about so well.

When the dinner gong pealed in the distant house, Charlotte thankfully corked her inkpot and wiped the steel nib of her pen. She had made good progress, but now she felt both tired and hungry.

Tibby was waiting in her room and showed Charlotte a brown and amber gown lying on the bed. "Miss Clara sent this for you to wear and keep." She smoothed the bands of tan lace at neck and sleeves with a timid anxious glance." I freshened it best I could."

"Thank you, Tibby. I'm glad to have a change of clothes." Was this her aunt's apology for the snake? Or only an expression of boredom from looking every day at Charlotte in her travel-worn grey dress?

"Your trunks—they be comin' soon, Miss Charlotte?"

"I certainly hope so. I'm told Cicero goes every day to the train depot."

After washing and having Tibby brush her hair, Charlotte donned the brown taffeta, arranging the cracks in the material inside the full folds of the gathered skirt.

When she descended to the dining table, Clara gave her a cool survey. "That's better. Cicero has word about your trunks. He should know more tomorrow."

Amy admired the brown dress and rose to show Charlotte another donation from Vanessa, this one a faded lilac muslin which made Amy look like a sweet-faced waif. Charlotte ground her teeth but praised it, anyway.

"It's kind of you both to keep us from a ragged state," she said, smiling with difficulty. "So generous of you."

Clara nodded majestically.

Vanessa pouted. "What good is it to take pains with our appearance when there are no men-folk here to admire us? That Devlin is gone again."

"I understand your feelings," Charlotte cooed, accepting a slice of duckling from the maid, then spooning orange sauce over mashed yams. "Therefore, you may be glad to know Amy and I saw Keith and Kathy Duncan sailing on the river. They are visiting Miss Beaulah and said they would be calling on us. On everyone at Stone Gardens," she added hastily.

As predicted, Vanessa was very interested in the new visitors at the Hartley plantation, which she said was called Roselands because of its extensive gardens.

From then on, she could talk of nothing else at the dinner table. "Mama, we must invite them all to tea, don't you agree? Tomorrow Cicero must take a note." Her glance swept over Charlotte. "I surely hope our servants won't have to dispose of any more snakes when they are sorely needed for other tasks." She giggled. "The servants, that is, not the snakes."

She took a sip of wine, regarding Charlotte over the gold-banded rim. "I do wonder about that viper. You didn't bring it in yourself, did you, Charlotte? Just to gain some sympathy?"

Charlotte's fork dropped on the china plate. "Now why would I want that? And where would I find a snake? Even if I could bring myself to touch such a frightful thing?"

Amy nodded indignantly, but Clara merely shrugged. "You do have an argument for everything, don't you, Niece? Pray let us drop the unpleasant subject. We are getting nowhere."

"Yes, Mama," Vanessa interjected with a pout. "Let's discuss the Duncans. What shall we serve at tea? Should we include Miss Beaulah and her husband? Though, really, that Charlie is such a bore. Can't talk about anything except his old roses."

The subject of the snake had been dismissed. A lot they cared that she had been frightened out of her wits, Charlotte thought, chewing angrily on a buttered biscuit. Probably Aunt Clara would say that she deserved it after her criticisms during the tour. Yes, Clara could easily have been the instigator of the snake's appearance. If she had ordered Cicero to do the deed, of course he never would admit to it.

When Vanessa carried Amy off after dinner, Charlotte retired to her room, preparing for an early night. The day's many events had taken a deep toll and quickly she undressed, then gave the room a comprehensive survey, even looking underneath the bed.

It felt unsettling to know she had an enemy. How could she handle it? She had no power here and no way to leave without money or another situation. She decided, finally, that the first thing was to watch her words, keep to herself,

and avoid further confrontations. Next, she must save every
cent and try to search for other work.

She would not mention any of this to her sister. The
child was contented in her role as Vanessa's handmaiden.
She was thrilled with Stone Gardens and all its beauty. And,
of course, her awakening womanhood had been stirred by
Martin Cord's attention, although Charlotte didn't believe
Amy had fallen in love—not yet. But the danger lurked
and the overseer seemed a determined man who had, by
some quirk, been aroused by Amy's innocence. He perhaps
saw himself as the first man to know her love and sweet
surrender.

That must be avoided at all costs! Charlotte picked up
her hairbrush and swept it fiercely through the long brown
mane of her unbound hair. If only she could talk to someone. Perhaps Beaulah Hartley? Or Devlin Cartright? Both
of them had shown a side of deep interest in other people
and a warm compassion.

As the strong face of the writer swam into her mind's
vision, Charlotte gazed dreamily at her reflection in the
dressing table mirror. What would Devlin think if he saw
her like this—the lamplight reflected in her eyes, her shining hair rippling over the full bosom which swelled the
thin material of her nightdress? She drew a trembling hand
down to her waist. Would he open her gown, press his big
male lips upon her flesh and wind determined fingers
through her hair?

Oh, good Lord, what ailed her? With a strangled cry,
she whirled away, running to the window and breathing
deeply of the cool night air. She never had felt like this
before. Not even when she had read the torrid love scenes
in his book. No, it was Devlin himself who had fired her
imagination. He was so masculine, so strong, with his deep-
scored face, the broad sweep of his proud shoulders, and

his voice, commanding, in control, yet showing sincere concern when he had comforted her.

She inhaled unsteadily. Here might be another danger she must guard herself against. He was her employer, nothing more. If he longed for anyone romantically, it would surely be Vanessa, with her flaunting beauty and determined pursuit. How could he be blamed if he desired her? He was a man alone here, married or not, and Vanessa was readily available. But just how far would she allow him to go?

It was a useless and unpleasant speculation and with an impatient exclamation, Charlotte turned away to seek her bed.

But before she moved, she heard a thin high cry come from beyond the window. A human cry of pain? At once, her mind recalled the injured figure at the studio and she spun back to lean upon the sill, her eyes straining in every direction.

Moonlight flickered on the lawn below and, just then, a figure staggered from the line of trees. A scarecrow figure with a bandaged head. His arms flailed the air and his footsteps wavered drunkenly as he tottered in a circle, uttering little moans before he collapsed upon the ground.

Swiftly, Charlotte whirled around. She thrust her feet into shoes, grabbed up her cloak, and tore from the room. Whatever or whoever he was, she must help him. He was a human being in dire need, first and foremost.

At the bottom of the stairs, she struggled with the chain across the side door, dismayed at how much noise it created. But no one came to investigate, and she raced across the lawn, halting at the spot where she had seen the injured figure.

Now there was no sign of him. She looked around and blinked. Has she been dreaming? Had her mind conjured up a figment of imagination and the cry been merely a lost animal? She gave herself a mental shake. No. It had been real, a human cry of deep distress. But how could he have moved all by himself?

She brushed back her long hair and called softly, "Where are you? Please come out, I won't hurt you. I have only come to help."

She heard a smothered sound and, heart pounding, she crept forward into the darkness beneath the interlacing branches of thick trees.

Then a deeper darkness separated itself from the rest and a tall figure stepped toward her. A figure in a cavalier's short cape, a wide-brimmed hat. A masked man with black curls falling to his shoulders.

"You!" Charlotte cried, her hand flying to her throat.

The Frenchman whispered harshly, "Please go, *mam'-selle*. At once."

She ignored his statement. Her head jerked from side to side. "I saw a man—he was hurt and cried for help. Where is he? What have you done with him?"

Another moan came to her ears, and though he tried to stop her, Charlotte darted around the Frenchman. There beneath the trees she found a pitiful scrap of rags and bones. She squatted down, her cape trailing on the ground. "Why, he is just a boy." She felt his head. "And burning up with fever. Good Lord, there is fresh blood running down his face!"

She sprang to her feet, confronting the masked man. "What does this mean? Why aren't you doing something? You are supposed to be a member—"

Instantly, one arm grabbed her and his other hand clamped across her mouth. "Silence! You will alert no one," he hissed gutturally, swinging her back against his chest.

Charlotte struggled vainly, while his arm across her breast increased in pressure. "You will not cry for help?"

Vigorously, Charlotte shook her head and he released her.

She spoke in a fierce whisper. "I have no intention of calling the slave catchers. What I do intend, is to see that this poor boy gets to a doctor secretly."

"I agree."

"That bleeding must be stopped at once." Charlotte darted a worried glance at the unconscious boy. "What did you say? You agree?"

He hesitated, then seemed to come to a decision, almost against his will. "Will you help me?"

"Of course. Anything."

The Frenchman hoisted the mercifully unconscious boy into his arms and led the way through the trees to a side road where a horse and covered buggy waited in the darkness. Charlotte opened the door and helped ease the boy onto the seat. She supported him while the Frenchman folded some strips of lint into a pad and secured it in place with a rough bandage.

He then took a scarf from his inside pocket and straightening up, looked at Charlotte with a shrug. *"Je regrete."*

The next thing she knew, he had bound her eyes from sight. Calmly, she accepted the need for secrecy. He could trust no one.

"Press your hand upon the bandage," the man whispered. "We go now to a doctor."

"I understand." The door closed and the buggy started forward with all speed. Charlotte took the boy's head upon her lap and braced herself to keep as much of the jouncing from him as she could. The road was badly rutted and grew even rougher when they turned into a narrow lane where branches slapped and scraped at the roof and further impeded their progress.

Finally, Charlotte had to do it. She tore away the scarf and saw the boy's eyes open but they looked blind and cloudy. To her amazement, he began to shout, "Don' hit my mammy any more. Please, Marse King, . . . oh, no, no . . ."

"Hush, hush," Charlotte whispered, patting the thin, trembling shoulder. "Lie still now. No one is going to hurt you or your Mammy."

The boy didn't see or hear her. He continued to relive some terrible, nightmarish experience. His patois was so thick at times, she couldn't understand this dialect of the deepest South. However, his tones of grief and terror made tears flood Charlotte's eyes as she realized that her attempts at comfort fell on deafened ears.

Sometimes he shrieked and then he sobbed. Then again, he would laugh and chatter with a girl called, "Sally Mae."

Finally, he gave one anguished cry: "Mammy!" His eyes dilated, then closed, and he grew still.

"Oh, what is it? Don't die, little boy!" Desperately, Charlotte shook the scrawny arm and patted his thin, cold cheek. When he gave no response, her heart began to pound with dread as she held him, pressing on the wound with a hand that shook while her eyes searched his face for the vanished signs of life.

Suddenly, the buggy halted. Quickly, Charlotte replaced the scarf across her eyes just as the door opened. Her voice caught on a sob. "Oh, dear God, I think the boy is dead."

She was aware of a hand feeling for the pulse, then he growled. "Not quite. Stay here, *mam'selle*." He lifted the slight figure in his arms.

When the door closed, Charlotte shrank back into a corner of the seat, pulling her cloak tightly around and shivering as much from nerves as from the dark night's coolness.

She shut her eyes and prayed that they were not too late. The tortured words of the injured lad still rang in her ears. His words gave only a hint of the conditions that had sent a young boy fleeing along the dangerous freedom trail.

What kind of inhumanity had permitted such treatment? Placing thousands of innocent people at the mercy of someone with unlimited control? Charlotte clenched her fists, nails biting into her flesh. How would it all end? Would the country be split in two, as some predicted? Slave owners against Abolitionists? North against South?

Questions without answers tumbled through her brain, mingling with concern for the injured boy. About to pull away the scarf with a frustrated gesture, suddenly the door jerked open, and the next instant, Charlotte felt the man's arms pull her close.

"He died, *mam'selle,*" the words growled huskily against her hair as he pressed her face into his coat.

Charlotte began to sob wildly. Brokenly, she repeated the agonizing words of the little slave. "What happened to his mother? Did she escape?" she implored.

"Dead," he replied. "I say no more."

She raised her head, tugging at the scarf across her eyes. "But you tried to help. I'm sure you are involved in—"

He caught her hand with a terse command. "You must know nothing." She felt his warm lips on her face. "Just this. I thank you." Then he kissed her for a long, heart-stopping moment while everything whirled in blackness and a strange lethargy engulfed her so that she sagged against him.

When he dragged his mouth from hers with a muttered growl, she caught his coat and strained against him. Her open lips found his. She surrendered to the breathless wonder with a dry sob, not even pulling back when she felt his hand slide in upon her breast, gripping fiercely until the thin stuff of her gown was no barrier at all.

It was he who stopped, thrusting her away with a muttered oath in French. He banged the door and shortly after he exited the buggy hurtled down the road.

Charlotte sank back in her corner, breathing hard. Did it really happen, she wondered? Did I kiss him like a wanton, permit him such liberties? Everything had a dreamy strangeness. The wild ride in the night, the delirious muttering of the dying child. The grief she'd felt had been overcome by the astonishing advances she had permitted, and with such excitement that she had only wanted more . . . Was that why he had done it? To help her deal with the night's horror? Or had an impulsive hunger overtaken him just as it had her? A longing to feel life in the midst of death and misery?

She dragged off the scarf and rode the rest of the way in a drugged torpor until the buggy stopped. He knocked his whip upon the door, but didn't leave his perch. Wearily, Charlotte climbed out and hurried to the house without a backward glance.

Only one clear thought filled her mind. No one, not even Amy, must ever know about this night.

Chapter 9

"Charlotte, our luggage has been found," Amy cried the next morning, bursting into the breakfast room. "Cicero just came back from the depot. The stagecoach left word there that they are holding our two trunks at the Railway Express Office in Charles City. Isn't that exciting news?"

"Yes, it is, Amy dear, but please calm down." Charlotte sighed. "I don't feel too lively this morning."

Vanessa drifted behind Amy in a billow of yellow ruffles, a little morning sacque of eyelet embroidery displaying a provocative glimpse of low-necked chemisette.

"Good-morning, Mama. Good-morning, Devi." She delicately suppressed a yawn. "I do declare, such a fuss about two old trunks." She tinkled the little handbell for a maid and dropped into a chair by Devlin. Her fulsome smile at him faded when she looked at Charlotte. "Is that really all you have, just one trunk each? However do you manage?"

Charlotte briefly shut her eyes and sipped the strong, hot coffee. "We only brought two trunks until we saw how

things worked out. Our other belongings are in storage."
No need to elaborate on the fact that the "other belongings" did not amount to anything important.

Amy touched her shoulder. "Don't you feel well, dear?
You are not eating much." She placed her own filled plate
on the table and slid into an empty chair. "That cornbread
and stewed fruit look delicious. Try some, do."

"I'm just not hungry," Charlotte muttered. "I had a
rather poor night. It must have been well after midnight
when I finally got to sleep."

Vanessa gave her a hard stare. She had lazily ordered
the maid to fill her plate from the chafing dishes on the
sideboard and was picking at her food. "Were you flitting
about outdoors last night, dear cousin? I thought I heard
the side door opening quite late and voices coming from
the garden." Her veiled glance darted between Devlin and
Charlotte. "A rendezvous, perhaps? Or a little unfinished
business in the guest house, perhaps?" she purred.

"Vanessa!" Aunt Clara exclaimed. "What an outrageous
question. Are you suggesting an impropriety?"

"Of course, not. I said *business,* didn't I?" Vanessa
dropped her long lashes as she placed a bit of ham between
her rosy, pouting lips.

Charlotte felt too disturbed by Vanessa's accusation to
frame an answer. If anyone knew that she had aided an
escaped slave, dire consequences would follow, the least
of which undoubtedly would be banishment from Stone
Gardens. Her wits seemed to desert her as she gazed at
her cousin's angelic countenance with its cold, blue eyes.

Then Devlin pushed back his chair and eased the
moment with a good-natured chuckle. "I trust I am not
that hard a taskmaster. You probably just heard a hoot-owl
in the garden." He gave a teasing tug to Vanessa's long
black curls, tied back with a trailing saffron ribbon. "You
look mighty fetching this morning, my dear," he drawled.

Instantly, Vanessa simpered and reached up to catch his hand. "Dear Devi, you have been so elusive lately. Take me for a drive this morning, do!" Suddenly, she clapped her hands. "I know! Let's go to Charles City and pick up those trunks so Amy and Charlotte can have some clothes to wear."

"What a sweet and thoughtful idea. So typical of you." He smiled across the table. "I have need of supplies there, but I wish everyone to go with us. It will be a good opportunity for your cousins to see the countryside."

Amy exclaimed with glee, her blue eyes sparkling.

"But what about my work?" Charlotte demurred, although longing to accompany them with all her heart.

"You shall have a day's vacation," he told her, ignoring the angry glance directed at him by Vanessa.

Aunt Clara said she had something else to do but offered the use of an open landau and supplied Cicero's young nephew, Ned, to drive them. She seemed in an anxious mood to please everyone, perhaps wanting to erase the previous day's unpleasant branding from their minds.

An hour later, the girls met on the front veranda. In the clear morning air, Charlotte's spirits rose. Part of it was eagerness for recovering her trunk. She never wanted to lay eyes on her grey poplin again and did not enjoy wearing Clara's hand-me-downs, either.

Amy had on the lavender dress with a borrowed stole and Vanessa was resplendent in a deep rose faille street costume complete with matching parasol and a green straw bonnet trimmed with lace, feathers, and velvet bows.

She clapped her hands in their little, crocheted mitts, almost prancing in her eagerness to be off. She had discarded her earlier annoyance and now was in a bubbly mood. "Oh, just wait until you girls see the fine shops in

Charles City. There is a yardage emporium two stories high and I vow at least four streets of shops. We have brick sidewalks and even gas lighting at night.''

"Incredible. I can hardly wait to view this southern metropolis,'' Charlotte said dryly, catching Amy's eye with a little wink.

Didn't Vanessa have the slightest notion of what New York City was like in this modern year of 1850? It had almost a million people, a great Broadway thoroughfare with brick and granite buildings of six stories, the street thronged with omnibuses, coaches, hackney cabs . . . nearly two hundred churches, the biggest library in the United States . . . the finest restaurants . . . museums . . . universities . . .

Charlotte suppressed a sigh. Did she actually feel homesick for the noisy, dirty, crowded, exciting northern city? *Yes, she did.* But she wouldn't think of that today.

In a few moments, Devlin and the landau arrived. Vanessa appropriated a seat beside him, Charlotte and Amy taking the places across from him. Devlin looked quite elegant this morning in a black serge jacket and white silk shirt above a striped vest and grey pantaloons. Charlotte surveyed him with an elevated eyebrow, but he seemed as unselfconscious in his finery as he did in his usual linen shirts unbuttoned at the throat and untamed hair tossing on his bare head.

He smiled at Amy and Charlotte's pleasure when they glimpsed the big mansions beyond wrought iron fences and the avenues of moss-hung oaks. "Someday we shall take a trip to Richmond and Williamsburg,'' he promised as they bowled along. "There are many fine historic buildings in those cities, including the capitol designed by Thomas Jefferson and a marble statue of George Washington that was displayed at the Louvre in Paris for eight years before being brought to Richmond.''

"Virginia can be proud of lots of things," Vanessa stated. "It's called the 'Mother of Presidents' because so many of them came from here: Jefferson, Madison, Monroe, Harrison, John Tyler—and, of course, George Washington—"

As she paused for breath, Amy twinkled. "Well, our new president, Millard Fillmore, is from New York, my home state."

Vanessa shrugged and muttered something like, "No-account Yankee," under her breath.

Charlotte grimaced slightly, but she had to admit that Vanessa had just cause for pride. This was the other face of Virginia . . . beautiful scenery, gracious homes, well-known statesmen . . .

Even the little town of Charles City had something to be appreciated. When they arrived, it was bright and busy with gigs, carriages, carts, and many elegantly-clad shoppers, the ladies in brocades and cashmeres, the gentlemen frock-coated and top-hatted. Most of them were accompanied by servants in turbans. They all moved in and out of the shops or hurried across the hard-packed earth to reach the tree-lined sidewalks of red brick.

Vanessa, loud in her priorities of where they should go first, bade Amy and Ned to accompany her to Greene's Emporium and other clothing establishments while Devlin and Charlotte collected the luggage. They all arranged to meet for lunch at the Maison Blanc Hotel, unless they ran into each other sooner.

Charlotte and Devlin walked down the street, but they had not gone far when he stopped to read a sign tacked to the front of a building:

"Slave Auction, October 10, 1850.
"A coffle of prime cargo just arrived from Louisiana. Twenty men, women and children, all of sound limb

and amiable disposition. Bodies unmarked by whip
or brand. We respectfully urge that you arrive early
for the best selections.''

Devlin chewed his lip a moment, then he took Charlotte's elbow in his hand and turned her down the side
street. "Come along. You have never seen a slave auction,
I'll be bound.''

Ignoring her resisting demur, he urged her forward to
the babble of upraised voices, and said firmly, "Part of
your Southern education, my dear. Besides, I need some
data for my book.''

His face had a hard, implacable light and Charlotte
ceased protesting, though the sight before her filled her
with distaste.

In a large, fenced area, a great crowd swarmed of loud-
voiced men, women and even children. The latter darted
in and out, excitedly playing games while they ignored the
poor wretches huddled together on a raised platform.

To Charlotte's dismay, Devlin forced a path up to the
front where they could clearly see the tear-stained cheeks
of mothers with young ones clinging fearfully, the men
standing stoically, gazing straight ahead. All seemed
dressed in new clothes and were scrubbed and polished
to put forward their best appearance. But not even the
auctioneer's frequently snarled injunction to "look smart"
could obliterate the terror in each pair of sad, dark eyes.

A sturdy buck was plucked out of the line and the auctioneer, a burly man in stove-pipe hat and gartered shirtsleeves, began to bawl, "Step this way, ladies and gentlemen. This here is Sam, a prime specimen if I ever did see
one. Twenty years old, strong and intelligent. Would make
a first-rate dining room servant or driver of a coach-and-
four.''

Charlotte was close enough to see the cruel pinch that

he gave the young man's ear as he growled hoarsely, "Smile, ye black devil, or I vow I'll give you something to look sad about."

The Negro stretched his lips in a taut grimace and the bidding began briskly. Finally, at a staggering $850, Sam was hustled off the platform while the rest of his companions were put on display. Prospective buyers were urged to poke and prod, look into mouths and ears, squeeze limbs. Some of the younger women cringed at the indignities, fighting tears.

Then came the children's auction, which to Charlotte, seemed even worse. Terrified, bewildered, eight and ten-year-olds stood alone, eyes imploring help, some gazing wildly through the crowd for their vanished parents. Already, they knew their sad plight, as some of the white boys scampered near the auction block yelling, "Nigra babies, tar babies," until cuffed away by the auctioneer.

One pig-tailed, little black girl, however, had a slightly happier ending to her story. A tall man, who had already bought several other slaves, had bent his head to his small daughter's whispered pleas.

"For my daughter's companion, how much is that scalawag in red calico?" he called to the auctioneer.

The transaction completed, the black child and the white linked hands and trotted off amiably. But Charlotte noticed a woman's tear-filled eyes follow them hungrily and heard her choked whisper, "Please, Lord, keep my little Mindy safe."

"Oh, Devlin, take me away," Charlotte moaned. "I've seen enough, haven't you?"

He didn't answer, but led her silently back to the streets of shops and well-dressed people walking in the sun and freedom of a different world.

"Well, now you've attended a slave auction," he said. "What did you think of it?"

She shuddered and wiped her eyes. "Men, women and children bartered like cattle! I'm so glad Amy didn't see it. Oh, Devlin, how can people be so unfeeling toward other human beings?"

"I'm sure many southerners deplore slavery," he replied gravely, "but they don't know how to exist without it. If all the slaves were suddenly set free and had to be paid wages, the South would soon be bankrupt."

"Couldn't it be done slowly, by degrees?" Charlotte suggested.

"That would be the sensible way, but only the most humanitarian and wealthy are willing to grant freedom to their slaves in any manner."

"It's very depressing," Charlotte sighed. "How will it all end?"

"Nobody knows, but it is certain to end someday." He pressed her hand that rested in the crook of his arm. "Put it out of your mind for now, my dear. Here is the express office. Soon you and Amy will have all your clothes and folderols."

"Such as they are." But Charlotte's spirits lifted when she spied their rope-tied, dome-lidded trunks. She produced the tickets and a drayer conveyed the luggage to their carriage down the street.

Afterward, she and Devlin wandered in and out of the various shops where he bought new steel pens and nibs, a quart of ink, and several reams of foolscap.

They found Amy and Vanessa in one of the dry goods stores and joined them to watch the purchase of bolts of cloth which Vanessa said their Lucalla could make up for her. *The Lady's Book* was consulted for styles and patterns while Devlin leaned indulgently against the counter, attempting to show the proper amount of interest when Vanessa pressed him for an opinion regarding the various merits of material called "satin veloute" in a color of rich

violet or "marron claire sultane," a silky cloth of shim-
mering beige.

Charlotte wished that she could afford to buy Amy something as she watched her sister pose before a mirror in a
bonnet of pink ruching tied with velvet ribbon that exactly
matched her eyes.

Reluctantly, Amy began to remove the hat, but Devlin
stepped up and returned it to her head. "I have never had
a little sister to buy presents for. Please allow me." He
paid the milliner amid loud protestations from them all,
especially from a jealous Vanessa. But Amy's pleasure in
her new bonnet soon brought smiles to every face.

Devlin appeased Vanessa with a fresh rosebud nosegay
in a lacy holder and a similar one for Charlotte which
they pinned on their shoulders before heading toward the
dining room in the Maison Blanc Hotel.

In the dim, subdued establishment, obsequious waiters
led them to a corner table heavy with damask, silver, and
crystal. Vanessa and Devlin ordered a full meal, including
goose stuffed with peanuts, cold venison and a molded
salmon. Amy and Charlotte were contented with a rook
pie and French salad, only allowing their appetites full
rein when the sweet cart arrived with a selection of open
jellies in whipped cream, Neapolitan cake a la Chantilly,
iced pudding, tipsy cake and a large, exotic Pine Apple
cut into enticing cubes on a bed of shredded coconut. It
was hard to limit their choice to only one, but Devlin
ordered several little cakes and tarts for sampling.

To Charlotte's dismay, she figured that the total bill,
including wine, must run over $8.00, but Devlin paid it
with equanimity and the excursion ended with them all
driving home replete with food and in a state of amiable
somnolence.

Chapter 10

Before Aunt Clara had a chance to invite Beaulah and her family to attend tea at Stone Gardens, a note arrived from Roselands.

With the exception of Devlin, they were all at breakfast when Cicero brought in the missive on a silver tray. " 'Scuse me, Miss Clara, this here jus' come by messenger from Roselands. Be waitin' on an answer." He handed over the note then stepped back and stared fixedly out the window.

Clara lifted the glob of sealing wax and read quickly, a flush of pleasure staining her long thin cheeks. "Oh, listen, everybody. We are all invited to tea this afternoon. Yes, yes, we'll attend. Girls, see to your toilettes. We must look our best, don't you know. Two guests are there and the Hartleys are quite wealthy. Cicero, tell the messenger we all accept."

Charlotte and Amy exchanged excited glances. "We must have our best gowns freshened," Amy breathed. "Charlotte, what do you think I better wear?"

Vanessa interrupted before Charlotte could reply. "Amy,

you must let me select your dress. It cannot be too fussy nor clash with mine."

In other words, Amy must stay in the background. Charlotte's own selection was meager, but she did have a rather nice bombazine . . .

Vanessa babbled excitedly. "Mama, should I wear my royal blue with the big lace collar? Or perhaps the pale green one? If only there'd been time to have my new material made up." She flounced around toward the sisters. "I knew Keith when he was a little boy, ten or so, and awfully handsome. He said I was his little sweetheart and he'd come back and marry me. I let him kiss me when he left. It was such fun." She put pink-tipped fingers against her lips as if reliving that childhood thrill. "Now he's returned."

Charlotte felt a stab of disappointment. She had hoped the handsome redhead might become interested in Amy, but it sounded as though Vanessa already had designs on Keith.

"Yes, little sweethearts," Clara echoed, laughing indulgently, but her eyes had a speculative gleam. "Beaulah says her sister married extremely well. They have nigh onto a thousand slaves, I'm told, a Greek-revival mansion three stories high and the finest stable in Kentucky. This summer they are all going abroad with the two younger children, a nurse, a maid and a valet."

"Oh, my, I can hardly wait to hear all about it," Vanessa breathed, placing a hand upon her chest.

"Sounds like you'll be very glad to renew acquaintance with this Keith," Amy twinkled.

Vanessa grinned and took a quick gulp of coffee. "You can bet your bottom dollar on that."

"Oh, Daughter," Aunt Clara gasped, "what a vulgarism. Where did you hear such an expression? From one of those common row bosses, I'll be bound."

Vanessa didn't answer, her eyes were fixed dreamily on the outside garden. "I just may have two gentlemen interested in me pretty soon."

"Who's the other one?" Charlotte asked. As if she didn't know.

"Devlin, of course," Vanessa snapped. "Anyone can see that with just one eye. Unless a person is an old-maid Yankee." Her lip curled. "Charlotte, didn't you ever have a beau?"

Charlotte was saved from answering by Amy's indignant intervention. "Of course, she has! Lots of them. My sister just didn't have time for getting too serious and she is very particular—"

"Well, so is my daughter," Clara declared. "There was just one time . . . That silly business with Martin Cord. I never could understand why you were so intrigued by him. Attractive in his way, but so far beneath you. It was purely scandalous the way you chased him last summer, until he told me bluntly that he wasn't interested in you romantically, and I should speak to you—"

"Mama, it wasn't that way at all." Vanessa thumped the table. "Didn't I tell you that he chased *me* until I had to slap his face?" She gave a quick glance across the table, her face flaming with embarrassment. Charlotte and Amy immediately became very interested in finishing their breakfasts.

Aunt Clara merely shrugged. "It doesn't matter, my love. You can get any man you want. I would say that Mr. Cartright seems mighty interested and Keith soon will be, too."

Mollified, Vanessa patted her back curls. "Mama, I vow I really don't know which gentleman I will prefer. We'll have to wait and see."

"Well, I think young Keith would be the better catch. My stars, we don't even know if Devlin has a wife—"

Vanessa answered smugly, "Mama, I know *all* about him.

He told me his wife is dead and they had no children. His papa was a judge somewhere in Virginia, and Devlin also took the bar, but he travels now and writes those wonderful, exciting books.''

"But a little too frank, I'd say," Clara muttered darkly.

"Oh, Mama, not at all. My friends adore them. They say the love scenes teach them everything they need to know for the big wedding night. Amy's reading one now and she likes it, too. Isn't that right, kitten?''

Amy glanced at Charlotte. "Well—uh—yes. They're quite well-written.''

"I just wonder where he gets all those romantic ideas," Vanessa said, running a tongue across her lips. "Amy, let's go upstairs and talk—''

"Just a minute," Charlotte cut in sharply. "I think we should prepare a dress to wear this afternoon. I imagine everything in our trunks needs pressing.''

"You're right," Amy said. "Excuse me, Vanessa, I won't be long.''

As the breakfast party broke up, Vanessa called after Amy who was hastening from the room. "Get that lazy Tibby to tend your clothes, you hear? I declare, every time I want her help, she keeps me waiting. I could give her such a slap.''

Charlotte imagined that the little maid avoided Vanessa whenever possible. How hard it must be to live and work under a hand of careless cruelty. If the child was free, at least she could leave Stone Gardens.

Tibby had become much more at ease with her, to Charlotte's contentment, and she had quickly gotten busy with the contents of the recovered trunk and dresses, petticoats and wraps already hung in the wardrobe.

On the bed reposed caps and bonnets which Tibby regarded with uncertainty. "Miss Charlotte, I did my best to fresh-up ribbons and steam the feathers, but I dunno—''

Charlotte sighed. "I'm sure there was nothing more you could do. They have definitely seen better days." She turned to her trunk and drew out the remaining articles, including a wooden box of medicines.

She had a sudden vision of the suffering runaway. Some of this salve might help his poor, scarred face. "Tibby, have you seen Elijah, the slave who was branded for running away?"

The neatly turbaned head nodded, small metal hoops trembling in her ears. "Yes'm. He's my brother."

"Your brother! Oh, Tibby, I am so sorry. How is he? Is your mother taking care of him?"

"We got no folks here, Miss Charlotte. Jus' me 'n him." Her young face looked pinched and worried.

"Tibby, why did Elijah run away? Was he being mistreated?"

The young maid withdrew a dress from the trunk and examined it, her face averted. When she spoke, her voice was low. "Our family was all right 'till Master Frank die. Then our folks was sold, and Miss Clara hire new, tough row bosses."

"Did you have to work in the fields at first?"

"Yes'm, but the new bosses drive awful hard. They got mad when I don't keep up and beat me. Then Elijah yelled and they beat him, too."

Charlotte gave a sympathetic exclamation. "Why didn't you go with Elijah when he ran away?"

"I was jus' too scared, and now I can work in the big house. Look what happen if you caught on the Freedom Trail!"

"I'm so sorry about your brother. Here, take this salve and put it on his cheek each night. It helps to heal a burn."

"Thank you, Miss Charlotte. Now, I'll see to these here

clothes." Arms full, she hurried to the door, very determined to please in "the big house."

Charlotte also had a place where she must give satisfaction and, at once, she sped off to the studio. Devlin was not there and she wondered where he went so often. Was it all research? He never wrote in her presence, but she figured that he must do it late at night, as every day a fresh pile of scribbled pages appeared on her table, bristling with notes, asterisks, and inserts on the back. It was not an easy task to decipher all his instructions. So far, however, she had not received any complaints.

She didn't stop for lunch, working straight through until the sun dipped low down in the sky. She had finished the required chapters and placed the finished pages in a neat pile with a pat of accomplishment before hurrying to her room.

Tibby had cleaned and pressed one of Charlotte's favorite dresses, a saffron bombazine with elbow length sleeves and a waist that fitted snugly. The only trimming was a row of brown velvet bows running from the v-neck to the hem and decorating the edges of the sleeves.

Charlotte bathed and dressed, twisting her hair into a loose coil at the back of her neck. Then, on an impulse, she ran down to the garden for a yellow rose to brighten her dark tresses.

She found Cicero also in the garden, a basket on his arm while he studied carefully each pink rosebud before adding it to his collection.

"Who are the flowers for, Cicero?" Charlotte called, strolling toward him.

He bobbed his grizzled head. "Why, for Miss Vanessa. She want to wear 'em to a tea party."

"I am going, too. That's why I'm here, looking for adornment."

"I should cut you some, too, Miss Charlotte?"

"No, I'll do it." A sudden thought struck her as his warm smile creased the dark brown skin. "Cicero, did you know my mother?"

"Oh, yes'm. Miss Rose. I helped pick flowers for her dear sweet self, time and time again." His voice sank to a hoarse whisper. "Those of us what knew her are mighty glad to see her chillun here. Except the working—" He broke off abruptly and bent over a bush. "These here roses be on their way out and that's a fact."

"Aunt Clara doesn't talk about our mother. No one does. She died when Amy was born, you know."

Cicero straightened up. "We all mighty sorrowful about that. Only time Old Missus cried."

"Why did they treat our mother so badly, just because they didn't approve of her husband?" Charlotte asked bitterly.

He looked at her sadly. "You has to know the Southerners, Miss Charlotte. So proud, so single-minded. And 'sides, they felt right sorrowful that she was going so far away from them. 'Twas hurt and anger all mix up, I reckon." He turned away, his basket full. "I hafta go, Miss Charlotte, but you mind, if ever you want my help—in any way—jus' ask."

"Thank you, Cicero."

He didn't answer, but his shuffling footsteps quickened out of sight. Somewhere in the house, a bell rang shrilly.

Charlotte selected several fragrant blooms and was inhaling their perfume when she noticed Devlin Cartright striding across the leaf-carpeted lawn. Suddenly, confusion swept her. What would he think of a sedate, spinster lady decking herself out with flowers like a blushing girl? Hastily, she flung the buds upon the ground and lifted her skirts, prepared to flee.

But Devlin called her name and loped toward her with his long, easy stride. He must have just returned from an outing as he wore fashionable narrow, tan trousers and a checked waistcoat beneath the black serge jacket that he had worn to Charles City. But his head was uncovered, the sun glinting on his thick brown hair as he brushed it back impatiently.

His frank gaze swept her up and down. "Very nice. Don't ever wear grey again. With your dark hair and creamy skin, you should choose rich colors like peacock, emerald, rose or wine. And yellow." He swooped upon the rosebuds. "Now, why did you decide not to wear these?"

Charlotte felt her cheeks flush beneath his scrutiny. "I— I was afraid of looking foolish—too girlish."

"Nonsense," he said bruskly. "It is true, you are not a callow girl, but you are still a young woman and a very desirable one. Now, turn around and let me tuck these in your hair. They add the perfect touch."

His will was stronger than her own and, meekly, she whirled around. His hands brushed her neck, sending an odd tingle down her spine, and he seemed to take a long time fussing with her hair. Then his warm breath fanned her ear as he clasped her shoulders and asked, "Don't you know that you are?"

"What?" Her voice came out in a startled gasp.

"Desirable." He bent his head to sniff the roses. Or did his lips brush her hair? His hands, warm and heavy, moved down her arms, pressing, stroking, his touch a force that seared right through her silky sleeve. It felt as though his bare hands touched her bare flesh, and he had turned her into a living statue. Unable to speak, her heart raced wildly, but she didn't move. And didn't want to . . . for some strange reason.

His fingers trailed down to her wrists, igniting a path of fire. Then his arm encircled her waist and she felt his body back of hers, strong, muscled chest and thighs pressing hard with an urgent masculine demand that even Charlotte, in her limited experience, recognized. *He wanted to make love.*

Quickly, she managed to jerk away and face him. Her breath moved rapidly in her chest, nearly suffocating her. Devlin's gaze dropped to her bosom, watching it. Charlotte stepped back, exclaiming hoarsely, "Mr. Cartright! You forget yourself."

"Yes," he answered thickly and managed to drag his glazed eyes up to her face. "Sometimes my writer's imagination overwhelms me." He studied her for a long moment. "Can you forgive me?"

Charlotte could only nod jerkily. Then they parted and Charlotte sought to calm herself. After all, what had he done? He hadn't kissed her or touched her in an unseemly way, as some of her former escorts had done during a dark walk in the park. Also, in these instances, their wet, panting kisses had been most disagreeable. Somehow, she didn't think Devlin's kisses would be disagreeable. No, not at all.

Dearest God, how vulnerable she was! She must be careful not to let their relationship get out of hand. They worked alone in a secluded studio, and he was a very attractive man. Extremely hot-blooded, too. That much was obvious from his books. Where did he get the material for those arousing scenes, if not from his own experiences?

Her own brief encounter with his hands and body, the whispered words—"You are very desirable. Don't you know that?"—all had actually been rather frightening. Not only because she sensed the rising passion in him, but because she also sensed it in herself.

Chapter 11

Charlotte had never imagined that she would be entering a home so beautiful as Aunt Clara's landau swept through the wrought iron gates. Above their heads, the word "Roselands" appeared in gold, surrounded by black iron roses intertwined through all the bars.

"Oh, it's just like fairyland," Amy cried, craning her head from side to side as she tried to see everything at once: the long, blue waterlily pool ringed with flowering bushes, an emerald lawn interspersed with graceful trees that swayed above snow-white Grecian statues.

At the end of the crushed shell drive stood a stately mansion saved from overpowering dimensions by the climbing roses on the tall, two-story pillars. A balcony ran along the upper floor and a servant stationed there immediately disappeared. This must have been a signal. By the time they left the landau, the front door swung wide and Beaulah Hartley came into view. A short, older man accompanied her, his face wreathed in smiles as his wife made the introductions. Clara and the girls received a hearty welcome and were led at once into a large parlor opening from the central hallway.

"What a beautiful room," Amy exclaimed.

Charlotte agreed wholeheartedly as her eyes swept the rich blue Oriental rugs on polished boards, the carved fireplace with its enormous gilded mirror, and three elaborate chandeliers sparkling with crystal prisms.

But, almost at once, the inspection became curtailed as the redhaired twins, Katy and Keith burst into the room. A babble of introductions arose. They both knew Clara and Vanessa, of course, from their childhood visits, and there were many exclamations regarding the changes apparent in each of them.

"I declare, you've become so handsome, Keith, but then I knew you would. How about me? Have I changed a lot?" Vanessa preened in her pale green lawn dress which she had lavishly trimmed with knots of rosebuds on hair, wrist, and waist.

"You were a beautiful child and now you're a beautiful woman." Keith laughed and kissed her cheek. "Seems to me you promised that you'd marry me one day."

"My stars, you remembered! Do you mean to hold me to that childhood vow?" Vanessa simpered.

"Oh, I imagine you have a dozen other beaus by now." His roving gaze strayed to assess the newest females. He smiled at Amy, but looked the longest at Charlotte. Her hair, throat, bosom, arms, and waist all seemed laid bare to his young male speculation.

Charlotte felt her face grow warm. Keith was undeniably handsome with his russet curls, bright blue eyes, fashionable grey coat and darker trousers. His waistcoat was of royal blue brocade and sported a watch and gold chain across the front. Ruffles on his shirtsleeves drew attention to an elaborate signet ring. He exuded wealth, good-looks and superb conceit.

His sister, much plainer with engaging freckles, had drawn Amy to a sofa for an animated conversation. Clara and Beaulah took chairs together, and Vanessa had again captured Keith with a blatant flirtation, at which he laughed indulgently.

Charlotte sat apart, feeling disappointed that her first impression of Keith as young and boyish who might appeal to Amy had not held up upon meeting him formally. Of course, she still didn't know much about the redhead, only that he didn't appear truly interested in girls as young as Amy and Vanessa. She received the impression of a boy who had had some experience with women and liked them to have it, too. He didn't seem overwhelmed by Vanessa, although he laughed easily and squeezed her shoulder, his arm draped casually behind her on the loveseat.

Charlotte knew she was the target of his interest because she was someone new, someone older, and perhaps, he might hope as experienced as he was. Her carriage, the fullness of her figure, and a cool, indifferent expression when she looked at him, all seemed to have fired his erotic imagination.

Charlotte turned her back and accepted tea and cakes from the hovering maid, then found Charles Hartley at her side. He beamed at her with a friendly nod of his bald head while he quickly consumed a strawberry tart and then took another.

"Try these, do, Miss Charlotte. I grow the fruit in my hothouse. Are you interested in horticulture?"

"Interested, yes, knowledgeable, no." Charlotte bit into the berry cake topped with whipped cream. "Delicious! How wonderful it must be to raise such things. I have never seen any flowers as abundant as the ones in Virginia. Is it true you have a famous rose garden?"

"Oh, yes, quite true. That is my hobby. Would you care

to see it?" He eyed her eagerly as he stuffed a macaroon into his mouth and then applied a lace-edged napkin.

Charlotte, out of the corner of her eye, saw Keith put down his cup and start to rise, lifting up his hand to signal her.

"Yes, let's go right now," Charlotte said quickly. "Before my aunt decides it's time to go."

"Oh, what enthusiasm! It will be such a pleasure to show—"

"Wait, Miss Charlotte." Keith had gained her side and took a too-familiar grip on her bare arm. "We're all going on a garden tour. I will escort you—"

"And Amy, too, of course." Charlotte smiled, ignoring a quick frown of annoyance. "And what about Vanessa? She has been dying to renew your childhood acquaintance and has talked of nothing else—"

"Plenty of time for that. Aunt Beaulah will take the children in tow, but you and I—"

"Thank you, but Mr. Hartley has agreed to show me his hothouse first."

Vanessa reached them at that moment and shot a venemous glance at Charlotte. "Keith, did you know my cousins are working girls and can't stay out too long? They had no place to live, so my Mama offered them jobs at Stone Gardens in return for room and board. They were ever so grateful," she purred. "Weren't you, Cousin Charlotte?"

"Certainly."

Keith looked undaunted, even happier than ever. He probably thought to himself: "Older, experienced, and *poor*. What a perfect target." His eyes strayed down to Charlotte's waist, but he let Vanessa tug him toward the door. He sent a wink across his shoulder.

Charlotte took a firm grip on Mr. Hartley's arm, and when they were on the veranda, she passed Keith without a glance. It was easy to dismiss him from her mind.

The other members of the tea party strolled in various directions, some lingering to examine the statuary or gaze into the pool dotted with pink and white waterlilies. Gardeners worked unobtrusively, melting out of sight like well-trained servants when approached. Were they slaves, Charlotte wondered?

Noticing the direction of her gaze, Charles Hartley said quietly, "We are setting our workers free, one by one, and it is a very expensive process, let me tell you."

"Very commendable. Will most of them remain here?" Charlotte asked. "This is a beautiful place to work."

He nodded. "They are used to it and it probably seems like home. We have never broken up the families and we have a teacher and a preacher once a week. So they have incentives to stay right here and receive wages."

"I should think so." She lowered her voice. "But I thought it was against the law to give Negroes the opportunity to read and write?"

"That's correct, it is," he responded, nodding, "but can you imagine the poor things without even the comfort of reading the Good Book? We will take our chances with the law," he added grimly.

"How difficult it all is." Charlotte shook her head. "This is my first experience with slavery."

"And you are appalled."

"Yes, even though I have only seen a little bit. I will tell you this in confidence, since by aunt does not believe as I do, but my father was Abolitionist."

"It is a fine movement; even they, however, do not fully understand the situation. Slave owners have a tiger by the tail—hating to hold on, but afraid to let go."

"I wonder how it will be resolved?"

They were walking underneath arches of climbing roses and it was a moment before Charles Hartley answered thoughtfully, "It may be resolved by force. There will be speeches, fights, arguments—all gaining nothing except an ever-widening gulf between North and South. The Mason-Dixon line surveyed between free and slave states still has the markers after a hundred years."

"But we are all part of the United States," Charlotte said in a troubled tone. "That must never change. You don't think the South would wish to set up their own government?"

"Secession? It would never work. We all need each other—industrial North and agricultural South. A way will be found. Someday. Somehow. When slavery is abolished, it will be a noble deed."

Feeling comforted by this good-hearted, intelligent little man, Charlotte was now ready to view the huge, two-acre rose garden stretching in neat, well-tended rows. A brick wall enclosed it on three sides covered with climbers. Grass paths, clipped and green, ran between the plots.

Square beds, triangular beds, horseshoe-shaped beds, each one held a special group of roses in colors ranging from dramatic scarlet to subtle pinks to salmon, white and yellow. Charles knew all their names, and like a proud parent, he pointed to several he greatly admired. "This is Old Blush introduced in 1793, Slaters Crimson China, 1790, and an intensely perfumed damask rose called Leda."

"Who cares for all this fabulous place?" Charlotte marvelled. "It must take so much work."

"I come out every day to supervise, but my helpers are well-trained in watering, fertilizing and weeding. The roses go dormant in the winter and must be pruned. I do that myself."

"Is the climate mild all year?"

"Oh, no, about eighty degrees in summer and thirty in January, but we have a lot of rain, between thirty and fifty inches." While he talked, Charles was cutting long-stemmed, partly-open buds. He had withdrawn a pair of folded clippers from his jacket. Charlotte imagined that he never was without them. When he had a large boquet stripped of thorns, he handed it to Charlotte with a little bow.

"Flowers for the fair."

"Oh, thank you." Charlotte buried her nose in the velvety satin petals, inhaling the deep rose fragrances.

"I see the others returning to the house, so perhaps we better join them and save the greenhouse for another visit."

"I hope I can return again."

"You'll be here sooner than you think," Mr. Hartley said as they turned their steps across the front lawn. "I believe the twins are planning some kind of a gala and, of course, you all will be invited, including Clara's houseguest. What is his name?"

"Devlin Cartright. I work for him. He writes books under the pen name of Rodney Rogue."

"Ah, yes. I only met him once and I am better at rose names than casual acquaintances."

"The roses are your best friends, I think." Charlotte twinkled.

Mr. Hartley chuckled. "Oh, I like people, too, especially when they show as much interest in my garden as you did."

When they reached the parlor, everyone was standing around, opening the creamy parchment envelopes Keith handed out.

"I want you all to help us celebrate Katy's and my twenty-first birthday. It's going to be one week from Saturday and will be a real gala. My sister and I will order an orchestra and caterers from Richmond. And Miss Amy and Miss Charlotte, you each must save three dances for me, you hear?"

"Well, I simply never, Keith Duncan. *Three dances?*"

Vanessa's eyes blazed blue flames. "Didn't I tell you that Charlotte and Amy are not at leisure?"

Beaulah Hartley turned to her as an embarrassed hush fell on the room. "Surely you don't begrudge your *cousins* a little social life?"

"Of course, not. No, indeed," Clara put in hastily.

"It's going to be a costume party," Katy cried. "Masks and everything. Won't that be fun? Keith and I have already ordered ours, but we won't tell anyone what they are."

Charlotte and Amy exchanged a worried glance. They couldn't afford to buy or even rent costumes!

As if to make up for her daughter's *gaffe,* Clara stated loudly, "Fortunately, our family has never thrown anything away. We have dozens of trunks in the attic filled with old ball gowns that can be used. Some of them date back to the Revolutionary Days. My nieces are welcome to anything up there."

As Charlotte and Amy thanked her, Keith began to strut around the room. "Let me see how I would dress each one of you girls if the choice were up to me." He raised a quizzing glass from his vest pocket and took advantage of the game to thoroughly assess each lady's charms.

Charlotte's lips thinned indignantly when she noted Amy's painful blush as Keith ran his hand slowly down her bare arm. "I see you as a shepherdess, young and shy. Lots of roses on glazed chintz, the skirt short enough to show a dainty ankle. A big straw hat tied under that cute chin and a crook with a big pink bow."

When he gave her cheek a little pat, Amy twisted out of his hands. "That sounds fine. I'll see what I can do. Why don't you dress like a woolly lamb so I could tie you up?"

Everybody laughed, and Vanessa said loudly, "He acts more like a marauding wolf, I'd say."

"In return for that remark, you shall be next, young

lady." Grinning, Keith swung around and grabbed her arms.

But she forestalled him by declaring, "I would like to go as Madame Pompadour and have all the men at my feet."

"I imagine you can do that without a fancy costume." Keith laughed. "You really should be a little older for a French courtesan. Perhaps you can find some rouge and eye makeup."

"Not in my house, you won't," Clara gave a gasping laugh which captured Keith's attention. "You should go as a queen, dear lady. Purple velvet, a train trimmed with ermine, and a jeweled crown."

"Oh, you silly boy! Anyway," she pursed her lips. "I'll think about it. Come now, girls, it's time to go."

Charlotte was relieved to escape Keith's attention and joined the flurry of farewells as they all headed for the hallway.

But he didn't permit her to escape. Catching her arm, he drew her back, speaking so low that no one else could hear. "Don't you want to know how I would dress you?"

"Not particularly," she answered coolly.

Undeterred, his blue gaze swept her up and down. "With that fine figure, what you should wear is . . . as little as possible. And that is something I would truly like to see."

"Never," Charlotte snapped. "And if I were not a guest in your aunt's house, I'd slap your face!"

She heard him laughing as she swung away.

Chapter 12

The imminent prospect of a ball had put Vanessa in an expansive mood and immediately after supper, she invited Amy and Charlotte to accompany her to the attic where they could look for costumes.

Accordingly, they changed into their oldest clothes, and each carrying a candle, followed Vanessa down the hallway on the second floor. Turning into the farthest wing, she opened a narrow door and shone her light upon a steep flight of stairs leading upward to the attics.

"Ugh, it looks as though no one has been up this way for ages. Just look at all the cobwebs." Vanessa ducked her head and batted at the dangling strands as she led the way. "I just hope the mice haven't gotten into the things we want."

"As long as the creatures stay away," Amy chortled, "this is fun. Charlotte, remember that book we read, *The Vanishing Corpse*, where they found a body in the attic trunk? Vanessa, has anyone disappeared mysteriously?"

"Stop that, Amy, it's spooky enough up here." Charlotte,

however, found it fascinating that all these things once belonged to living, breathing people—her ancestors. Early colonists, fearful of the Indians, everything so new and different from the homes they had left in England. Then the hard work, the slow building up of fortunes: an elaborate house, balls, carriages, buying slaves. Marriages, births, tears, and laughter . . .

Vanessa was not moved by any such sentimental musings. She walked forward briskly, surveying everything. "Just as I feared, dust and spider webs and mouse dirt. I wonder what they've left? Come on, y'all, help me haul these trunks out to the center of the floor so that we can look through them."

They set their candles on a dusty table, the flames flickering on the accumulated trash of centuries: broken chairs, their moldy velvet eaten by the vermin, rickety washstands with rusty basins, dust-covered stacks of mildewed books, boxes of letters, magazines and ledgers. And saddest of all, the toys of past children: a rocking horse with pealing paint, an eyeless plush bear, broken tea sets and an empty doll house wreathed in webs.

In a wooden box, Charlotte discovered a pile of china-headed ladies peering wistfully over the edge. She removed one faded beauty, stroking the matted wig of human hair and the raveled, pink satin skirt.

With a cry, Vanessa snatched the doll out of her hands. "Oh, give me that. Belinda darling, how I've missed you." She pressed the china cheek against her own. "I vow, if Mama hadn't sneaked you up here to the junk heap, you would still be in my room."

Charlotte stared at her. Did Vanessa have another side from the spoiled, selfish beauty? Perhaps she had been a very lonesome little girl who had focused on herself, making a kind of dream world where she reigned supreme and no one could compete. Was that why she kept shoving

Amy and herself into the background, Charlotte wondered?

"Let's take Belinda back to your room," Amy told her cousin with a smile. "I'll make a new dress from some scraps then clean her up."

"All right." Vanessa laid the doll aside with a final pat. "Now, let's see what we can find to wear in these trunks."

They raised the lid of the nearest one and the aroma of potpourri rose up to greet them. Herbs had been scattered over the clothes to repel moths and in this trunk, at least, they had done well. Silks, satins, brocades, and velvets arose from their shower of dried lavender and fennel, almost as bright as when they had been laid to rest so many years ago.

Charlotte lifted the clothes reverently. "These styles might have been worn over fifty years ago. Look at the panniers, Watteau trains, and overskirts. And the materials, aren't they lovely! Watered silk, lutestring, and this silky stripe is tabby cloth, I think. I wonder if there are wigs somewhere and face patches and fans . . ."

Indeed, there were. They discovered tarnished gauze scarves, plumed hats, paste jewels encrusted with dust, faded painted scenes on silken fans. The attic echoed to cries of each new discovery.

The candles had guttered low when Vanessa bundled up the most gorgeous costume of them all, a rose hand-painted satin trimmed with lace and artificial flowers. "This is mine," she declared. "Now I must go to bed. You girls stay and tidy up, will you?" She gave a yawn as she departed. "See that y'all do a good job when you pack the things away."

After she had gone, Amy giggled. "I felt as though we should curtsey and say, "Yes, mum. Anything you say, mum.""

Charlotte clicked her tongue and cast a swift glance

toward the doorway. "Now, Amy." She started folding up the gowns. "Have you found a shepherdess costume yet?"

"That Keith! Isn't he a caution? No, I'm going as something entirely different. I think that I will wear this Spanish dress with red ruffles and a lace mantilla. I can tie a black silk scarf to hide my hair and wear these long, jet earrings. Not a soul will know me."

She slipped the scarlet dress over her head and draped the black lace around her curls. "I wish I could see how it looks."

"It's beautiful, dear. There is a pier glass in that far corner if you want to see yourself."

With some difficulty, Amy made her way through the trash and furry dust toward the big full-length mirror. She wiped off the mottled surface with a rag, then giggling, she began dancing and clicking her fingers like castanets.

It happened in a second. As she whirled around, the flying mantilla caught on the mirror's edge. Slowly, it tipped over, shattering into dozens of splinters as it struck the wooden floor.

With a cry of horror, Charlotte rushed to Amy who had fallen on her knees. "Baby, are you hurt? Did you cut yourself?"

Shards of mirrored glass littered the satin ruffles, but only a tiny trickle ran down from Amy's arm. She sat up dazedly and Charlotte wiped away the blood with her handkerchief. "Thank goodness, it's only a small cut. What on earth happened?"

"The lace caught on the mirror's frame." Amy scrambled to her feet and started to gather up the pieces of broken glass, placing them in an empty box.

Charlotte righted the pier glass, examining the splintered wooden frame. "I hope this wasn't a valuable antique. However, it doesn't look like much." As she tried to shove it back, she gave a startled exclamation. "Amy, come look at this."

"What is it?"

"There's a hidden doorway here behind the mirror."

Amy advanced, peering over Charlotte's shoulder. "No, it's a closet. See the shelves."

"It just *looks* like a closet. The whole front is separate. The crash must have jarred the edge loose from the wall. There's a wide crack from top to bottom. Perhaps there is something in back of it."

"Or someone!" Amy squeaked and clutched Charlotte's arm. "Remember that story about the bride who was sealed up in the attic wall?"

"Nonsense, that was just a story," Charlotte answered sturdily. "Come on, help me. Let's see if we can move the shelves out farther."

With both of them tugging at the edge, the false front finally moved stiffly with a protesting groan, only wide enough for Charlotte to insert her head.

"What can you see?" Amy breathed. "Here, use the candle."

After a long moment, Charlotte pulled back, brushing off a cobweb. "Ugh, it's probably alive with spiders and other nasty things. But no bodies."

They both laughed rather shakily, then suddenly Amy cried, "Do you suppose it could be the lost passageway to the Stone Garden?"

Charlotte stared at her. "That's a possibility, all right. I'm going to explore it tomorrow, if I get the chance. I'm dying to see where it goes, aren't you?"

Amy shuddered. "You won't get me in there with all those spiders. But it's certainly an exciting discovery. I wonder what Aunt Clara and Vanessa will say when we tell them?"

Amy could hardly wait to announce the news. The next

morning at the breakfast table, she exclaimed excitedly, "You'll never guess what Charlotte and I found in the attic last night."

However, their discovery was received with only the mildest interest by Clara and Vanessa. The disclosure of the broken mirror created much more of a stir.

"Do you want to come up and assess the damage?" Charlotte asked uncomfortably. "I have to return to the attic, as I didn't select a costume yet."

Vanessa frowned. "Well, see that you don't break another valuable article while you're snooping around up there."

Charlotte's face flamed, especially when she noticed Devlin Cartright walk through the doorway.

"Did you break something?" His eyebrow quirked as he crossed the room to help himself to scrambled eggs and sausage.

"Amy and I broke a pier glass in the attic last night," Charlotte answered, hoping he wouldn't think her too clumsy to continue working for him.

"If you wish, Aunt Clara, I will pay for it out of my wages from Mr. Cartright."

Darting a swift glance at the writer, Aunt Clara hastened to say, "Oh, no. Forget it, do. I wouldn't think of making you pay for something that we never use."

Does that include my room, Charlotte wondered? She had offered some money for her board, but so far, Aunt Clara had declined to accept anything, adding that she might have to change her mind about it at some future date.

Now her aunt's generosity made Charlotte feel guilty and she said sincerely, "I am very sorry about the mirror. We will be most careful in the future."

The conversation became general for the rest of the meal, concentrating on the costume for the ball. "Oh, you should see mine," Vanessa raved. "Devi, it is absolutely beautiful. It has hand-painted roses on the skirt and the bodice is real tight. I wish we always wore our gowns that low-cut now."

"That dress belonged to your great aunt, Sara Mae," Clara said, "and you will have to tuck a fichu in the front or you will have Keith staring at you."

"No fichu," Vanessa muttered, stuffing a bite of spoon-bread between her rebellious lips.

"I'm sure you will all look lovely in anything you wear," Devlin said, pushing back his chair. "Now, you must excuse me, I am going to have a visitor this morning. Charlotte, wait for another hour before you come to work."

"Very well." Charlotte nodded then turned to her aunt. "Seeing those old costumes made me wonder about our ancestors. Why did Uncle Frank have the same name as your family, Bainbridge, that is?"

"We were cousins," Clara answered. "And when we married, he was delighted to make this his home."

"Do Amy and I have other relatives in the South? Our father was an orphan, so we have no one up North."

"There are not many of us left down here, either. Grandparents dead, my sisters and cousins scattered far and wide."

"Are there any portraits here?" Amy asked.

"A few. I'll show them to you some time." Clara smiled. "There are one or two who look like you, child—blonde curls, big blue eyes."

"I'd like to see them, too." Charlotte said. Her aunt nodded with a little less enthusiasm.

"I think I'll get a costume from the attic while I have the chance and can see better in the daylight. Amy, do you wish to join me?"

"She and I are going riding," Vanessa said quickly. "I

just have to show Lucalla what I want done with my costume."

Charlotte followed them as quickly as she could. This time, she intended to take a longer look at the secret passageway. With that in mind, she stopped in her room for a candle and a match and covered her sprigged calico with a voluminous apron. She also tied a scarf over her hair, and thus prepared for dust and spiderwebs, Charlotte mounted to the attic, her heartbeats quickening with excitement.

The matter of selecting a gown did not take long. She had seen one last night that reminded her of Devlin's remark about vibrant colors. It was made of lustrous material called "shot silk". Held one way, it looked emerald green; turned the other direction, a golden color rippled through it. The full, gathered overskirt split in the center to show a creamy satin petticoat. Yellowed lace trimmed the low-cut decolletage and hopefully could be revived with an application of damp cornstarch and sunshine. Side hoops dated it back to the Revolutionary War period, and in those days, hair was usually plastered with pomatum and white powder. She saw several frames on which to erect the towering headdresses of that era, but Charlotte decided to forego the messy business and just wear her hair naturally. She would adorn it with flowers and carry her mother's ivory lace fan. She even had inherited a dark velvet cloak which she could use as a wrap. With everything laid out in a pile, the time had come to investigate the secret passageway.

She lit the candle and made her way to the far corner. When she moved aside the pier glass, it seemed impossible for the unknowing eye to detect where the opening had been. What could have caused the false shelves to swing free when the mirror shattered? Did a spring jar loose, finally worn out over the long years? But a honeycomb of

perforated wood indicated termites might have under-
mined the wall. She had heard that they were the plague
of hot, moist Southern climates.

Brushing the dust from her knees, she rose and felt
around the edge of the shelves. Finally, she heard a little
click and something moved beneath her fingers. She
tugged and the false front opened for about a foot and
then would move no farther.

Charlotte lifted her candle into the dark void, wishing
Amy had come with her. Steps led downward in the narrow
space, and she hesitated for a moment. Suppose the closet
jarred shut again? Or someone came up and inadvertently
closed it? Visions of the bride walled up alive by a jealous
husband made her shudder.

Oh, but stories like "The Corpse in the Attic" and "The
Missing Bride" were befogging her common sense. No
one ever came up here. And a broken chair wedged in
the opening would surely keep it from closing accidentally.

When all was ready, Charlotte slipped inside the stairwell
and descended gingerly. The wavering candle threw shadows on bare pine walls, dangling cobwebs (fortunately
untenanted), and steep stairs without a railing, carpeted
with the thick, velvety dust of ages. At one place, the steps
hugged the brick wall of a fireplace and once she heard
voices and the rattle of dishes. An hysterical giggle rose in
her throat at the vision of their consternation should she
rap on the wall and moan a little.

As she crept downward, the stairs seemed endless and
there was a stale, musty smell in the narrow, confining
space that gave her an unpleasant, smothering sensation
. . . like being buried alive.

But how could she turn back now before she reached
the end of the passage? This was something built by her
own ancestors of whom she knew so little. Her heart
pounded and her palms felt damp and sticky when the

stairs finally stopped. The air seemed fresher and she found herself in a long hallway with a chink of blessed light outlining the far end.

Something scuttled away from her, toenails scrabbling frantically and Charlotte choked on a scream and nearly dropped the candle, visualizing a huge rat. Quaking, she swept up her skirts above her ankles. Should she go back? However. It was only a short way now to the chink of light, and though her teeth began to chatter, she soon covered the distance.

A flight of steps led to a box-like enclosure which Charlotte figured must be the little building connected to the summerhouse. As she raised her candle higher, she saw a wooden lever. She tugged it and heard a grinding gear, but nothing moved. Probably the mechanism had rusted or it required more strength to work it than she possessed.

About to lower the candle, suddenly she noticed something else. There were letters carved above the lintel, chiseled in the strange spelling of Old English:

Erasmus Mason, hee mayd the Stone Gardin for mee,

Fortescue Bainbridge, in the year of our Lord, 1652. With a blank astonishment, Charlotte moved her fingers over the carved letters.

The candle guttered, flared once, then smoked out in a pool of grease. With a gasp, Charlotte whirled around, about to leave when the sound of two familiar voices halted her in her tracks.

Amy and Martin Cord had just entered the summerhouse.

Chapter 13

Sparing only a fleeting thought to the fact that she would be evesdropping, Charlotte put her eye against the chink of light and saw the two figures face each other.

"I can only stay a minute," Amy said. "Vanessa expects me to go riding with her this morning. Martin, why did you ask to meet me here in the Stone Garden?"

"I didn't want anyone to see us." He put out his hand, but Amy stepped back out of reach.

"Amy, why have you been so cold and distant when I've tried to talk to you?"

"You must know. I can't forget that awful branding!" Amy's voice choked. "How could you order such a thing?"

"It's just routine punishment for a runaway. All the slave owners—"

"Routine! Oh, how can you be so callous? I thought at first you might be different underneath. I was beginning—"

"Yes?" In one eager stride, he closed the distance between them. "Beginning—to what? Like me a little?

God, Amy, don't you know how I've felt about you since the minute I first laid eyes on you? At night I dream about your tender beauty, yearn to touch you—'' With a hoarse groan, his arms swept her into his embrace and Amy's little cry was silenced by his lips.

Charlotte fell back against the wall, a fist pressed to her mouth. She longed to yell at them, but she also wanted to hear what happened next. Swiftly, she applied her eye once more to the crack.

"Stop, Martin," Amy gasped. "You must not do that!"

"Don't push me away—I love you," Cord groaned. "Oh, dearest, do you hate me because I dare aspire to you and yet I have no background, no wealth, no education?" His voice dropped to a grating whisper. "God knows I'm not worth a second glance from someone like you. You're as far above me as an angel is from Lucifer."

"I'm not looking for a man with wealth or position and I don't hate you. I only hate what you do here and the fact that it doesn't seem to bother you."

"I'd leave here in a minute, if you'd have me. We could go anywhere you wanted, I would work my fingers to the bone to give you what you want." He snatched her hand and pressed it to his lips.

"Martin, it's no use. I have to go. People will be looking for me. Charlotte would be furious if she knew you'd kissed me."

"Oh, yes, Miss Goody-Two-Shoes," he snarled, his face suddenly darkening. "Are you going to let her rule your entire life? When are you going to start thinking for yourself?"

Amy didn't answer, but Charlotte heard her running footsteps, then a deep curse from the overseer. After another minute passed in silence, the aroma of a cheroot drifted through the crack and his heavy footsteps crunched away in the distance.

Holding up her skirts, Charlotte retraced her way along the dark tunnel, her mind teeming. She must do something about Martin and her sister. So far, Amy had not encouraged him, but how long could she hold out against an experienced, passionate man who wanted her? He was very bold and visible every day with constant opportunities for seduction. And Amy knew so little about the world and its evils. Charlotte recalled the grim lines of a poem read long ago:

> Vice is a monster of such hideous mien,
> That to be hated, needs but to be seen.
> Yet seen too oft, familiar with its face,
> We first endure, then pity, then embrace.

The trouble was, Amy needed to meet other men. If only Keith Duncan had been a different sort, but he was definitely out of the question, as much a flirt as Vanessa. The two of them deserved each other.

When she reached the attic, Charlotte stood still, thinking hard. She better not speak to Amy just yet about the scene in the summerhouse. Rebuking her might lead to rebellion, especially if Amy recalled Martin's taunt: "When are you going to start thinking for yourself?"

Charlotte was afraid that threatening the overseer again would do no more good than it had the first time. It hadn't stopped his pursuit of Amy then and now he might try harder than ever to get his way with her. At the same time, he might use worse retaliation than a garden snake.

The matter required deep consideration, but right now Charlotte knew she must get to work. It would never do to lose her only source of income, especially since it took place where she could keep an eye on Amy.

She gathered up her costume in grimy hands and hurried to her bedroom, where she dumped the green silk on the bed. With a short gasp, she saw herself in the mirror: dirt-streaked face and apron, cobwebs dangling from her headscarf. She pulled off her dirty garments and rang the bell for Tibby.

"Some hot water, please," Charlotte requested when the little maid appeared. Tibby bobbed a curtsey, her widened eyes taking in Charlotte's dishevelment without a word.

When she returned with the can of water, Charlotte said, "Tibby, what is your last name?"

"Mason. I'm Tibby Mason, Miss Charlotte."

Charlotte nodded. She knew that the black community took last names from their masters or from some trade or characteristic. Mason was the name of the stonecutter.

"Was a stonecutter an ancestor of yours?"

"Yes'm, Erasmus Mason." Her head lifted proudly, nostrils flaring a little as she drew in her breath. She had never shown so much spirit. "He make the Stone Garden."

Charlotte stared at her. "Your ancestor carved all that? Does Mrs. Bainbridge know that your brother is descended from him?"

Tibby shrugged. She lifted the can and poured the hot water into the marble wash stand. "Why she care 'bout that, Miss Charlotte? It so long ago. Nothing to her." Then she added softly. "But my brother, Elijah, know. He cares." Quietly, she laid out towels and geranium soap. "You want anything else, Miss Charlotte?"

"No, thank you, Tibby. You may leave."

The door closed soundlessly and Charlotte dipped her wash cloth in the china bowl. Just as she had suspected— the descendent of that genius was now a downtrodden, runaway slave, with the additional ignominy, a brand upon his cheek. God in heaven, where was justice? If the man had been white, the first Erasmus would have become wealthy and famous. At the very least, he would have had his freedom, as well as all his family after him. Perhaps she could discuss this with Aunt Clara and convince her aunt to do something. She knew, though, that hopes in this direction were feeble ones at best.

When she had washed and dressed once more in her rose-sprigged cotton, with her hair tucked neatly into its white, crocheted snood, Charlotte made her way to Devlin's studio to tackle the morning's work. Outdoors, the wide sweep of lawns and trees seemed doubly beautiful, compared to the narrow, musty tunnel that she had just left. How terrible it would be locked up in a small enclosure like that for weeks, months or years, with only a tiny glimpse of the world outside. That's what jails were like and she had run the risk of imprisonment herself when she helped the Frenchman while he, with his Underground activities, was constantly exposed to the danger of arrest. Yet if he should require her help again, Charlotte knew that she would give it without hesitation.

The guest house had now come into view and she slowed her footsteps, wondering if Devlin's visitor had left yet. When the door opened, she took cover at a nearby weeping willow, staring in curiosity at a figure who emerged in a long black cape, wearing a heavily veiled woman's hat and white gloves.

Evidently, this woman was visiting in secret. Had she come on an illicit, romantic rendezvous with Devlin? But if so, how odd to visit him in the daylight when anyone might see her. Yet the guest house was discretely isolated. Perhaps it was originally designed for just such meetings.

Devlin followed his guest onto the porch and a whispered exchange ensued in which Charlotte only caught the words: "take care." A swift bow, then the figure in the concealing garments vanished into the grove bordering the James.

Charlotte waited for a minute while Devlin's narrowed

gaze swept the area, the lines taut beside his mouth. He wore a white shirt open at the neck, the sleeves rolled to the elbow. His dark hair tumbled in its usual tousled fashion upon his brow and he thrust it back impatiently. Was this the look of a man who had just finished satisfying his ardor with a woman? Charlotte bit her lip uncertainly. It hardly seemed likely that he would have chanced a morning assignation . . . unless they had no other opportunity.

When Devlin went inside and the door closed, Charlotte advanced briskly, knocked and entered. She couldn't help a surreptitious glance around. She saw nothing, though, to suggest lovemaking with a woman: no strand of hair, no scent of perfume, no pillows disarranged upon the sofa. Her eyes darted to the bedroom door. Closed, as usual.

She realized that Devlin stood beside her work table, studying her. "You look distraught this morning, Charlotte. Has something happened to upset you?"

Yes! The idea of him venting his passion upon some woman. *Good Lord, could she be jealous?*

She drew a quick sharp breath to clear her idiotic brain. Should she tell him about Cord's advances to Amy? No. That was too personal, especially for Amy. But she could tell him about the attic.

"I just had a rather strange experience. This morning, when I went to the attic for my costume, I discovered the long-lost tunnel."

His heavy-lidded eyes flew wide. "No! By gad, that's extraordinary. Did you tell Clara?"

Charlotte nodded. "Actually, Amy and I found the entrance yesterday when we broke the mirror. We told Aunt Clara just before you came in to breakfast."

"She must have been astounded."

"Not really. She said very little. The broken mirror overshadowed all."

"Have you explored the passage?"

"Yes, this morning. How could I resist? I've never seen a secret tunnel so I fought dust and spiderwebs all the way down several floors to the ending in the summerhouse."

"The one in the Stone Garden? Did you get out then?"

"No, the exit was blocked. I saw a lever but couldn't turn it. And then I saw something else. Above the door were carved words stating that an Erasmus Mason built the Stone Garden in 1652. Tibby told me that she and her brother are his descendents."

"Then he knows about his ancestor. That's a dangerous knowledge to have festering in his soul." Devlin stroked his jaw. "That may explain why he tried to run away. What frustrated resentment he must feel as well as hatred for all that Stone Gardens represents."

"How did he happen to be captured and brought back?"

"A free Negro, posing as his friend, turned Elijah over to the slave catchers for the reward. Charlotte, all of this ties in with my book. I must see this passage. Will you take me to it? Yes, right now. Don't shake your head."

Charlotte gave a rueful laugh. "I just got cleaned up."

"You don't need to go inside. Just come and show me where it is."

"Very well." Charlotte glanced at the pile of notes waiting for her pen. Today she would certainly be working late. However, Devlin was her employer, and she was being paid to honor his wishes.

Up to a certain point, that is! As she followed him out the door, she felt very aware of his strong, virile presence, her senses heightened by the image of him making love to some veiled woman. She had no doubt of his expertise in divesting them both of their clothing in short order. His lips would hold his partner captive in his arms while he carried her to the bed and pressed down on her naked body. Oh, yes, he had fully described such actions in his book, and Charlotte had read the passages several times while sustaining a guilty thrill at the images he created.

Only then, her mind had supplied no face to her imaginary partner and the details were still somewhat hazy. But now her lover wore a face. It was Devlin.

Fiercely, she struggled to subdue her startling thoughts, turning her eyes from Devlin's large, male form and rugged face with its sensuous eyes and determined mouth. To her relief, he introduced a diverting topic as they crossed the lawn and it immediately distracted her.

"What did you think of Keith and his sister?"

"Katy is full of fun. She's friendly and very cute. Keith is handsome and also very friendly, but I was a little leery of him . . ."

Devlin glanced at her keenly. "Why? Pray go on. As a writer, I am intrigued by people, good, bad or indifferent."

Charlotte answered carefully. "I think Keith, young as he is, enjoys great confidence in his ability to woo women . . . and succeed."

"I trust he wasn't offensive to you or Amy?"

"He only teased Amy indifferently. As for me . . . I can handle any of his juvenile attempts." But she knew Keith was not a clumsy boy trying out his powers. He appeared too self-confident, bold and brash. He could become someone it would be difficult to stop if he was determined enough. It was best that he had tried his wiles on herself, instead of Amy, who might not be as strong or ruthless in repulsing Keith. Or as aware of his intentions.

"Now it's my turn," Charlotte said, "what do you know about Martin Cord?"

"Very little, except that Clara depends on his judgment to a dangerous degree. The slaves are afraid to talk about him, even the ones whose confidence I have gained."

"I imagine they never interfere in white man's affairs. The gulf is wide and trust on their side very small. Even

Tibby—" She halted suddenly. "Oh, here come Amy and Vanessa, going riding, I would assume, from their attire."

The girls stopped for a moment, Vanessa giving all her attention to the writer in a useless attempt to inviegle him into joining them.

"I must decline with deep regret. Another time, I promise you. Research is swamping me and right now I am bent on doing some in the attic where Charlotte is going to show me the secret tunnel she explored earlier."

While Vanessa pouted, Amy looked at her sister with alarm. "You—you went all through it?"

"My stars, aren't you brave," Vanessa trilled scornfully. "You must have gotten filthy. Did you encounter any rats?"

Only in the summerhouse, Charlotte thought.

"Does it end in the Stone Garden?" Amy asked breathlessly.

"Yes, but I couldn't get the door open. Perhaps Mr. Cartright can do it."

"So you're getting atmosphere for your book?" Vanessa smiled, trailing her fingers lightly down the bared portion of his muscled arm. "Have you written any love scenes yet? Or do you need some inspiration? I could meet you in the garden after dark tonight . . ."

"Vanessa!" Amy laughed, sounding not a little shocked.

"Just for a discussion of how a woman feels," Vanessa said, continuing to stroke his arm.

Devlin pinched her rounded chin. "You are a little minx and asking to be kissed."

For an answer, Vanessa boldly threw one arm around his neck and pulled his mouth down to her rosy, open lips, where she clung quite unashamedly, although Amy gasped and Charlotte looked away uncomfortably, angry and astonished.

Devlin pulled down her arm, his face not even flushed. "Are you satisfied? It's a good thing I am an honorable man and aware of being a guest in your mother's home. But I'm warning you, Vanessa Wilson, you could easily get into trouble with some other man.''

Vanessa tossed her head, the azure plume on her hat dancing by her cheek. "I know who I am dealing with and can take care of myself.''

"That's what you think. And for your information, I don't intend to meet you after dark."

"I'll meet you in the sunlight, then." Catching Amy's arm, Vanessa pulled her along the path, laughing loudly with a new excitement in her voice.

That's what you would call a brazen hussy, Charlotte told herself, wondering how long Devlin's restraint would hold out against her beauty—and proximity. One thing for certain, it would be on his terms and not Vanessa's.

Charlotte watched Vanessa walk away and saw Amy glance back with a troubled expression that had nothing to do with her cousin. Amy suspected she had been overheard in the Stone Garden and now feared a confrontation with her sister. Or did she fear that Charlotte would tell Cord what she had heard and threaten him again?

Devlin broke into her thoughts as they walked toward the house, his tone one of wry amusement. "Do your cousin's antics shock you?"

"Sometimes, but I think she is just a silly girl. However, confidence in her charm is monumental, and since I have never known anyone that beautiful, it's hard for me to understand her.''

"A lot of men would make thoughtless love to Vanessa. I'll correct that—a lot would have sex with her, without a trace of love."

Charlotte caught back a startled breath. She had never heard the word "sex" used in such a context.

"The little ninny could indeed find herself in deep trouble," Devlin continued. "With an illegitimate child, blackmail, or physical abuse. Some men are brutes but hide it cleverly, until the woman is alone at their mercy."

Charlotte shuddered. "Dear me, Devlin, what can be done to save her?"

"Well, I'm sure Clara knows her daughter's nature and has no control over her. She also abets Vanessa's conceit by humoring and flattering her. I guess the best thing for Vanessa is marriage. Perhaps an ardent husband would cool her down, someone who would wear her out." He chuckled.

Charlotte felt faintly shocked by his uninhibited conversation. Did he enjoy the erotic images he had just painted of Vanessa cavorting in her wedding bed?

"How would you like to be her bridegroom?" Charlotte burst out impulsively, a taunting, angry smile upon her face.

"I certainly would not. A professional trollop would be much less trouble." He laughed, then sobered as they neared the house. "I've been married—unhappily, I might add. Then widowed after she ran off with another man and they both were drowned. She left me because she thought I was a dull fellow studying for the bar. She wanted excitement and she got it—for awhile."

"I'm sorry," Charlotte said. "how can a person think that just excitement will bring happiness to a marriage?"

He held the front door open, looking down at her. "There are many different kinds of excitement."

Charlotte halted. They were very close, very much alone as a quick awareness swept them. She knew his narrowed gaze assessed her up and down. He had said she was "desirable" . . .

Well, so was he.

When he didn't move, she tried to enter, her face suddenly on fire as her breast brushed firmly on his chest. At once, he caught and held her with one arm, pulling her hard and tight against his body so that she felt his heat, the beating of his heart, the aroma of clean male skin and his throat just inches from her lips.

A wonderful, sweet ecstasy engulfed her, then came weakness, a roaring in her ears, a blind desire to have him kiss her as Vanessa had kissed him.

She raised her head with heavy-lidded eyes that traveled to his harsh, flushed face, then rested hungrily on his lips. They opened while she watched him in a dream-like trance and saw his mouth move closer . . . closer. She felt his breath upon her face . . . but his mouth had barely touched her when a discreet cough sounded somewhere down the hall. They jerked apart and saw Cicero vanish out of sight.

Chapter 14

In silence, Devlin and Charlotte proceeded through the house without encountering a soul. Although she was almost blindingly aware of him, Charlotte's aroused state of a moment before had receded quickly, replaced by a deep sense of dismay. Dear heaven, she had been as eager as Vanessa for Devlin's kisses. What must he think!

She stole a swift glance at him, but his expression was unreadable. How easily he seemed to attract the opposite sex. Just today there had been the veiled woman, then Vanessa, then herself. What was it that drew them? True, he had a powerful, manly body, beautifully proportioned, but his face was more harsh than handsome, all the features large and rugged, topped by hair that never conformed to any discipline.

It must be something inward that women sensed. They must feel that he would be an exciting lover. In an agony of shame, Charlotte recalled how greedily she had waited to feel his lips on her. She realized his mouth was beautiful . . . the smooth, full lower lip promising delight and the rich masculine carving of the upper, promising imagination.

It was fortunate that they had been interrupted before she made a complete fool of herself. How could she have continued working for Devlin if she had let him kiss her . . . and he discovered how eagerly she responded? No matter how much she had desired it, she knew that now she must take care to act cool and businesslike in the future.

Devlin had not spoken a word nor looked at her since entering the house, but his brows formed a forbidding bar across his forehead, his mouth taut as steel. No doubt he regretted his brief flare of emotion and was determined not to repeat it. Well, he would find her of a similar resolve.

With this settled in her mind, Charlotte stepped briskly down the hallway at his side. They had nearly reached the attic stairs when Clara called out, coming from her room to join them.

Charlotte turned around. "Good-morning, Aunt. I explored the secret passage a little earlier and now Mr. Cartright wishes to view it, also."

"I trust you don't mind, Miss Clara." Devlin smiled suavely. "I'm hoping to gain some valuable background for my book."

"Oh, certainly. I'd like to take a peek at this passageway myself. Lead the way, Charlotte." She threw Devlin an arch glance. "Sometimes it's useful to have girls in the house who are both clumsy and curious. We might never have discovered it if they hadn't overturned the mirror. Imagine, the tunnel has been hidden for two hundred years! Well, maybe not that long." She wheezed a little, mounting the narrow attic steps. "Some of my ancestors may have found it, then sealed it up again."

When they reached the top and pushed open the door, Clara gave a gasp. "Saints above, what an awful mess! I'll have to bring a maid with me to handle this stuff when I pick out a costume.''

Charlotte pointed out the false shelves to Devlin who had no trouble pulling them away from the wall, then thrusting in his head. "I will need a candle to explore, it's black as pitch in there. By Gad, this is fascinating." His eyes were snapping with excitement.

"We left a candle here the other night." Charlotte soon found the taper with matches beside it in the pewter holder.

Devlin took it from her and pushed inside the opening. His voice was muffled. "Are you coming, ladies?"

Clara peeked gingerly into the passageway, then drew back with a shudder. "No, thank you. There's nothing to see except dirty stairs and spiderwebs. You can tell me about it later, Devlin."

"There is something else down there," Charlotte told her aunt. "Above the door leading to the summerhouse, there are carved words: 'Erasmus Mason, he carved the Stone Garden in 1652 for me, Fortescue Bainbridge.'"

"Oh, I knew that." Holding up her blue flounced skirt, Clara maneuvered her way across the cluttered floor, giving only an indifferent glance to the broken mirror. "That Erasmus was a slave."

Charlotte caught up with her in the hall below. "Did you know that Elijah Mason is his descendent?"

"No! That runaway? You'd think he'd have more pride. He's been well-treated here, but these people have no loyalty."

Charlotte bit back the words trembling on her tongue. They would only result in annoying her aunt and right now Charlotte wanted to ask a favor. She cleared her throat. "Aunt Clara, I know the South's reputation for hospitality and I have a friend in New York who would like to pay a visit to Stone Gardens. His father bought our bookstore and also owns several others in New York. Tim's young and charming and could escort one of us to the ball."

Clara turned slowly and Charlotte imagined the thoughts running through her mind. Young, charming, wealthy. An escort for Vanessa? Or possibly someone interested in Charlotte who might carry her away and relieve Clara of any responsibility.

She nodded graciously. "I see Rose instructed you in some of our traditions. Of course, your friend may visit us. I'll have Cicero send an invitation via telegraphic dispatch in the town. A room shall be aired and cleaned at once." She prattled joyfully all the way downstairs where she wrote down Tim Deane's address, then rang the bell for Cicero.

Charlotte hurried off to the guest house, well satisfied with what she had accomplished. The rest was up to Tim. She just hoped he hadn't forgotten Amy, and that when he came, Vanessa didn't try to snare him for herself—the way she did just about every man in sight. Oh, well, it was a gamble at best, and Amy certainly needed to be exposed to more young men. If Tim did not work out, perhaps she would meet somebody at the Hartley's ball.

Charlotte felt desperately anxious to have Amy distracted from the overseer who was someone so different from her former friends, besides being much more bold and exciting. Would Clara speak to him if he continued to pursue Amy? Charlotte was afraid Clara would not take the matter seriously, since flirting was a way of life down here. Especially if Amy had no complaints about Cord's actions, the matter would be brushed aside and another annoyance chalked up against the sister who was so like her "Yankee" father. Instead, the younger girl must seem like the sweet and lovely Rose who Clara had adored and sorely missed.

When Charlotte reached the studio, she worked steadily all morning and Devlin did not appear. The gong rang out for lunch at one o'clock and, at last, Charlotte laid down her pen and stretched her back. She wished she had told Tibby to bring her a tray out in the garden. It would have given her a longer interval in which to avoid Devlin. She knew that she must struggle to end this sense of strain around him, so she could continue working at his side. There must be only impersonal conversation between them. She felt certain that Devlin would make no further intimate demands. Perhaps, then, the former ease and friendliness between them could eventually be resumed.

On the other hand, he might dismiss her and try to find another assistant, a man, perhaps. Devlin might even be prepared to leave Stone Garden for another location. Then what would she do? How could she earn her keep? She hardly thought Aunt Clara would put her out in the cold. She was not that harsh, but things could become uncomfortable.

Well, she would just have to look for other ways in which to make herself useful. The garden, perhaps. Locking the door, Charlotte went slowly down the steps, gazing thoughtfully at the neglected flower beds: weeds, spent blooms that need pruning, drifts of fallen leaves, and straggling vines met her gaze. Yes, here might be an answer if she found herself dismissed by Devlin. The breath that escaped her was closer to a moan. The thought of never seeing the big, strong-willed writer who wrote so thrillingly about men and women filled Charlotte with a disturbing pain. The truth was, he excited her as much as his books. She also enjoyed his conversation, the sense of comfort near his maleness. She wanted to learn more about him. And if things were different and she were not dependent on him for employment, she would like another sample of his lovemaking, brief though it had been. There had only been the hardness of his arms, the lowering of his mouth to hers with its promise of something daring and arousing.

So engrossed was she with thoughts of Devlin, it took a minute before she realized what she was hearing. A song coming from the river, puzzling and familiar, and suddenly it stirred an image. Halting, now she heard the words:

"Go down, Moses, in Egyptland,
Tell old Pharoah, let my people go."

The song brought back a sharpened memory. After her mother died, Charlotte had attended meetings of the Abolitionists with her father. She heard the fiery William Lloyd Garrison, publisher of *The Liberator*. She heard John Quincy Adams, who nearing the end of his long colorful career, had spoken stirringly of freedom for every man, especially freedom of speech.

Then, one night, a colored woman was introduced as Harriet Tubman, the Moses of Her People. An escaped slave, she now devoted her life to helping others and had led three hundred slaves to freedom. When she came on stage, the audience rose as one and sang the forbidden song, the plea for help, the secret signal: "Go Down, Moses."

Now it was being sung beside the James in broad daylight. Charlotte hurried toward the grove of elms along the river, but checked herself when she heard the shout of men, the crack of a bull whip, and then abrupt silence.

While she hesitated, Martin Cord emerged from the band of trees. Lifting her chin, Charlotte faced him. "I just heard the song. You can't stop them. The cry for freedom is too strong."

He halted a few feet away and his lip curled back. "And if the brainless cowards get their freedom, what good will it do them? They will still be just ignorant slaves, working for any money they can get and, believe me, it won't be much. They'll have to buy their own food, housing and clothes. Is that what all the bellyaching is about? Let them see how far they get on their own. Some will starve. Some will try to crawl back to their masters, anxious to work for any wage."

"I've heard that argument," Charlotte replied. "But don't you realize that whatever becomes of them, it will be their choice. Sink or swim. Starve or return to the plantation. It's their own choice, not the will of someone else."

Martin stroked the whip he carried and eyed Charlotte insolently. "Everyone's a slave to something. Weren't you forced to beg for a job from your aunt? Don't you hate it here and wish that you were somewhere else? But you have no place to go, do you?"

Color burned in Charlotte's face, but instead of a reply, she turned the tables on him. "And you, Mr. Cord? Aren't you a slave to—to love? You desire my sister and would follow her in chains if she would have you."

"That's ridiculous," he growled and wheeled away.

"I heard you in the summerhouse," Charlotte shouted.

He turned around and blinked, jaw dropping. "Wh-what are you talking about?"

"Oh, yes. I heard you. I discovered the long-lost secret tunnel. It exists in the Stone Garden," she declared triumphantly.

He swallowed hard. "So what if you heard us? Maybe I would follow your sister willingly in chains, but so far, Amy doesn't know her own mind."

"She would never have you. You're coarse, rude, common and cruel . . . she would never love a rogue like you."

He stepped close, eyes on fire. "Don't be too sure. And don't you interfere or—"

"Or what? You'll put another snake in my bed?"

He looked blank. "What?" He gave a bark of laughter. "Who did that?"

"A stupid, senseless man-child consumed by futile hate."

Cord didn't answer, but his hard-bitten face purpled, his mouth worked soundlessly.

He would like to strike me, Charlotte thought, with a sudden stab of fear. He would like to turn that whip on me until he had me dead. I am a threat to everything he wants.

Unfortunately, when Charlotte spoke, her voice was husky. "You better watch your step. I may tell Aunt Clara, and she will not allow Amy to be insulted by the help."

It seemed as though her words struck him with a sudden wariness and he shouted after her as she spun away, "That won't be necessary!"

Breathing a little easier, Charlotte slowed her flight into a fast walk to the house. Her heart and lungs still labored with the angry fear engendered by her emotional encounter with Cord. How she hated the man! What could she do?

Just now, he had suddenly seemed uneasy when she threatened to inform Clara. He knew how fond she had become of the child who looked like Rose. Yes, for awhile he might tread softly as he worked out some new scheme. He probably would continue to keep Amy aware of him and his desires, but his seduction was slow and clever and patience immeasurable.

Amy would not be aware of what was happening until the tiger pounced.

The only hope Charlotte entertained was that, while the villain took his time, Amy would be introduced to other men. Especially Tim Deane, who was already smitten with her—if Charlotte was any judge.

She broached the subject of his arrival at the mid-day meal. Clara said the invitation had been sent by Cicero and a reply would be delivered to the house. Amy brightened at the information. Perhaps she, too, wanted a barrier against Cord's insistance. She must find it hard to cope with him.

His demanding kisses, his stalking, his arrogant strength and passion—all could be most frightening to a young girl like Amy. Charlotte hoped that Tim would soon become a buffer.

Vanessa, of course, was intrigued by a new man on the scene and she bombarded Charlotte with questions. "What does he look like?"

"Tall, slender, sandy-hair. Nice manners and appearance." Charlotte could hardly call Tim handsome, but his boyish enthusiasm and good health made him attractive and she tried to convey that to her cousin and aunt.

Amy also talked about him to Vanessa. Probably her own anticipation of Tim's visit was fueled by Vanessa's interest.

Devlin had not joined them at the table, and at last, Charlotte excused herself to return to duties in the studio.

When she hurried to her room to freshen face and hair. However, the first thing to meet her eye was a square paper, folded and sealed with her name printed on the front.

Another warning? Instructions from Devlin? With quickened interest, she slid her nail beneath the glob of red sealing wax and read the brief message:

My Dear Mam'selle,
Will you do me the great favor of a meeting tonight directly after curfew in the Stone Garden? It is a matter of the greatest urgency.
A bientot.

The note had not been signed. There was no need. Only "The Frenchman" could have written it.

And, of course, she would comply.

Chapter 15

In a fever of impatience, Charlotte waited for the day to end. Devlin did not appear, but she had plenty of work to occupy her time as she copied his copious notes. Sometimes she had to recopy them several times for the exactness he required. When he went over her work, he often made new revisions which she then had to rewrite the next day.

She found this book as gripping as the one she had read in New York. Her task in her eye, hardly qualified as work. Every day she eagerly read the escalating excitement as unrest rose among the slaves and passion flowered between his hero and heroine.

She had a few qualms sometimes about the success of a black and white romance in any Southern state. Liaisons like that were forbidden and marriages strictly against the law. Would there be shock and outrage when his book came out? Or more titilation than ever in the unusual duo? The handsome captain and the beautiful Aurelia were wonderful characters with brave, true hearts and strong intelligence and empathy, but their storm-tossed love found no happy ending until they sailed off to a distant land.

In spite of its controversial nature, Charlotte hoped that Devlin's readers would devour his new book, even if it might be hidden underneath the counter in a Southern shop. Since publishers didn't put pictures on the covers, people wouldn't know about the forbidden aspect of the lovers until they were deep into the book. And then, if Charlotte was any judge, they would not be able to put it down. She thought the new novel was even better than the other one she'd read. *From Dreams to Flames* also carried a strong message against prejudice and bigotry.

It was too bad other authors didn't turn their talents toward such injustices. Charlotte's father had told her about Harriet Beecher Stowe, daughter and sister of famous reformers and educators, who was working on a novel about slavery. However, he believed her title—"Uncle Tom's Cabin"—would never sell the book.

People needed to be told about the vast sea of slaves floundering on their shores. They should be made aware of the slaves's humanity and know that they felt love, hate, joy, pain and fear, just like any white person. Understanding and a desire to help were needed everywhere to end this festering disease that choked the South. Charlotte had heard that the transition period from slavery to freedom would be painful for everybody, both black and white. But she thought that, in the end, a society would emerge where all could work together.

As she had so much on her mind, it became an effort to concentrate on the work at hand. But, at last, her task for the day was finished. Deep purple shadows stretched beneath the elms as she made her way across the garden.

The sun had nearly disappeared and only a faint orange glow lit the sky.

As the slaves came home, occasionally a row boss shouted and heavy feet crunched on the paths, sounding weary with dispair. Charlotte wondered who had dared to sing the forbidden song this afternoon? Another slave grown desperate to escape? Would the Frenchman require her help in relation to this matter? Her impatience grew with every passing minute.

The family was gathered in the parlor when she entered the house and called her to join them in a glass of sherry. She agreed, hoping no one would notice her distraction. Fortunately, they had other matters to discuss—gowns for the Hartley's ball, guesses about who would attend . . . what food would be served . . . the kind of music played . . .

"I know they will hire an orchestra," Vanessa said importantly, "as well as extra servants. Some people will stay overnight if they come a right long distance and they may bring their own attendants, too. Oh, Roselands will be in an uproar, let me tell you. Amy, perhaps we should ride over tomorrow and see what is going on."

"Oh, yes, that is a good idea. They might need our help to work on something."

"Help? Work?" Vanessa yelped. "Believe me, I'm not about to join the nigras! That's their job. I just want to see the twins, discuss their costumes, and observe the decorating in the house and ballroom. I vow it will look stunning. And the refreshments will be wonderful. Mama, do you recall the Christmas gala we enjoyed there last year?"

Under cover of the ensuing babble, Charlotte bent to Amy's ear. "If you have finished, come into the garden for a minute."

Amy threw her an unhappy glance but rose immediately. Outside, darkness drew a soft blanket across the land. Stars began to prick the sky and sleepy birds flew chirping to their nests. The only light came from the downstairs windows as the sisters faced each other.

"What is wrong, Charlotte?" Amy asked. "I noticed your distraction today in the parlor. Is it . . . me?"

Charlotte sighed. "You're part of it, little one. I hope Tim Deane comes soon and shows you how a gentleman should treat a lady."

Amy's eyes dropped to the leaf-strewn bricks. "You refer to Martin Cord, I suppose."

"He's been bothering you, hasn't he?"

"No, Charlotte, I'm not bothered."

"Don't tell me you enjoy his liberties?" Charlotte demanded sharply, halting on the path.

"I will be more careful around him in the future."

"That's no answer."

Amy groaned. "Charlotte, dear, the attention of men is all so new to me. All I've known are boys. Can't you understand my curiosity?"

Charlotte caught Amy's shoulders covered in soft yellow dimity which made her look as young and tender as a daffodil. "Your curiosity is understandable, but also dangerous. Some of it must wait for marriage."

Amy moved away with an impatient gesture. "And then sometimes the wife is terrified and appalled at what is happening to her body."

Charlotte felt almost helpless, but she tried to marshall her wits. "Before marriage, you should know that you love and trust the man who is going to make you his. As for the act of copulation—" She paused, swallowing hard. "I—I've told you the basic facts."

"You did your best, dear." Amy smiled. "But the other things before the—the final act—I-I think they must be rather pleasant." Amy shot her a little upward glance.

"Of course. They can be, if you like the man sufficiently and know he is honorable and won't take advantage of you." Unable to halt the color that swept into her cheeks, Charlotte wondered miserably how far she would have let Devlin pursue his intimate attentions. She only knew that he had thrilled her more any other experience in her life. Then she recalled the Frenchman. Dear heaven, she had kissed him, too! Was she on the borderline of immorality?

Charlotte had to clear her throat as they walked on and she felt grateful for the concealing dusk. "Amy, dear, it's just that you are so young. You might start with hugs and kisses and end up being violated. Your mind and reason can be completely swept away by an unconscionable rogue, until you don't know what is happening."

"Have you ever met a man like that?"

"No, thank goodness. I know enough to stop a man if he becomes too familiar. I think Martin Cord is someone to be feared. So is Keith Duncan."

"Keith?" Amy gave a disbelieving laugh. "Why, he is just a boy."

"I didn't like his manner."

They were silent for a few moments, until Amy said in a low tone, "Mr. Cord met me in the Stone Garden. But you know that, don't you?"

"Yes. I know that he kissed you and then you had enough sense to run away. You must avoid him. I'm afraid he won't stop pursuing you. There will be other attempts. There's no telling what he might do."

"Well, if he gets too persistant, I shall tell Aunt Clara," Amy answered airily, not sounding one bit worried. She bent to pick a deep red rose. "Oh, what divine fragrance. Take this rose and put it in your lace collar."

Charlotte sighed and tucked the blossom in the opening of her dress. Nothing had been resolved, and Amy still seemed intrigued by the overseer. Perhaps Tim Deane would prove a most welcome distraction.

"We must go in," Charlotte said. "It's nearly dark. Hark,

there's curfew—three long chimes. I'd forgotten it came so soon."

"Now all the poor slaves must stay within their compound," Amy said. "Aren't you glad our life is different?"

"I am grateful every day. Coming South has given me a new perspective. None of the speeches or books can give the picture that you get from being right here in a slave state."

Before Amy could reply, Vanessa emerged from the veranda and called imperiously. "Where are you, Amy?"

"Out here in the garden with Charlotte."

"Well, come in now and play a few hands of piquet with me. I'm bored."

"Yes, mistress," Amy whispered under her breath. Then she said aloud, "Are you coming, Charlotte?"

"In a few minutes. I want to see if Devlin has come back to the studio to check my work. I have some questions," she added vaguely.

But when Amy disappeared indoors, Charlotte sped to the Stone Garden. She had a rendezvous to keep.

Chapter 16

Moonlight flickered in a darting pattern, turning the eerie stone objects into a nightmarish landscape, cold and hard. Apprehensively, Charlotte strained her eyes in every direction but saw no one. The Frenchman had evidently not yet arrived, so she sank down on a bench to wait.

This was not a pleasant place to linger, with darkness fallen and the moon so fitful. What had Devlin called the Stone Garden? Something about the death of dreams? He had not been in the guest house, and she wondered where he went for so many hours. Didn't an author gather all his research first and then sit down and write nonstop? She had met a few novelists in her father's shop but had always felt too awed for casual questioning.

Devlin also carried this same aura of importance, as though he would not take kindly to any probing in his affairs. Although he had vouchsafed a few words about his wife, she felt his face would close up tight, and he simply wouldn't answer if he didn't wish to. True, occasionally he had come close, touching her, murmuring in a manner she could only consider seductive. But to what end? Was he garnering reactions for his novels? That idea did not sit well and Charlotte frowned, although forced to admit that she found him attractive and had enjoyed the hands that had held her, the words growled in her ear. *"Don't you know that you are desirable?"* The time he'd pressed her against his body . . .

But it was foolish to sit here mooning. She sprang up and started toward the summerhouse. If the Frenchman did not come soon she would leave. However, at the first crunch of her steps upon the gravel, a whisper stopped her in her tracks. "That's far enough, mam'selle. Do not approach closer."

Charlotte strained her eyes, but he was only a darker outline in the night-shrouded summerhouse.

"You wished to see me?" she croaked and nervously cleared her throat. "What do you want?"

"A most great favor."

"What is it?"

"A precious cargo needs transporting tonight. Can you drive a cart?"

"Y-yes." Her heart was beating with excitement, and she found it impossible to speak calmly, even though his tones were slow and measured, probably to allay her fears, although he still used the concealing huskiness.

"I cannot go myself. Tonight, the good doctor needs my help. He has been betrayed."

"How terrible! What do you want me to do?"

"Drive the cart and its cargo along the River Road. It will appear beside the pier with someone who will give you instructions. *Comprenes?*"

"Not exactly, but if it is important—"

"Mais oui! And you, *cher mam'selle,* are my only hope. You must be there at midnight and sing, 'Go Down, Moses.' Do you know it?"

"Partially," Charlotte quavered, wondering how much danger was involved? Well, she had risked her safety for the cause once before. "How long will this take?"

"You should be back within the hour. The danger, it is small, but if you hesitate, I understand."

"What can you do if I refuse?"

There ensued deep silence, then he whispered, "Perhaps *le bon Dieu* will show a way."

How could she ignore the agony in his voice? "I will go, but would you do something for me? Tell me who you are. Show your face."

"Alas, anything but that," he growled.

"You do not completely trust me?"

He gave no answer.

"Even though I helped you once before? And let you kiss me?" she added.

"It is for your own sake. As for that kiss, I will return that so delicious favor."

The dark shape emerged from the summerhouse and demanded, "Shut your eyes, mam'selle."

Charlotte did as she was told, trembling in sudden thrilling expectation. The next thing she knew, she felt him tie a cloth tightly around her head, blindfolding her. His hands fell on her shoulders and drew her against his body where his long curls brushed her cheek. Beneath a soft shirt, his heart beat fast.

One hand moved suggestively down her body, pressing her hips closer to his own. She caught her breath, almost sobbing, and trembled again when he removed the rose and slid his hand inside her neckline to enclose the softness of her breast beneath his questing fingers.

She made no move to stop him, although the touch was almost more than she could bear. Her head fell back, hungry for his caress. He growled her name, not "mam'-selle" but "Charlotte." Back and forth his lips teased hers while she whimpered, blind and weak, only knowing one thing—his touch was flame and esctasy.

He ground his mouth against her lips, then pushed them open to admit his tongue. *Devlin, her mind cried. Yes, yes!* How long the madness lasted, she never knew, but through it all her mind sang Devlin's name and she never wondered why: at least, not then.

Soon she heard the words, husky, fierce. "You turn my limbs to fire. Quickly, let us seek my carriage—"

Like a cold wind sweeping her, Charlotte gasped and pushed against this wild, maurading creature with all her strength. "Never!" No matter that she had encouraged him . . .

"So?" The word was a silky rasp, but he dropped his arms and breathing hard, they both stood for a long pulsating moment, while Charlotte struggled to untie the blindfold. She heard the gravel crunch and his voice came from a little farther off. "Do not forget, mam'selle. The River Road at midnight." The passion for her had been conquered.

She knew that he had gone, and when she tore the cloth masking her vision, the emptiness confirmed it. Shaking in every limb, she stumbled to a bench and sank down, covering her face, trying to make sense of what had happened. What had she done? Why had she let this stranger invade her body as no one had ever done before? Where was her shock, her guilt, her shame?

She felt none of these, things, only bewilderment. She didn't love the Frenchman . . . why, then, had she felt such estatic pleasure in his lovemaking? She had wanted more, wanted him to never stop. It was only when he tried to take her to his carriage that she regained her senses and shoved him away, well aware of what his further advances would entail. The loss of her virginity had been imminent, and the thought appalled her. Thank God, they had regained control in time.

Wonderingly, she touched her lips with shaking fingers, then drew up the neckline of her disordered dress. It seemed as if she could still feel that passionate masculine invasion. His tongue on hers—dear God! Had she actually permitted that hot stroking—even enjoyed the astonishing intimacy? And the touch of his hand rubbing in the opening of her gown until her breast surged greedily against his palm? No man had ever dared approach these actions! Not by word or touch would she have countenanced such behavior. *Why now?*

Then she remembered something else. Devlin's name had been in her mind, his vision before her all the time. It had seemed to be Devlin's lips, his hands, his body pressed to hers. The Frenchman had been but a puppet, a fantasy for her. Imagination had done all the rest.

Charlotte opened her eyes wide and caught her breath. *Was she in love with Devlin? Did she actually desire him?* No, no, that must not be.

She started walking toward the house, her agitated thoughts awhirl. If Devlin should ever guess her feelings— even though it was a temporary insanity on her part—it would mean the end of her employment. She could just imagine the amazement on his rugged face. Then coolness, perhaps even disgust. Women came so easily into his orbit. First Vanessa, then the veiled woman and now Charlotte, the sober, strong-minded, no-nonsense woman. Her cheeks burned and she moaned aloud.

One thing certain: no one must ever guess how she had felt tonight. No one must know. From now on, she would be fiercely staid, aloof, all business around Devlin.

If anyone saw her now, perhaps they might become suspicious. Vanessa was always curious. As well as jealous. Charlotte smoothed back her hair, drew several breaths

and forced her footsteps to be slow even though she longed
to run once she gained the house.

Thankfully, she met no one and slipped unseen into
her room to wash and brush her hair. She stared into the
mirror anxiously. She didn't think anyone could tell what
she had recently been doing, even though her lips looked
red and fuller and breath still moved her bosom up and
down in agitation, pressing against the thin lawn of her
dress. The lace collar needed pressing, but there was no
time for that.

She noticed then that the rose Amy had given her to
wear, was no longer there. It had been removed by a
demanding lover.

Charlotte smiled a little. Undoubtedly, the Frenchman
was attractive and most virile, a true hero. But he wasn't
Devlin. And that's what she had wanted him to be.

Chapter 17

Dinner was served almost as soon as Charlotte entered the dining room, and no one gave her more than a passing glance and greeting. Chilled salmon, roast duck, asparagus in hollandaise, veal in cream, and brandied peaches made the rounds while all the talk centered on the imminent arrival of Tim Deane. Yes, he had replied with great delight and many thanks via electric telegraph, Clara informed Charlotte.

"Now there's still time before the Hartley's ball to have an outing at the caves," Vanessa said excitedly before Charlotte could reply to Clara. "Mama, what do you say? Timmie arrives day after tomorrow, so we can plan it—"

"Shouldn't you give him a chance to catch his breath?" Amy laughed.

"Well, the next day, then." Vanessa swallowed mashed potatoes with cream gravy and patted her rosy lips. "Let's decide what to eat on the picnic."

"After dinner, child," Clara smiled. "Pray, don't gobble so fast. There's lots of time."

"No, there isn't," Vanessa twitched impatiently. "We have to choose the clothes to wear, fix up Timmie's room . . . I'll put in some flowers, but you pick them, Amy. I might prick my fingers and I'm sure Timmie kisses ladies's hands like a true gentleman even if he is a Northerner—"

"Why do you call him 'Timmie'?" Charlotte exclaimed. "One would think you had known him longer than Amy or I."

"Well, I do feel like we might be kindred souls. Amy's told me all about him." Vanessa waved an airy spoon over her chantilly cream. "I know that he dresses nice, drives a right smart gig, goes to parties, concerts, dances—Oh, yes, we'll be most congenial, I am positive, in spite of everything."

Amy exchanged a speaking glance with Charlotte, then she said wryly, "Well, Vanessa, you might be right. After all, He's young, male, and unattached."

"And he likes *Amy,*" Charlotte snapped. "He's *our* friend." *Naturally,* no real closeness existed between Tim and Charlotte, but he had taken Amy to the park and escorted her to socials, gone on drives. . . . asked her to write . . .

"Of course, that's why he is coming, but I say, in all truth—wait 'till he sees me." She beamed around the table, noting Charlotte's frown, Amy's dismay, and her mother's tolerant trill of laughter.

"Goodness, child, but you do beat all! Is there no stopping you where men are concerned?" Clara chuckled richly.

"Why must you want so many?" Amy asked, pushing back her strawberry cream. "Tim . . . Keith . . . Devlin?"

"My stars, I was only joshing. But I guess I am an awful flirt." Vanessa tittered. "It's just the way I am. Men can't stay away from me."

Amy and Charlotte stared at her gloomily, knowing there probably was truth in the conceited observance. Talk returned to the coming excursion and, at last, Charlotte broke into Vanessa's babbling and demanded, "What are these caves you want to visit? It all sounds rather cold and dark to me. How can you picnic in a cave?"

"That's not what we'll do." Vanessa scraped her dessert dish and licked the spoon. "We'll go to an island in the river and picnic on the shore. After that, we'll visit the caves where Nat Turner hid and do some exploring. So exciting!" She pushed back her chair. "Come into the study, Amy, where there's ink and paper. You can make lists of the things to do."

She sailed out of the door in a swirl of creamy ruffles, but Charlotte caught Amy's hand and held her back. "Tim may not give a fig for Vanessa when he meets her."

"I never thought she'd set her sights on him," Amy whispered.

"Pshaw, any man with brains would find her silly and shallow." They both headed for the hallway, speaking softly.

"Yet Devlin likes her. They went riding in the dogcart all afternoon. And Keith's attracted to her. Why not Tim? *'Timmie!'*" Amy ground her pretty little teeth. "I can just see what will happen—"

"Men might be momentarily attracted to Vanessa, since she is lovely and so obviously eager for their attention. But, do you know what Devlin told me?"

Amy sighed. "What?"

"He thinks Vanessa is silly and conceited and her flirting might get her into deep water. He said he certainly would not care to marry her."

"Did he really?" Amy looked amused. "I think you and Devlin would make a good match. You both have brains and looks."

"My little advocate." Charlotte kissed her sister's cheek as they continued down the hall. For a minute, a hopeful surge swept Charlotte. Could there be a chance—ah, no. Ridiculous! Devlin was a mature, intelligent man of the world, educated in the law, son of a judge and finally a successful writer who had both fame and fortune. And if that wasn't enough, he was devastatingly attractive—not exactly handsome, just a strong, square face with heavy-lidded eyes that seemed to see right through you. And he had a wide mouth, controlled and firm, but capable of softening with amusement, admiration or compassion.

Which of those expressions had been directed toward her? Charlotte tried to remember. When he tucked a rose into her hair? Or comforted her after the branding?

"Charlotte, wake up!" Laughing, Amy shook her arm. "I've asked you twice how your work is coming."

"Oh—oh—fine. I'm just a little tired tonight."

"Is this new book as good as Devlin's other one that you read in New York?"

"I think it's better, but it may not sell as well. There's an inter-racial romance and Southern book sellers might be loathe to stock it for that reason."

"That would be too bad. He's such a fine writer."

"Oh, I see! You've read the book Vanessa loaned you." Charlotte sent Amy a sidelong glance. "Did the love scenes shock you?"

"No, but they were exciting."

"I certainly hope they didn't make you too curious about experiencing such . . . excitement for yourself. I really wish you wouldn't read things like that just yet."

"Oh, Charlotte, all the girls my age read adult romances. Do you want me to grow up ignorant?"

Helplessly, Charlotte shook her head. "Of course, not, dear. I know I can't keep you my little baby sister forever. It's just that . . . sometimes I worry . . ."

"Trust me, Charlotte. You have trained me well, and have given me the value of your good sense, so I am not a silly goose. There is just one thing we can't avoid—I will grow up." She gave her sister a laughing squeeze. "Now I best join Vanessa in her latest project: entertaining *Timmie!*"

"Good-night. I think I'll have an early bed." Charlotte tried to yawn convincingly.

They parted at the foot of the staircase, Amy going toward the study while Charlotte climbed up to her room. She really didn't fear that Devlin's book would lead her sister into any danger. Amy did show good sense most times. Look how she was handling Vanessa's coming encroachment on her swain. Was it because he wasn't that important? On the other hand, Tim might seem more important when Vanessa tried to capture him. Time would tell.

A little wearily, Charlotte entered her bedchamber and sank down in an armchair by the window. The scene outside looked dark and still. No singing from the slave quarters, not even any faint sounds of any laughter. What hopelessness their lives contained, worse than in her mother's day since Clara had now hired tough row bosses and was selling off some of her people, probably with no regard for splitting up families.

She wondered what her mission tonight entailed? Of course, "cargo" meant slaves. A wagon with hidden runaways. How many? From where? Was anyone on their trail yet? The Frenchman had said the danger to her wasn't great, but Charlotte felt uneasy because she would be on her own tonight. The Frenchman would not be at her side, and that was rather frightening. It must be imperative that the "cargo" be moved tonight.

Her mind turned to the doctor who had tried to help the injured boy the other time she had gone off in the night. How awful it was that he had been betrayed! Might he in turn name some of the other "conductors" on the Freedom Trail in order to get leniency? Probably not. The Frenchman trusted him so much that he was going to his aid, placing this emergency above all others.

Yes, Charlotte thought with a stiffening of her resolve. I can do no less than these brave people who daily risk their lives. Her father had instilled his own deep convictions in her, as had all the fiery speeches of the Abolitionists. And what a thrill she had in hearing Harriet Tubman who had conducted three hundred of her people to safety.

She wondered, as she had before, who this mysterious Frenchman really was? She flushed a little. The only thing she knew for certain was how skillfully he had kissed and touched her. Indeed, he was no novice at that titilating game . . .

The chiming of the gilt clock on the mantel startled her. Eleven! The time was fleeting. Then another thought struck her. Tibby usually came up with hot water and attendance. She must not find the room deserted. Undressing, she pulled on a nightgown and rang the bell.

The little maid appeared in a few moments carrying a heavy can of water which she had now learned to tip dexterously into the china basin. "Do you wish anything else, Miss Charlotte?" she asked, gathering up the discarded clothes.

"Thank you, nothing more tonight. I'm tired and don't wish to be disturbed. I'll see you in the morning."

"Sleep well, Miss Charlotte." Tibby smiled and glided from the room.

After waiting to be sure the maid would not return, Charlotte began her preparations. She selected a dark dress and cloak, sturdy shoes, and wound a shawl around her hair. In the bed she thrust a pile of clothes beneath the quilt, arranging it in the shape of a person. She even placed a night cap on a rolled up wad of dark stockings, then drew the covers high and tight. The door had no key, so she couldn't be certain that someone might not look in. Even Amy must not know about tonight's mission.

At twelve, the house was silent as a grave when Charlotte slipped out of her room and crept down the hall. She remembered how the door had squeeked downstairs the other time she had gone to meet the Frenchman, so with infinite care she eased it open.

Just then, a footfall creaked the boards in the hall behind her and she spun around, catching back a startled cry.

"You be comin' or going, Miss Charlotte?" Cicero whispered. "I just a-checkin' on the doors."

"Oh, Cicero, I—I have to go out for a little while."

He gave a stately nod. "You wish the door left dis-locked like I did before?"

"You—what?" Of course! Now she remembered that after being with the Frenchman and the injured boy she had had no trouble reentering the house. And never wondered why.

He smiled. "I sees you then, Miss Charlotte, but don' worry, I do anything to help Miss Rose's little girl."

"Thank you, Cicero. I can't explain—"

"No need. But, child, be careful."

"I—I'll try." Charlotte's smile wavered. What did Cicero think? Probably that she was going out for a rendezvous with—who else?—Devlin. After all, he had seen them embracing only the other day. Charlotte's breath fluttered a little at the memory. But this was certainly not the time to dwell on romantic interludes.

Quickly, she slipped outside and sped across the garden. Now that the time had come, her heart pounded heavily. If anyone caught her helping an escaped slave, she could be imprisoned. Aunt Clara's wrath would know no bounds, especially if it were one of her own people. A fine return for her hospitality, she might say, bringing shame to the whole family. Amy would be upset. Vanessa would have some stinging words. And Devlin? There would be nothing he could say or do to help.

But perhaps her worries were for nothing. The Frenchman had said the danger wasn't great. Charlotte grew a little calmer as she neared her destination. She must tell herself how fine it was to help some suffering members of humanity. Through her efforts, their life might become free and happy. Yes . . . she would do her best. Her chin went higher, her back stiffened. Now the river lay before her, rippling in a fitful moonlight, alternating between bright and dark. And at the pier, a wagon stood apparently as deserted as the landscape. Pausing in the grove beside the road, Charlotte sang, albeit a little huskily:

"Go down, Moses, into Egyptland."

No answer.

She sang again, her voice gathering strength:

"Tell old Pharoah, let my people go."

Something stirred beneath the cart's sacks and a man emerged. Climbing out, he repeated the song in low bass tones.

Charlotte stepped forward to meet him. "I have come to drive you to your destination. The Frenchman sent me." She did not give her name.

"Blessed be the Frenchman and you, too, mistress." He made a low bow from the waist. He was a large young Negro, with a face carved out of stone. Only his voice was soft. "Here's my pass, name's Jed. You are Mrs. White goin' to sell produce to the ships."

"You are the only one escaping?" Charlotte whispered.

"My wife and babe hide beneath a false floor in the wagon."

"Dear heaven, can they breathe?"

"Yes'm. We best go now. Pattyrollers due when moon gits high."

"Yes, let's go." Charlotte glanced up and down the long dark road. "You have seen no one?" She moved closer to the wagon.

"No 'm. Just one more thing. Ah has to drive."

Charlotte saw then that both his hands were bandaged and something that looked like blood seeped through in places. "No, indeed, you're injured—"

"Nothing, 'taint nothing. 'Twould not look right for a mistress to drive her slave."

He motioned her into the passenger side and she climbed up reluctantly. Evidently the Frenchman had been worried about Jed's injury, but he had not reckoned with his stubborness.

Charlotte put Jed's pass in her pocket and grasped the handrail as the wagon started rolling swiftly down the road. "How did you hurt your hands?"

"You best not know, mistress."

Another punishment, no doubt. "Can you tell me why you and your family are running away? Are you all from a nearby plantation?"

"We lives in Louisiana, married, with a year-old babe when Old Marse die. His kin all scattered. Only one son, Francois, come from France to take Dark Oaks. Trouble was—" he growled deep in his throat. "—he want My Luella, too."

For a moment, he couldn't continue, head sunk on his chest. "Luella married, has a child, meant nothin' to him. She so beautiful. Raised with Old Marse' girls. Can read, write, speak French . . . Francois don't recognize the marriage."

A Creole plantation, Charlotte thought, remembering how the Spanish-French had settled Louisiana and built fabulous plantations growing sugarcane. "What happened next, Jed?"

"Francois so cruel. Ah try to stop him—" Jed clenched his bandaged hands and winced. "He bring his own blacks to Dark Oaks, all jus' as cruel. Ah knew we has to run and at last got word to Moses."

"Moses?"

"Harriet Tubman who got us on Freedom Trail this far. Den Frenchman meet us, praise the Lord! Now we jus' has to make a ship at dawn." He snapped the reins and bent over the dashboard, teeth drawn back, fury and determination in his face. "Luella never can go back. We best pray now, mistress."

Yes, pray hard, Charlotte thought, feeling Jed's painful desperation and her own fright mounting. A whole family depended on her tonight, much more than she expected. She must strive to be calm—clever—strong—

Only a short time later, they both heard it. The pounding hoofs of iron-shod animals. The trumpeting call: "Halt at once! Halt or we will shoot."

"Go faster, Jed!" Charlotte screamed.

"Can't." He drew back on the reins and the wagon came to a creaking, rattling stop.

Chapter 18

Charlotte realized quite soon that a horse-drawn cart with four people could never outrun the thundering patrol of two men on huge, swift horses.

Jed immediately slumped down, looking smaller, defeated, dull of eye and brain, lower lip protruding. Charlotte marshaled all her wits. She, too, must don a disguise and should have thought of this before, but being stopped had been such a remote possibility in her mind. Maybe it was not too late.

Reaching swiftly to the floorboards, she found earth from their shoes, rubbed it hard into nails and hands, streaked a little on her cheek. Then she, too, cowered, mouth agape, eyes wide with exaggerated fear.

In a few minutes, two men on horseback drew abreast. Their mounts snorted, pawing, while the riders jerked hard on the reins. They both wore dark, peaked caps, a kind of similar jacket crossed by pistol holsters, a saber slung upon their saddles.

"Show us your pass, black man," one patrolman barked.

A thin cruel face peered at them closely. "And you, ma'am, state your business."

"Yes sir, yes sir," Charlotte croaked. "I'm Beaulah White goin' to sell vegetables to the ships. This here's my slave, Jed, and here be his pass." Fumbling, she withdrew the paper from her pocket, presenting it with a shaking hand, then ducking her head down on her chest, and hunching her shoulders.

"Just you two? The patrol received word of three runaways."

Another betrayal!

"No sir, no sir," Charlotte whined. "jus' us two. I'm a lone farm woman. Ain't got no more nigras. Only Jed here. And he ain't hardly worth his grub."

The other patrolman, older, tougher-looking, broke in. "I say we check this wagon." He wheeled his horse and whipped out his saber. Riding close to the wagon, he plunged his weapon downward. Once, twice, grunting with a kind of pleasure. He then rode to the other side, his partner following.

"Jed!" Charlotte breathed in agony, expecting to hear screams and see rivers of blood pouring on the ground.

"Sh—sh don' worry," Jed whispered.

The saber stabbed all through the vegetables while a strong aroma of onions rose into the air.

"My produce," Charlotte whimpered aloud. " 'Tis ruint!"

"Nothing here. Go on, old woman, move along."

"Just poor white trash," the other grunted with a laugh.

"And poorer black trash," his partner replied with a sneer as he tossed the pass back on the wagon floor. They wheeled their mounts and rode back the way they had come..to wait for other prey.

Jed snapped the reins and prayers of thanks tumbled from his shaking lips.

Afraid to speak until the road lay dark and empty once again, Charlotte finally asked, "What happened, Jed? Your wife and child? Where were they?"

" 'Neath a false bottom. Miz Tubman make this scheme and it work fine up to now."

"But someone may betray it for money, won't they? Just like someone gave notice you and your family were in the vicinity."

"Yes'm. That's the awful way of it." Suddenly, he raised his voice and called over his shoulder, "Luella, be you and little Jim all right? The patrol went on."

A faint reply issued from the wagon. "We fine, Jed."

"Praise the Lord," the big man muttered. "Now we must go mighty fast."

"How far is it to the ship, Jed?"

"Not too far, mistress." But Jed's voice sounded doubtful.

Charlotte licked the dryness from her lips. Evidently, the Frenchman had not expected Jed's whereabouts to be known. Someone, however, had found out and the search was on. Three slaves would be a tidy catch. Perhaps the new master had offered a large cash reward. He must be furious that Luella had escaped with her husband. Charlotte shuddered to think what revenge he would exact on the whole family if they were caught. He might secretly kill Jed and the infant, then imprison Luella, where no one but himself could ever find her. Charlotte's imagination ran through scenes of constant degradation and cruelty until the dry husk of the poor girl was discarded.

Then in the middle of her troubled thoughts, Charlotte heard a terrifying sound, high, hungry keening. At once, she knew. It didn't need Jed's gasp, "Bloodhounds!" to confirm it.

Their eyes met in mutual frozen horror.

"Is it the same patrol?" Charlotte stuttered.

"No'm. They comin' from 'cross the woods. Somebody else."

"Can—can we outrun those dogs?"

"Nothin' on legs can do that once they got our scent. And they bayin' like they has."

"Let's go into the river—"

"Can't. Too deep. They see us if we try to swim."

To Charlotte's dismay, he drew back on the reins and checked the laboring horse's flight. "Jed! Why are you stopping?"

"We gotta go on foot through trees and disguise our scent. Mistress, can you get home all right?" He alighted from the wagon and Charlotte jumped down after him, confused and frightened by this new disaster. How on earth could she help them now?

Tossing out the sacks of onions, potatoes, and corn, Jed tore at the planks. In a minute, he had his hysterically sobbing wife tottering in his arms. The babe lay in a basket unnaturally still.

"Luella, love, don' cry." Jed's voice shook. "We not licked yet."

"But—but I hear ze hounds—oh, Jed, they straight from hell, coming for us!"

"No, no, we'll fool 'em. We gotta run—"

"Can't—can't—Francois hurt me so last time. Oh, Jed, you promise I would die before you let him get me again. *Le bon Dieu* will forgive you if you do zis—" Her eyes rolled wildly toward Charlotte, but didn't seem to register her presence.

"No, not yet, honey-girl," Jed groaned." We gonna run some more. This here lady is a helper." He gently removed the clinging arms and Charlotte stepped forward.

"Just call me Miz White." Charlotte wrapped the girl's shawl tighter, noting dark bruises and dried blood on her arms and throat. Luella in spite of her almost witless terror was indeed a beauty, delicate of features with long-lashed liquid eyes and light tan skin. She looked helplessly at Charlotte, trying to form words. "My—my little Jim—"

Charlotte fetched the child and basket. "He's very quiet."

"I gave him herbs to sleep," Luella whispered. "I had to give it."

"Of course. A good idea."

Jed, meanwhile, had unhitched the horse and with a slap sent the animal back the way they had come. Then giving a mighty heave, he rolled the cart down the incline where it sank into the river. At Charlotte's cry, he turned to her. "Mistress, we has to get those dogs off our scent. We gonna smell of onions and then we gonna run."

"Mon Dieu, I cannot! Leave me—" With a gentle moan, Luella dropped upon the dusty road and didn't move.

"Oh, my God!" Jed cried, leaping forward.

Charlotte pushed him aside and felt the girl's limp wrist. "She's just fainted. Quick! Rub her with the juiciest onions, especially on her shoes. You, too. Then carry her."

Without a word, he obeyed instantly.

Charlotte rubbed the baby basket and the soles of her own shoes, hands, arms, face.

Jed hoisted his unconscious wife across his shoulder then reached out for the basket.

"I'll take the child," Charlotte said briskly, taking the basket and babe into her arms and finding them quite heavy. Which didn't deter her for a minute.

"But, mistress—" Jed protested. "you done enough for us already—"

Charlotte shook her head. "I am going to see you safely on that ship. You are still my responsibility. Now, let's make haste. Fast as we can go."

"Don' like to see you in more danger, mistress," Jed

gasped, as they all plunged into the dark forest. "Perhaps jus' a little way 'till Luella come to."

"We'll see," Charlotte answered, forestalling arguments. "Now no more talking, Jed. Voices carry in the night."

Darkness enveloped them like a tomb. A blessing in one way, hardship in another. They stumbled over roots. Caught their feet in holes. Branches whipped across their faces. Soon breathing became a labored torment. But on they went because there was no other choice.

Charlotte refused Jed's pleas to leave them. She wasn't sure what she could do if they were stopped again, but felt rather proud of her performance as "poor white trash." She couldn't pretend to be selling vegetables anymore. Perhaps she could say they were on their way to board a ship traveling up North for a new life, a white woman and her two servants. Why at night? Because the ship sailed at dawn and she had sold her horse and wagon to pay their way. None of it sounded very logical, but Charlotte's weary brain went round and round and came up with nothing better. Desperately, she prayed they would not be stopped and her story put to the test.

It wasn't long before the baying of the hounds grew louder, more hysterical. They must have reached the tumbled sacks of vegetables floating in the river, the scent of onions covering the humans's scent. The dogs must be terribly confused and now they seemed to fade away.

The fugitives didn't talk. Jed in the lead, stumbled sometimes, going slower. Charlotte, doing likewise, wondered how one small baby could become so heavy. At last, he stirred and whimpered. The sound was enough to rouse his mother.

"Jed, Jed," Luella moaned, her head lifting from his shoulder. "The child need me."

"Yes, love, we'll stop." Gently he lowered her to the ground, her back against a tree. "How you feelin'?"

"Better." She took a quavering breath. "Where are the dogs, *cheri?*"

"Reckon the onions held them for a spell." Jed grunted, brushing back her hair and placing a tender kiss upon her cheek. "We can rest a bit." He took the basket from Charlotte, giving her a smile of thanks and then withdrew the softly fussing boy.

There were cloths in the basket, a blanket, baby shirts, and in the bottom, a bottle of red wine which Jed tendered first to Charlotte. She sipped gratefully several times before handing it back, glad to be resting for a few minutes and relieved of her burden. After the child had been changed, Luella put him to her breast and Jed went off to the road to check their whereabouts.

Luella seemed to revive with rest and wine. She looked shyly at Charlotte who was lying on a nearby grassy mound. "You are so good, mam'selle, to help us. I think you save our life."

"I certainly hope so." Charlotte smiled. "You must have met many others along the Freedom Trail who also helped you."

"*Vraiment.*" She nodded. "Did Jed tell you about—about—" Her eyes dropped, lips trembling with shame.

"Yes, Luella. It sounded like a nightmare. That awful monster!"

"*Oui,* you name him well." Her head lifted, the lovely features hardening. "Not only did he force me to accept him, but when he couldn't—couldn't perform—*comprenes?*"

Charlotte nodded.

"Then he would hurt me to relieve his pain."

"Oh, how monstrous!" Charlotte shuddered. "It's a wonder he didn't come after you himself when you ran."

"Jed beat him and tie him up in shed before we go."

Her tone grew hard, teeth grinding with rage. "I hope he dies."

If he hadn't, perhaps the planter's son had offered a reward to spur on all patrols and encourage betrayers. So far, it hadn't suceeded, but the runaways would not be safe until they boarded ship.

Charlotte refrained from saying any of this to Luella, who was now patting the sleeping babe. "Where are you and Jed going when you get up North?"

"Canada," Luella answered happily. "Slaves are free up there and in Montreal they speak French, as I do. A place is waiting for us."

"Oh, that sounds fine. I'm sure you will have a good life there. Jed is strong and kind. You, too, are very brave to have endured so much and still kept fighting to survive."

"Ah, I must do it for our child. And Jed, he would not let me dispair. Jed is a fine man, that one. Me, I will teach him to read and write, French, too. His mind's quick, his heart's good."

"You both will be an asset to your community and gladly welcomed." She didn't add that Canada would be very different for them, especially the freezing winters. They probably would consider it a small price to pay, however, for freedom, after all they had suffered.

One thought troubled Charlotte. The enduring hatred of Francois. If he caught up with the runaways, his vengeance would be swift and terrible. After that, he might even boldly sail for France, knowing there would be small interest in the murder of a black family who had flouted the law by beating up a white man and then trying to escape.

Just then, Jed returned, crying hoarsely, "Quick! Under the bushes. Pattyrollers!"

They all huddled, shaking, while the thundering hoofs tore along the River Road. Closer and closer. Charlotte moaned to herself, her fear stronger than before. She had been lulled by the brief spell of rest and quiet. But now the earth trembled from the powerful patrol, trees shook down their leaves, and terrorized breaths rasped from each throat so strong it couldn't be controlled by Charlotte or the fugitives.

Then—as swiftly as they came—the patrol passed by. And all was still once more.

They sat up slowly, hardly daring to believe in their reprieve, while Jed clasped his wife, wiping sweat and tears from both their faces. He looked at Charlotte. "Ah saw the ship close by so reckon God still with us. How can we ever thank you, mistress?"

"You don't have to. I am just so glad you will be all right." Charlotte clasped his big rough hand, then embraced his wife. "I want you to send me a letter in care of the Book Nook, New York City. My name is Charlotte Davenport and they will forward it to me. Please send me word that all is well. Will you remember that?"

"Your name be written in our hearts forever," Jed said brokenly.

"And in our prayers, *cher mam'selle,*" Luella promised, her grateful smile a thing of beauty.

"Go now. I will watch from the trees to see you safely on board."

Jed led the way, and in a few minutes, they could see the harbor through the trees. In the flickering light of smoky pitch-pine torches, busy dock loaders hurried back and forth on the wharf. The shadowy figures went up one gangplank with cargo and came down the other, empty handed. One man who might be the captain, stared all around through a spyglass. He waved when the refugees emerged from the forest.

"That's our ship, praise be." Jed stood tall and proud.

After many more words of thanks, he and Luella proceeded to the dock.

Charlotte watched them, tears of joy streaking down her face, until the ship finally weighed anchor and two figures at the railing lifted their hands toward the trees.

Feeling renewed in strength and spirit, Charlotte turned her steps toward home. To her delight, she found the carthorse calmly grazing farther down the road. She gathered up the traces and had no trouble riding bareback, even with her limited experience, until they reached Stone Gardens. There she left him free for someone else to find.

The front door was still unlocked. Charlotte silently crept up to her room. She washed, shed her clothes and, in seconds, fell asleep.

Chapter 19

When Charlotte woke next morning, it was to feel an unaccustomed aching in legs, back, and arms. At once, the night's activities rushed back and she realized that her running through the woods, horseback riding (for practically the first time in her life!) and hours of fear and desperation had exacted a heavy toll.

However, it was a small price to pay for the lives of three human beings, and as she rubbed her painful limbs, she sent up a thankful prayer. Jed and Luella certainly deserved some happiness, after all they had endured, and she felt sure their brave hearts would find it at journey's end.

When she slid from bed, she saw a pot of tea waiting on a sidetable and at once both thirst and hunger assailed her. She gulped a little of the brew, but it was stone cold and must have sat there a long time. A pang went through her. What *was* the hour? She gasped to behold the hands on the French clock pointing to ten!

Hastily, she summoned Tibby who brought her tea, toast, and plum preserves all fresh and hot. "You had a mighty

long sleep, Miss Charlotte, but reckon you musta need it."
She poured out a steaming cup, then helped Charlotte
don a robe. "Early on, I stayed by your door and kept
everybody out from wakin' you."

"You did? Thank you," Charlotte gulped thirstily.

"Yes'm. Sat right there in the hall 'till little while ago
when I figure you was nigh to wakin'. Hear you toss and
mutter."

Had she muttered anything incriminating? Charlotte
wondered. Her mouth, full of toast and orange blossom
honey, she merely nodded until able to swallow. "What
did you tell the family?"

"Said you was so tired. They understood. Everyone
mainly thinkin' 'bout that Hartley ball."

"Did Mr. Cartright ask for me?"

"Dunno if he did or didn't."

"My sister? Do you know where she is?"

"Miss Amy and Miss Vanessa gone a-riding."

Tibby's eyes had an unusual gleam this morning, unlike
her usual shy, retiring manner. Did she know about the
runaways? And Charlotte's own assistance in their escape?
Probably not much news escaped the slave community. It
worked both good and bad. Help could be available for a
fugitive, but betrayal also was a constant threat. Even kin-
ship couldn't always withstand the dire need for escape
money.

At any rate, Tibby couldn't seem to do enough. When
Charlotte requested water for a bath, the zinc tub appeared
as if by magic, and several willing hands brought hot water,
lavender scent, and laid out soap and towels.

Charlotte slid her tired muscles into the welcome heat
and allowed Tibby's soft, little hands to wash her hair.

At long last, dressed in sprigged blue muslin with a towel
around her neck, Charlotte pushed open a French door
in the corner of her room and went out on the balcony.

There she found a chair and settled in the sun, idly brushing out her hair. Tibby had vanished. No human sound came from the garden, only twittering of birds, spent leaves rustling to the ground and a faint plash of the river on the distant pier as something stirred its current, perhaps a passing boat.

The recent night's events seemed unreal in this sunny, peaceful day. Had she actually ridden a horse? Had she controlled him, kicking with her heels to make him gallop, with one hand wound into his mane, the other gathering up his unbuckled trace? The docile animal had served her well. She would try to discover what had become of him, though surely every horse knew enough to return home if freed.

Just as the human "cargo" had been freed. They must have reached their next station by this time, and Charlotte saw them in her mind: the fragile, lovely young woman, the big, kind man, both now certain that a better life awaited them.

The hue and cry from Louisiana had followed them a long way. It was to be devoutly hoped that the fiendish Francois did not still pursue them. There wasn't much that he could do above the Mason-Dixon Line if the "conductors" passed them carefully along the Freedom Trail. At least, that's what she hoped.

If only she knew how to contact the Frenchman! There was so much she would like to know. However, the memory of their last amorous encounter sent a blush into her cheeks. What must he think of a woman who allowed a stranger the freedom of an intimate lover?

But, oh, how wonderful it had been! Still, it was not really the masked man she responded to with feverish kisses and embraces. The image of Devlin had inspired her, lured her, thrilled her . . . A dream lover so enticing she knew if the real man came to her, she would succumb to him with unequivocal delight.

And then she saw him coming toward her.

Pushing back the strands of hair across her face, Charlotte stared with a strange feeling of seeing her fate approach. Devlin strode along the leaf-strewn path until he reached the house. Then his head lifted and he saw Charlotte on the balcony.

"Good-morning," he called. The next minute, he mounted the iron-railed steps leading from the garden and joined her. The sun glinted on his dark tousled hair, and since the day was warm, he wore no jacket and had his shirt unbuttoned at the throat. He leaned against the railing, hands in his trouser pockets and stared at her silently for a long moment.

What was he thinking? What did he see? Flustered by his scrutiny, as well as her own recent thoughts of him, Charlotte pushed back her long hair, attempting some order among the unbound strands. No respectable woman of her age appeared with her hair down in such an abandoned manner.

About to excuse herself and retreat, his next words halted her flight and she sank back down.

"I wanted to see if you were all right," he said abruptly. "When you didn't appear this morning, I grew uneasy."

Charlotte blinked. "You said I could work at my own pace," she reminded him.

"Of course you can. But, evidently, there was some disturbance near here last night. I feared you were upset . . ."

Charlotte struggled desperately for calmness. "What happened?"

"It seems two slaves and their child were chased along the River Road and nearly captured by bloodhounds. They came from another plantation, but it was enough to set everyone's tongues to wagging and put Miss Clara in a tizzy.''

"They were not caught?''

"No. A Yankee trading vessel probably gave them aid, as one was sighted down the river. It's happened before. The fugitives simply vanished.''

"The Underground Railroad,'' Charlotte murmured.

"A lost horse was found wandering in the grounds. Cord asked me, but I had no idea who owned it. He placed the animal in the barns to wait for a possible owner.''

At least the fugitives had escaped. But would her own part be discovered? Suppose someone had seen her ride the horse into the grounds?

In her agitation, she dropped the brush and Devlin picked it up. "I—I'm nearly ready to start work,'' she stammered. "Just give me a moment to make myself respectable.''

Devlin stepped to her side and drew the brush down a length of her hair. "You don't seem disrespectable with your unbound locks like a silken cape about your shoulders. Do you know there are strands of gold in the dark splendor? It's a lovely sight—just the way a woman looks on the brink of her surrender . . . relaxed, warm, enticing . . .''

"Please—I must go in.'' She attempted to rise, but he pressed her back into the chair.

"Do you mind if I touch your hair? I've often wondered what it would look like out of that confined style you favor. Now I know. It's a satin, gold-shot waterfall.'' His voice had thickened and, suddenly, he gathered up a handful of her hair and held it to his face, the thick-lashed lids covering his eyes.

He inhaled deeply and murmured, "The scent is so fresh

and sweet. Lilacs, I think. How sensuous you are . . . warm and lovely.''

Charlotte stood up quickly, filled with alarm, fearing her response to his potent combination of male force and seductive tenderness.

But he wouldn't let her go. The brush fell to the floor and he thrust his hands into her hair to hold her face up to his as he growled, "I could drink from your lips and be intoxicated at the first sip.''

Though every pulse responded to his touch, Charlotte knew the danger of being observed in the embrace of her employer on Aunt Clara's outdoor veranda. She put her shaking hands upon his chest, feeling the warm skin through his shirt, the accelerated beating of his heart. She saw the slow descent of his lips, moist and parted by a quickened breath.

She swallowed hard. "Devlin—no! Someone might come and see us—''

"Let them!'' he gasped, then pulled her suffocatingly close and kissed her.

She couldn't help it. Charlotte melted into every contour of his body. His kiss was fire and lightning, all the wonder and excitement of the universe held suspended for an eternity in this man's hard kiss. His lips on hers demanded a response and when she kissed him back, he pushed his tongue between her lips, tasting greedily, groaning deep inside his throat.

His fingers clutched her shoulders convulsively, one hand moved to her waist, then lower so that even in the whirling, exploding darkness, she became aware of things she had never known before—the hardening of an inflamed man's body, the passion barely leashed and how powerless she could be to stop him if they were alone and she encouraged him further . . .

Forcing every reluctant muscle to obey her, Charlotte

slid her hands to his straining arms and pushed against them, twisting her lips from his exciting quest. "No!" she cried out raggedly.

Puny though her efforts were, he checked himself immediately. He released his breath in a long, shuddering sigh. "No? You mean it this time?"

"Yes," she managed with great effort. And he stepped back. How strange he looked. A man aroused to fever pitch. And she had been responsible. An odd elation filled her, a kind of gloating pride. She bent and retrieved her brush, the long hair falling like a silken curtain to hide her flushed and tell-tale face.

"That was my undoing," he grunted, "all that seductive unbound hair. No wonder that in medieval times maidens kept their hair covered until the wedding night."

Was that all it meant to him? Her long hair firing his imagination? "Perhaps I should wear a matron's cap in future," Charlotte ground her teeth.

He smiled slowly, maddeningly. "It was more than that and you know it. I also know you liked my kisses."

She tossed back her hair. "Yes, I admit you do that very well. It's the way you write, isn't it? Forceful, imaginative, knowing just how far a woman will let you go."

Anger swept his face. "You think I was testing your reaction so I could write about it?"

"What else? For me, it was an enlightening experience."

"What else, indeed?" He gave her a taunting glance. "Perhaps you'll see yourself in one of my books. You are indeed an exciting woman. Thank you for allowing my—ah—research." He gave her a mocking bow. "Now I think it's time we got back to work."

He bounded down the stairs and never once looked back while Charlotte watched the trees enclose him. Her hands were clenched for a long time, her breathing ragged. At least she had the satisfaction of knowing she had called a halt.

He was right, of course. She had enjoyed his embrace. Who wouldn't? No wonder he could write such devastating love scenes. He was a man possessed of an unparalled romantic imagination and in real life he obviously was as exciting as any of his heroes. Even with her limited experience, Charlotte knew that Devlin would be a thrilling and powerful lover, drawing a woman to partner his own unquenchable virility. He would do things she couldn't even imagine but knew they would swamp her senses with desire for him.

She had discovered that she was a different person in his arms, so filled with ecstasy that she teetered on the border of complete abandonment. How could this be? What had happened to the serious, upright spinster who had cautioned Amy about the dangers lurking in a man? Had she thrown caution almost out the door?

Would Devlin try to seduce her?

Would he succeed?

Did she want him to succeed?

Slowly, she turned, reentering her room and sank down at the dressing table. Hands in her lap, she stared long at her image. How odd, really, that Devlin admired her hair so much—Or said that he did. Perhaps the flattery was just part of an experienced man's seduction.

He must have been excited by her, though. The way he had kissed—stabbing with his long, hot tongue until she thought she'd faint. And then his crushing embrace, showing plainly how aroused his body had become. He had wanted her to know it. Oh, yes, she was not that innocent. He had wanted her with every fiber of his being.

The truth was ... she had wanted him, too, the way a wife wants the husband she adores.

With a shattering groan, Charlotte put her face down in her hands. Heaven help her! She was in love with Devlin Cartright—sensuous writer, forceful lover. Strong, arousing, exciting. And a devil underneath it all.

Chapter 20

Knowing that she was still dependant on Devlin for her livelihood roused Charlotte from her emotional mood and finally forced her back to a state of relative calmness. She had to face him. She had to do the work for which Devlin paid her so generously each week. Was she a mewing schoolgirl who could not control herself around a man she fancied? No, Charlotte fiercely told herself with a frown.

Standing tall before the mirror, she tucked every hair in place, then drew on the crocheted snood, which Devlin apparently didn't like. She raised her chin. Let him see that she had no intention of appearing "seductive." Wretched man! From now on, she would have to be conscious of her every word and act around him. How uncomfortable it would be. The only saving grace was that he seldom stayed in the studio very long when she was there.

Today proved no exception. Devlin had disappeared again, leaving as usual a stack of notes for her deciphering. The novel's pages had mounted to a respectable pile and, suddenly, Charlotte wondered what she would do when the work was finished. Would he start another book right away? Or would she be back to worrying again about a way to earn her keep? She couldn't do a servant's work when her aunt kept slaves for that purpose. A little gardening, perhaps? But winter was coming and she believed most plants would hibernate during the cold rainy season, especially the flowers.

If only she had learned a skill, such as nursing, sewing or teaching. Alas, so few doors were open to women, unless they worked at home doing piecework, like lace-making for a seamstress or hand-coloring pictures for periodicals and paper doll books to be sold in shops.

Well, she could still do clerical work and might find something as a shop assistant in Charles City waiting on customers or keeping records. With enough determination, she felt certain that she could succeed. She would work hard at any task and not be choosy.

But right now, she had a job to do. Firmly pushing aside every other thought, Charlotte applied herself to the careful copy writing in a clear and steady hand.

The morning passed without event, until Charlotte heard the laughing voices of Amy and Vanessa coming from their ride. In case her sister was concerned about her sleeping so late, Charlotte decided to step out on the porch and intercept her.

Vanessa had tripped on ahead toward the house while Amy had turned off on the path leading to the studio. But before she had taken a dozen steps, Martin Cord appeared from the trees directly in front of her.

Amy halted, looking adorable in an azure riding habit and white plumed hat. She smiled. "Good-day, Martin. How are you?"

"Not good, sweetheart. I'm still thinking about you night and day." His glance devoured her. "Won't you meet me soon? Let me take you for a drive? Or shopping? I do know how to act in town and have some decent clothes—"

Amy looked down. "I'm sure, but no one would approve of my going out with you."

He caught her slender arms although she gave a little cry and turned her face aside. He forced her head up to meet his anguished gaze. "Why do you need approval? You're nearly eighteen. Lots of girls your age are married and have children. Do you believe your aunt would mind if someone else supported you? I'm sure she'd be relieved."

Charlotte had been moving forward soundlessly and now she heard Amy answer. "Perhaps she would. But, Martin, Charlotte—"

"Yes, I know. That high-in-the-instep sister. Well, fry her!"

The next instant, he caught Amy up against his body, and before she could utter another sound or move away, he ground his mouth on hers.

Charlotte didn't hesitate a minute longer. She sped down the path, screaming, "You dastardly villain! Unhand my sister this instant."

To her dismay, Cord completely disregarded her, continuing to grip Amy in a passionate embrace, his lips glued to hers. His eyes stayed shut and Charlotte wondered if he even heard her.

Reaching him, Charlotte thumped his rock-hard arm with all her might until he raised his head, looking dazed, but he let Amy stumble back. Then his vision cleared.

"You!" he snarled so fiercely that Charlotte felt afraid that his raised fists would strike her.

"A few more minutes kissing Amy, and I could change her mind. If it weren't for you—"

Charlotte recoiled farther from his heaving, frustrated fury and called quaveringly, "Amy, Amy—go get help! Call Cicero—Ned—Clara—" Cord halted with a deep harsh breath while Amy hesitated. She looked bruised about the mouth, red of face, but otherwise unharmed.

"There's no need to get anyone, Charlotte. I'm all right." She turned to Cord with chilly dignity. "I warn you, Martin, as I did before, you must not force your attentions on me. I will stop speaking to you altogether if this continues, and then I really will have to tell my aunt."

"We'll tell her anyway," Charlotte shouted.

"No, let's not disturb her unless we have to," Amy said calmly. "Mr. Cord, do I have your promise?"

His hands opened and closed rapidly as did his mouth. Then he growled. "Very well. Just don't shut me out."

His hard black eyes swept Charlotte. "As for you, I know a thing or two about your midnight outings. But if you mind your own business, I'll mind mine."

Charlotte could only stare back dumbly and swallow. At last, she nodded jerkily. *He was blackmailing her.*

Cord stepped close to Amy, but didn't touch her. "We'll speak again," he whispered.

Amy didn't answer. He walked away with his usual arrogant swagger and Amy drew Charlotte toward the studio. "Dearest, you looked so shocked just now, at Cord's last words. What did he mean?"

Charlotte chewed her lip, pushing distractedly at her hair. *What did he mean?*

Amy sighed as they entered the guesthouse and sat down on the little sofa. "If you are meeting Devlin in the night, you don't have to tell me. You are old enough and wise enough to know what you are doing. But please be careful. Don't let Martin have anything to hold over your head."

"It's not what you think. I guess there's something I must tell you. You recall that man they call the Frenchman? Well . . I have assisted him to help some runaways escape."

Amy fell back on the sofa, one hand at her lips. "Oh, Charlotte, how? Why? It's so dangerous!"

"When we first arrived, I found an injured man—a boy, actually—unconscious in the garden. The Frenchman appeared and needed my help to take him to a doctor. Unfortunately, the poor child died." She paused and Amy moaned.

"You went again last night, didn't you? That's why you slept so late."

"Yes, but Amy, you must not breathe a word of this. Promise me—I could be in a lot of trouble—"

"Of course. How can you think that I'd tell a living soul? But does Martin know?"

"He must know or suspect something. Last night, I had to drive a wagon carrying three refugees to safety on a ship sailing to the North. Cord might have seen me riding back."

"Charlotte—Charlotte—" Amy wailed, beating her hands together. "You could be caught and jailed. Oh, why have you taken such a chance?"

"Indeed, I know the danger full well. But if you had seen those suffering people . . . and last night I put them safely on a ship with their little babe. Oh, Amy, how could I refuse when he said there was no one else available—"

"Did the Frenchman tell you that? How do you know it was the truth? It might have just been a lever he was using."

"No. I trust him."

"I knew it! You're in love with him! Ever since he kissed your hand."

"No, no. Oh, Amy, it is Devlin that I love." The words were out. Amy's jaw dropped as she straightened up.

Charlotte's face burned and she mumbled, averting her eyes. "Now you know all my secrets. Please promise that you won't tell anyone, especially not Vanessa."

"Especially not Vanessa," Amy promised, staring hard.

She gripped her sister's trembling hands. "Don't worry, dear. Please trust me."

"I do. You had to know about the Frenchman in case Cord starts talking. I didn't want you taken by surprise."

"Have you found out who he is? The Frenchman, I mean."

"He hasn't dropped a hint. He is always masked and speaks in a disguised, gruff voice. Whoever he is, I do admire his courage and the caring nature that sends him constantly into direst danger just to help someone he's never met before. I think he must be a wonderful person."

Amy gave her a sly glance. "You have a dreamy look when you speak about him. Has he kissed you again?"

Charlotte turned her head aside. "It meant nothing. Gratitude, perhaps."

"Gratitude? Fiddlesticks! Now, tell me more about you and Devlin."

"There's really nothing to tell. Come, it's nearly time for lunch." Charlotte rose. "You'll have to change, won't you?"

Amy followed her as they went outside and Charlotte locked the door. "You're not getting off so easily, sister of mine. Devlin, now—how? When? Details, please."

Charlotte's breath caught on a laugh. "Oh, I—I can't."

"Charlotte!"

"He—he kissed me on an impulse. He is probably lonely. Anyway, I was thrilled and then I realized that I was in love with him."

"And? Did you let him know?"

"Of course not. He told me he was attracted to me. He became rather overwhelming, and I had to pull away. I accused him of doing research for his novel."

Amy shrieked in pain. "I can't believe this. Even I would know better. That's no way to make him love you."

"What does it matter? We're complete opposites. He is

very masculine, very sensual. Probably likes lots of women. You know the unrestricted way he writes. And I—I am a repressed old maid.''

Amy stamped her foot upon the leaf-strewn path. ''That is utter nonsense. You are filled with love—and sympathy—and courage. You say he's sensual. I'm not sure what that means, but I can guess. Do you know what I think? I think you are perfect for each other.''

Charlotte couldn't help the tiny flare of hope. But then it quickly died. She had to change the subject. ''What are we going to do about Martin?''

''Please let me handle him. He's proud and you treat him like a naughty boy.''

''A naughty *man*, you mean.'' Charlotte snapped.

''Don't you realize how hard this must be for him? I doubt if he's been in love before. He's not sure how to act, but his feelings swamp him. Oh, yes, he is almost out of his mind.''

''You sound pleased. Surely, you don't enjoy his vile attentions? He kissed you like an animal. I tell you, he's a cad. He wants you for one reason only and we both know what that is.''

Amy didn't comment on the last statement but said thoughtfully, ''I think you'll have to agree that we must not antagonize him. He might have some very damaging information. Even a hint to Clara that you were helping slaves escape would send her through the roof—to say nothing about what the patrol might do to you.''

''Do you intend to allow his kisses, then, as a bribe for his silence?'' Charlotte asked indignantly.

''I think just my friendship might suffice.''

''You are such an innocent,'' Charlotte muttered. ''I don't like your even speaking to that odious cad.''

''And I don't like your helping the Frenchman. Let him take care of the Underground Railroad himself. He knows what to do. He's one of the conductors, isn't he? What did he do before you came?"

Amy halted on the path with a hand upon her sister's arm. "I shall be sick with worry if you don't promise not to get involved anymore with the runaways."

Charlotte sighed deeply. "All right. I know it would be bad if I were caught—bad for everyone. I won't chance it anymore. Though I wish . . ."

"What?"

"That there was some way I could help these people who are so miserable, through no fault of their own. They lead such a terrible existence, with no hope for improvement."

"Perhaps there is something both of us could do. If Clara will allow it."

"Tell me."

"Why couldn't we visit the slave quarters once a week? Take a little special food, supplies, make jackets for the babies. Talk. See what is needed."

"Amy, dear, you have hit upon a wonderful idea. Your sympathetic heart found a way to do something that never occurred to me."

Amy smiled as they entered the back door to the big house. "Actually, Cicero gave me the idea. He told me that our mama used to do that every week, and all the slaves worshipped her. They called her the Princess of Joy and Beauty."

"Really? Oh, how I love to hear anecdotes about her. No wonder everyone dispaired so when she left. I imagine Clara never inspired such feelings in the slaves."

"There's one thing, though," Amy said hesitantly. "I don't think Mama would ever have helped a slave escape. She would have tried instead to iron out the problems here. For her sake, Charlotte, you, too, must try another way."

"You're right, little one. You have really surprised me with your wisdom." But Charlotte's mind was troubled. If she was asked to aid a runaway and there was no one else to help, could she refuse and turn her back? She only hoped her new resolution would not be put to the test.

When she and Amy joined the family a little later in the parlor, however, she felt devoutly glad that she hadn't turned her back on Jed and Luella. For there sat a strange man sipping sherry. Small and elegantly dressed, he had a narrow seamed face, the lips turned down beneath a little black moustache, a goatee on his chin. His eyes on Amy and Charlotte looked cold and calculating.

Aunt Clara, seeming somehow flustered, herded the girls forward and introduced them. Her next words sounded the knell of doom and dread as she continued. "This gentleman is Francois Savon who has come all the way from Louisiana to track down two runaway slaves."

mouth. Surely she hadn't known Francois, his features, of all the world . . . her eyes met the man who turned to his feet and looked and only come to Amy. He looked as though his movements pained him, then began to walk, his face to her small face for him long enough? He patiently gazed at her for a time, that time, that Amy, in a place beside him, his hands tightly gripped, demanding bottle. Amy, she said thickly, "We will come shortly, we have to meet and announced firmly.

"Amy is too delicate," said Charlotte. "I wish I were able to stay more time with her." She was too choking in her throat.

"I will present to Jed first," Savon said. "I'll run the relief, but that you were going to be there, should no . . .

Francois Savon's cold glint his eyes, then he raised no fear no matter nervous about explaining. Amy moved a step near, caressing her with her face.

Chapter 21

Charlotte's tongue seemed frozen to the roof of her mouth. Surely guilt must suffuse her features for all the world to see. But the man who struggled to his feet and bowed had only eyes for Amy. He winced as though his movements pained him, then eagerly pressed his lips to her small hand for too long a period. He merely glanced at Charlotte, then drew Amy to a place beside him, his beady black eyes devouring her. *"Enchante,"* he said thickly. "My so-tiresome journey was worth it to meet such unusual beauty."

"Amy is my companion," Vanessa cut in with a venemous glance. "Though I swear she spends more time with her sister than attending to my needs."

Amy jumped to her feet. "I'm sorry, Vanessa. I'll return the riding habit that you were kind enough to loan me."

Monsieur Savon cried quickly. *"Non, non,* you must not go just yet. I wish to question everyone about ze runaways."

Amy moved a step away, regarding him with wide blue

eyes. "I have not heard a word about them. Did they come
from Louisiana?"

"*Oui,* I will tell you all." His claw-like fingers, heavily
ringed, fastened like a vice on Amy's arm as he drew her
back to a place beside him on the horsehair sofa.

Amy threw a shrug toward Vanessa, who fumed and
twitched, but didn't protest again. Clara looked uneasy
and Charlotte shrank back on a chair somewhat removed.
She tried to school her face to blankness, but her heartbeats had quickened rapidly. What did this devil know?
Could he possibly find out that she had aided the runaways
to escape on the Yankee's ship? She must guard her every
word and expression in his presence. He looked shrewd,
as well as determined.

Fortunately, however, the Frenchman bent all his attention on Amy. "My father died recently and I came to
America from France two months ago to claim ze plantation, Dark Oaks. *Ma foi,* so rundown it was! I sell nearly
all ze slaves and buy new ones, just keeping ze best. Zed,
so big and strong and a woman he had, Luella, were among
them."

The thin face reddened and his voice suddenly grew
husky. "*Mon Dieu,* such a beauty—too good for a *chou* like
him. So I place her in my protection." He shrugged and
sent Amy a sly glance, perhaps wondering what she would
read behind his words.

"And they repaid you for this honor by running away?"
Clara intervened, her tone and face expressionless.

Charlotte wondered what her aunt actually felt about the
situation. The Frenchman certainly was an unprepossing
man. In spite of rich clothes and cultured tones, his face
showed ugly lines of depravity and dissipation. No one
would welcome his attentions. His interest in Amy had
been quick and greedy and Charlotte knew that a beast
lay buried beneath his satin clothes and jewelry. She felt

that an aura of the most evil nature surrounded him and
prayed he would soon go on his way. Back to Louisiana
or France, where he could give up his desire for vengeance
on the runaways.

Savon shot Clara an inimical glance. "You speak true,
madame. *Oui*, ze run away. But my men track well and I
have followed as soon as my wounds allowed.

"You were hurt?" Amy asked politely.

He ground his yellowed teeth. "Zed beat me! You cannot
believe it? I see your face is shocked. But it is true. I nearly
die, but *le bon Dieu* spared me for revenge. And this time,
both of them shall pay!" His voice rose.

Clara shifted but said coolly, "Well, monsieur, I regret
that they aren't here. We cannot help you." She rose and
held the sherry bottle poised above his glass which he had
placed on a nearby taboret. "More wine before you—"

"Non, non," he snarled and waved his hand. "I tell you,
madame, ze are nearby. My last information was ze were
headed for a Yankee trader ship. Where is it, I want to
know?" He rounded on her. "Zed and Luella probably
are in hiding. Perhaps right here." His eyes bulged. "I
want them found."

Clara flushed and drew up regally. "I repeat, monsieur,
I cannot help you. I have not seen them. If they were
anywhere nearby, it would have been reported to me. That
is all that I can say. And now—"

At once, he tried to placate her with shrugs and out-
spread hands. "But, of course, of course. Forgive my anxiety, but certainly you would feel ze same if two valued
slaves mistreated you and then vanished—poof! Like ze
air. *Non*, madame, I will pursue. Now I must seek rooms
in ze village." He managed a wistful glance around the
parlor. "You have a so-lovely home and very large, *n'est-ce
pas?"*

Decades of Southern hospitality would not be denied,

even to an unpleasant stranger, and Clara inclined her head stiffly. "You can have a room, here if you wish, and one for your servant above the stable." She jerked the bell cord rather strongly.

"Ah, such cordiality! You are too kind, madame." He leaped up and kissed her hand. A bright fire lit his eyes as they roved to Amy. "May I escort you to your room, *mam'selle?* You wish a brief rest before *dejeuner, hein?*"

If he thought to discover where Amy slept, she soon foiled that blatant attempt. "No, thank you, I wish to stay here and converse with my sister and cousin."

He gave a strange low laugh, almost as though he liked her uneasiness, then he bowed to all. When Cicero appeared, he followed him from the room.

At once, the remaining family drew closer, Charlotte going to join Amy on the couch. Vanessa and Clara moved up their chairs.

"I don't trust that man an inch," Charlotte hissed. "If ever I saw villainy in a face—"

Amy shuddered and exchanged a glance with her, knowing from their former conversation that Francois Savon was after the runaways Charlotte had helped, on whom he would undoubtedly inflict the cruelest punishment.

"I don't like him, either," Vanessa muttered. "Do you know what he did, Mama? He put his tongue upon my palm while pretending just to kiss it. I could have slapped his ugly, leering face, I swear."

"I thought he held your hand too long," Clara exclaimed, tapping her foot. "I don't envy those slaves of his, if he captures them. Especially the girl he fancies."

Charlotte glanced at her in surprise. For once, was her aunt showing sympathy for escaping slaves? Would wonders never cease?

"I was appalled at the way he looked at my sister," she

said, frowning. "Amy, I think you better sleep with me tonight."

"I think you're right. It seemed to me as though he lives by a terrible set of rules, which he twists to suit himself, and cares nothing for the rest of the world's opinion. In just a few minutes, he set his sights on both Vanessa and myself."

Clara stirred uneasily and took another splash of wine into her glass. "Believe me, we shall all lock our doors tonight. I wish he had departed, but what could I do? I had to offer him hospitality."

"The code of the South." Vanessa nodded solemnly. "But stars above, how long do you think he'll stay?"

Clara took a gulp of wine. "I vow tomorrow I'll get rid of him. Tim Deane will be arriving and I'll just tell Monsieur Savon that we are expecting other guests and I can't accommodate him another night."

Vanessa expelled her breath. "That should work, all right. Bravo, Mama. Don't you wonder what he did to those slaves he's chasing? A woman and her husband. Do you suppose he forced her to his bed and then the husband attacked him?"

How close to the truth Vanessa had come! Charlotte held her breath, afraid to comment. Fortunately, the signal for lunch sounded just then, and they all adjourned, Amy hurrying upstairs to change her clothes. The Frenchman joined them in the dining room, and at least there the conversation proved less unpleasant, as their guest talked about his chateau on the Loire in France and then his parents's plantation which he now possessed.

"Will you stay there?" Clara asked him, carrying the main burden of the conversation, as Amy and Charlotte contributed but little. As for Vanessa, she talked in a supercilious, disdainful manner that brought frowns to the seamed, dark face.

He, therefore, conversed mainly with his hostess and replied now that he would, indeed, spend the winter in Louisiana and stay on for Mardi Gras. His hooded eyes moved to Amy who concentrated on a dish of chicken pudding, which consisted of browned fowl baked in puffed batter served with giblet gravy.

"Perhaps I could prevail upon you, Miss Amy, to visit Dark Oaks in ze spring." Catching Clara's glare, he coughed and cleared his throat. "All of you. Have you ever attended ze Carnival, *ma petite?*"

In spite of herself, Amy looked interested. "No. What is it all about?"

"It begins on January 6 and is celebrated in many Roman Catholic countries. 'Mardi Gras' is similar to 'Fat Tuesday' in English, called that because a fat ox was led through ze streets of Paris. Ah, in Carnival time, all is merriment— balls, parades, such food, such wine. Everyone wears ze costume. A King Krewe and his Queen rule everything, and all is romance." The black eyes swept Amy and he said thickly, "You must come. I would dress you like a princess. You, too, Miss Vanessa," he added quickly, darting a glance across the table.

At that, Vanessa and her mother both regarded the little Frenchman with more interest.

"That is a long time in the future," Charlotte snapped. "The South may be on the verge of war."

Immediately, Clara gasped and loud denials burst out from everyone but Charlotte and Amy. Seeing the upset she had caused, Charlotte now kept a still tongue in her head, while Amy placated all with a question regarding the Carnival and its customs.

"It is ze tradition to serve a King cake," Savon continued. "And he who finds a ring inside his slice is king for a day and may choose a slave to cater to his every whim." Suddenly, his eyes glazed and he whispered hoarsely, "Last spring, I arrive in time for Carnival and my slice of King Cake gave me ze power. I chose Luella—ze most beautiful I have seen."

"But then she ran away?" Charlotte asked in an icy tone.

He shrugged. *"Quel dommage!* Slaves do that, no? He ground his teeth even while he laughed.

"How will you find them if they get up North?" Charlotte persisted. "Many Abolitionists will aid them there."

"Bah, my money always gets results."

Dessert was brought in just then, and Clara pounced upon it, apparently glad for an interruption. "Ah, Mississippi Mud. My favorite dessert. Shall I tell you how 'tis made? Vanilla ice cream, equal parts of black coffee and bourbon all beaten together and served with lady fingers . . ."

She prattled on, but Savon looked bored and soon excused himself. However, he made one more effort to determine Amy's boudoir, no doubt intending a visit later on. "If I could see you to your room, *petite,* we might continue our discussion, no?"

"My sister and I have matters we must attend to," Charlotte said, and making no further excuse, took Amy's arm and they marched from the room without another glance.

"Let us hurry," Amy whispered, lifting her skirts of flowered lawn as soon as they were outdoors. "I can't abide that lecherous smirk another minute."

"Nor can I," Charlotte shuddered. "He even makes Martin Cord look better."

The afternoon sun was still warm and Charlotte suggested the Stone Garden would be cool and deserted, which it was.

"You knew about Francois Savon, didn't you?" Amy asked as soon as they sat down on a bench out of the sun.

"Yes." She related the tale.

"How vile he is!"

"Finally, Jed made inquiries about the Underground Railroad and escape plans escalated. They ran off, aided by Harriet Tubman. Have you heard of her?"

"Yes, Cicero told me she is a brave and clever woman who was an abused slave herself. She received such a blow as a child, she still has spells of blanking out and stands, unable to move or speak, until it passes."

"What a tragedy, yet she hasn't let it hamper the efforts she makes to help her people. She devised a cart with a false bottom and Jed used it to hide Luella and their child. Thus we escaped the patrol. Amy, you would have laughed to see your sister with dirt on hands and face, whining that she was just a poor farm woman and Jed her no-account slave."

Amy stared. "I don't feel like laughing. Heavens, Charlotte, how could you be so cool and resourceful? Weren't you scared to death?"

"Well, yes, but I had to do it. And when I saw that little family safe on board the yankee ship, I felt proud and happy. Exhilirated, actually. I've always been so prim and proper and here I was, having an adventure!"

"I think you started on the road to adventures when you sold the shop and brought us to the South, not knowing what awaited us at Stone Gardens. Just don't go too far. I don't like this Frenchman—" Amy giggled. "Not Savon, though I don't like him either, but I mean the other one, the slave conductor. I don't want you risking your life for him."

Charlotte didn't answer. She had promised not to help him and hoped he wouldn't ask her. She could face the dangers, if it were just for herself, but if she should be caught, what would become of Amy?

"Let us prepare some baskets later to give the mothers and children tomorrow," she told her sister. "Perhaps we can follow in our mother's footsteps."

"Yes, let's," Amy said with alacrity. They rose to leave and Amy shivered, glancing around at the cold, silent stones of the unreal garden. "Don't you find this place depressing? I should hate to spend the rest of my life here. No wonder Vanessa is so anxious to meet men. Perhaps she will marry the first one who asks her."

"Keith? Devlin?" Charlotte wondered, feeling the familiar pang at the thought of Devlin succumbing to the beautiful Vanessa. She shook her head. "Well, tomorrow Tim Deane arrives and we shall see how he reacts to a determined southern belle."

They both laughed a little ruefully and parted, Amy going in search of Vanessa and Charlotte heading for the guest house.

Chapter 22

Devlin was not in the studio, and he didn't appear all day, not even coming to dinner that night, which was attended by their new guest, Francois Savon.

He seemed extremely agitated and constantly crumbled the bread between his heavily-ringed fingers, so that it spilled unheeded on the damask tablecloth.

His eyes darted around the table, although he directed his words to Clara. "Did you know, madame, that a stray horse has been brought to your plantation? No bridle, no saddle, just ze cart straps dangling and signs of so-hard riding from a long way off."

Clara sipped her wine and hesitated before speaking. "My overseer mentioned it. Rather odd, but not important, I would venture."

"It is important!" he banged the table. "A riderless horse not seen before? Not a usual occurrence, you must agree. Who brought him? And where from? Me, I know—it was ze runaways! It come from Dark Oaks!"

"How can you know?" Vanessa sneered. "Do you have

magical powers, monsieur? If so, you must know where your slaves have gone."

He bent across the table, his face flaming. "Someone from here has helped these slaves. *Vraiment,* I do know it and your Monsieur Cord concurs."

Amy and Charlotte exchanged swift glances of dismay.

"And what did the all-knowing Mr. Cord say?" Charlotte asked, mastering her fear with an effort and looking at the Frenchman squarely.

He had never paid Charlotte much attention and tonight was no exception. He shrugged, accepting the next course of breaded trout. "Cord had no names for me, but agreed ze horse could only have been brought by someone who lives here. A slave perhaps, or—who knows?" He cast a swift narrowed glance at them all, even including Cicero hovering in the shadows.

The butler glanced at Charlotte but sent no message. If he suspected her involvement, he might take the blame if she were accused before he'd let "Miss Rose's girl" get into trouble. Of course, Charlotte knew she could never let that happen to him.

Fortunately, the matter of the lost horse was not pursued. Savon said he believed the fugitives had taken ship to Ohio above the Mason-Dixon Line, but he intended to follow the trail while it was hot. Therefore, at the dinner's end, he thanked Clara for her hospitality, saying he was departing before dawn next day.

Charlotte felt that an inaudible sigh of relief ran around the table. She had no chance to speak privately with Amy, as Vanessa carried her off to attend a musical evening at a nearby plantation. A note had come from Keith and Katy Duncan in the hope to see Amy and Vanessa there. If Charlotte's name had been included, her cousin did not choose to mention it.

Charlotte really didn't care. She felt drained and only wanted sleep, hoping that she wouldn't dream of Devlin.

She had no memory of her dreams. The next morning, however, Devlin in the flesh had to be faced. She went to the studio early and found her heartbeats quickening when she stepped upon the porch. What would he say about their last encounter? Perhaps nothing. On the other hand, he might even tease her. How awful that would be! She had no experience in such titillating games and knew his expertise could make her feel like a fool. One thing was certain—she would keep him at a distance, no matter what he did. Drawing a quavering breath, she tried the door. It wasn't locked so she knew Devlin was inside.

She found him seated at his worktable, writing swiftly. He wore a white shirt fastened with a string tie at his throat. A black waistcoat matched the dark hair falling unheeded across his brow.

When Charlotte stepped inside, he turned to look at her with a slight smile, as though recalling their encounter of the day before and was curious about her present mood. Was his smirk the satisfaction of a male who had made a woman respond to him? Charlotte wondered. Alas, there was no doubt she *had* responded. She couldn't control the wave of heat that burned her cheeks, but she managed a cool, unhurried greeting while moving to her own chair and table where numerous pages awaited her attention.

"Charlotte—" he began, rising to his feet.

She cut him off. Let him see that she only wished to be all business. "Perhaps if you intend to work in here today, it might disturb you less if I take my copy writing into the house. The library is usually deserted."

"You disturb me no matter where you are." He gave a low, short laugh. "But I'll say no more on that subject, as I can see that today we have the no-nonsense, dedicated worker here. So be it. I am going out, so stay here and work as usual. This is more convenient for you." He turned away, donned a wide-brimmed hat, picked up his jacket and vanished out the door, ignoring Charlotte's faint reply, "As you wish."

With him gone, Charlotte leaned back and exhaled her breath. Thank heaven, he was always gone so often. No doubt about it, from now on relations would be strained at best. It was impossible not to be constantly aware of things that had passed between them. It would always be lurking in her mind. When he was absent, it seemed simple to pretend that she could avoid all pitfalls that might arise. In all honesty, however, she had no certainty that she could resist Devlin if he really tried to seduce her.

Obviously, they had no future. She was in love with a man who drifted around the countryside and made no permanent attachments. Probably Devlin had no desire to marry again or to settle down.

The problem must be faced. Since she wouldn't take him for a lover, what alternative remained? First of all, a cool remoteness must be maintained on her part in order to discourage any of his attempts at intimacy. She would perform her duties on his novel, that was all.

Although her savings were accumulating nicely, she felt reluctant to live on them just yet. She had no real idea of how difficult it would be to find other work once she left Stone Gardens. For the present, she would bide her time. With this settled in her mind, she went to her copying.

The morning passed quietly, until Amy arrived at the door. After a gentle knock, her merry little face peered inside. "May I interrupt?"

Charlotte flung down her pen and stretched. "Of course, come in. I'm nearly finished. What have you got in those baskets?"

"Some things for the slaves. Remember? We were going to visit the quarters today."

"What a good idea. Thank you, little one. I had quite forgotten. I think you are a great deal like our sweet, caring Mama used to be."

"Oh, I hope so. See, Charlotte, in this basket I've put medicines, bottles of juice for anyone who is ailing. And in the other one are some dishcloths for diapers or infant sacques. Do you think the mothers know how to sew?"

"A few probably can. Who else would make their dresses or the men's pants? Clara or Vanessa? Not likely."

They both laughed a little wryly.

"Where did you get all these things, dear? I see you even have paper and pencils. Do you intend to teach some writing?"

Amy sighed. "I wish I could, but Aunt Clara would'nt approve. Besides, Vanessa keeps me too busy. No, don't look so indignant. It's my job. As for the other things, the cook, Aunt Beckie, helped me assemble everything."

"But why paper and pencils, if not for teaching? And a pair of scissors?"

Amy dimpled. "They still are for the children, only I am going to make paperdolls. Remember how much I used to play with them? And I don't imagine anyone gives out toys."

Charlotte corked her ink, wiped the pen nib clean, and took her finished work to Devlin's desk. "Let's go, Amy. I am anxious to see what we will find."

As they left the guest house, each carrying a basket, Amy shook her head. "Vanessa could do so much good here, if she wished."

"Well, she doesn't wish it."

"You don't think I could interest her?"

"No, don't waste your time. I suppose she's busy today preparing for Tim's arrival?"

"Heavens, yes. Hair washing, gowns appraised, constantly checking on his room. There was lots of yelling and running back and forth going on. You'd think royalty was arriving. I could hardly wait to slip away."

"Maybe she'll stop persuing Devlin now, if Tim proves interesting."

Amy threw her a sidelong glance. "Are you feeling a teeny bit jealous now that you have—ah—feelings for him yourself?"

"No," Charlotte answered a little too emphatically. She added, then, "Really, pet, I have no claims on Devlin. He has never said that he loves me . . . only that I disturb him."

Amy nodded. "Very good."

"That's good?" Charlotte had a strange feeling that in some matters of the heart, little sister had the advantage. "Why do you say that, Amy?"

"You want him disturbed, thinking uncertainly about you. The worst thing is indifference."

"Good Lord, how on earth have you learned so much, you innocent little infant?"

Amy chuckled. "Innocent, yes. Infant, no."

They had now reached the slaves's compound, and as before, only very young children and very old people were about. A little girl with a grubby finger in her mouth called her granny to come out.

A wizened crone appeared on the porch, leaning on a stick, a corncob pipe between her teeth.

"Dis be Granny," the child lisped. "Ah'm DeeDee."

Charlotte introduced herself and Amy. "I've brought some things to give out. DeeDee, can you call all the other women and children?"

"Only a handful of us ole women," Granny wheezed. "But go, Dee, git the rest. Ah'll fetch some chairs for the young missies."

Soon a silent throng surrounded Charlotte and Amy, some with startled curiosity, others with eyes on the ground. The children ranged in ages from naked babes-in-arms to girls and boys of five or six. The women were all old, but none as aged as Granny.

After determining there were no sick ones today, Charlotte obtained a knife, peeled the fruit, and distributed a bit to each child as far as it would go, feeling appalled at the large group who received nothing.

Amy busied herself drawing paperdolls, just little figures already clothed. There was no time to make additional outfits and she ran out of paper before half the children had received a toy.

"Oh, Charlotte, we need so much more for them," Amy moaned when they stood up to leave.

"We'll have to find a way to take turns giving to the others," Charlotte said as she waved to the subdued group. Only those who had received something showed a timid smile.

The children followed them until they reached the fields. There, they turned back, calling, "Goodbye, missies, goodbye."

"We'll come again," Charlotte promised, but the little ones were already running, with bare, dusty feet, back to their quarters.

When Charlotte and Amy reached the gardens, Beaulah Hartley surprised them, striding down the path. She waved a hand and called, "Yoo-hoo, girls! Charlotte, I was just looking for you in the studio."

"My stint is over for the day. Amy and I have been distributing odds and ends to the children."

When she learned of their endeavors, Beaulah shook her head. "You're right. They need so much. Training and guidance, mostly."

"And learning to read and write," Amy put in as they walked together through the garden. "Stories told . . . Oh,

Charlotte, that's something else. Someone should tell Bible stories, to teach them right from wrong."

Beaulah gave her an approving pat. "So much like Rose. When your Mama lived here, a preacher came on Sundays, but no longer. His visits ended when Clara took charge."

Charlotte frowned. "What was it, the money?"

"Partly. A preacher must be paid. Clara is having a hard time, but now I think she is afraid of rebellious ideas being hatched. I've told her that more strictness and more splitting up of families do the most harm, but she doesn't want to hear that."

They had reached the house and Amy sped away, looking a little worried because she had been gone for so long.

"You girls have come at a bad time," Beaulah said. "Both of you being put to work—" She clamped her lips. "Heigh-ho, I talk too freely sometimes. Charlotte, put your worries behind you for a spell. I've come to take you to Roselands. Charlie's waiting out in front. He wants to show you his conservatory."

"Oh, how lovely! Thank you, Miss Beaulah. I'll just get my hat and leave word for Aunt Clara."

Charlotte sped indoors, hearing the excited bustling sounds which Amy had described. She freshened her face and hair, donned a wide-brimmed straw hat and flung a lacy shawl around her shoulders. She couldn't take the time to change her deep blue muslin morning gown, so it would have to do. After all, Beaulah was wearing a simply tailored grey jacket over a white blouse. Clothes probably were of little interest to her, as long as they were well-made and comfortable.

Charlotte rang for Tibby and instructed her to tell Aunt Clara that she was on her way to Roselands for a short visit at Mrs. Hartley's request. She then hurried out to the front of the house where Beaulah and her husband awaited her. Charlie was driving his open landau and gave Charlotte a delighted greeting. Soon, they were speeding down the road, with Mrs. Hartley chattering a mile a minute and Charlotte feeling as though she had run away from school for an unexpected outing. "Are Keith and Katy home today?" she asked, suddenly remembering the event Amy had attended the previous evening.

"Oh, yes, they are home, for once." Beaulah chuckled. "They are nearly always doing something. Such energy! Racing their horses, playing games, rowing on the river, bringing in everyone they can find from nearby homes. They have made a lot of friends."

"I forgot to ask Amy about the musicale, but they must have had a pleasant time."

Beaulah's expression sobered. "Well, yes, but Katy got a little peeved at her brother. It seems he sneaked outside with Vanessa for several hours and when they came back, Vanessa had been crying and wouldn't speak to Keith." Beaulah sighed. "I didn't say anything to the boy. Katy does enough of that, though all he does is laugh at her."

"Perhaps he and Vanessa had a little spat." Keith might have tried for more than kisses in the moonlight, but whatever else she was, Vanessa was not a fool and probably would guard her reputation until she snared a husband.

"I guess they went outdoors for a little sparking," Beaulah said. "Keith says Vanessa is an awful flirt."

Charlotte didn't answer. It was evident that Beaulah had a blind spot when she looked at her beloved grandchildren.

When they arrived at Roselands, Keith and Katy were on the lawn playing croquet. They immediately bounded over to greet Charlotte with glad cries and tried to coax her into their game.

"No, no, not this time." Charlie waved them off. "As soon as I have the horses put away, I am taking Miss Charlotte to see my conservatory."

Katy then persuaded Beaulah to join them in croquet

and bore her off where wickets, balls and mallets rested on the lawn.

Keith hung back as soon as Charlotte was alone. Today he wore a frilled white shirt and a bright blue satin vest which matched the color of his eyes. With sunlight burnishing his copper curls, he looked handsome enough to draw many a female's second glance.

Charlotte, however, had no interest in even a first glance and took a step away from him, intending to reach the porch.

At once, he blocked her path. "I wish you could have come with us last night. I missed you. Someone performed on the pianoforte and another on the harp. So romantic. It only needed your presence to make it perfect." He reached out to straighten Charlotte's shawl and allowed his fingers to take the opportunity of moving on her neck.

She twitched away. "I hear you were otherwise occupied with Vanessa. Did you go too far, I wonder? Was that why she cried?"

He gave a delighted crow. "By Jove, the girl is jealous! I do admire a young lady who speaks her mind. There's no pussyfooting around with you, Miss Charlotte, is there? Now admit it, I interest you. Suppose I appease your jealousy with a kiss? Come here, you little dickens!" Chuckling, he slid his hand beneath her shawl, eyes glittering as they focused on her mouth.

The conceited fool! She ground her teeth. "Let go of me this instant. Mr. Hartley is coming."

"What of it? He's seen me kiss girls before." Keith dropped his hand. "I'll see you at the picnic tomorrow. Lots of fun in those big dark caves, eh? I can hardly wait. Wear a thin dress." He ran back to the lawn, throwing a laugh across his shoulder.

"Was he bothering you?" Mr. Hartley asked, a little anxiously, seeing her flushed and angry face.

With an effort, Charlotte smoothed her features. "No, Keith was just being silly."

Mr. Hartley gave a sigh of relief. "He's such a high-spirited lad. Can't keep away from the girls. Oh, well, let's hurry now. I'm so anxious for you to view my treasures."

Charlotte was glad to leave the vicinity of Keith as soon as possible. Would he prove a nuisance tomorrow? Should she bow out of the coming picnic?

Well, she didn't have to decide that now. She thrust Keith from her mind and with happy anticipation she accompanied Mr. Hartley across the lawn where a glass building sparkled among the trees.

Chapter 23

Charlotte found the conservatory at Roselands every bit as wonderful as Charles had claimed. The big glass building rose about two-stories high with several rooms, the first ones holding shelves on which stood clay pots brimming with the most extraordinary blooms Charlotte had ever seen. The colors were breathtaking, mostly lavender, purple, pink or white—some with contrasting markings. The central "throats" rose between wide petals, some as big as a lady's hand.

"These are called cattleyas," Charles said, puffing out like a proud parent at Charlotte's wide-eyed admiration. "All are orchids, of course."

"Of course," Charlotte murmured although she had never heard the term before, much less seen any.

"They originally came from the tropics, Africa, India, South America and Australia, where it is hot and moist. I grew all of these from seeds, which are brown and as tiny as a grain of sand." Charles poked at the moss surrounding each fleshy stalk and added water carefully from a jar.

"They actually feed on air. Some hang loose on trees, the way they grow wild in the jungles." He pointed upward where a rough-barked banana tree supported several vines, their roots shooting into the air while above them grew a multitude of pink and white flowers which Charles called vanda orchids.

"Something smells like vanilla." Carefully, Charlotte followed Charles as he moved into another room.

"This plant, indeed, furnishes real vanilla," Charles nodded toward a big-leaved vine with tiny rootlets clinging to a nearby tree. "See those long pods, or beans? When grown commercially, they are harvested after three years, boiled with water and alcohol, then dried in the sun. It's an expensive process, but no flavor equals real vanilla. What you are smelling are a few beans I am curing in the sun."

"I had no idea vanilla flavoring came from flowers," Charlotte exclaimed.

"It does seem strange, doesn't it? These orchids take so many forms. One variety contains a nourishing starch."

The sides of the greenhouse were all glass-paned windows and now Charles pushed one open. "I have to stimulate jungle conditions," he explained, "by circulating damp, warm air."

He indicated a tray of tiny brushes. "In the jungle pollination is done by insects, but here I have to do it by hand to stimulate the blooms. That central 'throat' is called a lip and in the wilds, insects are drawn to its necter, carrying pollen on their bodies in the process. Each variety of orchid has its own special insect and they never get mixed up and go to a wrong flower. What do you think of that!"

"It all leaves me breathless," Charlotte gasped. "Aren't these orchids a lot of work?"

"Not especially. They are pretty hardy. Anyway, I love it. It's a nice hobby for an old fellow who had to give up raising horses. My doctor said I must slow down, so we gave most of the horses to my daughter and son-in-law. Now Beaulah interests herself in the animals we retained and I am happy raising flowers.''

He fished out his tiny silver scissors and cut a pale lavender flower with a ruffled purple throat which he handed to Charlotte with a little bow.

"Oh, how beautiful! Thank you. Wouldn't it be amazing to see orchids like this growing wild in jungles, hundreds and hundreds of them?''

"I have often thought of that. Perhaps some day I can persuade Beaulah to accompany me to the Amazon.''

Holding her flower carefully in both hands, Charlotte moved with him through the other rooms, which held towering trees up to the roof. Beneath them grew strange bushes also containing exotic flowers, but none were as fascinating as the orchids.

When they had completed the tour, Charles invited her to stay for lunch, but she refused, telling him that a guest was arriving from New York.

"You must be sure to bring him to our ball,'' Charles told her.

Charlotte promised to do so, and after thanking him warmly, was driven home by one of the servants. She arrived just in time for the mid-day meal, but first, she had to run upstairs, put the orchid in a glass of water, and tidy herself.

Lunch was very different this day from the usual heavy food, only vermicilli soup, chicken salad, hot rolls, and blanc mange. This was more like the noon meals Charlotte always had up North and she wondered if Clara would be amenable to a suggestion for lighter fare? Probably not, she finally thought. Old customs seemed to be the rule here in the South.

The talk was all of Tim's arrival and the picnic on the morrow. No one mentioned Charlotte's trip to Roselands.

"Aunt Beckie promised to fry chicken the way I like it.''

Vanessa smacked her lips. "She soaks it first in beaten egg, milk, and a little tobasco sauce, then rolls it in flour."

Clara agreed. "Men all like pan-fried chicken, and it tastes good cold."

Vanessa flashed a quick look at Amy. "I suppose you know Timmie's preferences. Why don't you tell me what they are then Mama can confer with Aunt Beckie."

"Oh, he seemed to eat anything. I can't remember any of his dislikes."

"Did you and he go out a lot to fancy places?"

"Not often. Tim liked simple pleasures: skating or riding in the park, rowing on the lake, listening to music . . ."

"And parties, of course." Vanessa nodded happily. "My stars, he sounds exactly like me."

Charlotte hid a smile. Vanessa liked simple pleasures? They would probably bore her to tears. Whatever it took, Vanessa seemed bent on catering to Tim's every wish and making him another suitor.

Charlotte looked at Amy and raised her eyebrows, but Amy only looked amused. At any rate, she didn't appear to be worried about Vanessa, so Charlotte decided not to worry, either. There was no way of telling what would happen when Tim arrived.

Clara showed an unusual bit of humor. "Well, since the young man likes simple things, why don't we have hog jowls and turnip greens for dinner tonight?"

"Mama!" Vanessa shrieked. "That's the nigras's food."

"Sounds good," Charlotte remarked.

"I was only joshing. I think a real Southern dinner, don't you? Country baked ham—"

"Cornbread dressing," Vanessa chimed in.

Clara nodded. "Scalloped oysters. Why not crab soup to start?"

The mouth-watering suggestions flew back and forth,

ending with persimmon pudding, tipsy cake and the favorite Mississippi Mud."

"Good heavens," Charlotte exclaimed faintly. "So much rich food, though it all sounds delicious."

"Poor Tim." Amy chuckled. "He won't be able to move after eating all that."

"Oh, he can just taste everything, if he's a picky eater." Vanessa pursed her lips. "Well, I want him able to go on the picnic tomorrow. Let's see, how many men will be along? You said we could take Martin, since he knows the caves."

That was bad news to Charlotte. No wonder Amy was indifferent to Vanessa's pursuit of Tim. Her cousin's next announcement sent a thrill through Charlotte both pleasant and apprehensive.

"Devlin's coming. That makes four men, Keith, Tim and Martin." She exhaled happily. "And all attractive, I do declare. The girls are Katy, Amy, Charlotte and me. Why that comes out exactly even. We should all go with a partner."

"That's not a good idea," Charlotte burst out. A vision of Amy going off with Martin hit her. Also her own possible pairing with the unsettling Devlin . . .

"Well, I never!" Vanessa exclaimed. "Whatever is your objection?"

"I—I just think pairing should come naturally. Devlin might starting talking to Martin, getting information for his book. Amy, Katy or I might want to visit together—"

"Oh, wonderful!" Vanessa crowed. "That leaves three men for me."

"I really think you should let Tim and Amy visit by themselves."

"Oh, yes, some of the time." Vanessa bounded to her feet. "I must get ready to greet our company. I intend on going to the station with Cicero. Amy, I suppose you—"

"Yes." Amy pushed back her chair. "I am certainly going with you. Charlotte?"

"No, I'll wait until he comes here. I want to do a lot of work this afternoon, so I can be free tomorrow."

Train travel was still unpredictable. That evening, a weary group arrived back at Stone Gardens with their guest, in time for a late supper. Clara and Charlotte had waited in the parlor for the past hour when finally Cicero ushered in the two girls and the young man from New York.

Tim, however, seemed to recover quickly as he strode into the parlor behind Vanessa. He went at once to Charlotte with a wide grin and gave her an exhuberant greeting. "By Jove, Charlotte, you look blooming. This Southern climate certainly seems to agree with you and Amy."

Charlotte rose, shook his hand and presented him to Clara who surveyed his well-cut Norfolk jacket, short plaid cape and wide-brimmed hat with curly edges. Her smile approved it all.

"So kind of you to invite me," Tim told her. "I've never been down South, you know. I want to see as much as possible."

"Oh, we'll show you everything," Vanessa babbled. "Sit down by me. Cicero, will you take our wraps? I'll pour out the sherry."

"Hold supper for a few minutes," Clara instructed her majordomo. "Mr. Deane, you've had a tiring journey, I imagine."

"Lord, yes." He groaned. "Cinders blowing in the windows, crowded cars, constant stops. But, please, call me Tim, Miss Clara. I feel as though I know you all, from Amy's letters."

With a batting eye, Vanessa edged closer to him on the sofa. "What did Amy write about little old me?"

"Just that you were sweet and beautiful and, by Gad, she didn't lie."

Vanessa simpered. "Well, I do declare you are just as I imagined. Handsome, suave, cultured—"

"Oh, come now, Miss Vanessa." He took a hasty gulp of wine. "I say, this house—it-it's really champion." His brown eyes roamed over the entire room from crystal chandeliers and marble busts to the worn but glowing Persian rugs. He praised everything, winning a smile from Clara.

Charlotte decided the time had come to claim Tim's attention since Amy had allowed Vanessa to take the center of the stage without a challenge. "Tim, how is business at the bookstore?"

"Quite well," he answered eagerly. "Things have been turned around since my papa bought it—lots of new furnishings, all the latest books, advertising . . . Incidentally, I've brought new books for everyone."

"Why don't we see them later." Clara rose majestically in her softly gleaming garnet satin. "There will be lots of time later, but now I suggest we go in to supper before it's ruined."

The meal, while perhaps not at its best, was gobbled up by Tim with every indication of enjoyment. He captured Amy's attention with the latest news about their friends, after he apologized to Vanessa and his hostess, who were left to talk among themselves for a few minutes. Charlotte hid an approving smile. Tim had turned to Amy at the first opportunity. So far, he hadn't lost his head despite Vanessa's obvious attempts at flirting.

When the meal was over, they all returned to the parlor, where Tim opened a valise he had left in the hallway and distributed books to everyone. The first one was a beautiful book of art reproductions. He handed it to Clara, while her eyes brightened with appreciation.

Next, he turned to Charlotte. "Here is a fascinating new

novel by Nathaniel Hawthorne, the best book I've ever read. It's called *The Scarlet Letter*."

Vanessa leaned over to stare. "What is the scarlet letter?"

"It's an 'A' worn for adultery. A person convicted of that sin in Pilgrim times had to sew the letter on their clothes. Charlotte, I trust you won't be shocked by this story."

"I wouldn't be shocked," Vanessa cried, reaching out to grab the book.

Charlotte tugged it away from her. "No, I'll read it first. Nathaniel Hawthorne is very much admired, but Aunt Clara should also pass her judgment on it."

Clara eyed the slim volume with interest. "Indeed. I shall decide if it is proper reading for my daughter."

Vanessa pouted, but quickly changed her manner. "Oh, Timmie, I just knew you would be a man of the world. What have you brought for me?"

"I have two new books of poetry. You and Amy can decide which ones you want. The first is by Edgar Allan Poe, who died last year after a mental breakdown. I've heard he had been depressed since his beloved wife passed away in '47. His poems are often sad but very powerful.

"The other is a new book by Elizabeth Barrett Browning called *Sonnets From the Portuguese*. Critics are already saying they are the finest love poems ever written. In spite of the deceiving title, they actually relate her adoration for her husband, Robert Browning, and his for her."

"I'll take that," Vanessa cried. "Amy, perhaps I'll let you read it later." She opened up the gilt-edged pages greedily.

Amy held the book by Poe and thanked Tim for his thoughtfulness. "Your choices are all wonderful."

Tim reached over and captured Amy's hand. Vanessa was so absorbed in her book she paid him no heed, not even when he kissed Amy's wrist and smiled into her eyes.

Charlotte didn't let a single gesture escape her eagle eye. Tim must still be interested in Amy, maybe even in love. Hadn't he just made a long, uncomfortable journey to see her?

He seemed more attractive than heretofore, Charlotte thought, casting a critical eye over his lanky but well-dressed person. As Vanessa said, he did appear more suave and cultured. Perhaps it was the contrast between him and Martin Cord and Keith. The latter two lacked any attributes to be a possible suitor for Amy. Whereas Tim . . . well, it remained to be seen what would develop. How long would Tim stay here? Charlotte recalled her mother mentioning visitors who remained for months, since the far-flung plantations hungered for some social life and had to depend on guests for it.

Tim began to seem a little weary and Clara suggested that he might like an early night. He willingly agreed, and after more gratitude was expressed, they all trooped up to bed. All, that is, except Charlotte and Amy who, after an exchange of speaking glances, remained behind, ostensibly comparing the gifts they had received.

"Chapter One. The Prison Door," Charlotte's book began, but her eyes read nothing more. "Amy," she said softly, "are you pleased to have Tim here? Do you think Vanessa's pursuit of him is serious?"

"Yes, to the first question. Maybe, to the second." She opened her book and read aloud:

" 'Once upon a midnight dreary
While I pondered, weak and weary.'

"Hmm, just the way I feel." She looked up and glanced around to see if they were alone, then hissed, "Vanessa makes me sick."

"Oh, Amy, you've known all along the way she is. Tomorrow she'll be after Keith. Well, maybe not him . . ."

"Why not?"

"Beaulah told me they had a quarrel at the musicale. Did you notice anything while you were there?"

"Well . . . they slipped outside for part of the program, but I was listening to the music and was glad for once that Vanessa was quiet when she returned. There were lots of nice young people there and I enjoyed myself."

"You've missed going out just for fun, haven't you, little one? I'm glad Tim is here. I think he still favors you. Just don't let Vanessa get the upper hand."

"I can't be too assertive around Vanessa and make her angry with me."

"Oh, go fry Vanessa!"

"Charlotte, such language." Amy giggled weakly. Then she yawned. "I better get to bed. Tomorrow will be a big day."

They embraced and parted, Charlotte going to her slumbers torn between anticipation of Devlin's company at a day-long outing and worry about controlling her feelings. It was going to be impossible to avoid him.

She had no inkling that tomorrow would bring a time when she would yearn for Devlin to appear with every fiber of her being.

Chapter 24

The morning of the island picnic promised a Southern day of beautiful fall weather. A day to wear full-skirted cottons with only shawls and hats to mitigate the elements which might intrude.

She would compensate for sunshine or an errant breeze, Charlotte thought, by tying a green satin bow beneath her chin. She surveyed her matching wide-brimmed straw hat with satisfaction. In keeping with the casualness of a picnic, she wore her hair in loose waves upon her shoulders—no snood today.

Excitement sent a surge of color through her cheeks as she smoothed the hair so free and shining. Would Devlin admire it as he had before?

Or did she appear too youthful? Perhaps she had tried too hard. Biting her lips, she took another length of ribbon and tied her hair back at the nape. There. That looked more like her usual self. A tiny sigh escaped her. Had she ever been as carefree and young as other girls? She knew the answer, but raised her chin defiantly. Today held the promise of seeing Devlin, a day to laugh and chatter, to fling off worries.

She heard a knock at her door and whirled around to see Amy dance and twirl into the room in a froth of yellow organdy and violet ribbons. Charlotte clasped her hands with a happy cry. "Oh, little one, you look enchanting! As lovely as a spring bouquet."

She circled Amy, touching the curls tied on each side with velvet bows. "Are you going to wear a shawl and bonnet?"

"Oh, I don't think so. It's so mild today and I want to run and climb on rocks and go into the caves without any things to hamper me."

Charlotte suddenly remembered Martin Cord begging Amy not to wear a hat the day he took them over the plantation. Had that influenced her to go bare-headed now?

Amy studied Charlotte and was lavish in her praise. "You look so lovely and cool in all that green. And I like your hair loose down your back. It's much softer, more feminine."

"You don't think it's too youthful?" Charlotte peered anxiously into a mirror.

"Of course not. Oh, this will be a day of such fun. Listen! I hear voices below."

Hastening to the window, they saw Tim and Vanessa who called and waved, telling them to hurry. Snatching up her shawl, Charlotte followed her sister into the garden. They were just in time to see Keith and Katy arrive, then Devlin.

All were introduced to Tim, who had dressed casually in a wide-brimmed hat and loose jacket. Its checks nicely complimented his tan trousers and low brown boots.

"I say, how smashing everybody looks," he beamed. "Amy, you remind me of every sweet daffodil and tender violet in the spring. While you, Charlotte, are a woodland nymph in leaf-green.''

''My stars, Timmie,'' Vanessa giggled. ''You certainly do turn a pretty compliment. Girls, he called me trailing arbutus. Did you ever?''

It was true that Vanessa's rosy skirts trailed on the ground like the flowers, causing Charlotte to wonder how she would fit them into a boat. Were they taking more than one vessel?

It seemed that they were. Katy loudly proclaimed that their own sloop from Roselands must be ready now at the dock and also another rowboat.

''Here comes Martin back from the landing,'' Vanessa cried prancing forward, one hand managing to hold up her skirts, parasol and shawl, while keeping a firm grip on Tim's arm. ''I sent Martin down early to get things ready. Timmie, you must sit by me. I know all the sights, the homes, the people, and things like that.''

Tim stretched back his hand to Amy. ''Come along—''

''I tell you, she doesn't know the river.'' Vanessa gave his arm a jerk. ''Don't you want my company?''

''I'd be honored,'' he drawled, but gave a little wink across his shoulder.

Amy merely smiled and fell in step with Keith and Katy who were full of their usual laughter and enthusiasm.

Martin's black eyes swept the group, lingering on Amy. He seemed to swallow. ''If everyone is ready, let's be off. Ned is loading up the boats. Don't dally. I noticed a few clouds on the horizon.''

''Oh, you're a worrywart,'' Vanessa trilled. ''I vow I never saw a more perfect day.''

Martin shrugged and strode off, everyone falling in behind him, chattering and laughing. Devlin walked beside Charlotte, looking casual and relaxed and exceedingly attractive, Charlotte thought, noting his soft white shirt open at the neck, brown waistcoat and matching trousers. As usual, he was bareheaded.

Two boats were at the dock, the sloop filled with rugs and baskets of food. Benches beneath a striped awning were soon appropriated by Vanessa, Tim and Amy, with Keith and Katy right behind. Martin directed the management of the sails and ropes to the men who had come with the Hartleys's boat, two husky Negroes dressed in seamen's jerseys.

Charlotte felt Devlin's hand upon her arm. "Shall we sit in the other boat?" he asked. "And leave this one to the children?"

Charlotte could see no reason to refuse as, indeed, the sloop was jammed with excited, bubbling youth. "Are we the chaperones?" she wondered, letting him assist her into the rowboat where Ned sat at the oars.

"Not at all," Devlin laughed. "Today I feel as carefree as a boy. And you look as young and vibrant as Amy." Devlin shed his jacket, adjusted a pillow behind Charlotte's back, and settled his long legs beside her.

Ned grinned at them, then pulled out into the sunlit water, a short distance behind the sailboat and rowed them easily into an unhurried procession.

Charlotte felt all her apprehension about being close to Devlin melt away and just enjoyed the pleasure of sitting calmly next to him. Neither of them spoke for a while. The peace and beauty seemed to cast a spell. Even the noise from the boat ahead softened to voices calling back and forth, as they exchanged remarks and comments on the countryside.

Above, mossy, rock-strewn banks, tree-shaded homes, fields and orchards could be glimpsed. Some had wrought-iron gates and tall hedges beyond the river. All the lawns were still green and flowerbeds lingered into fall, alive with many colors. They made an entrancing foreground for the mansions of red brick or white-painted wood. Sometimes, they saw fields of workers picking cotton or tobacco and then the smell of drying sheds mingled with pine trees and fresh grass.

Since Vanessa's narration of the scenery didn't carry back to the rowboat, Devlin began his own discourse. His eyes looked dreamy as he leaned back on the pillowed seat. "I love Virginia, in spite of the plague of slavery. You see, I grew up around here."

At last, Charlotte felt she might learn something personal about her reticent employer and she dared to ask some questions. "You have very little Southern accent. Have you always lived in Virginia?"

"Lord, no. I went to school at Harvard and met my wife in Boston. My father wanted me to come back home to practice law, as he had done." His face grew strained. "I did. But I told you about that. How my marriage fell apart—"

"Yes," Charlotte answered quickly. "So then you started writing? Did your family encourage you?"

"They were outraged. I think my father would have cut me off completely, but I was the only son, the heir to a large estate. My father abhorred my feelings about slavery, which had grown stronger when I met so many Abolitionists in Boston. Our arguments raged uselessly, until finally, I left for good. I corresponded with my mother while she was alive, but never with my father."

"Do you have any other family?"

"Just two sisters who both married well and are older than I am. Neither of them had any use for my anti-slavery views, my broken marriage or my abandonment of my law career."

Charlotte put a hand upon his arm, remembering the warmth and comfort of her parents when they were alive and how much she valued her sister's love. "I'm sorry, Devlin."

He took her hand and held it in both of his. His eyes looked somberly at the passing shore, but with a certain peace upon his face. "I think I grew stronger after I left. I wrote, traveled, and formed my own ideas everywhere I went. Yes, I've been lonely, but . . ." He smiled a little. "The characters I wrote about always became very real to me. They lived beside me night and day, and I missed them when the books were finished."

Finished! A sudden pang swept through Charlotte. "How near are you to completing your current book?"

"Quite near." He turned to look into her eyes with a searching glance.

"You'll leave, then?" Charlotte's voice was husky.

He nodded. "I suppose so. Although . . . this time I don't relish the idea. Would you miss me?"

"Of course." Charlotte lowered her glance to their clasped hands. He probably had no idea how much.

A silence fell between them. The boat moved slowly. Ned rowed in a dreamy fashion, as though he had all day and relished being on the water. He seemed to be humming underneath his breath. Voices and laughter drifted back from the boat ahead. Birds called from the trees along the bank, where little waves added their own harmony.

In spite of all the beauty, Charlotte felt like crying. Nothing mattered but the man beside her and soon he might be gone. Devlin looked at her, then put his arm around her waist, drawing her close to his side and not caring who might see. "Let us enjoy this time together, my dear girl."

"Yes," Charlotte whispered, gazing at his throat, and the strong line of his clean-shaven jaw. How she longed to kiss the hard planes of his face . . . feel his lips engulf her own . . .

With an effort, she spoke calmly. "You started to tell me about Virginia."

"Ah, yes." His eyes roved far and wide. "America began right here. The first permanent English settlement started at Jamestown in 1607. In 1619, the first legislation met. And in that same year, Dutch traders brought in the first Negro slaves. The good and the bad had begun. The land grants from England had created huge estates."

He gestured toward the passing scene. "Many of these old homes were built in the early Colonial days, so well-made, so simple and elegant, they are all still as good as new."

Impressed, Charlotte murmured, "They are beautiful." She wondered where his own home was located, but feared it might reopen a painful subject, so she stayed silent while he continued.

"The colony thrived with forward-looking men who built the first hospital in America, the first university, William and Mary College, which Washington and Jefferson attended. Then came the first capitol building in Williamsburg and here also the first theatre and the first law school."

"So many firsts!"

"It was all beginning. John Rolfe found a way to cure and export tobacco, which grew so well that everybody rushed to plant it. And that led to more slave labor and bigger, wealthier estates."

"And now that seems to be destroying everything."

"I think the South will have to industrialize when slavery is banned. The land is being worked to death. There is increasing unrest everywhere among the slaves. More and more are trying to 'make free.'"

"I guess you haven't been aware of the unsavory person who visited Stone Gardens recently, a Frenchman named Francois Savon, from Louisiana. He has been tracking two slaves who ran away from him and he gained information that they had passed this way. He seemed suspicious of us all.''

"He didn't catch them?'' Devlin asked sharply.

"Not to my knowledge. He left still in hot pursuit, even intending to follow the trail up North. I certainly hope he doesn't find them. I'm sure he would be a master to be feared.''

"This Savon should be stopped,'' Devlin growled. "If I had met him, there would have been unpleasantness, believe me. His treatment of the girl and desire for revenge seem to border on insanity, in my opinion.''

"Do you think there's any chance he will find them up North and bring them back?''

"There always is a chance that an informer can be paid enough to track them down. Judges can be bribed to send back slaves, even when they have been granted freedom by some former owner. Once back in the South, an unscrupulous planter can keep them deep in some plantation, making them labor with no chance of escape from carefully guarded premises.''

"I wish Aunt Clara would give Elijah Mason his freedom. Don't you think the family owes him something for the work his ancestor did on the Stone Garden?''

"That has to be your aunt's decision. I cannot give any advice.''

Neither should I, Charlotte thought rebelliously, but am I not also an heir to Stone Gardens? No, came the next reply. Mama was disinherited when she married Papa.

Devlin put a finger underneath her chin, turning her face up to his. "You must not have any long thoughts today, dear girl. I want you to be happy and carefree.'' His head dipped lower and Charlotte gasped as she felt the light, warm pressure of his lips, tantalizing and exciting, recalling other more intimate encounters. As he had before on her aunt's balcony, Devlin didn't care about a possible spectator.

Charlotte drew her head back and forced a shaken laugh. "You're a bold, bad pirate, like the heroes in your books."

"Aye, lass, I want what I want when I want it," With a teasing growl, he regarded her beneath lowered lids, then whispered in her ear. "And I can't be near you without wanting everything about you."

At the image his words conjured, a tide of heat swept Charlotte and she couldn't speak. There was no doubt about his desire for her . . . but why didn't he say that he loved her?

Chapter 25

There was no chance just then for further discussion. Their destination had approached unnoticed. The widened river now held several small islands. All appeared thickly wooded but uninhabited, at least no chimneys reared among the trees and no animals or people were in evidence. The rocks and vegetation came right to the water's edge and the lack of beaches probably prevented any place to land a boat.

This was not so, however, at the island of Vanessa's choice. Waving wildly, she called shrill unnecessary instructions to the men who manned the boat, and it was soon obvious that they would be landing on the largest island. A place of rocky hills and wind-gnarled trees, at least it had a small crescent of sand and a natural cove.

The two boats bobbed slowly forward, carefully maneuvered between rather alarming boulders dashed by spray, until they rested safely drawn up on the shore.

As Ned steadied their craft, Devlin stood up and reached for Charlotte's hand. "Well, here we are."

Charlotte clutched her skirts and stepped out on the beach. "How dark the hill looks. Rather forbidding, don't you think? An odd choice for a rollicking picnic."

"It will be all right." Devlin stared around. "The sun has just gone behind a cloud. It will be back in a minute. I suppose the famous cave of Nat Turner is in that hill somewhere?"

"Yes, Vanessa seemed intrigued by the idea of exploring it," Charlotte muttered, plowing through the sand toward the other boat. "I don't know if I care to go in a labyrinth like that. There's something about this place . . . I don't know . . . it makes me feel uneasy."

"Oh, you'll have to go exploring with the rest. I'll stay at your side and never let go of you."

"Well, all right." Charlotte threw him a fleeting smile. A dark cave with winding tunnels and Devlin. It sounded rather romantic . . . When they reached the others, Charlotte's eyes went swiftly to Amy. She was pleased to see that both Keith and Tim were vying for her sister's laughing regard.

Everyone seemed to be arguing about the best place to put the rugs and baskets of food. Soon Martin stepped ashore, leading the servants, and Charlotte saw his quick glance take in Amy and her swains. Charlotte frowned, wishing he could have stayed on board the sloop, but she knew he had been brought along because he understood the caves. Thank goodness, Tim seemed anxious to keep Amy for himself.

Vanessa was darting everywhere, finally halting on the smoothest part of the beach. "We'll sit here in a circle," she proclaimed. "Then we can all laugh and talk together, I reckon. Later, we can pair off when we go exploring." She pulled off her rose-covered bonnet and shook out her curls, dropping gracefully on one of the rugs. Coyly, she patted a place beside here. "Come right here, Timmie-honey. Let the servants set out the lunch. Ned, put that tablecloth in the center. That's right. I swear to goodness, I'm purely perishing for food. Are the rest of y'all hungry, too?''

Among the chattering and settling of skirts and shawls, Charlotte saw Keith moving purposely toward her. Quickly, she pulled on Devlin's arm. "Sit by me, please," she hissed.

With a quick glance at Keith, Devlin sat down obediently and put his arm possessively around her shoulders. "We'll foil all attempts to board this vessel. Today, my beauty, you are my sole companion. Is that what you want—I trust?''

"Yes, but Devlin, just don't be too—too obvious. People will make remarks.''

"Very well. I'll be close but not obvious.''

Charlotte knew he was laughing at her skittishness. Well, she couldn't help it. She had never been in love before and didn't know how she should act. It still seemed remarkable. At her age, too. Most young women felt romantic urges much earlier—such as Amy and Vanessa.

In spite of the prevalence of such tendencies among the young, it seemed to Charlotte that it posed an awful problem. Attraction ripened far too often into yearnings much deeper, and if given in to, the consequences could be dire indeed. Marriage during adolescence was almost impossible without some form of security or income. Besides, characters were barely formed so young. How could they know who they would be in a few years hence?

Perhaps it was better to feel love at a later date such as she herself was. Oh, yes, she knew her heart. She even thought she knew Devlin's. He might be in love with her, but he couldn't or wouldn't settle down. It was on the tip of her tongue to blurt out a question about his future plans. And that would have been disastrous. Fortunately, the bowl of chicken legs appeared in front of her.

"Have some," Devlin spoke thickly and swallowed.

Katy, on Charlotte's other side, giggled. "Oh, they look delicious. Hurry, pass them on, do."

Soon everyone began to gobble up the picnic, which consisted of varied edibles crowded on their big china plates. Besides the fried chicken, sliced beef and ham loaf, there were salads such as mixed fruits, vegetables, potato and egg. Many ingenious appetizers also appeared: cheese baked in piecrust, deviled pecans and liver paste on crackers. Besides all this, Ned handed round a platter of dainty sandwiches: cucumber, watercress and crab. Accompanying the food were bottles of lemonade, ginger beer and cold tea nog, a spicy beverage of the rind and juice of oranges and lemons.

Groans issued from the assembled throng when they received fresh plates for the array of tempting desserts: white cake, chocolate cake, pecan or apple pies. Then a tray of frosted cookies topped with nuts and chopped glacéed fruits. But in spite of protestating, everyone ate everything.

"How is it that you Southerners aren't as fat as balloons?" Tim asked, then laughed.

"Well, heavens to Betsy, we don't eat like this every day," Vanessa protested, licking icing from her lips. "This is in your honor, Timmie-honey. Oh, and for Keith and Katy, too. I wager at the ball, you'll outdo this simple food. Am I right?"

"Oh, I don't know about that," Keith drawled. "Food is not the thing I'm looking forward to ... it's holding lovely ladies in my arms."

Vanessa giggled. "If you don't beat all! Such a tease."

"I'm not teasing." Keith raised his voice. "Miss Charlotte, I want to claim you right now for the first three dances."

Vanessa opened her mouth indignantly, but Charlotte said hastily, "Don't you think it's a little soon to select partners?" She cleared her throat. "Listen, I'd like to change the subject. Is everybody going into the caves now that we have finished lunch?''

No one had a firm reply. Some had fallen back upon the sand with moans of having over-eaten. Others struggled to their feet reluctantly, looking to Vanessa for direction.

"What are these caves?" Katy queried, shaking sand from her white dimity skirts.

"Well—" Vanessa began.

"Pardon, miss, if I can have everyone's attention, I will explain." Martin Cord stepped firmly into the circle. During the picnic, he had sat apart, not too near the guests nor associating with the three servants. Still, Charlotte noted uneasily, he was never too far from Amy.

She thought he seemed like an animal, leashed but still extremely dangerous. Amy's avoidance of him seemed studied, almost teasing, as she openly flirted and encouraged Tim while tossing off-hand glances at the brooding overseer, then laughing with Tim, whispering in his ear or slipping a piece of fruit from her own plate into his mouth. While Cord grew steadily grimmer.

When he stepped into the center, everyone sat up or gathered closer. Cord raised his chin and pushed back his hat, looking proud and cocky. Even Amy riveted her eyes on him when he began to talk.

"Nat Turner was a slave preacher born in Southampton County in 1800. He wasn't badly treated by his master, but he began to say voices were telling him to take revenge on whites because they had enslaved his people. He gathered a large following and, in 1831, they all ran amok and slaughtered fifty-one innocent people.''

Everyone gasped and murmured in shocked tones, even though most of them must have heard the story, which had so terrorized the South, many times already.

Cord continued, his narrowed eyes swiveling from one face to another. "Turner was eventually captured right here on Ferris Island where he had been hiding in the caves. After he was executed, the South passed stricter laws to keep the slaves in line which, believe me, were long overdue.'' Cord finished in a cold, hard tone, grinding his teeth together.

''Do y'all still want to go into the caves?'' Vanessa quavered.

''Follow me, if you want to come,'' Cord said, his mouth twisting. ''Perhaps Turner's ghost will step out of a tunnel and say 'boo!' ''

Katy gave a little shriek, but everybody laughed and followed Cord as he led the way across the beach. Amy and Tim were right behind him and Charlotte hurried to keep up. It would be just like Cord to lure Amy into some byway in the caves and keep her to himself, perhaps pretending they were lost, so he could again force his odious attempts at lovemaking on her.

They halted at the entrance to the caves, and Cord ran his eye over everyone while he waited for the stragglers. ''So the story of Nat Turner hasn't scared you off?'' he sneered, his eyes lingering on Charlotte.

''Well, it's a nasty tale,'' Keith drawled. ''No wonder you people in Virginia lock your doors at night.''

''Don't you?'' Cord snapped.

''Gad, no. Our slaves would never dare to turn. Owners keep them . . .'' His voice hardened. ''. . . terrified.''

''You and Francois Savon sound just alike.'' Charlotte said, wondering if the Hartleys knew about Keith's sentiments.

''Oh, yes, let us hear from our dear Yankee.'' Keith had a strange light in his eyes. Had her avoidance of him finally touched a tender spot and turned his admiration into hate?

''Who is Francois Savon?'' his sister asked.

Several voices answered her, both Vanessa and Amy sounding indignant, although for slightly different reasons—Amy because she knew he was a cruel, deranged tyrant to his slaves and Vanessa because he dared to attempt liberties with her, even though he was so old and ugly.

When the babbling faded, Cord spoke up, drawing on his cheeroot. "I met him. He had right on his side. Two of his slaves had run away. One of them was a woman he had honored with his attentions and showered with jewels."

Charlotte had to clamp her lips together to keep from saying too much. Gasps went up and Cord was instantly bombarded with eager questions.

Charlotte drew Amy to one side and murmured in her ear. "I imagine Cord and Savon would make a perfect match."

Amy said nothing as Tim looked at them curiously, but Charlotte said no more, knowing it would be dangerous. It made her distinctly uneasy that Cord had talked to the Frenchman and Savon had been suspicious of nearly everyone at Stone Gardens. Cord had also hinted to Charlotte that he had seen her out at night and knew more than he was telling. She had a feeling that blackmail from him might be imminent, leaving him able to pursue Amy undeterred.

Suddenly, Vanessa pushed up to the front and clapped her hands. "All right, everyone. Martin is going to lead us through the caves now. They are long and winding and very dark farther back so don't go wandering off, you hear? Girls, stay close to one of the men." She started toward Tim, but her trailing skirts impeded her progress and Tim took the opportunity to draw Amy's hand beneath his arm. Charlotte smiled, thankful that so far Cord had not found some scheme to escort Amy.

Tim glanced at Charlotte with a gallant bow. "Will you accept my other side?"

Before she could reply, Devlin spoke behind her. He grinned when she turned around. "If I hold your hand inside the caves, will it be too . . . obvious?"

Tim and Amy looked merely puzzled, but Charlotte laughed and slipped her hand into the delightful warmth of Devlin's clasp.

Keith, with a rather bored expression, came along between his sister and Vanessa. His eyes flickered with an unreadable expression when he saw Charlotte standing so close to Devlin. Could the silly boy be jealous? she wondered. There was no doubt in her mind that Keith could be extremely unpleasant to anyone who incurred his anger. Tiresome puppy!

She met Devlin's gaze as they started toward the entrance. "I couldn't have stood this excursion without you," she murmured.

His thumb caressed the soft mound of her palm and his lips blew her a soundless, teasing kiss.

"Devlin," she admonished with a smothered laugh.

"What's the matter?" He chuckled. Then he whispered in her ear. "Leave your hat here on the beach. It might get in the way."

She didn't ask him what he meant, but her pulses tingled and her heart began to race. Devlin was such a constantly exciting man. With just a hinting word he could send thrills coursing through her entire body.

"Get in the way," he had said.

Did he mean what she thought he meant? Kissing, perchance, in a darkened tunnel where no one could observe them?

A reckless feeling swamped her, and she decided to enjoy whatever Devlin had in mind. She loved him, after all, and their days together might be drawing to a close. No, she couldn't bear to think of that. Not today.

When they stepped inside the shadowed cave, she had to force her thoughts from Devlin and try to observe the strangeness of their surroundings. Which were very strange, indeed.

Chapter 26

The first object to catch Charlotte's eye was a yellow gourd hanging above the entrance. She would have thought little of it, except that Cord snatched it down and flung it on the ground, grinding with his heel.

"What's the matter? What is that thing?" Charlotte exclaimed.

Amy and Tim had vanished inside the caves without being aware of the gourd, but Charlotte and Devlin stopped and stared at the angry overseer.

"It's the sign to a fugitive slave for a safe place," Cord said, annoyed greatly. "From that damn Frenchman, I'll be bound. I'd like to get my hands on him, believe me." His fingers opened and closed spasmodically as though in his mind they clutched somebody's throat.

Charlotte felt her heart skip a beat. Swiftly, she glanced at Devlin to see what he made of this. "Have you ever heard of the Frenchman, a conductor on the Underground Railroad?" she asked him, trying to conceal her apprehension.

"I've heard about him." Devlin's face looked stony as he stared at the smashed insignia. His mouth clamped shut.

What was he thinking? Charlotte knew he had no sympathy for slavery. He had said as much. And his book showed it, too. But did he believe in helping slaves to escape their lawful owners? This was a ticklish question for many people. Besides, Devlin was a Southerner by birth and inheritance, no matter what his recent views.

With a muttered curse, Martin stomped ahead into the cave and Charlotte heard him calling her sister to wait for him and not get separated. A sudden wind stirred up the sand as the others arrived on the scene and once again the sun disappeared. Charlotte took a quick look at the sky and saw to her dismay a rolling darkness.

"Oh, Devlin, I fear a storm is coming!"

"I think you're right. We better make this exploration short."

"Bring up that pitch torch, Ned, and put it near the entrance so we can get some light in here," Vanessa called, holding her blowing skirts as they all crowded forward. "My stars, isn't this the strangest place! I haven't been in here since Papa was alive. He told us all about the pools and rocks and things. Gather close, now."

As Vanessa began talking, Charlotte stared at the sandy floor where tide pools could be discerned, gleaming darkly in the flickering light of Ned's pitchpine torch. Strange water creatures darted back and forth.

"Those round things in the pools are made of sand covered with limestone," Vanessa pointed out. "And the little white fish are really blind. See, they have only pinpoints for eyes."

There was a general murmuring and bending closer, then Katy asked in a tone of awe, "What are all those pillars and spires growing from the roof of the cave?"

"I'm not sure what they're called," Vanessa said, tipping back her head. "Except they are made of limestone."

"I believe they are caused by water dripping," Tim said, a little shyly. "I've read about them. The ones hanging from the roof are stalactites and the ones formed on the floor are called stalagmites."

"My, aren't you the smart one." Vanessa looked a little miffed. "Well, if you have seen enough, let's follow Martin."

Devlin let them all go by, then he took Charlotte's arm and without a word, drew her into an inky, unlit tunnel.

"Devlin, what are you doing?" Charlotte gasped.

He caught her in his arms, holding her tightly. "This is why I came. All day I have envisioned you pressed against me. Even clothed, our bodies know and respond to each other. Can you feel it? I know I can. Your swelling breasts, your pounding heart, your hips beneath my hands, thigh to thigh . . ."

When he breathed her name, Charlotte shuddered and pressed, as close to him as she could get, all her body hungry for his touch. She dragged his head down to reach her gasping mouth. His lips pressed fiercely, then his hands dug into her flesh, pulling up her skirts. His touch was hot, intimate and moving everywhere.

Charlotte clung frantically, knowing she would sink to the ground if he let go. All her senses whirled and she could barely speak. "What . . . what . . . are . . . you . . . doing?"

"Don't worry. I'm not taking your virginity," he growled against her lips, then thrust his stabbing tongue inside her mouth, over and over in a rhythm duplicated by the movement of his hips and hands.

A wild joy swept through Charlotte, stronger than anything she had ever known. It was as though here in this dark secret place all barriers were down. A need arose in her for something she couldn't understand. Her body jerked and throbbed while she sobbed his name.

Then, suddenly, it was over. Like an explosion in her brain, she went limp with a great surge of relief.

For a few moments, Devlin held her tightly, panting, his cheek pressed to hers. "That's a taste of what a marriage can be like, my love. Oh, yes," he groaned, "I do love you. And I know that you love me."

"Yes, I do." Charlotte raised her head. "But why then—?"

"Why don't I propose marriage? There are several reasons, but I can't tell you any of them. Not now." He withdrew a folded handkerchief and wiped her face, smoothing back her hair. "Did you enjoy that?" he whispered thickly.

"Oh, yes, you know I did." She expelled a shaken breath. Confused, she wondered if a man felt the same as she had without performing the actual act? Or had Devlin just coaxed a response to give her pleasure?

And what pleasure it had been! Charlotte straightened her clothes, suddenly shy, bewildered. What to say? What to do next? Dear God—his hands, those wonderful dexterous fingers! What they had done . . . where they had touched . . .

She swallowed hard. "Won't everyone wonder where we are?"

"We've only been away for a few minutes." He laughed softly. "You responded so quickly, my lovely girl. Well . . . I guess we better join the others."

Charlotte fumbled for his hand, feeling weak. Feeling wonderful. He said he loved her! Something would work out for them. It must!

When they reached the main cavern, several others were hurrying toward the entrance, looking worried. It became apparent that the storm had descended in earnest. Beyond the cave could be seen a drenching torrent while thunder rolled and lightning flashed.

Nobody seemed exactly frightened, but the thought of being on the river in a little boat made Charlotte catch her breath and look fearfully to Devlin for direction.

"Is everybody here?" he shouted above the din of storm and chattering voices.

"Tim and Amy?" Vanessa looked around. "No, and Martin's not here, either. Someone call them. We'll all catch our death if we don't get out of here. The river can rise and fill the cave!"

"Go now, Vanessa," Devlin barked. "Take the men, Keith and Katy. Charlotte, you go with them in the sloop. I'll bring Amy, Tim, and Martin in the rowboat."

He darted back inside the cave and the others surged away, all but Charlotte. No way was she going without Amy. And Martin might be brewing mischief to still get Amy for himself in some dark tunnel.

A swift shame engulfed her as she thought of the intimicies she had recently enjoyed with Devlin. Above all, Amy must never know about her sister's indiscretion. Now she had to push the thrilling memories from her mind which still flamed with a desire for more. But this was no time for such yearnings.

Stumbling, she raced across the cave, until she came to a side tunnel. Far away, she thought she heard Devlin shouting and now she began to call herself. "Amy! Tim! Where are you? Answer me. We have to leave at once!"

Were Tim and Amy secretly embracing? Was that why they didn't answer? Had they sneaked so deeply into the labyrinth that they couldn't hear the voices calling them? Feeling close to panic, Charlotte continued shouting, fumbling her way along one black tunnel after another. When she paused for breath, she had to tell herself that it was impossible to get lost. She hadn't come that far and surely someone would hear her voice.

But then she realized her folly in going off alone. A hard body bumped against her. Hands went out in a painful grip. They went across her hair, face, and body in an insulting survey.

"So, it's you," Cord snarled. "I might have known big sister would come looking. Well, Yank, I don't know where Amy is, and it's all your damn fault if she is lost." He shook her fiercely.

Charlotte stood her ground and pushed at his hands until he freed her. "What happened? What have you done? As God is my witness, I'll make you pay if you have harmed her."

"You ask what I have done? You meddling fool! Why did you bring that puppy down here to upset Amy? She was almost ready for me." His voice roared off the walls filling Charlotte with a quickening fear. Was the man insane?

She attempted to speak calmly. "Why shouldn't Amy have a friend come visiting? What business is it of yours?"

"My business is wanting Amy, and you know I am going to get her. With or without a ring!"

"You—you're talking about rape!" Charlotte gasped. "Do you think anyone would let you get away with that?"

"What could you do?" he sneered. "Once I show Amy how I can love her as she's never been loved before, she will give herself willingly, gladly." He expelled a gusty breath. "All night I can love her, days and nights on end until she can't stand."

"Stop, stop, you monster!" Charlotte screamed, trying to hit him with her flailing fists. "I'm going to tell Aunt Clara and believe me, you'll be banished from Stone Gardens at once. We'll have the law on you if ever you touch Amy again, a girl of only seventeen—"

"Damn you to hell! If you try to tell anyone, I'll do some talking of my own. I know who the Frenchman is and when Savon returns next week, I'm going to tell him. As well as how you helped his slaves escape."

Stunned, Charlotte fell back and clutched the rocky wall. "What are you saying? I don't believe you. How do you know who the Frenchman is? If it were true, why wouldn't you have turned him in?"

"I just found out. Now my information is going to the highest bidder. Unless . . ."

"What?"

"Unless you stay out of my life." The next instant, he pushed her so roughly that she nearly fell. Then the crunching sound of rocks beneath his feet grew faint and Charlotte knew she was alone.

At first, she felt too drained and frightened to move. She couldn't see her hand before her face. She tried to call but only croaked. Then tears came in a wild rush. Amy—at the mercy of that fiend! She would kill him first before she'd let Cord ruin Amy. His tireless, horrible assaults could destroy a tender child like Amy. He was not one whit better than Savon.

What could she do? She must find a solution. She could be imprisoned if she confessed everything to Aunt Clara, but she could stand that if it meant saving her sister. If all was out in the open, Cord could no longer try his blackmail scheme and certainly Clara would send him away at once.

Cord might also name the Frenchman, but that wily hero surely could escape. He might even help Charlotte to escape.

Yes. The first thing was to tell Clara all that Cord had said. If by some quirk, he was not dismissed, perhaps Tim could be prevailed upon to take Amy for a visit to his family up North. If they decided to marry, so be it. Charlotte would not stand in the way of Amy's safety.

She began a stumbling return along the passageway, calling now for Devlin, wanting him with all her heart and soul. On and on she went until her hoarse cries elicited a faint response. The shouts grew louder, the tunnel widened. Thank heaven, she was back in the main cavern.

Amy and Tim rushed toward her, but Devlin reached her first. Nearly fainting, she embraced each one in turn.

"Where's—where's Cord?" she croaked.

"Gone down to the sloop," Devlin said. "The rain is letting up. Let's get to the rowboat. It will just hold the four of us."

"Amy, where were you?" Charlotte scolded, arm about her sister as they struggled along the beach. "Didn't you hear us calling you?"

"Not for a long time. Oh, Charlotte we discovered a lake—"

"Did Mr. Cord find you?" Charlotte interrupted.

"No, Devlin did. He seems to know these caves quite well. Ugh, Charlotte, I'm so c-cold."

They huddled together in the rowboat with the men's jackets around their shoulders, but even when the sun came out and they reached Stone Gardens, everyone was soaked and shivering.

Charlotte felt relieved that Amy was safe for the time being . . . but how long would it last? Her sister didn't know the danger she was in. A ravenous beast desired her. And his appetite grew wilder by the minute.

Chapter 27

Keith and Katy had sailed back to Roselands in their sloop by the time the occupants of the rowboat landed at Stone Gardens. Tired, wet, and cold, no one felt like much conversation. Devlin hurried to the guest house while Tim, Amy and Charlotte made their way across the garden, dodging dripping trees and soggy piles of leaves.

Inside the house, pealing bells summoned servants and Tibby ran to Charlotte's aid, bringing hot water in a pitcher. Charlotte decided to forgo a tub, more interested in donning dry clothes and mopping her wet hair.

Finally, she flopped wearily on her bed, knowing she had a lot to think about. If only she could have flown into Devlin's arms for comfort and advice. But he also had presented her with a problem, saying he loved her, yet couldn't propose marriage. Was his writing the main hindrance? His need to travel? Other writers had wives and families. Besides, she would have been happy wandering with Devlin at her side.

Well, that obstacle would have to wait. Right now, the

biggest worry was Martin Cord's blackmail scheme and his ominous threat regarding Amy. The matter must be discussed with her sister as soon as possible, since she had no idea of the danger creeping toward her.

Probably Vanessa, as usual, had Amy on the run helping to repair the ravages to her appearance. Charlotte wondered if her cousin was annoyed because Tim and Amy had gone off together in the caves. Probably. But what did she expect? A singleminded kowtowing to her own beauty while Tim slighted his companion from New York? Yes, that undoubtedly had been Vanessa's plan, self-centered and vain creature that she was. In her eyes, no one existed more important than herself. And she hungered for masculine attention.

At first, she had centered on Devlin, who had seemed interested to some degree, but not sufficiently for Vanessa's demands. Was that what had prompted her to place a warning note in Charlotte's bed? Jealousy? Somehow the act seemed more like Vanessa's style than anybody else's . . . heedless, selfish and demanding.

After Devlin, Vanessa's interest veered to Keith, but evidently he had not met her demands, either. He wanted the game of seduction without any strings attached.

When Tim arrived, her hopes rose again, in spite of his being mainly interested in Amy. Again, Vanessa met with disappointment. Charlotte could almost feel sorry for the shallow beauty who was so anxious for a suitor that she tried to snare any half-way attractive man who came her way.

Tossing restlessly, Charlotte abandoned her thoughts regarding Vanessa. There were more important matters to consider—mainly Martin Cord. How could he have learned the Frenchman's identity? He even knew her own part and now he held it like a weapon to keep her from stopping his pursuit of Amy.

Charlotte clenched her hands until the nails dug in her palms while red hot waves of anger swept her. How dare he brag about what he could do if he took Amy? The villain was so certain of his prowess. Did he think they were all fools who wouldn't interfere? Yes! He believed Clara, Charlotte and Amy would be too afraid to fight him because his knowledge could put Charlotte behind bars and disgrace her aunt and sister.

Hope flared briefly: what proof did he have? Then her hope died. He didn't have to prove a thing if he confided his suspicions to Francois Savon. That odious creature would not wait for the law. He would take matters into his own hands, after Cord told him about the stray horse belonging to the runaways, which Charlotte had been seen riding. Cord had also claimed he saw Charlotte on the River Road that night. Savon already believed that someone at Stone Gardens had helped his escaping slaves.

Cord would not act, however, until he had Savon's money in his pocket. Or, would he keep silent if Amy came to him? If Charlotte interfered, his vengeance would be swift. First he would tell Savon, then the slave patrol.

What could she do? Twisting and turning, no plan came to her and at last she swung out of bed and rang for Tibby. She drew on a dark serge dress with a white knit shawl and told the maid to ask Clara and her sister to meet her at once in the study. "Tell them it's very urgent," she added.

Eyes wide but unquestioning, Tibby flew off on her errand and Charlotte made her way downstairs relieved that there was no sign of Vanessa or Tim. She hoped they both were napping and would keep out of the way. The coming confrontation promised enough nervewracking anxiety without an added audience.

Amy appeared first, but Charlotte wouldn't answer her questions until Clara joined them. She had a grim expression on her long face as though she expected nothing less than bad news from this "Yankee" neice.

She and Amy sat down in two arm chairs, but Charlotte stood rigid, her back to an unlit fireplace. "I want to tell you both about a very disturbing conversation I had today with Martin Cord—"

"Oh, Aunt Clara knows about Martin," Amy interrupted swiftly. "A while back, I told her he was flirting with me and she said if he persisted, she would reprimand him."

"Flirting!" Charlotte spat. "Today in the caves he bragged to me that he intended to have you—with or without a wedding ring."

Amy looked uncomprehanding.

Clara pounced on the word "wedding". "Are you saying he has the audacity to think Amy would marry him? A mere servant?"

"If she doesn't marry him of her free will, he said he intends to ravish her until he bends her to his passion."

Clara gave a little scream and Amy cried, "Oh, that's ridiculous."

Charlotte frowned at her. "No, it isn't. He encountered me in the caves today and was very explicit about his intentions. He is furious because Tim has come to pay court to you and blames me for the visit."

"He doesn't mean it," Clara scoffed, but her face had paled. "He would never dare—"

"I could tell you his exact words, but they were so horrible I don't like to repeat them. Believe me, he was not making idle threats."

Amy stood up, her voice choked. "It's true, then. I think he intends to kidnap me and force me to surrender." She swallowed hard and clasped her hands. "I didn't want to believe it, but now ... He cornered me in the garden yesterday and said Vanessa told him that Tim had come to court me. Martin threatened to do something awful. I thought he was overwrought and jealous and I tried to soothe him. I can see it didn't help, especially after Tim and I want off alone in the caves." Her lips trembled and her wide blue gaze sought Charlotte. "What do you think he will really do?"

"I'm glad you finally are frightened," Charlotte said tightly. Amy must realize now the true nature of the beast she had encouraged, thinking her gentle ways had kept him tame. Instead, his passion fed on every sight and sound of her, maybe stimulated all the more by her resistance.

"There is something else. Cord intends to blackmail me so that I won't interfere."

Speechless, Clara's and Amy's eyes flew to Charlotte's face.

"Cord told me today that he knew who the Underground Railroad conductor called the Frenchman was when undisguised. He also said that he knew I had helped him with escaping slaves." Charlotte drew in a long quavering breath. "As I really had. On two occasions."

Amy ran to her. "Oh, Charlotte, are you sure he knows?"

Clara made an inarticulate sound of rage. Her eyes flashed fire. "You say all this is true? You wretched, ungrateful girl!"

Charlotte flung out her hands. "Oh, Aunt Clara, I am not ungrateful. You took us in when we had nowhere else to go and would never let me pay you anything—even though you were having a hard time here. I never would harm Stone Gardens. It would be an affront to my mother's memory. The slaves I helped were not from here. The first was an injured boy on the Freedom Trail who needed aid. The other two belonged to Francois Savon. They had a babe-in-arms and it was the mother he had desired and savaged. Now that I've met him, I know I did a good thing."

"My God," Clara said weakly and sank back on the sofa. "Do you realize the position you are in? I understand how you would want to thwart that awful Savon, but think what will happen if your part comes to light. The disgrace and shame will affect us all."

"Yes, I know," Charlotte whispered and closed her eyes. "I'm sorry. Realizing that, I promised Amy I would do nothing like that again. But saving Amy will be worth it even if I am sent to jail. Or exposed to Savon's wrath by Martin Cord."

"No, no," Amy moaned. "We must keep Martin from exposing you and the Frenchman. Why does he want to tell Savon?"

"For money. Savon is rabid to discover the people responsible for helping Jed and Luella. He'll pay anything."

"And if Savon finds that you are one of the culprits," Clara asked. "What will he do?"

"Kill me, I'm sure."

Clara gasped.

"I'll go to Martin," Amy cried, "reason with him. Say that no matter what he does, I could never love him. I'll beg for mercy—"

"Mercy!" Charlotte scoffed. "He doesn't have a drop in his whole body. Besides, he's not a fool—although mentally deranged, I'm sure. He wouldn't believe a word you'd say, Amy. He thinks his lovemaking would change your mind. He thinks he's been patient up to now, but Tim arrived and he immediately moved up to your side."

Clara knit her brows. "I just remembered something. Savon sent me a letter recently saying he would pay us a visit on his return. It could happen any day. He also said that his searching had been fruitless."

"Coming here again shows he is still suspicious of us," Charlotte said.

"What proof does Martin have?" her aunt asked.

"He claims he saw me ride in at midnight when the two

slaves got on the boat. The horse I rode had belonged to Savon. Cord also said he had knowledge of my other activities with the disguised Frenchman. Add that to my Yankee upbringing and there is proof enough for Savon or the slave patrol."

"Charlotte, we must leave at once," Amy begged wildly. "Go back up North where Savon can't touch us. We'll hide. Tim will help us. I know he will!"

"Let's think calmly," Clara said, raising her hand. "Nothing can be gained by panic. We must consider everything before we act. I agree that Martin has become a threat. I do not believe your assessment of him is wrong, Charlotte. You are too level-headed as a rule. Except," she muttered, "when you helped the Frenchman. That was wrong."

"But, Aunt, what could I do?" Charlotte asked miserably. "If you had seen that little family—the bruises on Luella's throat, the terror in her eyes—"

"You took an awful chance, Niece, and I hardly can condone it, though it's not surprising you should feel as you do, being your father's child. But you are also Rose's child and for that reason, I would not put you into the hands of Francois Savon, a villain of the first water, if I am any judge."

"Thank you, Aunt," Charlotte said humbly. "But now I think it would be best if I leave Stone Gardens. Maybe Amy should go, too . . . Perhaps she has the best idea."

"Let us not be hasty. First, of course, I shall dismiss Martin—"

"But Martin won't do anything," Amy interposed, "until he sees what Charlotte does. He also wants to wait for Savon's visit."

"Yes," Charlotte said, "I agree with Aunt that we must think this through carefully, or we'll have Cord pouncing before we make our plans."

"Perhaps I could tell Martin that I despise him," Amy said, "and never want to lay eyes on him again. I could even say I am going to marry Tim."

"What!" Clara and Charlotte both jerked their heads to gape at her.

"Oh, no. He hasn't even asked me yet. And, besides, I'm not yet ready."

"Humph." Clara looked relieved. After a silence, she said. "How on earth did Martin learn the identity of the Frenchman? Charlotte, do you know who he is?"

"No, Martin didn't tell me, but he must have spies. Someone helped him find Elijah when he ran away."

"Martin always did his job well," Clara mused. "He seemed honest and hard-working, but kept to himself in private. Although he was never soft or kind, this latest action of his astonishes me—threats regarding Amy and saying he would sell information about my niece to Savon!"

"Perhaps he doesn't realize what Savon is really like," Amy ventured.

Charlotte clenched her fists. "Good Lord, child, how long are you going to keep on finding excuses for that man?"

"Calm down," Clara said. "I understand how Amy feels. Martin is the first man to say that he loved her. She can't dismiss that in an instant."

How surprising Aunt Clara could be, Charlotte thought. First, she had forgiven her own actions in helping the conductor—or at least excusing them because of her Yankee father. Now Clara showed an astonishing understanding of Amy.

But Amy must not be lulled into a false feeling of security. She still might run to Martin and beseech him to let her be. And beg compassion for her sister. Amy didn't realize how far beyond that point he had gone.

"I think Amy and I should leave," Charlotte said. "There is no other way."

"Yes, you may be right." Clara threw Amy a worried glance. "When Martin finds in the next few days that Amy is not going to see him, he could do two things: kidnap Amy and throw Charlotte to the wolves. But I think he will wait for Savon."

A heavy silence fell. Charlotte felt that her own heartbeats must be heard, they pounded so loud in her ears. She must think clearly. Ideas tumbled through her brain one after the other . . .

Amy hit on the main problem when she faltered, "How can we escape Martin? He or his spies will watch our every move if we try to leave . . . won't they?"

"I think I know a way," Charlotte said slowly. "In one more day, the Hartley ball will be filled with masks and people in disguises. And we can blend right in. No one will know who we are until the unmasking at midnight. And by then, Amy and I will be on our way."

"Leaving Stone Gardens could be a problem," Clara gnawed her lip. Her face looked pale and drawn. She must have hated the idea of losing Amy but was terrified of Martin and Savon.

Charlotte looked pityingly at each of them in turn. Safety lay in her own plan and her own effectiveness in carrying it to a conclusion.

"I have an answer all worked out," she said firmly. "Trust me."

Chapter 28

"Aunt Clara, I will speak to you again about this matter. Until then, I beg you not a word to anyone." Charlotte rose and beckoned Amy to her side. "My sister and I have plans to make. She must confide in Tim, as we need his help. Above all, Vanessa must be kept in ignorance. She is jealous of Tim's preference for Amy and might even divulge our plans to the wrong person."

"I understand." Clara's lip quivered. "So you're both really going?"

Amy ran to hug her. "Dear Aunt, I'll come back when all this is over. I promise."

"Yes, please do and write, won't you?" When Charlotte came to her a little timidly, she embraced her, too. "You're Rose's child, after all. I see it in your bravery and the love you've given Amy."

The girls left, then, Amy wiping tears, but in the hallway, Charlotte halted. "Listen! I think someone's hurrying away, perhaps not wanting to be seen. I wonder . . ."

"What?" Amy shrank fearfully. "Do you think somebody was listening at the door?"

"It's possible . . ."

"Who? Vanessa?" Amy whispered.

"Or one of Cord's spies. A house servant could be in his pay as well as anyone."

"Not Tibby!"

"No, but her brother, Elijah, hates Stone Gardens and all it stands for."

"Oh, Charlotte, we must be on our guard and watch every shadow."

They hurried upstairs to Charlotte's room where she turned quickly to her sister. "We have a little time before dinner. I wonder if we should summon Tim and confer with him about our plans?"

"Suppose Vanessa sees him coming in here? Won't she wonder why? No," Amy said slowly, "I think I should arrange a meeting with him later. It's hard to realize that we may be leaving here for good. We never may come back, in spite of what I said to Auntie."

"I know that." Suddenly, Charlotte's eyes became suffused with tears. Unable to suppress a sob, she ran to her handkerchief box upon the dresser and pressed a cambric square against her streaming eyes."

"Oh, dearest, you've been through so much with Martin Cord. I know you're frightened and bewildered, trying to figure what is best to do."

Amy led Charlotte to the bed and sat beside her, patting and soothing until the tears petered out and Charlotte drew a deep, quivering breath.

"Oh, Amy, the thought of leaving Devlin! He said today that he loved me, but there was a reason why we couldn't wed."

"Oh, that's wonderful that he loves you, though I thought his wife was dead so why—"

"She is. It's something else. Perhaps because he travels all the time seeking backgrounds for his books. I don't know—"

"That's not a very strong reason. I think he'll change his mind. Are you going to say farewell to him and tell him of our plans?"

"Yes, I can trust him," Charlotte said heavily.

"You can write to each other."

"Perhaps."

"Now tell me your ideas for our getting away," Amy said briskly. "Let's sit by the fireplace. Your hands are icy."

"I have a plan, but it is dependant on good luck—as well as our skill at disguising. The voluminous costumes are godsend. We can be completely covered and underneath we must be dressed for travel, money in an inner pocket. We'll wear capes and masks. I think—yes—I'll go up to the attic and prepare a wig. Your hair will be hidden by your black scarf and the mantilla. Everyone will know we're at the ball, but they won't expect us to run away in our costumes. We'll discard them somehow before we slip away with Tim."

Amy looked worried. "Why don't we just leave Stone Gardens in the dead of night?"

"I think that we'd be stopped. On the night of the ball, however, we'll leave here in two coaches and at the ball no one will know our identity. Before midnight, you and I and Tim will slip away, discard our costumes, and flee to the first train stop.

"Please ask Tim to find us a room somewhere, so we can hide in New York. I have saved enough money to tide us over while I look for work. Tonight or tomorrow I will confide my plan to Devlin." Her lips quivered before she firmed them.

Amy spoke up quickly. "I think it is a good plan and will work very well. Devlin will surely want to keep in touch with you. I believe he loves you deeply. I could see it on the island. His eyes on you, his warm regard, the way he stayed so close and held your hand. I wager he even stole a kiss in some dark tunnel. No, don't answer. Your face is tell-tale enough."

Charlotte smiled. "Didn't Tim kiss you? No, never mind. You also show the answer in your face."

Amy laughed, but quickly sobered. "These days could have been so much fun if it hadn't been for Martin. What did I do to make him become so crazy? Did I encourage him? I didn't mean to—"

"Perhaps you did, but not intentionally, little one. The seeds for an unbalanced nature must have always been there, and his mad desire for you just set it off. He had no rational behavior to call on. All his life he'd depended on force to bend slaves to his will. You would have been treated the same way."

"Like a slave?" Amy looked a little skeptical.

"Like someone to be cowed or disciplined, if necessary. He probably would have beaten you if he became displeased."

"Oh, I can hardly believe that, Charlotte. He seemed to really love me."

"Perhaps he did, but when you turned to Tim, his love could become hate just as easily. They are the two most powerful emotions we humans possess: love and hate. And they account for most of the murders in the world."

Amy shuddered. "I am becoming terrified."

"And you must remain that way. I saw the beast in him at once. But you were blinded by your first encounter with a man's passion."

Amy ran to the window and pulled back the drape. "It's so dark out there. Do you think he's watching . . . somewhere?"

"We're safe here in the house. Just stay close to someone all the time. And speak to Tim as soon as possible. Oh, there's the gong to meet downstairs. I'll just pat a little rice powder underneath my eyes. Do you think anyone will notice that I've been tearful?"

"Of course, not. You just look a little tired, as we all do after that excursion." Amy took Charlotte's arm going down the stairs and brought up the subject of the interesting caves so that they were both talking easily upon entering the parlor.

Clara looked grim, but she never had a carefree expression. Everyone else was chattering brightly, sipping sherry while warm flames leaped behind the black iron grate. Devlin's eyes moved to Charlotte, but he only gave a little nod, though he seemed to stare a long minute at her wan expression. Charlotte looked away, wishing she had pinched her cheeks to give them a more pleasing color. Her plain gown didn't help matters either. But no one had chosen to dress tonight, and for that she could only feel relief.

Tim sat on the sofa next to Vanessa, but he held out a chair for Amy on his other side. "Vanessa just asked me what I intend wearing to the ball. I am going as the slave conductor called the 'Frenchman.' Amy wrote me all about him."

"Oh, Tim," Clara exclaimed. "That's not really a good idea. Someone might become incensed and start a fight with you."

"Well, they'll have a hard time," Tim chuckled. "Three of us are going in the very same outfit—Keith, Devlin and myself. I already have my costume. Brought it with me from New York: black curls, plumed hat and all. Should look dashing, eh?"

Charlotte lifted her sherry and shook her head. "Devlin,

do you think it's wise to poke fun at such a disliked person?''

"That's the best kind of person to poke." His dark eyes held a teasing light, but then it faded and he leaned closer to Charlotte as everyone started talking loudly once again. "Is anything wrong? You look upset—"

Her answer was a mere breath, "Yes. I need to talk to you."

"Come to the studio after supper," Devlin said.

She nodded. Talking would be all they would do. She knew the seriousness of their conversation would preclude any lovemaking. Already, those moments in the cave seemed like part of another life now irrevocably behind her.

She forced herself to glance away and was startled to see Vanessa's eyes on Amy, glittering with icy anger. *Had she been the one listening at the study door?* If so, all their careful, desperate plans would go for naught, and the danger would be doubled.

At that moment, Cicero announced dinner and they all moved off to take places around the table, with its snowy damask and old, well-polished silver. The lavish food held no appeal for Charlotte, and she scarcely tasted the gumbo soup, deviled crabs or veal croquettes in sauce.

All she could think about was the perilous time ahead. One slip, one suspicious person, a hitch in transportation and all the trouble would descend from Martin Cord and Francois Savon, two evil, vicious men both bent on vengeance for their thwarted passion.

There also was no telling how long Cord would wait. One more day? Two? Until Savon arrived? Or would he grow impatient, perhaps sneak into the house, abscond with Amy, then alert the slave patrol to Charlotte's and the Frenchman's activities.

Charlotte knew that she must try to think of every possible contingency. Her eyes went swiftly around the dining table, then lit on Cicero standing on duty in the corner. He nodded at her with a little smile, almost of reassurance.

When the meal ended, Charlotte lingered, then drew close to him and whispered. "I need your help. Will you come to my room as soon as possible so I can talk to you in private?"

She had dropped her handkerchief in case anyone was watching, and when the elderly servitor bent down, he breathed the words: "At once, miss." Bowing, he said louder, "I trust you enjoy your dinner, Miss Charlotte?"

"Very much. Thank you."

She noticed Tim and Amy move toward the study while the others proceeded to the parlor for an after-dinner cup of demi-tasse or brandy. Vanessa was chattering to Devlin, but it would not be long before she noticed the absence of Tim and Amy and decided they were wooing. Charlotte hoped they would speak swiftly and rejoin the others before much time elapsed.

Charlotte hurried to her own room, knowing she, also, must act quickly. When Cicero knocked softly, she beckoned him in, cast a glance up and down the hall, then closed the door.

"A grievous problem has arisen, Cicero. Mr. Cord has formed an attachment for my sister that she doesn't wish."

"I knows that, Miss Charlotte. 'Twas plain to see and worrisome to me."

"I agree. He has become very determined to have her. Amy has tried her best to discourage him, as I have, also. But today he made some terrible threats. I fear that he may try to spirit her away and bend her to his will."

"Oh, Lordy!" Cicero fell back a step and gaped at her, then he straightened and firmed his chin. "You want that I be on the watch . . . for trouble?"

"Yes, oh, yes. If you could see the house is locked up tight each night—"

He inclined his head. "And perhaps Ned should sleep outside Miss Amy's door?"

"Thank you. I would be so grateful—"

"Anything you wish, Miss Charlotte. You is Miss Rose's child and so is Miss Amy."

When he left, Charlotte knew the time had come to visit Devlin at his studio. She would confide her plans in him, then see what he would say. Flinging a dark scarf over her head, she sped into the night, unable to halt a swift stab of fear. Was Martin Cord abroad, hiding nearby, watching their every move? Or did he have an ally posted in the shrubbery who would report to him if she and Amy tried to flee?

However, she met no one, saw no one, and panting, reached the studio. She knocked, but received no answer. Seeing a light, she pushed the door ajar, then entered, calling Devlin's name.

No one answered. As her eyes roved around, she saw that for the first time in her memory, his bedroom door stood open. Could he be sick? Injured? Her recent experience with Cord made any frightening event seem possible. The overseer had become a deranged villain in her eyes.

But no one was in Devlin's bedchamber. She saw only a few bare essentials: a wardrobe, a straight-backed chair and lamp burning on a nearby table. The bed was made up smoothly with counterpane and pillow.

She had always felt curious about this locked room. Now she saw it held scattered papers, piles of books . . . perhaps he kept the door secured because he liked to write in here undisturbed.

Then on one of the papers, her eye lit on something completely out of place.

A limp, faded rose.

And something roared into her mind. Not a question, but knowledge, sure and blinding, as though a voice spoke in her ear.

Chapter 29

Pressing the dry, rose against her heart, Charlotte closed her eyes. It still held a sweet fragrance as it had the night the Frenchman plucked it from her dress so he could slip his hand inside the opening. Although his warm fingers had found her breast a throbbing eagerness, Charlotte only saw Devlin in her mind. She had imagined it was he embracing her and she thrilled and hungered for all he gave.

Why had she seen Devlin's image?

Because he was the Frenchman.

It had taken her a long time to solve the mystery of the elusive conductor, but now the signs seemed clear. He had appeared on the Stone Garden's grounds twice—no, he'd been there three times, counting the rainy night he had brought Charlotte and Amy to their destination.

Devlin traveled frequently. What better excuse for delving everywhere than a writer searching for material? Only he was searching for abused slaves who needed help along the Freedom Trail. The veiled woman at his door could easily have been Harriet Tubman or any other female informant, alerting him to the plight of Jed and his wife.

The rose she now held in her hand must have been kept by him the night he sought her help. With his romantic imagination, he had cherished the flower, remembering the bliss they both had shared. She did not recognize him that night, but her excitement and delight had been just the same as on the other occasions when Devlin had kissed her. Yes, yes, always it had been Devlin. There was not the slightest doubt in her mind that he was the Frenchman.

Charlotte looked around the bedroom—always so carefully locked! She couldn't discover any incriminating articles of clothing but saw a locked chest, which perhaps contained the wig and hat of his disguise.

He must have left in extreme agitation. A terrified sob caught in her throat. The danger! Oh, the awful closing of the net now held by Cord. He thought payment could be had from Savon in return for knowledge of the ones who had helped his two slaves escape. Yes, Savon would surely pay him well.

Her thoughts churned wildly. She felt faint and dizzy. Not much time remained. Every minute increased the danger. Blood pounding in her ears, Charlotte ran back to the main room and peered out the door. Cord or an accomplice could be watching their every move. She strained her eyes in every direction but saw no one.

She retraced her agitated steps, wondering what to do? Should she leave a message? She must be careful. Anything incriminating could precipitate Cord's actions.

Going to the table, she immediately discovered something. A note was propped against the ink bottle:

Beloved—

Forgive me, but an urgent matter has come up and I must be gone awhile. I shall try to return in time for the ball, where we will meet and talk.

Devlin

Charlotte crushed the paper in her trembling hand, then thrust it in her dress. What "urgent matter"? Another trip on the Underground Railroad? Oh, dear Lord, protect him! Soon his forays would have to end, and they must escape together. Two men had marked them both for retribution. Cord and Savon, animals of the lowest order. Thwarted by their desire for a passionate possession, they wanted to exact the highest penalty on the ones responsible. Charlotte and Devlin would be their prey.

Charlotte's hands clasped her face, almost sick with fear. The escape that she had planned seemed suddenly a puny effort in the face of these determined, evil men. She had no doubt that both Cord and Savon could kill them all, without a moment's twinge of conscience.

What could she do? Who could help her? No one! She had only her own wits to use and at all costs she must think clearly and keep calm, avoid panic and mistakes. A note to Devlin? Yes. She took up a pen and wrote:

Dearest—

I want to see you as soon as possible. My heart is burning with words which must be uttered.

Charlotte

There. If Cord was able to enter the guest house (and she felt sure he could), the missive from her to Devlin could be construed as merely a love note. On the other hand, Devlin might realize the wording didn't sound the way she usually talked, and he would guess she had something vital to convey.

She laid the rose on top of the paper. Would he see the significance? Maybe yes, maybe no. Devlin was so clever. His mind must race in a thousand directions. He had escaped capture for months. What courage the man had! What powerful convictions against prejudice and slavery. And, all the while, he managed to write a wonderful novel—and make her fall in love with him.

Her heart swelled with a floodtide of emotion. Then, she checked it abruptly, suddenly alert to danger. She had heard a footfall on the gravel. Swiftly, she turned out the lamp and cracked the door ajar. Thank heaven, a fitful moon showed that the porch and path looked clear. But she must not tarry any longer. She locked the door, then crept toward the main house, keeping off the gravel and muffling her footsteps on the grass.

Again she heard a step and this time, she ducked beneath a tree. The sound grew closer. Then she saw him. *Elijah!* and beyond him stood the figure of his sister. Charlotte strained to hear their voices.

"You promise Miss Charlotte be all right?"

"Sh-sh," the brother rasped. "You fool girl! Cord jus' want Miss Amy. Now git back in the house and keep on listenin' 'till I calls you."

A few more muffled words, then the figures blended in the darkness, Tibby to the big house and Elijah going quickly toward the slave quarters.

For a long moment, Charlotte stayed beneath the tree, trying to absorb this new development. *Tibby? and Elijah?* Tibby must be supplying information to her brother. And he must be in the pay of Martin Cord.

How could Tibby have betrayed her! She had seemed so sweet, so anxious to do well. Charlotte clenched her hands, shock replaced by anger. The overseer had chosen well. A timid girl swayed by her only relative and Elijah, who may have been promised a chance to escape and money in return for information. The young man probably hated everyone in the Stone Gardens family and would be glad to see them suffer.

Charlotte swallowed hard as quiet and darkness descended once more on the garden. What did Cord plan? How much had the two young Masons told him? Had Tibby been the one lurking in the hallway when Charlotte discussed her plans with Clara and Amy? Tibby might know that they were planning to leave but not how or when. Charlotte had kept the final plotting between herself and Amy and they had spoken softly.

There was only one more day to go, and Cord could not act until Savon arrived and paid for the information. If only Devlin would return soon so they could talk. But suppose this time he was captured before he could get back? She might never see him again. Oh, dear God, no, no! It was all she could do not to break into wild sobs.

Clenching her hands, she breathed deeply several times. Think, plan, she told herself as she sped toward the house. Tibby would be in her room by this time, waiting to prepare Charlotte for the night, perhaps wondering at her absence. How would she explain it? Any hint that she was in the garden just now could bring suspicion from Tibby and Elijah that they were overheard and accelerate Cord's attack.

She would need some excuse. Suddenly, she recalled the wig she planned on getting from the attic. Hunting up there would explain her whereabouts since dinner.

Charlotte turned down the hall and sped to the top floor. She found the attic dark and dusty, lit only by a fitful beam of moonlight, but the candle and matches still reposed where Devlin had left them after his explorations. By the wavering beam, she easily found the box of wigs and dragged it open, giving a sneeze as sixty years of filtered dust wafted upward. The white wigs were grey and dirty and she had no time to clean them, even if she had known how. A red wig? Yes, that didn't look too bad. A good brushing and the addition of some plumes and flowers would make it quite presentable and a good disguise.

Tibby might know the costumes she and Amy would be wearing, but no one would expect them to escape at the ball. Secreting the wig beneath a length of velvet shawl, she doused the candle and crept down the stairs.

She found Tibby waiting in her room and dismissed her quickly. "I don't need anything tonight. So go, you must be tired, and I know it's late."

"I been waiting here, Miss Charlotte, a long time," Tibby faltered.

"I've been busy in the attic looking for a wrap to wear." She indicated the velvet shawl, then thrust it in the closet.

"You want I should clean it?"

Charlotte waved her back. "No, thank you. I just want to get to bed."

Tibby's lips seemed to quiver, then she slid away and shut the door.

In a few minutes, Charlotte heard a soft knock at her door. Had Tibby returned? But it was her sister who moved quickly into the room, her hair in braids and a long quilted robe clasped around her narrow waist.

"Amy," Charlotte exclaimed, "just the person I want to see."

"I came several times, but only Tibby was here. Where have you been? It's very late. Oh!" her face lit up. "I expect you were with Devlin."

Charlotte put a finger to her lips and gave a swift survey of the hallway, then led her sister to a chair beside the fire and took another chair across from her.

"I did not see Devlin tonight. I went to the studio, but

he had gone away, leaving me a note. He may not return until the ball.'' She was not going to reveal Devlin's identity to anyone, not even her sister. It was too dangerous. The fewer people who knew he was the Frenchman, the better it would be. His very life hung by a most precarious thread.

"I wonder where he goes so often?'' Amy mused. "When does he have time to write?''

"He makes the time.'' She quickly changed the subject, lowering her voice to a whisper. "Amy, I made a serious discovery tonight. While in the garden, I overheard Elijah telling Tibby to keep on spying in the house.''

"What!'' Amy smothered a small scream with her hand. "Tibby! I can't believe it. Do you think she heard us in the study speaking to Aunt Clara?''

"I wouldn't be at all surprised. Tibby seems unhappy about her deception.''

"Why do you suppose she did it?''

"She's weak and young. Elijah is her only kin and he probably hates everything about Stone Gardens. I imagine Cord gave him some money and Elijah will try again to escape.''

"We'll have to be more careful than ever,'' Amy said.

"Did you speak to Tim?''

Amy nodded with a faint smile. "Yes, indeed. He wanted to rush right out and challenge Cord to a duel or something.''

"Dear heaven! How foolish. Dueling has been banned in most states and if a person is killed, the other party can be tried for murder.''

"Well, I talked Tim into acting rational.''

Uneasiness rippled over Charlotte. Could they really trust Tim not to make a disastrous move? They actually didn't have any idea how he would act under pressure. Charlotte wished they hadn't had to confide their plans to him, but she wanted someone strong at Amy's side. They would be in constant danger until they arrived up North. Suppose the train should be stopped and searched, acting on Savon's disclosures?

"We should have thought about another disguise when we leave the ball," Charlotte fretted, jumping to her feet.

Amy pondered a minute. "Why don't I dress like a boy? And you—perhaps a mourning veil, a black bonnet . . ."

"There are some up in the attic and tonight I brought down a red wig to wear, but your bright hair might be a problem."

"I shall cut it," Amy decided. "I must if I am to wear a cap and try to look like a boy."

"Oh, dearest, your lovely hair!"

"Never mind. It'll grow again. Perhaps you should cut yours, too, so the wig will cover it completely."

Charlotte agreed, remembering with a pang how Devlin had admired her long, unbound hair. "Ah, well," she shrugged. "I guess the sacrifice of our hair is a small price if it will help to conceal our identity. Now let us plan what I should wear beneath my costume."

A thin dress, dark and plain, was decided on with part of Charlotte's money divided into two purses tied around their waists. The rest was secreted in her cape.

"We'll dispose of our costumes in time to catch the train. Tim will ride in a carriage with you and me. I heard Clara say we must take two conveyances, due to the big costumes, hoops and so forth."

"Where can we change so no one will see us?"

Charlotte bit her lip, then cried softly, "I know the very place: Roselands's conservatory. I'm sure it will be deserted. We'll plan it when everyone is going in to supper. Tell Tim to secret a jacket and trousers for you in the carriage then bring them later to the conservatory."

Amy suddenly looked bleak. "Oh, Charlotte, do you

really think all this is necessary? Isn't there some other way? What will we do up North? How will we live?"

"I'll find work. We have a little money now, and Tim can help us, I am sure." Charlotte put out her hand and patted Amy's knee. The child was shivering.

"Oh, little one, I know how hard it is for you to leave Stone Gardens. It's meant warmth, beauty, and security for both of us. And for me—" Her voice broke. "Here I found my love."

"I know, dear. It just seems so dramatic. Escaping in disguise. How everyone will wonder! What can Auntie tell them?"

"That is the least of our worries. Amy, we both had the misfortune to become involved with terrible men. Inflaming Cord's desire for you was not your fault. You didn't seek it. But I ignored the danger when I helped the runaways— although having a person like Savon appear on their trail was an unexpected disaster. I believe when he finds out who helped his slaves escape, he will try to kill me."

"No, no! Oh, Charlotte, do you truly think so?"

"I'm sure of it. Can you imagine a creature like that turning me over to the law? Why, they might set me free, say there wasn't sufficient proof. And Savon is rabid for revenge, almost to the point of insanity."

Charlotte's tone grew harsh as she leaned back, staring at the flames. "Think how much easier it would be for Cord if I were dead. Then nothing would stand between you and him. He is certain that he could seduce you with enough of his lovemaking. Amy, he told me to my face that he would force your body to his will night and day, hours on end until you crawled upon the floor, unable to stand upright, your spirit completely broken."

Amy moaned and covered her eyes with a shaking hand. "Are you sure he meant it?"

"I'm sure. Do you think what Cord feels for you is love?

He wants to satisfy his overwhelming lust by using force, if necessary. He is cruel and cares nothing for how you might be hurt, mentally and physically.''

Amy began to sob. "Everything is turning into a nightmare!"

Charlotte comforted Amy, and when she became calm, led her off to bed. But Amy looked so upset, Charlotte began to worry. What did Amy feel for the overseer? She had seemed curious about sexual relations, and this was her first encounter with a domineering man's passion. She probably felt flattered by the force of his desire.

Was it possible that Amy still believed she could reason with that animal? It had just been Cord's threats against Charlotte that had made her agree to leave. If it had only been his pursuit of herself, no doubt Amy would have continued to play with fire—until the flames consumed her, ruining her innocence and youth forever.

Ned slept near Amy's door and Charlotte nudged him with her toe. "Let me know if Amy leaves her room," she whispered into his ear. "And don't let anyone go in, except the family.''

Drowsily, he muttered, "Yes'm.''

Charlotte wondered if he had even heard her, but it would have to do. It was highly unlikely that Cord would come inside the house and approach her sister's door.

Charlotte didn't think that she would sleep, but in the morning, she knew that she had dreamed of Devlin lying in a grove of trees, severely injured.

She found her face was wet with tears.

Chapter 30

As soon as she was fully awake, Charlotte leaped from her bed, flooded with instant awareness of the problems this day presented. She breathed deeply of the still, cold air, then shivered. No fire had been laid as yet, but first light filtered palely through the curtains.

Dressing quickly, she hurried down the hall to Amy's room, her eyes darting in every direction. She could see no sign of Ned, and when she burst into her sister's room, she found to her dismay that it was empty. Since she saw no evidence of a struggle, Charlotte told herself not to panic.

Amy always kept her room in order and it held very few possessions—dresses in the wardrobe, a bonnet or two, some shoes . . . However, her cape did not hang on its usual hook.

Something else seemed odd. The basket she had taken to the compound children sat upon the bed lined with a linen napkin as though waiting to be filled. How could she intend going there today, after all that just happened?

Perhaps there existed a perfectly simple, harmless expla-
nation for Amy's absence. An errand for Vanessa? Some
flowers to be gathered for the ball?

Yet all the while, as she strove for calmness, another
dreaded possibility loomed in Charlotte's brain. *Could Amy
have gone to see Martin Cord?* Perhaps in an effort to reason
with him? Foolish, foolish child!

Clenching her hands, Charlotte ran into the hall and
nearly knocked down Ned whose arms held a bowl of fruit.
They both uttered startled cries.

"Oh, Miss Charlotte—"

"Ned, where's Amy?"

He craned his head toward her room, looking fearful.
"She tole me to get some fruit from the orchard for her
basket. Took me a right long time, not much fruit left.
Mebbe she gone lookin'—"

Charlotte cut him off and jerked the bowl out of his
hands so she could set it on the floor. "She wanted to get
you out of the way. Come on. Show me where Martin Cord
lives. She may be there."

"Lordamercy," Ned muttered with a gulp.

They ran down the halls and out into the silent, dewy
garden with not a soul in sight. What she intended doing
if Amy was at Cord's, Charlotte had no clear idea. She only
knew there was no time to spare, and if the beast had
harmed her sister, she would see that he paid dearly for
it.

She couldn't bear to consider the possibility that Cord
might have abducted Amy, yet it must be faced. And even
if Amy had gone to reason with him of her own free will,
Cord might not let her go.

"There, Miss Charlotte," Ned suddenly exclaimed,
pointing a shaking finger toward a small house isolated in
the trees. "You want I should come in with you?" He

shrank to one side of the leaf-strewn path, looking decidedly apprehensive.

"Sh-h, just wait here, but don't leave. Understand?"

When he nodded, Charlotte crept forward onto the little porch. The windows were closed, the curtains drawn. Choked sounds came from the interior, but when Charlotte called, she got no answer. Her hand flew to the lintel above the narrow door. Yes, a key was there just as one was kept at the studio.

With a shaking hand, she forced the lock, and burst inside. Her wild eyes swept the room and saw no sign of Cord. But Amy was tied up in a chair, a gag between her lips, cloak on the floor, her gown ripped open to the waist.

"Amy! Amy!" Charlotte flew to her. "Oh, dear God! What has he done to you? Are you hurt?"

Amy shook her head, making sounds deep in her throat. until Charlotte tore out the gag, then she gasped, "We must get out of here—he went to get a carriage. I'll tell you all when we g-get safe."

"He—he did this? These bruises?" Charlotte choked out hoarsely. Amy merely nodded.

"Ned," Charlotte shouted, "Come here. Help me." She drew her sister's gown together as best she could, feeling ill.

Ned's bulging eyes darted frantically around the cabin, but he quickly undid the cords that bound Amy to the chair. Then he stayed by the door, evidently fearing the return of Martin Cord.

Amy stumbled into Charlotte's arms, but she was anxious to get away and when questions were put to her, she only sobbed, "Later, later!"

Realizing she couldn't face Cord by herself, Charlotte hurried Amy back to her room. "Ned, get Cicero and Miss Clara," Charlotte gasped and shut the door. She dragged off the torn dress, fastened a robe around Amy's shaking form, and led her to the bed. "He didn't touch you, did he?"

"There wasn't time." Amy covered her face. "D-don't be angry with me. I know I acted like a fool, but—but I couldn't leave Stone Gardens without explaining things to him. I really thought he l-loved me."

"Didn't I tell you—"

"Yes, yes, I know. Please just listen, Charlotte."

"Go on," Charlotte said tightly.

"I told him you were afraid of what he might tell Savon. He said he wouldn't say anything if I would marry him, but I couldn't agree to that and tried to leave. He became enraged. Grabbed me, tied me up and began to make love." Amy gave a sob. "Oh, he was awful—hurting, savage, not listening to my pleading. I screamed and then he put a gag in my mouth."

"Wait until I get my hands on him," Charlotte cried.

"Suddenly, he jumped up and said he was going to take me away and—and never let me go. That's when he ran off to get a carriage. Oh, I was so frightened—thank heaven you came! B-but what shall we do now?"

Before Charlotte could reply, a knock sounded at the door. Cicero and Ned stood there behind Aunt Clara. Her face looked white, her quilted robe askew like the nightcap tied beneath her trembling chin. She shut the door after telling the two servants to stay in the hall.

"God in heaven, what has happened? Cicero only said there had been trouble." She flew across the room and took Amy in her arms, looking horrified at the bruises and listening aghast as the story was related to her.

"You crazy child! Thinking you could reason with Martin Cord. Even if he had agreed to your demands, how could you believe he'd keep his word and never turn in your sister?"

"I didn't realize how upset he was," Amy faltered. "He suddenly seemed to have lost all reason."

"He has where you're concerned," Charlotte told her. "You are lucky you're unharmed."

"What will he do when he returns and finds Amy gone?" Clara stood up, gripping her hands together . . . "He'll know that she will tell me." She swept back to the door and flung it open. "Cicero, fetch the sheriff. I'm going to have that devil put in jail. Ned, stay here in the hall. I want someone with Amy every minute, do you hear? And why is there no fire in here? No hot chocolate?" Angrily, she gave several jerks on the bell pull.

"Miss Clara," Cicero sighed. "They's more bad news. Tibby and Elijah ran away las' night."

Clara exchanged startled glances with her nieces. "What's being done?" she snapped.

"We jus' hear it. 'Spect Marse Cord's gone after 'em." Cicero said. "What you want I should do, Miss Clara?"

"Go get the sheriff anyway. Charlotte, you and Amy must tell him everything that happened. When Martin comes back, I want him taken into custody."

And as soon as he saw the sheriff, he would denounce Charlotte and Devlin. And where was Savon all this time, Charlotte thought, with an added stab of fear. And Devlin? Was he again masquerading as the Frenchman?

A servant crept in then to start the fire while Clara paced worriedly. "Charlotte, I'm going to summon Tim and Devlin for a conference after breakfast. We need some strong men at our side. But first, I must get dressed." She spoke a few more words to Amy, then went out the door, looking pinched and white, quite different from her usual self-confident demeanor.

Charlotte sank down on a corner of Amy's bed. She groaned and rubbed her head. "I can't seem to think clearly or make new plans. I fear we're both in more danger than ever."

"It's all my fault—"

Charlotte sighed. "Not all of it. I, too, share the blame."

"I wonder what Martin will do now," Amy said in a high shaking voice. "I guess we're all wondering that."

"One thing for certain, I will not let him get his hands on you again." Charlotte jumped to her feet. "You heard Cicero say that Cord went after Tibby and Elijah. I believe that he helped them escape because they knew too much about his plans for you."

She drew an unsteady breath. "When Cord finds you have escaped, he'll fear the consequences and perhaps go into hiding. A lot depends on whether he's talked to Francois Savon yet and received any money from him."

"Aunt Clara said Savon wrote her that he hadn't found his slaves up North," Amy ventured. "I wonder why, then, he wants to come back here?"

"He probably still thinks someone here at Stone Gardens aided Jed and Luella. We must avoid him at all costs."

She turned back to the bed. "Amy, stay in your room and wear a scarf to hide those red marks Cord inflicted." Angry tears welled in her eyes. "Oh, how I long to make that villain suffer!"

"He'll suffer when he finds we are gone."

"Not enough." Charlotte brushed her eyes, then firmed her lips. "Shall I get some salve for your bruises?"

"No thanks, dear. I just want to rest." Amy's voice sank to a whisper. "You don't think we could leave *now*?"

"Instead of at the ball?" Charlotte shook her head. "Cord might be watching us. If we go to the ball as planned, he won't expect us to escape from there in our costumes and there would be no way he could approach you."

She frowned and bit her lip. "Actually, I think Cord will want to take me instead of the patrol. He knows Savon would not show me any mercy and Cord desires revenge as well as money. I'm sure they met when Savon was here, but we don't know what they have planned."

She sighed and turned away. "All we can do now is wait and watch."

"Remember, Charlotte, we must cut our hair."

"We will do that just before we leave. Avoid Vanessa. The less she knows, the better though you can tell her about Cord. It will be a good excuse to stay clear of her prying eyes. You better lock the door behind me. I am going to speak with Devlin."

"All right," Amy whispered.

Ned still sat in the hall and Charlotte told him to fetch tea and toast for Amy, then resume his post.

Since food held no appeal for her, Charlotte hurried outdoors and headed for the guest house. Dawn colors streaked the sky and now she could hear distant sounds of life: row bosses shouting in the fields, babies crying in the compound, dogs barking, birds chattering.

Charlotte's eyes, wide and anxious, swiveled in every direction. Cord might still be around, cocky and conceited on the surface, angry and vindictive underneath—trying to see Amy and hoping to placate Clara through her need of him. He might even have Savon with him, ready to accuse Charlotte or do something worse.

Her feet sped faster, longing for Devlin's safety and concern with all her heart and soul. She would tell him everything and ask for his advice. Of all the people at Stone Gardens, he had the coolest, keenest brain. It had served him well on all his dangerous excursions and now it might help Charlotte with her own plan for escape. He knew a lot about disguises.

She prayed he would be in the guest house. And he was.
He stood beside the table, her note held in his hand,

his hat and jacket on the chair, as though he had just arrived. His face lit up when Charlotte entered.

With a sob of joy, she flew into his arms. "Oh, Devlin—Devlin—I'm so glad you're back. I've been terribly worried. There's trouble with Cord. A-and Savon—and runaways from here—"

He held her closely for a minute, then said, "My dearest heart, sit down. Try to tell me calmly. But first drink this."

He led her to the sofa, handed her a glass half-full of sherry and waited silently while she drank it. His arm stayed around her shoulders and finally she sagged against him, feeling the drink begin to warm and soothe her shaking nerves.

"I don't know where to start . . ." Suddenly, she raised her head. "Yes, I do! *You're the Frenchman, aren't you?*"

He stared a moment, then nodded. "How did you find out?"

"It was a lot of little things which finally added up." She listed them and finally added, "I found you had kept the rose from that night we kissed in the Stone Garden. Oh, Devlin, I felt at the time as though I were *kissing you!* Yet I wasn't suspicious then."

"I wondered what you were feeling." He brought her closer, puttting his face down in her hair.

"That's why you were reserved when we first met and why you said we couldn't marry."

"Yes, I travel on a dangerous road."

Charlotte put her hand beneath his chin and raised his head. His eyes held the drowsy tenderness she had seen before, but she knew this was not the time for lovemaking.

"There is something more that I must tell you and it is very serious."

His look deepened then, echoing her anxiety, and when he removed his arm, he clasped her hand in both of his.

Charlotte inhaled shakily. "It concerns Martin Cord. He

and I had an unpleasant, most disturbing encounter in the caves."

"That is what you wanted to tell me last night? I'm sorry—I received an urgent message and had to leave—"

"That's all right," Charlotte interrupted. "Listen, Devlin, Martin Cord said he knows who the Frenchman is and also that I have been helping him. He threatens to expose us both unless I allow him to have Amy."

"What arrogance," Devlin ground out. "I wonder if he's bluffing?"

Charlotte's voice shook. "I don't think so. I told Clara and Amy that we must run away—go back up North—"

"Wait, not so fast. Where is Cord's proof?"

Charlotte told him everything that had drawn Cord to his decision. "The worst part is that he intends to sell this information to Francois Savon, who will readily believe him, I am sure. When he was here, he said he thought someone at Stone Gardens had helped the runaways as the horse from Dark Oaks had turned up here. I fear Savon is rabid for revenge."

Devlin's face looked grim. "Mainly suspicion, but still enough to alert inquiries."

"Amy went to see Cord this morning, in hopes of changing his mind." Her voice faltered, but she told him all the sordid details, including their fears about what would happen next.

Devlin caught her close. "Oh, why did I allow you to get involved with the escaping slaves? And now Cord's using it for blackmail. My God, where is the villain now?"

"Oh, dearest, I had to help. I feel the same as you do. As for Cord, I think he's hiding somewhere and sent the word that he was going to search for Tibby and Elijah, who ran away last night. Did you know that?"

He nodded. "Those are the ones I waited for along the Freedom Trail. At my sound of the whipporwill signal, they

responded, and I gave them directions to a new route
where I don't think they'll be caught. However, if Cord
knows of my activities, I fear my days as a conductor are
over."

"Oh, yes, Devlin, you must come with us." Charlotte
clasped his shoulders. "Listen to my plan."

When he had heard her out, Devlin stared thoughtfully
above her head, his face a dark, taut mask. Finally, he
nodded. "Yes, it just might work. Of course, you and Amy
can't remain here. Savon and Cord present a real danger
to you both."

"And to you, also," Charlotte cried. "You must join us,
Devlin. Oh, promise me!"

He touched her cheek. "I will try, dearest, but we must
watch our every move. I want to try and stop that meeting
between Cord and Savon. So far, I think Cord is the only
one at Stone Gardens who knows about our activities."

Charlotte could only say, "I hope you're right." But she
felt an uneasy feeling flicker over her that perhaps another
person knew their secret. But was it a friend or foe?

Chapter 31

The rest of the strange day proceeded swiftly, for which Charlotte felt grateful as her nerves seemed almost at the breaking point.

Not wanting any breakfast, she just rang for a cup of hot chocolate and sipped it by the window when Vanessa burst into her room. The yellow muslin morning robe she wore looked wrinkled and her unkempt hair straggled down Vanessa's back, obviously lacking the vanished Tibby's care.

For once, Vanessa's toilette was not uppermost in her mind. "Amy just told me about Martin," she gasped, grabbing at a bedpost. "Stars above, I never heard the like! Why, Amy is so scared she wouldn't even unlock her door to me. And I don't blame her. Where is Martin now, I want to know? And what is being done about him?"

"He seems to be hiding out somewhere—probably alarmed after finding Amy gone. Your mother sent Cicero for the sheriff." Charlotte put down her cup, then rose

and said through gritted teeth. "I never did trust Martin
Cord, and his obsession with Amy terrified me."

Vanessa's blue eyes bulged and she licked her lips. *"Obsession.* I vow it's just like one of those romance novels."

"Only this is *real life,*" Charlotte snapped. "Don't you
realize the danger?"

Danger to Amy and myself as well, if Cord informed on
me, Charlotte thought, clamping her teeth together on a
shudder.

"Listen, Charlotte, we can protect Amy right here, but
Martin probably hates you. Yes, you should go, but by
yourself. I know you are considering it."

"What do you know about my plans?"

"I heard you talking in the library." Vanessa tossed her
head defiantly. "Yes, I evesdropped. Why not? A person
needs to know what's going on. But you must not think
of taking Amy away with you. I don't care a fig if *you* go.
I warned you once that this was not the place for you."

Charlotte's voice choked. "That snake—the note—"

"Oh, yes." Vanessa waved an impatient hand. "You
don't fit in here—always speaking out against slavery.
Mama told me how you complained when Martin took you
all on a tour of the plantation. And then you got Devlin
so interested that he never had time for me anymore. I
even saw Keith whispering in your ear." Her face grew red
with anger. "Amy has always spent too much time with
you. So if you go, I insist that Amy stays."

"Suppose she *wants* to leave with me?"

"Persuade her not to. If you don't, you may regret it."
With that, Vanessa flounced out of the room.

A threat! What did it mean? What could Vanessa do?
Charlotte turned blindly to the window. How unfortunate
that Vanessa had overheard part of their plans. At least
she didn't know that they intended to leave during the

ball. Only Amy and Tim knew about the final phase and neither of them would confide that to Vanessa.

A soft knock sounded at the door. It must be a servant. Vanessa never knocked. But when Charlotte called, "Come in," Amy slid into the room, now dressed in a simple morning frock, but still looking pale and wan.

"Vanessa came to see me," she whispered. "I didn't let her in and only told her about Martin as you said I should."

"Yes, she was just here, demanding that you stay and that I go back to New York alone."

"Heavens, how did she find out about our plans?"

"She evesdropped when we were in the library. She knows we want to leave but not how or when."

Amy sank down shaking in a chair. "Have you spoken to Devlin about this?"

"Briefly. He knows how Cord attacked you and that Savon is suspicious of me."

"Did he approve your idea for escape?"

"Yes." Charlotte couldn't tell Amy about Devlin's involvement with the Underground Railroad until they were all safely on the train. His very life would be in danger until then, and someone could be evesdropping even now. Charlotte sprang up and thrust her head into the hall. Empty.

While she hesitated, Amy sighed and said tremulously, "How I wish that we could leave right now."

No, Amy could not bear any more bad news. Charlotte returned to Amy's side and pressed the little, trembling shoulder.

"I know the waiting is hard, but soon we'll be out of here and on our way to—" Her words were cut off by a loud knock at the door. "Who's there?" Charlotte demanded.

"Your aunt." The next instant, Clara swept into the room. Although looking neatly garbed in a dark maroon morning dress trimmed with bands of black beading, her face was drawn and worried. "Girls, please come down to the parlor. Sheriff Sweeny's here and wants to speak with both of you."

"Has he found Martin Cord?" Charlotte asked as they hurried out into the hall.

Clara merely shook her head, lips clamped tight.

The house seemed oddly deserted with not a servant in view anywhere. However, a fire had been started in the big, red-carpeted parlor and Tim stood leaning on the mantel with Vanessa talking to him earnestly. Her hair had been brushed in its usual glossy ringlets and she wore a starched blue muslin with a double lace-trimmed skirt. She evidently had found a satisfactory replacement for Tibby.

Frowning, she turned around, but before she could speak, a stocky man stepped forward. He carried a peaked cap and had a holster across his tan uniform. Clara hastily made the introductions while his gimlet eyes examined Charlotte, softening only slightly as he observed Amy's trepidation.

"This may be painful, ladies, but I would like to hear what happened from your own lips. Shall we sit down?"

He flipped open a notebook and began writing, not looking up at Amy while she described the incident, her voice trembling. "He seemed to have a romantic interest in me, which was getting out of hand in spite of my efforts to discourage him. When my friend, Tim Deane, came here to visit, Martin was enraged and I became afraid. So I want to the cottage in the hope of reasoning with Martin." There was silence in the room as Amy's broken voice told everything that had ensued.

The sheriff's face looked sharp with anger, but then it was Charlotte's turn, and she tried not to show her fear and hatred of the overseer, not wanting the sheriff to put her down as hysterical and over-protective. So far, this lawman had no suspicion of her activities on the Underground Railroad. How terrible it would be if she had to stand accused before him. Would he show any mercy to a "Yankee"? She thought not.

When finished, the sheriff turned to Clara. " As I told you, ma'am, Martin Cord seems to have disappeared into thin air. I have a man posted on the grounds. He will stay the night, but after that, your own people will have to be on watch. I can't spare more men at this time."

"We also are short-handed," Clara told him. "Two of our slaves escaped from here last night."

He shrugged. "That's a matter for the slave patrol. As for the missing overseer, your row bosses can control the workers for the time being. Good-day now, ladies. I must be off."

As the sheriff headed for the door, Tim called after him, "No one knows what Martin Cord will do, but I intend to keep my own watch for the villain."

Sweeny grunted. "Don't do anything foolish, boy. Only the law has the right to use force."

When he left, Tim clenched his hands. "Condescending boor! Calling me 'boy'. No force, indeed. How can I apprehend Cord, unless I overpower him and tie him up?"

"Perhaps you should say, 'Please, sir, don't bother Amy anymore, or I may have to slap your wrist.'" Vanessa giggled, but Charlotte thought it had an angry sound. Amy was now the center of everyone's attention and concern, and Vanessa clearly was annoyed.

Tim didn't deign to answer her but came to Amy's side. "Do you want to have some lunch, dear?"

Amy nodded and took his arm. Charlotte heard her say in a low tone, "Please don't get into any trouble on my account."

Charlotte noted the new strength in Tim's face and hoped the anger he displayed could be tempered with wisdom. Of course, she was grateful for his help. She knew that Amy must have told him everything about Cord and Savon, but surely she had left out Charlotte's participation in the Underground Railroad. That knowledge was too dangerous.

"Yes, let's all go in and eat," Clara said wearily. "I think that's what we need. At least Aunt Becky is still here to cook for us."

At the table, she and Vanessa chattered about Tibby's defection, finding it more amazing than the fact that Elijah had again tried to "make free." "We always treated Tibby real good, I swear," Vanessa mumbled while buttering a beaten biscuit. "Why would she want to leave all these comforts? A warm pallet in the kitchen, left-over food from our own table? And she never got a real hard beating, just a slap or two."

"I guess her brother influenced her," Charlotte said, finding the creamed crab cakes and eggplant medley were stimulating to her appetite. She took a sip of tea nog. "Although after Elijah was brought back the first time he ran away, Tibby told me she was scared of the Freedom Trail."

"I think somebody gave them money to run away," Clara said.

"Why?" Tim asked. "Who would do that?"

"Oh, some Abolitionist sympathizer," Vanessa sneered.

Meeting Vanessa's suspicious gaze, Charlotte frowned. "Well, I certainly have no money for anything like that."

Vanessa pushed away her plate and leaned across the table. "We all know you want to get away." She darted a quick glance around the room, but not even Cicero was in evidence. "If you promise to leave Amy here, I could give you a few dollars to help you out up North."

Amy dropped her fork. "Charlotte must not leave without me. I can't stay here after Martin acted so terrible. It puts everyone at risk, including you, Vanessa."

"Yes, you should leave for a little while," Clara agreed, "but Martin will either be apprehended by the sheriff's men or he'll go far away and never be seen again. After a safe interval, Amy, surely you can return."

"It's up to Charlotte." Amy's troubled gaze went from one face to another. "I always follow her advice."

Vanessa's face grew thunderous, but Clara intervened. "This is not dinner-table conversation. Let us change the subject."

After the heavy midday meal, Tim went outdoors and the women repaired to their boudoirs. In a short time, bells began to peal throughout the house, and servants clattered up and down the stairs as preparations started for the ball. Tubs were filled with scented water, instructions floated from open doors aimed at the costumes and the coaches.

After she had bathed, Charlotte dismissed the maid, and wearing a robe, hurried down the hall to Amy's room with a pair of shears wrapped in a towel.

Her sister greeted her with a quavering sigh. "Oh, Charlotte, I'm getting more worried all the time. I'm afraid Martin is just waiting for darkness, then he'll spring from somewhere—maybe with some slaves to help him capture me."

"Now, Amy, get hold of yourself. We must keep our wits about us and not give way to panic. Sit down in that chair. I'm going to cut your hair."

Amy moaned and shut her eyes until the snipping stopped. Charlotte wiped off Amy's neck and said, "You can look now." She held out a handmirror.

Amy gulped. "It—it's not so bad." She blinked a few times, then rose with a determined air. "All right, sister mine. Now it's your turn. Are you ready?"

A little later, Amy and Charlotte surveyed each other.

"It's actually cooler and more comfortable," Charlotte said stoutly. "My hair was so long and heavy. See, now it even curls a little."

Amy nodded. "You're right. I will hide my own shorn locks in a tight black scarf beneath the lace mantila."

"Do you want me to help you dress?"

"No," Amy replied. "I can do it. How about you?"

"I'll be fine. My costume laces down the front, so that part is easy. I'm only wearing a single hoop, the pannier style that extends on each side instead of all around." Charlotte gathered up the brown and gold locks on the floor, wrapping all in a towel which she thrust in a far corner of the armoire.

She was determined not to moan about the loss of a "crowning glory" and dusted her hands briskly. "Stay in your room with the door locked until it is time to go. You can pack your belongings for Clara to send later on. Don't let anyone see the costume, if possible. Wrap up securely in your black cloak and bring the mask Clara gave you. I shall do likewise."

She gave a glance at Amy's desolate face and embraced her swiftly. "We must be strong and brave, little one. I am sure we can get through this time if we keep our wits about us."

Amy raised her chin. "You're right, as always, dearest. I shall be aware every minute and I promise to keep a cool head and a smile on my face, so no one will get suspicious."

"That's my girl."

Charlotte eased the door ajar and went swiftly back to her room, meeting no one. She thrust a chair beneath the doorknob since there was no key. Then she proceeded carefully to dress.

She had already sewn part of her money in the cloak, the rest she folded into a little purse and pinned it securely to her waist where the billowing costume would disguise any bulk. The traveling dress had to be thin and dark with its neckline tucked down as low as possible. A few beauty pins should anchor it. Then the ball gown. The creamy satin underskirt was attached to each side of the green and gold shotsilk skirt and bands of gilt lace extended all around the edges and trimmed the flowing sleeves. Knots of ribbon and French silk roses were everywhere, and after carefully adjusting the red wig, Charlotte tucked a wreath of roses on the crown.

She then examined every inch of her attire until she felt satisfied that not a speck looked out of place and covered her traveling dress completely. When she wrapped the black cape around her bouffant gown, a small amount of green-gold silk was visible at the hem, but it could not be helped. She soon would be mingling with a throng of exuberant party-goers, her cloak abandoned, her identity unknown.

Would Devlin make it to the ball? How could she leave him behind, not knowing his fate? She hoped and prayed that he would be at her side, so they could escape together. She sat down to wait, uncomfortably aware that her hands were damp and her heart now beating fast.

When the time came to leave, there still had been no word from Devlin.

Chapter 32

The driveway to Roselands was thronged with vehicles disgorging guests. Carriages, open landaus, and coaches halted at the entrance where footmen in green velvet livery escorted the costumed guests up to the open doors.

Lanterns had been strung along every tree and pathway so that glimpses could easily be had of the fantastic throng. People laughed and chattered blending with music which came in resounding waves from somewhere deep inside the house.

For a few moments, Amy and Charlotte stared in awe, exchanging little smiles. Who could help responding to so much gaiety and beauty, even in the midst of an uncertain future?

When they alighted at the marble steps, Clara's face likewise filled with awe. "Girls, did you ever imagine such a scene? The wealth required to furnish so many out-of-season flowers—orchids, lilies, gardenias everywhere. And just see that fountain in the foyer, the colored water is divinely scented, I do declare." She inhaled deeply.

Amy pointed to drapes of rosy tulle and satin ribbons covering the walls. "Listen—I hear birds singing among the folds."

"They are artificial." Charlotte smiled. "Yes, this is truly wondrous. I just hope . . ." She didn't complete her sentence—that they might not enjoy it to the utmost. Besides, Vanessa and Tim arrived just then.

Servants took their wraps, then Vanessa surveyed Charlotte's green and gold ballgown. "I thought you would select that costume. It was the best one next to mine and when I went up to the attic later on, I found the gown was gone."

Charlotte felt her nerves grow taut. Had Vanessa told anyone what she would be wearing? Before she could frame the question, Vanessa, Amy and Clara had joined the receiving line. The Hartleys, garbed as Robin Hood and Maid Marian, gave everyone a hearty welcome, pretending not to recognize them.

Before entering the ballroom, Tim drew Charlotte to one side and bent his head down to her ear. "I want a word with you, but don't tell Amy." He was wearing a cavalier's costume, a wig of long dark curls, a plumed hat, and short brown velvet cape tied across one shoulder with a golden cord.

Seeing the costume of The Frenchman, made Charlotte think of Devlin. *Where was he? When would he come?*

She made an effort to speak calmly. "What is it, Tim?"

"While I watched in the grounds this afternoon, I saw Vanessa slip outside and hurry to the grove. She looked around to make sure she wasn't observed, so I think she meant to meet someone."

"Who?" Charlotte gasped.

"I don't know. I had to keep out of sight as much as possible and I lost track of her in the shadowy trees. I waited and finally Vanessa ran back toward the house. I checked the grove clear down to the River Road but could find no intruder, so I went inside the house to get ready for the ball. All I could learn from the servants was that Cord had cleared out all his belongings and taken his own horse from the stable."

"If Vanessa met him, she could have warned him away," Charlotte said slowly. "On the other hand, she might have let him know we were all coming here tonight."

"She certainly would not put Amy at such risk?" Tim exclaimed.

"Not Amy, but Vanessa holds no love for me. Perhaps in exchange for his promise not to hurt Amy, she told Cord what I would be wearing. Cord hates me for interfering with his pursuit of Amy. We all must stay alert."

Looking worried, Tim hurried to the ballroom. Charlotte didn't follow him. First, she felt it was urgent to check out the conservatory and make sure it was unlocked. Pushing her way through the hordes of clowns, fairies, dancing girls and noblemen and women, she darted down the steps and sped toward the rose garden.

She saw no one in this part of the estate, and when she gained the conservatory, it, too, was deserted. She grasped the door and found it locked. She felt along the lintel. No key. Heart pounding, she shook the door with all her strength.

And something tumbled at her feet, narrowly missing her head. A gourd! Mind awhirl, she remembered the island cave. A gourd had been above the entrance and someone said it was usually placed to show a slave the way to safety. She picked up the yellow dried fruit shell and stared. She saw an empty hook above the door. Was it possible—?

Charles' voice spoke behind her. "I see you recognize the symbol." The little man in the green velvet tunic surveyed her calmly. "I left the receiving line when I saw you run outside. My curiosity was aroused and now yours is, too. I am not a conductor, but this is a way station on the Freedom Trail. No one in our family knows this, except my wife. Devlin said that I could trust you."

Charlotte dropped the gourd and caught his arm. "Have you see him? Where is he?"

"I have no idea, but I know the undercover work he does. Were you looking for him? Are you in trouble?"

Charlotte drew a deep breath. "Yes and I believe that I can trust you." She told him about Martin Cord, and he shook his head, lips tightening. Then she admitted helping the runaways and Savon's desire for revenge.

When she described her plan for escape, he nodded. "I will help you. You now have proof of my own sympathies." He pointed to the gourd, then unlocked the conservatory door. "You can discard your costumes and stuff them out of sight in the tool closet. I can get them later. You say you will have transportation? Do you need money?"

"Oh, no thank you. But I'm so worried about leaving without Devlin."

"He will be all right. He's survived a dangerous deception for several years. If he said he's coming, be sure he will. But I fear his days as a conductor are over. Try not to worry. Now I must get back to welcoming our guests before someone comes searching for me." He pressed her arm, then scurried off.

Feeling reassured by the encounter, Charlotte waited a few minutes then returned to the festivities. She greeted her hosts, picked up a dancecard, and after slipping the black silk cord around her wrist, she entered the ballroom.

It was a blaze of lights from crystal chandeliers which sparkled everywhere on whirling couples clad in imaginative, rich costumes: satin clowns in vari-colored suits decorated with big pompoms, gypsies dressed in rainbow hues, kings and queens in jeweled velvets, dancing barroom girls and demure shepherdesses, even bears and tigers in fur suits. Gilt chairs and plush sofas lined the mirrored walls, which were entwined with more ropes of exotic flowers and, at the far end on a fern-decked dais, a group of musicians played loud, merry rhythms.

After asking her permission, several young men signed her dancecard, but before their turns came, the orchestra took a rest and left the dais.

At that moment, Keith approached her unmistakable with his usual cocky swagger. He, also, wore a cavalier costume, but his red hair was not covered by a wig. He picked up her wrist and began scribbling his name on her card. "I'll just take several of these blank spaces and I shall also be your supper partner."

"No, thank you. I'm not sure yet about supper." Charlotte tried to pull her hand away, but Keith's touch tightened.

"Must you always resist me?" He laughed. "The hoity-toity Miss Charlotte. Oh, yes, I knew you right away. That queenly carriage, the full pink lips and creamy throat leading down to even more delights." His voice thickened as he stared at her. "Come, let us have a glass of punch before the music starts again. You have made my imagination set me afire."

In spite of her reluctance, Charlotte suddenly realized that she felt parched, also, after her running through the garden, so she nodded and accompanied Keith to a corner area where crystal cups contained a frothy syllabub. Ice floated in a huge cut-glass punch bowl and two maids worked rapidly to refresh the thirsty throng.

As she drank, Charlotte scanned the crowd with ever-increasing worry. Why didn't Devlin appear? Even though disguised, surely he would make himself known to her. How could she leave without him when the time arrived?

As she turned to accept the refilling of her cup, she

noticed that Keith had moved a few feet away to face an angry Vanessa.

"Do you mean to say you've given Charlotte *three* dances and only one for me? And you won't take me in to supper? We'll see about that ! I swear, I'm mighty vexed the way she is monopolizing you."

Keith laughed. "What can you do about it? I'm not complaining."

Vanessa's face suffused with angry color and she hissed, "Just you wait and see."

She whirled away in a froth of rose-painted satin and Charlotte followed her example, edging through the noisy throng until she reached Tim and Amy resting by the wall. She gave what she hoped was a reassuring smile. "I visited the conservatory and, so far, all is well."

Tim nodded alertly but Amy faltered. "No sign of— *them?*"

Charlotte shook her head. "No sign of Devlin, either." When she saw quick alarm whiten Amy's face, she added very softly, "But we have another ally here. Someone who knows all about us."

"Who?" Amy breathed and Tim moved closer.

Charlotte spoke carefully. Many strangers were nearby. "I spoke with Charles about his flowers, especially the gourds. You might want to visit his conservatory after awhile."

Amy and Tim exchanged glances and Charlotte knew they understood.

The musicians resumed their places and a pierot in a black and white diamond-patterned costume came to claim Charlotte for his dance.

Chapter 33

The evening wore on, a noisy, multi-colored blur while Charlotte's anxiety grew with every passing minute. She was so preoccupied during her dance with Keith that he became disenchanted and did not return to claim her for the others. Perhaps Vanessa said something about her impending departure—if so, it was fine with her.

Charlotte hovered by the door, searching the foyer constantly for a sign of Devlin. Her eyes checked the clock. Were the black hands standing still? They didn't seem to move.

Several times Amy or Tim approached her, murmuring reassurances. From her place on a sofa, Clara caught Charlotte's eye and nodded gravely, sadly, and Charlotte knew she was bidding her farewell. Not in relief, but with a look of regret that her sister's girls must have this troubled departure. She had always accepted Amy, but now both girls had become wrapped in fondness.

Charlotte's eyes filled with tears and her lips trembled. If she hadn't been so frightened about the two men seeking vengeance, her sorrow about departing would have swamped her. Stone Gardens had been a beautiful sanctuary at first, with comforting glimpses of her mother's early life. Then she had met a wonderful man and fallen deep in love for the first time in her life. What would happen to them now?

She forced herself to inhale deeply. She must not allow herself to be disturbed about her future in New York. Amy had told her earlier that Tim would have a room for them at his mother's house for as long as needed. How good he had been, Charlotte thought. Involving himself in their escape with no concern about any danger to himself.

Suddenly, she felt a hand upon her arm, and when she jerked around, Vanessa stood behind her. "A servant just brought me a message from Devlin Cartright. He wants you to meet him in the rose garden at once."

After the first rush of joy, Charlotte hesitated and questions began to surface. "Why did Devlin not send the word to me? Why you?"

Vanessa's lips thinned and she leaned close. "The slave did not know you. He brought the message to me by word of mouth asking which one was Charlotte Bainbridge? I said that I would tell you. My stars, you stand there like a ninny asking questions. Don't you want to see him?"

"Why can't he come in?"

Vanessa threw up her hands. "How on earth should I know? I guess he wants a secret rendezvous. Shall I go out and keep him company?"

"No. I'll go now." Heart pounding, Charlotte picked up her skirts and ran outside, keeping to the shadows. When she reached the rose arbor draped with ghostly blossoms, a young moon sent its beams fitfully here and there, leaving dark patches when scudding clouds obscured the sky.

Charlotte stared frantically in every direction. Devlin!

Where was he? Should she call his name? The earlier uneasiness swamped her. Suppose Vanessa had tricked her and *Cord* was hiding in the bushes waiting for his hated enemy? What would he do? Overpower her and take her to the slave patrol or sheriff? Then come back for Amy?

Not moving, Charlotte clutched her throat. She dared not leave in case Devlin really came. Perhaps he was waiting to make sure it was safe for him to appear?

She put one foot before the other and glided forward. "Devlin? she whispered hoarsely. "Where are you?"

Suddenly, a shape appeared at the end of the arbor. Long black hair, a plumed hat, a short cloak . . .

"Devlin, is that you?" Throwing caution to the wind, Charlotte darted forward only to halt abruptly. This wasn't Devlin. He was shorter, slighter. Then she saw the cruel face. His lips curled downward, with eyes glinting like a feral beast.

Francois Savon!

Charlotte stumbled backward with a muffled shriek. The heavy costume with its thick skirts hampered her escape just long enough for the villain of her nightmares to leap upon her. Forcing her to the ground, he gripped her arm and flicked a glinting steel dagger against the white flesh of her throat.

"*Zut!* One word, one scream and you are dead," he snarled. "But first I take from you what you deprived me of with Luella. Zen we talk about what you did with my slaves. *Mais oui,* you shall tell me all.

After violating her, Charlotte knew he would kill her no matter what she did. Blindness swirled around her, but she must not faint or panic. In spite of his threat, she continued struggling, pushing at his drooling, ravening red mouth while shrieking all the while.

Nothing stopped the beast's assault. He managed to shove up her heavy skirts and, panting, he fell prone upon her struggling body. "Ah, oui," he grunted. "I like ze fight. "But not too much, or—"

Charlotte felt a sharper stab. Desperately, she raked his sweating face, tore at his hair, screaming all the while. But the gardens seemed deserted, the noise from the ball engulfing everything. Savon would soon attain his goal, then kill her and escape. Never for an instant did she stop fighting him, even though her strength was ebbing fast.

Suddenly, something happened. The monster gave a gurgling cry and slumped upon her body, a dead unmoving weight.

Gasping, Charlotte shoved him off and saw two figures. One, an old man, feet wide apart, held a leather-covered weapon. The other, dark-skinned, young, jerked her assailant onto the path.

"Oh, Miss Charlotte, oh, Miss Charlotte—" he croaked over and over.

"Ned! Thank God!" Her eyes bored the other figure. "Who—who—"

"It's Devlin. How are you? Were we in time?" Swiftly, he knelt beside Charlotte and took her in a fierce embrace, his face pressed against her cheek, his hands running over her.

Charlotte clung to him and it was several minutes before she was calm enough to tell him all that happened while Ned tied the Frenchman's hands and feet with his own scarf and belt.

Devlin listened with a deepening frown. He was almost unrecognizable with his straggling grey beard, low-brimmed hat, and nondescript long dark coat. Finally, he rose and drew Charlotte to her feet. "I think you'll be all right now. Can you continue with your own plans if I leave you?"

"Oh, must you go? Is he . . . dead?"

"No, just stunned. I hit him with a blackjack. He will be

sick and unconscious for a long time. Ned and I will put
him in a rowboat and let the current take him. Perhaps
he will be rescued, but I am sure he will not return.''

Charlotte gripped his arm. ''And Cord?''

He shook his head. ''I don't know where he is. This has
been a game of hide and seek. I have much to tell you,
but it must wait and you should go back now to the ball
before someone comes out searching.''

''When will I see you?'' She swallowed hard.

Devlin pulled her close and kissed her. ''On the train,
my love. I promise.'' Slowly, he stepped back.

Charlotte looked at Ned. ''Thank you for helping us.''

''Uncle Cicero ask me to watch over you, Miss Charlotte.''

''You did good, Ned,'' Devlin said. ''Now we must
remove this carrion. Charlotte, you may still be in danger
from the patrol, as I am if Cord alerted them.''

''Oh, Devlin, come away now!''

He shook his head. ''Ned can't handle this alone. Never
fear, I'll follow you . . . somehow. Be brave, my dearest,
and may God be with you.'' He shouldered the inert body
and vanished in the shadows, Ned scrambling after him.

Still trembling, Charlotte drew several deep breaths,
then fled back to the house, still engulfed in noise and
laughter. She must find Tim and Amy. The time for
unmasking was drawing close. Her own mask lay on the
path, torn off by Savon.

To her surprise, she found Vanessa standing on the
pillared porch. She stepped in front of Charlotte and stuttered, ''What happened to your throat? Did you see
Devlin?''

''I ran into Francois Savon and he attacked me,'' Charlotte grated. ''Were you lying? Did you know he would be
there?''

Vanessa fell back. "No—no! I swear I didn't. Not Savon. But you're all right, aren't you? I thought—"

"What? Perhaps you expected Martin Cord to find me?"

Vanessa shook her head, looking the soul of guilt, but just then a bell began to toll and shouts came from the ballroom. "Time to unmask," she gasped and fled.

Charlotte realized she couldn't afford to question Vanessa any further. It probably would be fruitless. She hurried to the ballroom's entry, seeing Tim and Amy push their way through the jostling throng.

Amy caught Charlotte's arm. "Quick! We must leave."

"I'll get the carriage." Tim ran off, and after securing their cloaks, the sisters sped to the conservatory.

"Have you heard from Devlin?" Amy panted as they rushed along the deserted paths, holding up their skirts, cloaks billowing behind.

Fortunately, Amy hadn't noticed the knife scratch on Charlotte's throat and she decided there was no time now to add another burden to the task before them of trying to escape without detection.

Charlotte blurted out a few words to the effect that Devlin had appeared and promised to join them on the train. Amy seemed satisfied. In fact, now that the time had come for action, she seemed to become more excited than fearful.

"I wish I could have said goodbye to Vanessa," Amy said when they were inside the conservatory, pulling off their costumes.

"Write her a letter," Charlotte advised tersely, buttoning up her traveling dress. "We must hide these ballgowns in that tool shed. Listen, Amy, Charles Hartley knows about us."

"What!" Amy yelped. "That's what you meant about a gourd!"

"Yes, he told me Roselands is a station on the Underground Railway, but no one in the family knows, except his wife.''

"For heaven's sake,'' Amy breathed, her mouth agape. Slowly she drew on the knickers Tim had provided.

"Hurry, child,'' Charlotte urged. "Fix your hair. We're not out of danger yet.''

They heard Tim's whistle in a few minutes, and soon he had the carriage bowling along the main road to Beauville. With a little time at her disposal, Charlotte now filled in Amy with the recent events. However, she made a lighter tale of Savon's assault and said Devlin and Ned had rescued her and then made off with Savon.

"How did you happen to be out in the rose arbor?''

"Devlin sent in a message for me to meet him. He didn't know Savon was anywhere around.''

Amy mulled this over with a worried expression. "And what about Martin? Has there been no sign of him?''

"None that I know of.'' Charlotte peered out of the window, but the road was dark and deserted. In the town where Tim stabled the horses, only the railroad station was lit, with a few weary passengers waiting.

Finally, with a roar and puffing, the train arrived and all climbed aboard. Charlotte's heart was pounding, but no one stopped them. There was no sign of Cord.

Neither was there any sign of Devlin.

Filled with mounting fear, Charlotte gazed in every direction, then pulled down her veil and took a plush seat several places back of Tim and Amy. Would a hard-faced patrol enter before they left the station and penetrate the disguise of two young men and a shabbily-dressed mourning woman?

A whistle shrieked. The conductor bawled, "All abo-o-ard!'' Wheels began to groan. But just before the train moved out, an old man ran along the platform and swung onto the steps.

Charlotte gave a sob of joy. "Devlin!"

He slid into the seat beside her and clasped her hand, pressing it against his lips. The train roared out of town with a screaming whistle, wheels clattering. The few other people settled down in the dim lighting to catch some slumber on their journey.

Charlotte leaned against Devlin's shoulder and tears of relief streamed down her face. "Are we safe?" she whispered.

"I'm sure that we are," Devlin told her softly, using his handkerchief to wipe her cheeks. "We'll soon be above the Mason-Dixon Line, and I saw no sign of any patrol before we left, did you?" He drew a flask out of an inner pocket. "I took the precaution of bringing a little calming brew. At the next rest stop, we'll get some food. They have concessions along the line, and some should be open for this train."

Charlotte took several sips of the sweet brandy and felt it run warmly through her body, bringing renewed strength. "Tell me what happened earlier today."

"Well, Ned told me that Cord had cleared out all his belongings and then disappeared. I felt certain that Cord would not leave until he had obtained some reward from Savon for his information. But he had to get away from Stone Gardens."

"I took a horse and rode to where the ship from up North would dock. It came in early, however, and all was confusion with passengers and cargo getting off when I arrived. There must have been a meeting between Savon and Cord, and Savon learned that he could find you at the ball. Probably Cord suggested that Savon use my name to lure you outside. I arrived later, just in time to hear you screaming." He frowned and drew her closer.

"Is Cord really gone? Do you think he spoke to the patrol?"

"Perhaps, but they won't find us now and they have no authority in the North. I imagine Cord collected some money from Savon and then hightailed it out of town. He could see that Clara had posted some sheriff's men around the grounds. At that point, he knew that Amy was lost to him, and all he could do was run as far away as possible."

"I wouldn't be surprised if Vanessa told him how I could be identified at the ball. Tim saw her going to talk to someone in secret, but he couldn't determine who it was. But I'm sure she didn't betray Amy."

"You may be right, but evidently, Cord decided it was too risky here and he was satisfied by giving Savon all the information about you."

"What finally happened to Savon?"

"He didn't regain consciousness, but he was alive when Ned and I set him adrift on the river. He will be rescued and feel sick and disoriented for a long time, even after he returns to Dark Oaks. Eventually, his evil nature will do him in, you can be sure."

"Did you know Charles Hartley was involved with the Underground Railroad? He told me tonight."

Devlin nodded. "I knew he had a station at Roselands for runaways. Alas, my own days as a conductor are over in the South. Whether Cord actually discovered my secret or was merely bluffing, I don't know, but I can take no more chances. We will be married soon and I'll have other responsibilities, my dearest."

"Are you asking me to marry you, Devlin?"

"Would you?" He picked up Charlotte's hand and kissed it, looking deep into her eyes. "I love you more than I ever dreamed possible. Would you marry me, Charlotte?"

With tears in her eyes, Charlotte nodded. "Yes. Yes I will marry you."

Charlotte snuggled closer. Devlin would be at her side, and that was all that mattered.

Chapter 34

Three years later, in New York Charlotte received a letter from Amy, postmarked Leichester Square, London, England.

Charlotte put down little Rose to coo and gurgle on a blanket in the flower garden then settled on a bench to eagerly peruse her sister's letter.

Dearest Charlotte,

As you see, Clara and I are still in England, but Lord Winston is making plans to escort us to his summer villa on the Riviera for a house party. Won't that be fun? "Jolly good!" as the British say. Due to Clara's generosity, I am becoming quite an anglophile, after nearly six months of this pleasant social life. But, dearest Charlotte, I long to see you and little Rose who must be nearly one year old! I hear occasionally from Vanessa, who constantly complains about Keith's neglect. However, she is living in the lap of luxury and I never thought they were terribly in love, did you? At least, she will soon give her husband the wanted heir, though

*I can't see Keith as a devoted papa. I am glad Devlin is
still writing, even if it's only for the Abolitionist periodicals.
Someday, I hope he returns to fiction, which he did so well.
I think in these troubling times we all need to escape into
a world of makebelieve occasionally.*

*Do you ever hear from Tim? Our correspondence has died
out. He mentioned a new young lady, and I think he is
romantically interested. You know I was not in love with
him, but he will always be very dear to me.*

*My life is so full and happy that I cannot be serious
about marriage yet, even after the several proposals which
I wrote to you about. My only unfilled wish is to see you
and your family. However, I must take advantage of this
wonderful opportunity. Clara has been so generous and
kind. I am glad she sold Stone Gardens. It was getting too
hard for her to run it by herself. She will go to live with
Vanessa when she returns.*

*Until then, we are having the most wonderful time in
the world seeing so many famous places and people. I even
saw Queen Victoria one day in a gilded coach!*

*I am keeping a journal, as Devlin suggested, but I long
to talk with you face to face. So much to tell and so much
to hear about your own new life, which sounds so happy.*

My deepest love to you all,

Amy

Hearing footsteps on the garden path, Charlotte looked
up and saw Devlin strolling toward her. "What are you
reading, my love?" He sat beside her on the bench and
Charlotte handed him Amy's letter.

"You have kept our coming visit a secret, I trust?" He
laughed.

"Yes, only Clara knows and she wrote me that Lord
Winston has invited us to be his guests."

"I think the trip will do us good and I know how much

it means to you to celebrate Amy's twenty-first birthday. I also intend to contact some publishers in England who wish to reprint my books.''

Charlotte leaned into Devlin's arms. She never would forget Stone Gardens, but she had no wish to see it ever again.

Charlotte often wondered what happened to all who she met there. She had known that Tibby and Elijah had been betrayed themselves by Cord but were hopefully living safely and freely in the North. She had no interest in discovering the happenings of Savon, although Aunt Clara indicated that he may have had a mortal riding accident. All she wanted to remember was the beautiful yet sad stone sculptures and finding her true love. Devlin and their daughter were her life and with her family it became more wonderful every day.

PASSIONATE ROMANCE
FROM BETINA KRAHN!

HIDDEN FIRES   (0-8217-4953-6, $4.99)

LOVE'S BRAZEN FIRE   (0-8217-5691-5, $5.99)

MIDNIGHT MAGIC   (0-8217-4994-3, $4.99)

PASSION'S RANSOM   (0-8217-5130-1, $5.99)

REBEL PASSION   (0-8217-5526-9, $5.99)

DANGEROUS GAMES   (0-7860-0270-0, $4.99)
by Amanda Scott

When Nicholas Barrington, eldest son of the Earl of Ul-combe, first met Melissa Seacort, the desperation he sensed beneath her well-bred beauty haunted him. He didn't realize how desperate Melissa really was . . . until he found her again at a Newmarket gambling club—being auctioned off by her father to the highest bidder. So, Nick bought himself a wife. With a villain hot on their heels, and a fortune and their lives at stake, they would gamble everything on the most dangerous game of all: love.

A TOUCH OF PARADISE   (0-7860-0271-9, $4.99)
by Alexa Smart

As a confidence man and scam runner in 1880s America, Malcolm Northrup has amassed a fortune. Now, posing as the eminent Sir John Abbot—scholar, and possible discoverer of the lost continent of Atlantis—he's taking his act on the road with a lecture tour, seeking funds for a scientific experiment he has no intention of making. But scholar Halia Davenport is determined to accompany Malcolm on his "expedition" . . . even if she must kidnap him!

ROMANCE FROM HANNAH HOWELL

FROM ROSANNE BITTNER:
ZEBRA SAVAGE DESTINY ROMANCE!

#1: SWEET PRAIRIE PASSION   (0-8217-5342-8, $5.99)

#2: RIDE THE FREE WIND   (0-8217-5343-6, $5.99)

#3: RIVER OF LOVE   (0-8217-5344-4, $5.99)

#4: EMBRACE THE
    WILD WIND   (0-8217-5413-0, $5.99)

#7: EAGLE'S SONG   (0-8217-5326-6, $5.99)

Available wherever paperbacks are sold, or order direct from the Publisher. Send cover price plus 50¢ per copy for mailing and handling to Penguin USA, P.O. Box 999, c/o Dept. 17109, Bergenfield, NJ 07621. Residents of New York and Tennessee must include sales tax. DO NOT SEND CASH.